I Am Alone

WALTER MACKEN, novelist, short story writer, playwright and actor, was born in Galway in 1915. He first began to write at the age of eight. When he left school in the 1930s he became a member of the acting company at the Taibhdhearc. It was there he met his wife, Peggy Kenny; they worked together in the Taibhdhearc until their marriage in 1937, after which they lived in London for a while.

Returning to Galway in 1939, Walter took up the post of theatre manager with the Taibhdhearc. At this time, he began to write both in Irish and English. By 1946 his first play in English, *Mungo's Mansion*, had been successfully staged at the Abbey Theatre in Dublin and his first novel, *Quench the Moon*, had been accepted for publication.

In 1948 he joined the Abbey for three years. A year later his second novel, *I Am Alone*, was published, and in 1950 his third novel, *Rain on the Wind*, brought him international recognition, winning the Book of the Month Club award in the UK and the Literary Guild award in the USA. A successful US theatre tour gave him the impetus to return home to Galway to establish a career for himself as a full-time writer.

In 1957 he embarked on his most ambitious writing project: the three historical novels, *Seek the Fair Land*, *The Silent People* and *The Scorching Wind*, and in 1964 his first children's novel, *Island of the Great Yellow Ox*, proved to be one of his most popular books. In all, he produced a body of work which finally came to ten novels, seven plays, three books of short stories and two children's books; most of his novels have been translated into many languages.

"Essentially, all my works are dreams on paper. One hundred years from now, people will read them and say: So, that's how people lived."

Walter Macken

I Am Alone

BRANDON

Published in 2000 by
Brandon
an imprint of Mount Eagle Publications Ltd.
Dingle, Co. Kerry, Ireland

First published by Macmillan and Co Ltd., 1949

10 9 8 7 6 5 4 3 2 1

Copyright © Walter Macken, 1949

ISBN 0 86322 266 8

This book is published with the assistance of
the Arts Council/An Chomhairle Ealaíon, Ireland

Cover design: PUSH, London
Typesetting: Red Barn Publishing, Skeagh, Skibbereen
Printed by Zure, Spain

1

'**A**nythin' to declare?' asked the little fat man, raising his eyes from the closed suitcase in front of him to regard the traveller.

'No,' said the young man; 'I don't think so.'

'Any perfume or paraphernalia, wireless accessories or dogs-bodies, soap or cigars, tobacco or nuts, tripe or tribulations, watches, clocks or penny-farthing bicycles, puddens, black or white, stuffed and stamped in *Déanta in Éirinn*? If so, say, I do declare; and if not let you forever hold your peace and no wise-cracks,' he went on in a splurge of talk as was his custom, all the time his hand hovering over the suitcase with the chalk held in it, ready to descend, and his tiny intelligent eyes examining the young man from top to toe, fixing him into a category. No danger, said his mind, nothing to declare except youth and eyes with a glint in them. A would-be exile, about twenty years of age, from the country. Overcoat new. Suit underneath not so new. New shirt and tie. Bet I could tell you what's in the case.

His hovering hand didn't descend.

'Open it up,' he said, indicating the suitcase.

The young man's hand moved and clicked the catches on the suitcase. Clean hands, clean fingernails, thought the fat man. No callouses. White-collar worker. One of the lower middle-class, poor but honest, dip in the dip and leave the herring to your daddy. Clean curtains, clean floor, white-scrubbed tables and slack bellies. Clean shirt on Sunday morning and the smell of black polish. As I thought. His hands were rumpling the clothes in the inside of the new cheap imitation leather suitcase. Two

shirts, seen better days. Underclothes. Ho-ho: middle-class ath-
letic vests and two trunks, washed white but frayed. I never had
those at his age. Pull on the britches and hope for the best. Razor
and brush alone, just thrown in, another suit with the smell of the
cleaners off it. Extra pair of shoes. Piece sewn into the side, socks
darned. Few bits of clitter-clatter. Books, how are yeh!

His quick, pudgy fingers flicked at the stuff, pulled back the
top cover of the nearest book. My God, William Shakespeare!

His eyes darted at the stamped inscription imposed on the
white inner page. Presented to – the name written in ink –
Patrick Moore, and then on, third place in English literature.
H'm, not at the top of the class so. Looked quick enough, but
you never knew. Sometimes the really brilliant men didn't win
prizes at all. Look at himself! Could have taught them all about
it, but nobody presented him with a volume of Shakespeare's
plays for being third in the class at English literature. The things
he could write if he had time to sit down and work it all out!

'I hope,' said Patrick Moore, 'that I don't have to declare poor
oul Shakespeare?'

'What's that?' asked the other, his mind working all the time.
Soft voice, fairly well educated, from the north, south, east, or
west? Yeh, from the west. They drawled a bit and put in an extra
vowel or two. My God, the things I learn from being a customs
officer! Isn't it only wasting my time I am? I should be a bloody
Professor of Intuition up in the college there. All I have to do is
to look at a guy and I can tell you how he was sired, where he
lives, how he lives, and how he'll die; and I'm down here openin'
idlers' cases for contraband when I should have long grey
whiskers and be lecturing the young university squirts about the
facts of life – not the vulgar facts that they know before they
should, but other facts about judging a man from the appearance
of his underwear, and that. God, talk about wasting genius! 'All
the world's a stage, and all the men and women merely players.
They have their exits and their entrances, and each man in his
time plays many parts.'

He said this aloud, much to Patrick's amazement. 'What's
that?' he asked.

'Pass on,' said the customs officer, getting tired of it all, 'and take Willie with you. Next please!' I shook him, all the same, he thought, as he moved to the next suitcase. I bet I shook 'm! 'Anything to declare?' he asked, his hand hovering with the chalk and the tiny eyes going up and down and over his next victim.

Pat Moore clicked his case closed, had a look back over his shoulder at the little fat man, and then, grinning, made his way to the gangplank. He refused to have his suitcase carried by one of the brawny men with the blue gansies and the name of the company written across the chest in red wool, like a branded sheep, Pat thought. He noticed that they did not importune him, asked from habit, but their eyes had already seen and summed up, and they probably knew how much his total wealth amounted to, so for charity's sake they left him alone to make his way on to the ship.

He was excited and his heart was thumping.

He noticed the difference the minute his feet got on the deck: the slight feeling of insecurity which hits the body as soon as the legs leave the solid land. Besides, it was a little rough in the harbour and the boat was moving lazily at its moorings; but when he walked through the corridor, or whatever they called it, and got over the other side, he could see that the sun was shining and glinting off the white-tops. He dropped his case and leaned his arms on the rail. It was pleasant. The houses lining the harbour and the hills behind rising mightily. Not like the hills at home, but passable all the same. And the harbour was dotted with the moored yachts, big, small and indifferent, and they rode the waves like corks, their slim, stripped masts looking indignant in their disturbance.

That's all very well, Pat thought, but what about me? Aye, what about me? Well, as soon as this ship pulls away, I will be officially an exile. Not that anyone gives a damn, but it's exciting all the same. He turned then and looked about him. The ship was becoming fairly crowded; mostly, he decided, people who had been in Ireland for a holiday and were going home again, or Irish who were going over to England on a holiday. He couldn't see many who had the look of himself. Mostly well-dressed people with imposing-looking leather suitcases and rugs, and stomachs on the men that hadn't grown overnight, but had been carefully nurtured over a period of years. There was a nice smell too of cigar-smoke coming from a group at the railings below him. A tall man with grey hair, a smoothly shaven face, a brown suit with a yellow waistcoat. A very good suit, Pat thought, the price of the one I'm wearing wouldn't have bought the waistcoat even. There was much loud talk from here and there, most of which he found it difficult to distinguish, since they were talking with very English accents, and his only real acquaintance with the English had been in the history books, which didn't exactly show the English in a favourable light.

As the place where he was standing became more crowded he looked around, saw the stairs going up, and mounted them to get out on the top deck of the boat, which was comparatively deserted. There was a strong breeze up here and it felt good on his face.

I shouldn't have come Saloon, of course, he thought. Apart from the fact that it cost an extra quid, which probably he would need very badly, he didn't feel comfortable. It would have been better to have done it on the cheap, and chatted with the others in the Steerage class, who, he was sure, were off to England like himself to try and make a living. But then he had promised sister Cissie. He smiled as he thought of Cissie. The intense look of her. She had never been out of their town in her life and when she thought of a ship at all, she thought of the famine ships going to America with the hundreds of Paddies crowded and dying in the holds and the steerage. So out of her little she had dug a pound, just so that he would go Saloon on the boat! She didn't mind third on the trains. That was fairly all right, since quite rich people went third, who'd be damned if they'd give a few extra bob to the bloody railways. But like all the respectable poor, Cissie was a snob, and since she was actually quite serious about it, he had taken the pound and had promised her.

The engines rumbled in the bowels of the ship and the deck vibrated. He couldn't see from where he was, so he went to the other side of the ship and watched as men shouted and threw hawsers and freed lines, and bells tinkled and water poured out of the side of the ship, and then almost before he was aware of it all, the boat was nosing out into the channel and the figures on the wharfside became tiny-looking puppets, standing there look-ing after them with their hands on their hips, their attitudes one of great gratitude, as if to say, Well, thank God we've got rid of that big bitch and let's hope she doesn't come back for another twenty years.

It was only when his eyes shifted to the land that he really real-ized for the first time that he was leaving Ireland. When distance had ceased to make the size of the big city overpowering and when he could see the land behind it, then he realised and it left him cold. So what, he thought, am I expected to feel? Sorrow, tender-ness, a lump in the throat, a knot of jumbled Irish emotions in the guts? Listen, he said, inside, you can stuff it up your jersey and if you have room in the same place you can squeeze Caitlin Ni hOulichaun along with it. He felt a great excitement in him that he was leaving. He was young and his heart was beating fast. He looked back at his life, all twenty-one years of it, in which there were few highlights, mainly rather dull shadows which had not left a mark on him, and he knew that however badly off he might be in England, he couldn't be much worse off than he had been at home.

What, he said with a grin, looking down at the very green water going by in giant undulations, no lump in the throat? He cleared it but it was free, so he gathered a spit between his teeth and threw it at the water. The wind took it and whipped it away so that it might have landed on the distant hills. Well, they can have it, he thought.

'Going to England?' a voice asked beside him. He was star-tled, and turned to look at the man beside him.

He was a well-dressed man, small and stocky, a grey hat on his big head and a brown striped suit covering his well-padded frame, a double chin of prosperity, and a thick neck caught by a hard collar, decorated by a plain tie with a small pin holding a diamond that twinkled.

'Yes,' said Pat, 'I am.'

'Holiday?' asked the man, leaning on the rail beside him. He had to stretch his short arms a lot to get to it.

'No,' said Pat, a little put out by this questioning. The man had an English accent.

11

'Another emigrant, what?' he went on then.

'Well, I'm going to work there,' Pat answered.

'I thought so,' said the man. 'Have you been out of Ireland before?'

'No,' said Pat, 'I haven't.'

'I thought not,' said the man. You'd easily know, he thought. He liked the look of the young man. It was the glint of his teeth that had attracted his attention, strong pointed teeth in a generous mouth. He looked very young with his brown wavy hair, broad forehead, and very blue eyes, around which humour wrinkles were already being engraved. He was tall, head and shoulders over the man, but he was not built very big; his body was lithe and looked graceful as he leaned indolently on the rail. His face was tanned from the sun and his skin had the cold, clean look of youth.

'I hope you don't mind my asking you those things,' the man went on. 'You're probably thinking that I'm old enough to have sense, and not to be sticking my nose into other people's business.'

Pat laughed.

'Not at all,' he said. In fact he had been thinking just that.

'I've just been to Ireland for the umpteenth time,' the man told him. 'I'm not Irish, but a grandfather of mine was. Have to go back and forth sometimes on business. I like it very much.'

'If you want to know me,' said Pat, 'come and live with me.'

'That's what they say, the people who leave it,' said the man. 'Sometimes I don't blame them. I went once to the village where my grandfather was born and died. Amazing. Away back in the Middle Ages. No wonder they emigrated from it. But you don't come from a village, do you?'

'A glorified one,' said Pat. 'It's got all modern conveniences; shops, cinemas and scenery, and the few people with money invest it all in English factories and businesses. A good idea, so that when the people breed they can send their kids to follow the money. I don't give a damn. I think it's great. I love going to England.'

'Have you a job to go to?' the other asked.

'Sure,' said Pat, thinking that the inquisition had gone too far.

12

'Where?' the other asked.

'Oh, London, I suppose,' said Pat, wishing that the man would go away and leave him alone. He wanted to be alone, to appreciate all this that was happening to him. It would only happen once, and he knew that he ought to take it and enjoy it on that account. But not with a little man beside him asking him questions, making him think about the future when he didn't want to think about it, until he had to.

'Here's my card,' said the man, taking the pasteboard slip from his pocket and holding it out. Pat took it and glanced at it. 'It might come in useful sometime. I'm in insurance, as you see. Maybe that's why I talk so much and ask strangers questions.' His eyes were creased now in a smile, and Pat thought that he was a nice little man after all.

'Thanks, Mr Johnson,' he said, looking at the card.

'You've had a decent education, I see,' said Johnson. 'I can tell from the way you talk. You might be useful to me, you know.'

'Thanks,' said Pat, but you can go to hell, he thought under his breath. What the hell is insurance and did people actually make a living out of it? Johnson went then, saying, 'I see the wife over there. Well, so-long,' wondering as he went what on earth had impelled him to go and talk to the young man at all. Just that he had liked the look of him and he had looked lonely there looking back at the land. Johnson had thought he might have been a bit sad or something. What a hope! 'There you are, Jeanie,' he said then to his plump wife, taking her by the arm and going towards the saloon. 'Come on and we'll have a quick one.' And she said, 'Who was that young man, Dick?' And Dick said, 'He is a young fella going to England. He looked lonely, and I thought I'd chat to him, but he seems to be well able to look after himself.'

Pat watched them out of sight and then turned to face the breeze.

They came into the outer harbour and met the force of a strong wind, that made criss-cross waves which raised the bow of the boat and crashed it into a trough. Pat's stomach went up and down once or twice and then settled. He had been in very small boats on rough seas before when they were out fishing for pollack and mackerel, and for a second his mind flashed back to the other bay, with the seas sweeping into it and the glitter of sun on silver sands. Yeh, he thought, and the glitter of sun on stale margarine and bread, because you couldn't afford to buy any-thing else; and he had a picture of sister Cissie in her flowered apron, bent over the range stirring things in a pot, her hair brown like his own, but grey hairs in it, even though she was only a few years older than he; but then he didn't have to have five children in a short time, just because her husband loved her very much, and although Cissie would say after each one, 'Now, we mustn't have any more, Jim,' and Jim would agree and say, 'How in the name of Christ can I afford any more?' Yet they were very much in love and they were poor and they didn't have to pay any-one anything for going to bed and having a bit of fun, forgetting their troubles by exercising the privilege of the poor, believing implicitly when the Church told them that God would provide, while all the rich tarts could go to bed whenever they liked because they could afford to buy and read *The Laws of Life*, whereas when Pat himself tried to explain to Jim what it was all about, about how you do it this time and not another time, and count up this and that and whatnot and you'd be all right, and Jim looking at him with his mouth open, totally unable to under-stand all these bloody figures and more than slightly shocked that a boy of Pat's age should be talking about things like that, and he a Catholic into the bargain, and about his own sister too! Pat smiled now as he saw Jim's face again, with the outraged look on it and the sweat of embarrassment on his brow. Jim was nice, and a good husband and he loved all his kids. Since it was the only thing he could create he probably got satisfaction out of it, and quite possibly, Pat thought, God would provide. He'd want to, because poor old Jim was a council scavenger with £2 6s. a week less stamps for unemployment insurance. So what? So to hell with it! And he looked around at the life of the ship.

He enjoyed every minute of the way across to the Welsh port.

He was driven from his high place on the ship by the number of people who came there with grey, tortured faces and looked forlornly at the buckets provided for their discomfort. He watched their faces turning green and the awful spasms of their bodies as they leaned over to retch into the containers, sitting back after the spasm, very cautiously, the expressions on their faces saying, 'Surely to God that's the end of it now.' The sight of their suffering sent chills up and down Pat's straight stomach. He didn't even get any satisfaction from the sight of fur coats getting as sick as anyone else, so he went downstairs. He sat in the cold comfort of the lounge, with its hard furniture bolted to the floors and the imitation fires that gave no heat. Here more bodies lying stretched, covered with rugs. So he left that and walked the decks, and it was good to feel the breeze on his face; but the throb-throb of the engines made it hard to think. He went into the saloon and had a glass of beer but the whole ship seemed to be permeated with an air of caution. Admittedly it was rough, but everyone on the boat seemed to be afraid to do much in case they became the victims of the waves. Downstairs it was worse, with sick men rolling on the free bunks and the awful smell of disinfectant and men's leavings, so he went to the front of the ship again and watched the sea, and distinguished later the land rising out of it like a bank of cloud.

It was the signal for the resurgence. As the ship nosed its way into the calmer waters, the corpses arose with strained faces, tidied disordered hair and crumpled clothes. There was a great rushing around and the gift of speech was restored to the silenced throttles, and the hefty men with the blue jerseys appeared like rabbits from burrows, looking disgustingly healthy with their leather faces and placid stomachs. It was amazing the way the ship suddenly came to life. As they entered into the harbour they lined the ship's rails and pointed out such a place to one another, and Pat looked at the screaming, hovering gulls and thought, Well, they are exactly the same, anyhow, as the ones at home, and it was a link. Soon there was a shivering in the ship and some controlled shouting and a heaving of lines and a closing to the wharf, and before he knew where he was, Pat, with his suitcase clutched in his hand, was standing on foreign soil for the first time in his life.

It was a bit of a sell.

He didn't know exactly what he had been expecting, but this was too much the same as the other side. The same long, draughty shed with customs officers dressed much the same and the chalk in their hands. This one didn't even bother to raise his eyes to look at Pat. He just took one look at the cheap new suitcase and marked it disdainfully, saying, 'Next, please,' in a tight, controlled way that showed he was probably thinking of his wife or his mother or some other fellow's sister, or a million other things, anything at all but what he was doing. Pat saw Johnson again in the shed. He smiled at him and got a wave in reply, and then he was out on the platform looking for a seat in a third-class compartment.

It was a very long train and comparatively empty. He was surprised at the third-class. It was almost luxurious, with arm rests and whatnot, and his behind was unused to the soft comfort of the seat, and he thought of the other third-class seat in the train to Dublin. Hard stuff that covered it, and if you hit it you were enveloped in a cloud of dust. And when this train started and pulled away and got up speed he was surprised at that too, being used to an Irish engine that seemed to have a severe dose of asthma, and the ambling pace of it that would infuriate even a bishop; and he thought of the times when he was at school and they were going on excursions, and the milling multitude of schoolboys swarming over the train and the destruction they wrought on it – surreptitious smoking of cigarettes when the monk's back was turned and some chap firing a burning butt out of the window and it being blown back and going down inside the window and starting a fire, and how they laughed and were frightened by degrees, and how they finally put out the fire by urinating on it, which was very easy because the food at the end of the excursion had consisted of ham sandwiches and lemonade – oh, lots and lots of lemonade. He could still taste it.

He regarded the landscape. Why, he thought, slightly shocked, the fields are green! Then he laughed. Another illusion gone. Naturally enough. You heard so much about the green Emerald Isle, and all the green banners and flags, and St Patrick in his green robes, and the green shamrock, and the green uniforms of the army, and green kilts, and his own town a great combination of grey stone and green trees. Wasn't it only natural in a way that you unconsciously came to believe that Ireland was green and that therefore every other country must be a different colour? Well, what had he expected? Had he expected the green

fields of England to be coloured red or a mixture of the Union
Jack? But they were unmistakably green. The houses were different. Two-storey or three-storey houses here and there
amongst the farms slated. The stupid-looking cows that raised
their heads from the grass to look at the passing train were just
as stupid-looking and raised their heads in the same way as the
cows outside Athenry. The horses that started at the train's
approach and ran away from it with flashing hooves and tails laid
out on the breeze of their own making were the same. Men who
came to the doors in shirt-sleeves and with a pipe in their gobs,
idly watching the passing of the train, were no different to the
men with pipes in their gobs who had watched the passing of the
Dublin train. Well, what had you expected them to be like?
Hydra-headed monsters? Pat laughed again, and then his attention was caught by the high, crane-like yokes raising themselves
above the landscape.

Well, there's something new anyhow, he thought. Never saw
them before. Then he thought where he was and realized that he
was looking at the part of the land where the coal came from. So
them's coalmines now, he said, very knowledgeably, and laughed
again, and felt the thrill in his stomach and said to himself, God,
I am enjoying this, so I am.

The train pulled to a halt at a large station. Porters shouting
and the train hissing steam and chaps going by standing up at the
front of trolleys that went by themselves. That was some thing.
He also thought that you could have fitted the whole station at
home into a small corner of this one, where lines of rails seemed
to stretch away out of sight. Before the train went, two men got
into his empty carriage. They spoke funny and he found it fairly
hard to understand what they were saying. Very clean shaven and
hard white collars and creases in the pants that you could have
used for a knife. Bald, gleaming skulls and brief-cases, so he got
up and went into the corridor and made his way to the dining-
car. White linen on the tables and gleaming cutlery and waiters,
or whatever they were, in short white coats. Very natty, and they
called him 'sir' for the first time in his life and he tried to pre-
tend that he was a rich man hopping over for a short trip to London, and that he had more money than he knew what to do with,

but that was a hard thing to imagine when he could still get the smell of the cleaners from his best suit, the cuffs of which had been carefully darned by sister Cissie, and he thought of the overpowering wealth burthening his inside pocket – nineteen pounds, eleven shillings and a few coppers. He thought of the hard job he had had saving that out of his two pounds five a week as a temporary clerk, and just for a few seconds he let his heart fall to his boots when he thought of himself off to London with a small sum like that, no definite prospect of a job, and nothing but the address in his pockets of the brother of Cissie's husband Jim.

Then he said, To hell with it, I'm not going to think about it. I'm young and I'm strong, and I can't be worse off than I was at home; so he tucked into his soup and his roast-beef and the square of Yorkshire pudding, and the bread pudding with the raisins in it and the custard on top, and after that a cup of tea and a rectangle of cake, and the bill was three shillings and sixpence, and in a moment of great magnanimity he also gave the chap who had called him 'sir' a tanner for himself, and he thought that he was a very big noise indeed.

Later he stood on the station at Euston, appalled at the size of the thing and remembering the miles of backs of houses through which the train had passed, standing up alone in the middle of the bustle, the hiss of steam and the chug of trolleys and the funny-looking lines of taxis, and enormous voices booming over loudspeakers and neon signs on this and that, and he looked at the bit of London he could see through the great opening of the railway and he thought, Where the hell do I go from here? People were meeting other people and there was much loud talking and kissing and hugging, and he felt as alone as a fly in the middle of the Atlantic Ocean, and for one awful moment of weakness he wished that he was back where he had come from. But then he tightened his lips and said, What the hell, and he opened his coat and took out the envelope with the address on it, looked at it, reached out and caught a hurrying porter by the arm.

'How do I get from here to Ealing?' he asked.

The porter stopped. 'Tike the tube, mite,' he said, waving his arm.

Pat didn't know what he was saying.

'What's that?' he asked, holding tight to this bit of humanity.

The porter took pity on him. 'The tube, mite,' he said slowly, as if he was talking to a child, and then as the light of understanding failed to dawn on Pat's face, 'Over there,' he went on, waving an arm, 'underground.'

Pat's eyes followed his arm. He saw the sign UNDERGROUND with all the funny dots surrounding it, and the stairs leading down apparently to the bowels of the earth.

'Oh, thanks a lot,' he said, releasing the porter, who went his way.

Pat scratched his head before he bent and took up the suitcase. I'm as wise now, he thought, as I was in the beginning, but he made his way to the sign and cautiously descended the stairs.

He was bewildered below: Signs saying TO THE TRAINS and maps on the walls. He looked at them, the different colours that meant they went to different places. He found Ealing after a lot of striving, but he was as badly off then as ever. Ealing Broadway and Ealing Common. Were they the same or what were they? And was the place he had to go anywhere near them? The lighted lists of names with the fares to each of them were little help to him either. There was an office with a chap shooting tickets at people. He waited until there was a lull and then went over to him.

'Look,' he said, slowly, as if the chap was an eejit. 'I want to get to this address,' holding it out. The man bent to look at it.

'Forty-eight Acacia Avenue,' he said. 'Never heard of it. Near Ealing, is it?'

'Yes,' said Pat.

'Don't know,' said the other. 'Give you a ticket to Ealing, if you like. Not much help though if you don't know where you're going.'

'I'm afraid I don't,' said Pat.

'Best thing you can do, chum,' said the other, 'is to go by bus.'

'How do I do that?' Pat asked.

'Outside the station,' said the man, 'hop a bus to the B.B.C., get a Green Line coach, and bob's your uncle.'

'Thanks,' said Pat, passing on.

'You're welcome,' said the other, shooting another ticket to the customers held up by Pat.

Pat went up the stairs again, slightly bewildered. Apart from the fact that he didn't know where the B.B.C. was or what a Green Line coach was, or what the chap meant by 'bob's your uncle', he was doing fine. He got mad for a moment and thought, Christ, Jim's brother could have sent someone to meet me, and then he had to laugh, because Jim's brother didn't know him, or he the other. They just knew he would be coming and that was that. Anyhow, he wasn't a child to be frightened by silly things like this, so he toughened himself and went out and found a bus to the B.B.C. To his surprise it was all quite easy because there were the green buses lined up ready to proceed, and when he asked one of the conductors which was the bus to Ealing, the other told him, and not only that but the conductor of the Ealing bus knew exactly where Pat wanted to go and promised to let him down there, and soon he was sitting in the bus, looking out of the window with his mouth open as he tried to screw his neck to see the tops of the buildings through which he was passing.

Then he thought about his trip in the first bus and he felt his face getting red and the sweat in his armpits. It had been very embarrassing. He got on the right bus. The conductor was a man with a big stomach and a red, cheerful face, the cap of his worn back on his head. Pat noticed that the creases in his fingers were black from handling coins. He said where he wanted to go and asked if the other would tell him when they got there, and then handed over his coppers.

'Here,' said the conductor, 'what's this? Tryin' to put one across me, mate?'

'What is it?' Pat asked.

'Pennies with bloomin' chickens he gives me,' said the conductor, turning and addressing the other passengers. There were a lot of them and they all looked back, enquiringly first, and then, as Pat saw the grins coming on their faces, he felt himself going hot first and then cold. 'Now, I ask you! Good King George ain't good enough for this bloke. Has to have his pennies with chickens on them!'

'I'm sorry,' said Pat in a sort of whisper, wishing that the bus would run into a ravine and go down into a great blackness. 'It's Irish. It's a mistake.'

'I'll say,' said the other, grinning largely. 'Can't have that, you know! Not that it ain't pretty! A bloomin' hen and her clutch. Could do with it for my supper, I could.' His audience laughed at this sally. He handed back the penny again. 'Look, you keep it, mate. Come in handy when you're hungry sometime. Me, I'll stick to His Majesty, I will. What'll you Irish be up to next? Pennies with hens on them! Coo, love a duck!' and he went on to the next passenger.

Pat frantically took the loose change out of his pocket now and scrutinized it. No; it was all right. No Irish money left. He didn't know how the penny had escaped his attention. He thought he had got nothing but English money left. He put back the change and looked out the window again. He could see that conductor's face and would probably see it for the rest of his days. To have attention drawn to him like that! Mother a God! Then he had to grin as he thought about it further, and the sweating he had done and the crinkles around the conductor's eyes. He laughed then when he thought that it was a damn good job he hadn't tendered an Irish shilling. What would the conductor have said to the imprint of a bull on the coin? A bull with all his faculties. That would have given the conductor something to be funny about!

He brought his attention back to London. It was so big that it was overpowering his small-town mind. The wide streets, the milling multitudes, the masses of machinery, the policemen with the white things on their arms, colossal shops, towering buildings, flashing traffic lights, and miles and miles of streets, never-ending, twisting around corners into other streets that appeared never-ending. He thought of his own town. It had seemed quite big really, with its long, winding main street and the streets off it. It seemed quite a walk to go from one end of it to the other on a summer's evening when you were parading to see if the lassies were around and there might be one you might click with. Now in retrospect it was a weeshie thing, small and narrow and village-like, and the country people with their baskets and the horses and carts and the donkeys seemed like things out of another world and so far, far away. He liked this. He liked the bigness of it. Millions of people and you didn't know one of them. And not one of them knew you.

Away the bus flashed through the streets where the big buildings became fewer, into suburbs almost all alike. A row of houses and then a shopping centre and a cinema and then another long row of houses and then another shopping centre. All the shops in the different centres seemed to be exactly the same, the same names over them and the same things in the windows. The cinemas seemed to be replicas of one another, except that the names were different on some and the same on others. Narrower streets, and then the big buses that were like other double-decker buses except they had yokes out of the top of them like the trams in Dublin, although these were running on tyres instead of tracks and they went along with just a whine out of them instead of the grinding bite of steel on steel.

Pat thought he had only been in the bus for a few minutes when he felt the conductor tapping him on the shoulder.

'This is where you get off,' said the conductor.

'Thanks,' said Pat, hefting down his case and going to the door.

'Up that street there and first on your right,' pointing.

'Thanks a lot,' said Pat, dismounting.

'You're welcome,' said the conductor, closing the door and pressing the bell, and Pat stood there watching it until the bus went from his sight around a further corner. It had been the first friendly thing he had met and he wanted to hold on to it.

Then he turned his face to the long street before him.

2

It seemed to stretch to infinity, that street, and the early summer sun was going to bed at the end of it. It wasn't a street actually: a broad, macadamized road, smooth and gleaming, with cars and lorries and motor-cycles tearing up it as if someone had poured scalding hot water on their tails. Houses exactly similar. Brick, brick, brick. Brown brick and red brick and yellow brick, with here and there a lacing of concrete to break the monotony. Gardens in front of each house, small gardens with wooden gates and concrete pillars with knobs on iron chains stretched between them. Rose trees and bushes and flowers and a scattering of green hedges. The numbers on the doors made him smile: 486, on the other side 485. God, imagine that! A number 30 at home would have been a phenomenon. The paths were as regular as the houses, square blocks neatly laid, gullies regular, concreted and cleaned. Just dust and pieces of paper and an odd empty cigarette packet. At home it would have been dust and wisps of straw and hay and what the asses, horses, jennets, sheep and pigs that passed through the town would leave after them.

He stopped his thinking and hurried on. The first turn on the right? Sounded simple, really, but as he realized by the time he came to it, the first turn on the right was at least a mile up the road, and he felt that his fairly light suitcase was packed with lead weights by the time he reached it. He stopped there and wiped the sweat off his forehead and opened his coat. Yes, there it was, the name of the road: written on iron painted white, fixed against the wooden palings. Not many people about here;

seemed to be a sort of secluded backwater. On the other road all the people seemed to be in cars. An old lady standing at her door talking to a man whose bicycle was parked at the kerb. A few vans with firms' names on them delivering parcels.

He took up his case and went right: 48, hah? He looked at the numbers on the nearest doors. My God, 346. Sweet hour! That meant he still had a few miles to go to get to 48. He felt cheated somehow and annoyed at the size of the things. He smiled rue-fully and went on. If I can feel annoyed, he thought, it must be a good sign. On and on and on, like a pilgrimage to Croagh Patrick; but all pilgrimages must have an end, all travail must sometime cease, so there he stood with his hand on the gate of 48. No different from the other houses, but it seemed to Pat that it was a special fairy house built in the clouds. Bay windows with austere curtains behind them. The garden in front trimmed and pruned and primed like a virgin for confirmation. Windows and door painted a pale green, like Mother Eire's cloak. He grinned, reached down, and fumbled at the funny little latch on the inside of the gate, opened it, closed it primly behind him again, and walked lightly up the concrete path. Two steps up to the door and a gentle rap on the small knocker.

He was excited again. He didn't know what Jim's brother was like. All he knew was that he was married, had been in England for a long, long time, had no children. Jim had sat down to write him the letter (Jim, who hadn't much schooling, frowning over the paper, the penny pen clutched furiously in his hand, the look of absolute concentration in his whole body – good old Jim: he hated anything to do with the written word, but he had gone through it all for the sake of Pat). Well, they had an answer back saying yes, Jack would be willing to take him in for a few weeks until he had got a job. It wasn't exactly what one would call a terribly enthusiastic letter, but then maybe Jack was as bad a writer as Jim, although Pat didn't think so. However, here he was, five or six hundred miles from home inside twenty-four hours, and destiny holding out a fingertip to him. No wonder his heart was beating faster than usual!

He turned as the door opened. A woman was looking at him. She was smallish and thinnish and her hair, worn loose, was brownish and her eyes were blueish. In fact, as Pat came to realize later, there was a lot of -ish in her. Just nondescript. Fairly old, with an apron on her very clean. A blouse over that and her chest flat-ish. There I go again with the -ish, he thought.

She smiled tentatively. Her lips were pale and it made her teeth look yellow, but he liked her smile. It was quiet.

'I'm Pat Moore,' he said.

It took a few seconds for her to sort that out, and then she smiled with her eyes too and stepped back, opening the door wider. 'Come in,' she said. 'We were expecting you. We didn't know whether it would be today or tomorrow. I thought you were someone selling something. They always are.' A little colour had come into her pale cheeks.

'Thanks very much,' said Pat, stepping past her into a small hallway with hardly enough room for the two of them in it. She closed the front door and then leaned forward to open another one beside her.

'Won't you come in?' she asked.

He went in. It was a sort of living-room—dining-room. Two windows. The one in front and the one at the side looking at the side of the nearest house. Wireless on the table under the front window. A sort of hard-looking couch in front of the fire. Two fireside chairs, and at the back of that a table with chairs. Table laid for two. Knives and forks and cups and things. On the walls, to his surprise, many holy pictures, the same as at home. The Blessed Virgin, and Our Lord Crucified and with the bleeding heart. A Little Bit of Heaven, he thought, like home, sweet home.

'Jack isn't home yet,' she said, 'but he'll be here very soon.'

'Hope I'm not troubling you,' said Pat. It was the smallness of the room. With all the furniture and the pictures and the ceiling that seemed to be very near his head and him with his case and overcoat on, it felt as though there wasn't room to breathe.

'No,' said she and then, as if reading his mind. 'They are small houses. This is only a bungalow. Big enough for the two of us.'

'I noticed that,' said Pat. 'The street below is all two-storey houses.'

'Yes,' she said, 'that's right. Won't you take off your coat?'

She puzzled him. She seemed to be a little lost, like a ship without a . . . how was this it went? Like a rat without a tail, like a ship without a sail.

'I'm sorry Jack isn't here,' she said.

Is Jack the sail? Pat wondered.

'Thanks, I will,' he said, dropping his case and removing his overcoat.

She took it from him. 'I'll leave it in the hall,' she said, going out slowly as if glad of an opportunity of getting away from her obvious embarrassment.

Pat sat on the couch in front of the fire. There were book shelves on either side of the fireplace. He looked at them. He was surprised. They were all religious books. Talk about the lives of the saints! Thick books too. Practically every saint in the calendar. He lifted some of the smaller ones. They were all of them religious too, thin little sixpenny volumes about *Christian Marriage, Youth and Sex, The Fallacies of H.G. Wells, Christ amongst the Lepers, The Chinese Missions.*

She came back again. There was another taut silence as they looked at one another. For the life of him Pat couldn't break it. She succeeded with an obvious effort.

'Did you have a nice journey?' she asked. Her voice was small and gentle, as if she was afraid of hearing her own voice. She sat on the edge of the couch.

'Yes,' said Pat. 'It was grand.'

'How is Jim?' she asked.

'Oh, Jim is fine,' said Pat, glad of something he could talk about. 'Full of life and children. He sent you all his love.'

'I never met him,' she said.

'He has a picture of you,' said Pat. 'A wedding picture.'

'Oh yes,' she said. 'I remember that.'

Pat couldn't remember it. Just a woman in a long skirt, with a big hat pulled down on her head; hardly see her face at all.

'Would you like to wash?' she asked, after another silence. 'I'll have the tea ready as soon as Jack comes.'

'I would indeed,' said Pat, standing up.

She went out another door beyond the fireplace. He followed her, carrying his case. There were three doors facing them. One was open. It was the kitchen, he could see. A white scrubbed table, tiled floor, a range, a sink, cupboards, and more holy pictures.

She opened one of the other doors. 'This is the bathroom,' she said; and then, opening the one beside it, 'This is where you'll sleep. It's a bit small, I'm afraid. That's ours.'

It was small and bare. Cream walls, a window looking out on the back garden, where growing potato stalks reared their heads. Hedges of peas or beans. A small wooden bed with blue-coloured blankets.

'This is nice,' he said, heaving down his case.

'We meant that for the children,' she said surprisingly, 'if they came.' There was some sort of look in her eyes. He felt sorry for her suddenly. She looked at him. 'Jim has a lot of children, hasn't he?'

'Too many,' said Pat heartily. 'Crawling all over you. Can't get a sleep on a Sunday morning.' But he was smiling as he thought of them milling on his bed and he laughing just as loudly as any of them.

'They must be nice for him, all the same,' she said. 'Well, come back when you're finished. Jack will be in soon.' She went then, closing the door behind her.

He stood awhile. He felt as if he wasn't part of himself at all, as if he was acting in a part of a dream. That was being tired, of course. So little sleep and the anti-climax of the excitement. Ah, forget it, he said then, and set about opening his case. He didn't unpack it, just threw it on the bed and then went into the bathroom. Very small: just the bath and the W.C.; no room to swing a cat, but well up on the house at home, Jim's house. No bath there. Bath in front of the fire on a Saturday night when everyone else was in bed, standing in the zinc bath, trying to swing your arms around to get at your back. It would be good to have one lying down. W.C. in the house as well: civilized. At home you ran outside the house hoping that you wouldn't get pneumonia in the middle of the night. Pat laughed and sank his face into the soapy water. He felt much better when he was cleaned. Wondering at the amazing amount of dirt one could collect on a journey. He brushed his teeth too, to make a job of it, straightened his tie, and

27

ran the comb through his thick hair. You'll do, Pat, he said to the man in the mirror then, and opening the two doors went back to the other room.

She was putting milk and sugar on the table. She looked up and smiled at him.

'Jack just came in now,' she said. 'He's in the kitchen taking off his working clothes. He'll be in in a minute.'

'That's good,' said Pat, sitting on the couch. He was barely there when he heard the door behind him opening. He got up from the couch again and turned to face the door. He found himself looking at Jack.

Bald all up from the forehead to the back of the head, the rest of his hair clipped close to the skull. Grey hair. A long, thin hard neck going into the collar of a working khaki shirt, a waistcoat and blue trousers with slippers on his feet. His shirtsleeves rolled and showing thin, muscular arms browned by the sun. He was taller than Pat, thinner but tougher-looking. His nose was thin and whitened when he opened the thin lips. Eyes pale blue. He held out his hand; Pat took it.

'You got here, I see,' said Jack, not terribly enthusiastically.

'Yes,' said Pat.

'You should have stayed at home,' said the other, passing him to sit on the sofa in front of the fire. 'England is no place for young Irish fellas.'

'It doesn't seem to have done you any harm,' said Pat.

A sidelook from Jack's eyes. 'Aye,' he said, leaning forward to stir the fire. 'But I'm different. God was in my heart, so He was, since I left home, and I kept Him there.'

Pat was stumped.

'You go and get the tea, Mary.' This to his wife without even a look over his shoulder. She moved to the kitchen. Pat felt that she had been waiting to be told what to do. Did that apply to everything, he wondered. 'I've seen what happens t' them,' Jack went on then. Pat noticed idly that he hadn't lost his Irish accent. He sat on the chair near the fire.

'Aye, I've seen what happens t' them,' Jack went on, raking at the coal with the poker. 'Good Catholic boys. Off they go. No Mass on Sundays. Then they drop the altar, too. Then they drop their religion. Whoring and drinkin' in the sight a God. Shame on their race and their religion. Eatin' meat on Fridays.'

Pat just managed to stifle a laugh. Then, he thought, It's not really a laughing matter at all. The man actually means it. There was an intense look on his face as he watched the sparks from the disturbing poker. He noticed that the hands were big, with heavy veins on the backs of them, and the fingers spatulate and powerful looking.

Pat felt he had to say something. 'They're not all like that, surely,' he said.

'No, not all of them,' said the other. 'A few like meself that has t' be prayin' to God for them, the bastards. It's a wonder the Mother a God doesn't be smitin' them out a the sky with balls of fire.'

My God, Pat thought, what is this? 'It's their own life, isn't it?' he asked.

'It is not,' said the other, turning to him. 'They come to the land a the pagans, and they should show be their example that there is a little Christianity left in the world. Not them. One look at the fleshpots and they have their faces stuck into them like pigs' snouts in a trough. It'd drive yeh mad, I tell yeh, looking at the small churches here, and they too big for the people that go into them, when the Irish should be packin' them from door to door, grateful to St Patrick for rescuing them from hell's fire. No, they turn around and throw their religion back inta the teeth a God.'

'Have a fag,' said Pat, holding out the box, thinking this might provide a diversion.

'I do not smoke,' said Jack, 'and I do not drink.'

That's one up my la-la, said Pat to himself. But he took out a cigarette all the same and put it in his mouth and put a match to the end of it. He blew smoke out then and said, 'Well, I like a smoke myself.'

'I suppose you drink too?' the other asked.

'An odd one,' said Pat.

'Well, I hope you'll be sober while you're in this house,' said Jack bluntly. 'I spent me life makin' this a house a God, and I'm not goin' to have it any other way. You'll keep drink out a this house while you're in it, and women too.'

This is a great welcome to the exile, Pat thought, feeling his neck getting red. If only, he thought, I had anywhere else in the world to go I'd rise now and I'd get my case and I'd walk out of this house. My God, he thought, maybe I'm in bed dreaming all this. He managed to swallow and speak.

'You're not much like your brother Jim,' he said pleasantly, keeping the bite out of it.

'No,' said the other, 'and I'm grateful for that. I do not want to be, like Jim, a scavenger for a local council all my life. I came here to be something and I am something. Jim never had anything in his mind but go-a-day, come-a-day, and God send Sunday.'

'He's happy,' said Pat.

'Pigs like to roll in dirt too,' said Jack.

'I don't think you know your brother very well,' said Pat, biting back bile. 'He's one of the happiest men I know. Money doesn't mean a lot to him. His happiness is coming home from a hard day's work, eating his tea, and rolling around with his five kids.' That's hitting under the belt now, me brave Jack, he thought, and I hope you like it.

Jack looked at him sharply. Pat's face was as bland as a baby's.

'God sends crosses to every man,' said Jack, after a time. 'I can bear mine with fortitude.'

Knowledge, fortitude, piety, and the fear of the Lord. My God, Pat thought, the man is living his life out of the penny catechism. It just didn't seem possible. A wave of depression came over him as he looked at the smoke from his cigarette. Why did he have to be like that, he wondered. When he had thought of coming to Jim's brother at all, he had thought of a welcome smile, and how's Jim, the old so-and-so, and what's he doing, and how's his kids getting on, and tell me all about him and all about yourself, and how did you like the trip over, and did you see anything of note. And Pat had pictured himself in front of a fire, pouring away all the enforced silence of a traveller, the difference between this and that, and what it had meant to him. And here he was now, he who always loved to talk and to hear others talking, stultifying under the roof of this man, who from all the appearances was on the point of becoming a religious maniac. Maybe, Pat thought, the surly bastard has made it a house of God, but God isn't in it, there's nothing in this house but a great emptiness and fear.

'I have it ready now,' said Mary, coming in with the tray.

Indeed, she's afraid, Pat thought. I wouldn't blame her. But it was obvious to him, who had only been here for a short time, that whatever personality Mary had had was beaten into the holy pictures hanging on the wall. That is the voice that is afraid to lift itself. Had she ever fought, he wondered, as he pulled his chair over to the table on a gesture from Jack. Had there ever been a time when she had felt like hitting him on the head with the shovel? If so, she had failed. And probably, he thought, it is far too late for her to save herself now. She probably wouldn't even realize it if you pointed it out to her. He thought of Cissie at home and Jim. There was a house that was overcome with happiness, raptured in near poverty, the caressing eyes of Cissie resting on Jim, and the way he would lay his work-stained arm on her shoulder for a second, curly hair falling over his forehead and his kindly eyes twinkling.

'What were you thinkin' a doin'?' Jack asked him, pushing a sausage into his mouth.

'I don't know,' said Pat. 'Anything, I suppose. I was a clerk at home.'

'Well, you won't clerk here,' said Jack. 'Clerks here are twopence a dozen. The best thing you can do is come in on my job.'

'What's your job?' Pat asked.

There was a pause as Jack masticated his sausage. He was sitting opposite Pat, with Mary silently eating her meal at the side of the table. It was a nice meal, well cooked. Sausages and bacon and eggs and nice funny pancakes, which Pat had never eaten before. Hot tea, bread and butter, and honey. Pat was hungry but couldn't eat. He only ate when he saw Mary's soft wondering eyes regarding him, and then he pushed the food in lest she might be offended.

'Well,' said Jack, and Pat lowered his eyes from the sausage grease on his chin. 'I'm a foreman for a big building contractor. We're at the extension of a railway now, a few miles from here. I can get you on there.'

'Doing what?' Pat asked.

'Working,' said the other, and paused again to take a sip of his tea. He sucked it. 'Not, of course, the work you have been used to.' There was a slight sneer there, Pat felt, and was conscious of the other looking at his smooth hands. 'You'll have to work hard with your hands.'

'I'm not afraid to work,' said Pat.

'Why should you,' Jack asked, 'when God said that by the sweat of our brow shall we earn our bread?' Pat silently hoped that God was taking a poor view of Jim's brother. 'Besides, you haven't much choice, have yeh?'

'No, that's true,' said Pat. 'I haven't much choice.'

'The wages is about three-ten with overtime,' said Jack. 'That'll leave yeh nicely off. You can pay Mary thirty shillings for boarding you, and you'll have enough over to buy yourself things.'

'That seems all right,' said Pat.

'We'll see how yeh shape,' Jack said. 'If you're good you'll last. But I can't guarantee anythin'. Just because yer me brother's brother-in-law won't save yeh from bein' sacked if yer a slacker.' Don't let him bring You into it again, God, thought Pat. 'The laws a God is that every man shall do an honest day's toil commensurate with his wages,' Jack went on despite Pat's plea.

'Yeh can come down with me in the mornin',' said Jack, 'and let the boss look you over. Then you can start next week.'

'Thanks,' said Pat.

He helped Mary to wash up, despite her soft protestations. Anything at all to get away from Jack.

Mary tried in her quiet way to let him talk about his journey, but it was no good. He couldn't do it, and she hadn't the necessary mental equipment to get him out of himself, to break the crust of despondency that was around his heart. The kitchen was small and very clean: a coal range, with the metal parts gleaming, and a kitchen press, and a lot of doo-dahs, and the inevitable pictures on the wall. Jack was apparently patriotic as well as religious, because the walls here too were painted green. In fact, thinking of the green sea and his surprise at the green grass and the green buses and the green-tiled roofs of the houses and green gates and palings, Pat was beginning to think that he had to leave home in order to really appreciate what the colour green meant to man.

'Working on Jack's job will be very hard for you,' said Mary suddenly, handing him a plate for drying.

'I don't mind,' said Pat.

'You're not used to it,' she went on. 'I can see that from your hands. Maybe you oughtn't to take it. Maybe you ought to wait around and try for something else.' She said this a little fearfully, lowering her voice. Poor Mary, Pat thought.

'No,' he said, 'I'll take this. I haven't a lot of money. It is easier to take this, and then if I don't like it look for something else while I have it. I was out of work since I left school. Odd jobs here and there at home. I know what it is to have one job and lose it and then watch the few quid you saved from it dwindling along with it. That's worse. It's bad for your soul so it is. If I did that, I would be afraid, watching and waiting. That's not good.'

'No,' said Mary, with a sigh, 'I suppose it isn't.'

He patted her on the shoulder with his free hand.

'Don't worry,' he said, smiling into her eyes. 'I'll be all right.'

'Pat,' she said then, 'Jack is the way he is because he's disappointed, you know, about children. He always wanted children.'

'I know,' said Pat.

But he knew she was wrong. Jack was that way because that was the way he was made, and if he had seven legions of children he would still be that way. Pat thought how popular Jack must be as a foreman. He didn't have to leave home to meet Jack's type. A smattering of education, unimproved by reading books which he didn't properly understand and never digested. Jack was like a reformed boozer or a reformed prostitute or a reformed criminal – the outraged condemnation of their former habits! But Jack was worse because he probably had never been boozer or a prostitute or a criminal. It he had been he might have been a better man in the long run.

'We'd better go in now,' said Mary. 'Thanks for helping me.'

'It's a pleasure,' said Pat, drying his hands.

'Wouldn't you like to go out awhile,' she asked, 'and look around?'

'No,' said Pat, 'I wouldn't.' It was dark and they had the lights on in the house. The street outside to his imagination was so long and you would have to walk and walk to get to the end of it. 'I'm tired and I want to go to bed. Besides, I'll see it all tomorrow in the light of day. It's nicer that way. Things are never the same at night.'

They went back to the room.

Jack was reading a book. It was probably about a saint. He didn't look up from it when they came in. Mary sat on the couch and started to darn socks. Pat sat on the chair and smoked a cigarette. There was little conversation. Now and again Mary asked him in her quiet voice about Jim and the children. Pat answered her, told their names and their ages and a few of the cute things they could do. He said those a little louder, because he knew that Jack was listening and he wanted to give him a pain in the craw if he could. All the same, as he looked at the hard profile presented to him he thought how lucky Mary was that she didn't have any children. He thought what a grand time they would have in this house, the grey hairs she would have protecting them from their father. He thought how the broad leather belt Jack wore around his trousers with the brass buckle on it would have been brought into play. He had seen Jack's type before and he didn't like him. A grand prospect for the future, he thought. The sadistic pleasure the brave Jack would get out of beating a bare bottom.

I shouldn't be thinking like this, he thought then. Maybe the man is a saint for all I know. The business about the job had been a challenge, he knew, though Pat hadn't intended becoming a labourer except as a last resort. He had a good education and a quick brain and he had thought that he would have got something else. He couldn't see that there was any need to work with his hands when he would be better with his brain, and as he knew from home, the danger of becoming a labourer was that you might find it harder to become anything else afterwards. However, to hell with him he thought, I'll show him; and then he knew that he was foolish. That was the danger of the man, that he could trap a better intellect than his own for the most paltry reasons. Looking at Mary, he wondered how she had come to marry him. She had a nice forehead and she spoke nicely and she looked as if she shouldn't have been so subdued as she was. A far cleverer woman than her husband, he thought, and yet he had her beaten into a tame mouse. I wonder, is that it, beaten? Is that the word? He wouldn't put it past him, Pat thought.

About half an hour afterwards Jack issued another challenge.

'We'll say the Rosary now,' he said, closing his book. 'Get me me beads, Mary.'

Mary rose dutifully and got the rosary beads from the sideboard and handed them into his hands. Jack rose, preparatory to getting down on his knees.

'We always say the family Rosary,' he said. 'I hope ye do at home. Or is that place becomin' as pagan as the next?'

Pat rose to his feet.

'You'll say it without me, I'm afraid.' he said. 'I'm tired. I'm going to bed.'

'It only takes ten minutes,' said Jack, his thin lips tightening.

Pat saw Mary looking at him, a plea in her eyes. It was a silly issue in a way, but he felt that it was an issue.

'You can give ten minutes to your God, can't you?' Jack persisted.

'I can,' said Pat. 'To my own God. Not yours. My prayers are always private.'

There, he thought now, it's laid at your feet and what are you going to do about it? His eyes were steady as they looked into the pale blue eyes opposite him. He thought that Jack became pale about the jaws for the few seconds that the tension lasted. Now is your chance, Jack, he thought. You wield the power. Open the door and say, Go into the night, you bloody pagan, and never darken me doors again. He could do that. It was the only weapon he had. Let him use it now if he likes, Pat thought, and to hell with him!

Jack's eyes shifted first. 'Well, that's your own business,' he said then, turning his back and letting himself down on his knees, and ostentatiously blessing himself with the cross of his beads, saying, 'In the name of the Father and of the Son and of the Holy Ghost, Amen.'

Pat was out of the room before he started the preliminaries.

He sat on the bed and found that he had been very tensed. I won that round anyway, he thought. He was sorry for Mary's sake. It was nothing to do with the Rosary either. He wasn't particularly religious and any night at home he happened to be in when they were saying the Rosary, he always joined in, although it was very funny there with the kids supposed to be saying the Rosary too, and they crawling all over everybody and Pat tickling them surreptitiously, and Cissie pretending to be very cross and then giggling at a sally, and Jim saying, God forgive ye, and making bloodcurdling threats which nobody thought he meant. Maybe it wasn't very devout, but at least in its own way it was holy. Far holier, he thought, than the empty austerity of what goes on out there.

Pat stripped himself to the accompaniment of the droning voices, switched off the light and got into the bed. It wasn't a very comfortable bed, but the mattress was no harder than the one he had at home. He put his head under his arms and thought over the day with his eyes closed. At first he felt the unsteadiness of the boat and the smell of it, and then he saw the telegraph poles flashing by in front of his eyes, and he was surrounded by all the noises of the great city; and then suddenly and unaccountably he was flooded with a terrible depression so that to his shame he just managed to hold back tears that forced their way almost to his eyelids. He shook that off, and said, My God, what sort of an eejit are you at all, at all? The end, he thought had been so different to his imaginations. The rest of it had more or less come up to scratch. But then, he thought, wouldn't Jack depress even a bishop? He thought that was good, and it made him laugh into the darkness.

Well, I'm here, anyhow, he thought, and maybe I have learned a lesson. That things will never be the same as your imagination pictures them to be. That's true. Then he wondered what sort of work he would have to do, and hoped that it wouldn't be too hard altogether. After all, he was barely three years finished with the secondary school. His jobs since had been soft, if not too frequent, but he had never had to work very hard. Certainly he had never had to work his body, apart from playing football and hurling, which couldn't be regarded as work in a proper sense.

I'll face it when it comes, he said, and turned on his side, pulling the bedclothes up to his chin.

Maybe, he thought then, I shouldn't have been that way about the Rosary, but I was right about it, I know I was. He hoped God wasn't offended, but he was sure He wasn't. Pat had a picture of God as a nice man with a quirk to His lips as he watched Pat's efforts at analysis of the soul. So, just to assure Him that he hadn't meant anything personal about the Rosary he crossed himself and started to say a Hail Mary.

He was asleep before it was finished.

3

The sun wasn't hot, but it shone on the clouds blanketing the earth, and had the same effect as a fire in an oven.

Pat paused to wipe the sweat from his forehead. He didn't straighten his body, because he knew the excruciating agony that the straightening would have caused him. He just dropped the head of the pickaxe in the bottom of the ditch he was digging, rested his left arm up on the handle carefully, and raised his other hand to his forehead as if he was an old man of a hundred and two, crippled with all the diseases of the bone that affect old age. He was wearing only a singlet and trousers, with the ends of them pushed into rubber boots with the tops turned down, which was then the fashion for what the well dressed worker should wear on a hot day. He was wet with perspiration, and the only ease he got from the heat was when the wet singlet flapped in and out from his body.

He took his hand down then and looked at the palm of it. A revolting sight, he thought. It was covered with three days of blisters. Will they ever get hard at all? Pat wondered. The others had assured him that after the first day everything would be all right. The second day's work burst the first day's blisters and set up some of its own. Today's work had burst the blisters of yesterday and the day before and the whole top of his palm below the fingers was a pulpy mass of purple and red. Black blisters about to burst and the white ones, from which the water was oozing, all mixed up with the dried dirt of the ditch. His hands were very painful. They were not too bad, he discovered, if he kept them constantly wrapped around the handle of the pick, but once he removed them from a position to which they had become accustomed and tried to straighten them from the crooked way they were fashioned, sharp pains shot through them and went up his arm to merge with the groaning of his tendon muscles.

He never knew that there were so many muscles in the body. Now he reckoned that there were about three thousand four hundred, and every one of them was acting as if it had been beaten separately by a rubber mallet. He straightened himself a little and groaned. The ones in the back were the worst, he thought. They started somewhere below the neck and went right down the body, so that when you moved one, ripples of pain shot up and down your back like the waves of the tide on a shore. It was the same way in front, where they started at your neck and went down your chest, so that every move of your sore arms pulled the muscles of your breasts and they sent the good word along to the padded muscles of your stomach.

He thought it wasn't as bad today as it had been the other two days. At least today he could more or less think about it and try and make it out. He only remembered the other two days as a blinding blur of agony. He sneered now as he thought of himself coming on the job the first day. The healthy way he had thrown off his coat. My God, the eejit! Dig a ditch he was told, along here, it's all marked out for you. Two by four. He winced as he thought of the way he had tackled it. With might and main. Take a look at the torso of a Samson! Watch the way the mighty muscles ripple in the arms and the back! I'll show them! Silhouette against the sky. The answer to a maiden's prayer.

Don't go down the mine, daddy. He had seen a few grins on the faces of the other workers. He had thought, Have those bastards nothing else to do all day but stand up there? I'll show them how money should be earned. Mostly Irish they were, too. One look at them was enough to tell him that. The Irish kissers of them! Country boys in the main. There are two classes of country boys in Ireland. The people in Dublin refer to everyone outside the Pale as country people. The people in the small towns refer to all the people outside their own walls as country people. So that even though Pat in Dublin would be a country boy, he from the fastness of his town, with its population of twenty thousand, regarded the men from Connemara as being very country boys. He'd show them how a civilized man could work. That was practically all he remembered.

When the break came he remembered sitting on the side of the ditch, with his bloody hands hanging between his knees. When a voice asked, 'Are you comin' down for yer dinner?' he had just enough energy to shake his head; and it had seemed only like a second until the call came again. Lay in on it now. Back to work again. He had managed to stand up, anyhow, and after that the only other thing he cared to remember was the sound of a voice behind his head. 'Here, for Jaysus' sake, take it aisy, will yeh? D'yeh want t'puncture yersel, do yeh?' Then the pick was taken out of his hand and he was lifted up out of the ditch as if he was a child, and he had been taught how to dig a ditch by Seamus. To Pat's hazy eyes Seamus was like a giant out of a fairy tale. A monster of a man, stripped to the waist, as brown as a sod of dried turf, with arms like legs, shoulders like a Hereford bull's and a smile like sun breaking through clouds. 'You let the oul shoulders do it,' Seamus had said. 'And when you dig with the effing shovel yeh push with yer bloody knee, and not with yer arms. Ye'll pull them outa the sockets and end up with a rupture, so you will, if you keep on that way.' Pat had muttered and got back into the ditch and the rest wasn't even a memory. Just home and sleep and groaning the next morning.

He put the next morning out of his head and the one that followed it. The sound of his stretched muscles screaming as he let himself down carefully on the bed, and after that, oblivion. Yesterday had been a dream too. Not as nightmarish as the first day, but still a dream. Voices speaking to him. The big face of Seamus looking at him anxiously. 'Are yeh comin' for yer dinner?' A shake of the head and a sitting in the ditch. Home and bed and oblivion, with the anxious eyes of Mary somewhere in the background.

He dug the point of the pick into the yellow, stone-littered earth. The stones were the worst, he thought. When the point of the pick hit them, a jar went back from it up your arms and right through your body. He was cautious now. He looked for the stones, dug the point of the pick beside them or behind them and jogged them loose, bent his back, stretched his arm, and scooped them out of the hole, so that there would be nothing left for the lift of the shovel but the soil. Not too bad. He was learning, but holy God, he was learning the hard way. Throw the pick aside then with as little energy as possible, just raising the heavy head and pushing the handle gently after it. Then reaching behind without looking (that would stretch the muscles of the neck) and finding the handle of the shovel, the wood on it shining from use, so that you had to gather a spit in your mouth and transfer it to your aching hands so that you would be able to get a grip on the shovel. Forward with the left knee, rest the handle of the shovel on it, push the blade of the shovel under the soil, heft it on your knee, joggle your knee, twitch your body and it was gone, and you proceeded with the next bit.

The whistle blew for dinner.

Pat dropped the blade of the shovel, wrapped his arms around the handle, and rested. That's something, he said, I didn't sit down. The thought of how the muscles of his behind would hurt if he did so might have something to do with it, but all the same he thought that he was coming on. There was a slither on the piled dirt beside him and the same voice said, 'Are yeh comin' to dinner?'

'I am,' said Pat, turning his head to look at the questioner.

It was Seamus.

'Yah-hoo!' roared Seamus. 'Yer comin' on so? Not so bad today, hah?'

'I don't know about that,' said Pat. 'There's no surcease from pain, but at least my brain is not numb.'

'All that means,' said Seamus, 'is that you're learnin'. Have a fag.' He held out a packet of Woodbines. Pat stretched and took one and lit it from the match Seamus had in his hand. He blew the smoke from his lungs then and grinned.

'I'm a terrible eejit, amn't I, Seamus?' he asked.

Seamus thought it over seriously, bending his great head.

'No, begod, you're not,' he said then, judiciously. 'You know, if it was any other man had tackled the job the way you did the first day he'd be a corpse now, so he would. Lookit, forget it.

Come on an' we'll go down to Jack's for a bitta mate, and we'll talk over it then.'

'All right,' said Pat, levering himself carefully out of the ditch. Seamus stretched one of his hands and wrapped it around Pat's arm and pulled. Pat roared like an impaled bullock. Seamus pulled his hand away again as if it was scorched.

'The oul muscles still bad?' he asked.

'Frightful,' said Pat, hauling himself out.

'It'll take another few days,' said Seamus, 'and then they'll be all right again. You haven't done work like this before, have you?'

'I don't have to answer that one, do I?' Pat replied.

Seamus laughed. A great boom of a laugh he had, that ended in a cough from the smoker's frog in his throat.

'No,' he said. 'Wan look at you diggin' a ditch 'd put an honest workman off his dinner.'

Pat stood up then, and felt like Napoleon when he crossed the Alps. Triumph. Alone I did it. Then he realized how hungry he was.

'My God,' he said. 'I could eat a fourteen-year-old child!'

'I don't think you'll get a child in Jack's place,' said Seamus, 'but you'll get a bellyful, anyhow.'

Pat slipped on his shirt and the coat over it, and then they slithered down the railway embankment they were creating. During this operation Pat noticed, almost for the first time, the masses of machinery surrounding them. The tall cranes raising delicate steel fingers to the sky, colossal concrete mixers, giant scoops on tracks. He stopped Seamus with his arm then.

'Listen,' he said, 'with all these huge yokes at hand, how does it happen that a feeble man like me has to be digging a ditch?'

Seamus laughed.

'They can't do everything,' he said. 'They can do most things. Some a them can nearly talk. But they's always a few holes and corners that only the hands a man can get inta.'

'I see,' said Pat grimly.

They went through the gate, joining a stream of other workers coming off the job. All dressed like themselves. Trousers tucked into the rubber boots with the tops turned down. Various headgears, the most popular being berets of different colours. All

43

laughing, smoking, cursing, and mostly in Irish accents. Sure my God, Pat thought, I needn't have left home at all. A few men with bowler hats and clean clothes. They would be the gangers. Most of them with English accents. Not English exactly. English with flattened consonants and broadened vowels.

'Up this way,' said Seamus.

They turned up a road under a bridge and saw the place before them. A large board building it was, painted yellow, with JACK'S PULL IN painted on it in great black letters. A terrific smell coming out of it of all sorts of food, the smell of boiled meat being the main ingredient, a sort of a stewy smell. They entered. It was crammed with workers, all talking in loud voices and laughing, and a fug in it of choice blend – Woodbines and roast beef. Two or three girls in soiled white coats, pushing their way through the throng with raised trays, avoiding the fingers that came out to pinch their thighs, screeching with loud voices above the din, 'Here now, none of that now! Cawn't you see I'm busy?' Taking the order and shouting to the place at the back with the counter where a man presided, a huge fat man with a red face streaming with sweat, hearing the call of the minions and passing it through a partition at the back. 'Roast and two for four'; 'Steak and kid for three'; 'Oh ky; oh ky, comin' up now, comin' up.'

It was a delightful confusion that Pat enjoyed. After all, dammit, I have been here for nearly a week now and all I've seen is the four walls of the house where I'm living and the job. Seamus pushed his way to the top. Anyone who might have been inclined to argue about his pushing methods took one look at him and decided to be friendly. Shouts of 'Here, take it aisy, Seamus!' 'Who the hell are yeh pushin', yeh bastard?' But all very friendly. And Seamus would say 'Lo, Joe. Howya, Jim. Ha-ha, Tomás,' raising his big palm and cracking it down on the back of some unfortunate with a forkful of food raised to his mouth. Spluttering curses and laughs from the others. A grand procession. Then at the top a small table, only big enough for two. Sitting there, squeezing the body into the hard wooden chair. The table covered with check oilcloth, soiled with the last eaters – bits of spilled stew, a bit of kidney, cigarette ash, and tea.

Seamus roaring, 'What yeh havin', Pat?' throwing a large thumb at the blackboard at the counter, where the menu was written in chalk. Pat reading: *Rst Bf and Two Veg. 10d. St. and Kid Pud. do. 11d. Irish Stew. 9d.* And down the list, *Custard and Apple Tart, Bread Pud.* He made it up quickly. You could have a great meal for a shilling and threepence.

'I'll have the oul roast beef,' he said.

Seamus turned his head and roared at the fat man.

'Here, Jack,' he said. 'Mate and cabbage, double distilled and the usual.'

Jack waves a large arm. 'Oh ky, Shymus, oh ky,' and then roars in the partition. 'Roast and veg, one once and one twice, C and A to follow. Char and cheese cike!' Then back to Seamus. 'Oh ky, Shymus?'

Seamus raises a hand.

'Oh ky, Jack,' imitating him and laughing.

'He's a great fella, that Jack,' he said then, turning back to Pat. 'Wait'll yeh see what yeh'll get! Great grub, so it is.'

'Isn't it very cheap?' Pat asked.

'Sure, it's the same everywhere,' said Seamus. Then he looks around for one of the girls, half rises to his feet and roars, 'Here, Rosy, come on up to hell here ou'r that and attend t' two gintlemen and don't mind the bloody pigs down there!' A screech from Rosy and loud and profane protestations from the insulted diners. A few dirty remarks thrown back in loud voices about Seamus and his ancestors, and then Rosy wriggling her way up to them. A tall girl, thin, with blonde hair black at the roots; lipstick, big eyes, with long lashes; a thin nose; prominent teeth; and slightly nasal tones. Her busy hand wiping at the table with a cloth.

'You didn't really ought to be shoutin' like that, Shymus. We 'eard you the first time. It ain't polite to be roarin' like that at lydies.'

Seamus saying, 'G'wan ou'r that, Rosy!' and slapping her on the bottom with a hand like a meat plate. Rosy screeching, ''Ere, Jack, see what 'e's doin'!' quite in good humour. The loud chuckle of Jack. ''Ere, Shymus, leave the ladies alone. Rosy ain't robust. You 'it Rosy again, and there won't be nothin' left.'

Laughter. Seamus: 'Sure she loves me, don't yeh, Rosy? Go on, give's an oul kiss.' His arm around her thin waist. Rosy: ''Ere, how am I supposed to get the grub?'

And then the grub. Steaming on plates. Piled with food. Metal forks and knives, still warm from the cleaning. Splash of salt. Pepper. Sauce. A dig with the fork. An open, anticipating mouth and the clash of white teeth. Um. Excellent. A cleaned plate. Eating as if he never saw food before. Realizing the awful emptiness of his stomach. Forgetting the pains and aches that had racked him. Wincing a little as the scattered gravy with the salt found its way into his bleeding hands. A clean plate and a sitting back to rub a stomach. Seamus packing it away. Double helpings. He'd want it, Pat thought, with a body like that. Then the apple tarts, with the creamy custard over it. After that a cup of tea with the sploshed saucers. Sugar, sure. And the cheesecakes. Oh, grand: big round things with strips and strips of stuff all mixed up on top of it. Very filling and sweet and nice. All for one and fourpence. Pat couldn't believe it.

And then the glory of a lighted cigarette and the pulling of the smoke into the lungs and the leaning back in the chair and pointing the plume of smoke to the low ceiling. Content? Practically.

Eventually they were finished eating. Some of the men had gone and the Pull In was more bearable: less smoke, less fug, and you could hear yourself talking.

'I don't think that Jack likes you, Pat,' said Seamus then, leaning his elbows on the table.

'Well, after giving me a meal like that for one and fourpence,' said Pat in reply, 'It seems to me that Jack loves me like a brother.'

'I don't mane that Jack,' said Seamus. 'I mane Jack the ganger.'

'Oh, him,' said Pat.

'Is he a relation of yours?' Seamus asked.

'His brother is married to my sister at home,' said Pat. 'I'm staying in his house.'

'I see,' said Seamus. 'Y' know that he's riding yeh, don't yeh?'

'Is he?' Pat asked. 'How?'

'Be makin' yeh dig that ditch,' said Seamus. 'Listen, no man born would set a raw hand like you diggin' that bloody ditch unless he had something special in for yeh. You should be attending the concrete mixer or even unloading gravel. Diggin' a ditch you're a total loss, so you are. And it's a cruel thing to do. Listen, would you like for me to give 'm a puck in the kisser for yeh?'

He said this earnestly, leaning forward and holding up a closed fist that could have burst in the door of a bank.

Pat laughed.

'No, thanks, Seamus,' he said. He paused then. 'I know he's riding me, and I know he doesn't like me, because it's mutual. I can imagine the holy satisfaction he has got out of the past two days. He wanted me to retire. He wanted me not to be able to do it. To go up to him and say, "You can stuff that oul job up yer gansie." Then he'd be right. Out I go into the night. A letter home to Jim. "Your brother-in-law is a no-good son of a gun."'

'I see,' said Seamus.

'No,' said Pat with determination; 'I'm going to dig that bloody ditch if it's the last thing I do. I have it nearly bet. I don't feel as bad at all today. And if I can turn around and dig this ditch I will have beaten him too, because he didn't think I would. And after that I'll tell him what I think of him. With the help of God.'

'Good man,' said Seamus then, leaning back with a smile on his face. Pat noticed once again the white teeth of him, big teeth that seemed just right for that big jawbone. He had a very kind face, Pat thought, for a young man. 'I'm glad too. You know the lads been bettin' on yeh. Five to one against that you wouldn't stick it. I knew you would. First minute I saw yeh I knew ye'd do it.'

'Thanks, Seamus,' said Pat, smiling and feeling good.

'What the hell!' said Seamus. 'Aren't yeh from me own part a the country? Heard your accent. Galway, says I at once. Amn't I a Galway man too? Listen, I sez to thim others, a Galway man is better than two a ye bogmen any day in the week. That's what I said. And isn't it true for me. The oul backbone is there, I tell yeh. No fancy-pantses come out a County Galway, that's what I said.'

'Are you long in England, Seamus?' Pat asked him.

'Two years,' said Seamus.

'Do you like it?' Pat persisted, wondering.

'Yeh,' said Seamus; 'I do. Sometimes mebbe I get lonely for a look at the sea. And I think how nice it'd be to be out in a currach in the sea at Rosmuc. And you miss the smell of the turf fire. But listen, I wouldn't change. You know what it's like there? Hard work and potatoes and salt. Fried mackerel and the arse out a yer trousers.'

'You work hard here too,' said Pat. 'It seems to me that all the hard labouring work is being done by Irish chaps like us.'

'Listen,' said Seamus. 'You wouldn't call that work. And look at the pay you get for it. Enough to eat on. And you can go and see films, can't you? And you can go and dance, can't you? And you can have a drink. You can see a bit of life. You can earn a bit of money and send it home to them at home. I send more money home to them now, money that I don't even miss, than we earned altogether there. What was it? Pull your guts out at the turf. Pull your guts out at the hay. Some months of the year break stones on the bloody roads for them at thirty bob a week, and you expected to get down on yer knees and thank them for it. Fellas gettin' up on the Dáil and shoutin', What are ye givin' all these lazy bastards in Connemara money for? Sugar? You come into the town. You have a Connemara accent. You wear a báinín and you talk Irish and they hate the sight of yeh – like the primitive man. Here there's a bitta dignity being a workman. They don't give a damn who yeh are or where yeh kem from or what way yeh talk. Can yeh work? they ask. And if yeh can work you're as good as the next man and better than most. So what's the answer. This is!'

There was silence then while Seamus rubbed his hand across his forehead and Pat digested what he had said. It added up, he thought. He became more interested in Seamus.

'God,' said Seamus, 'I wish I had a drink. Talking makes me thirsty. I don't talk that much always. It must be your face that med me.'

Pat laughed. 'I don't think so,' he said. 'It seems to me, Seamus, that coming to England was good for you if it makes you think.'

'I don't want t' think,' said Seamus, rising. 'All I want t' do is to live and have a fairly good time at it. Come on back. We'll be late, so we will. So-long, Jack,' turning to the man behind, busy cleaning the silver-looking yoke that made the tea.

'Bye, Shymus,' said Jack. 'Come again.' Then chuckles, his double chins shaking, his belly up and down.

'We'll consider it,' said Seamus. 'Oh, Jack, this is Pat.'

'Hello,' said Pat.

'Another Englishman, I presume,' said Jack, shaking bands. This was very funny. He laughed terribly at this. Pat grinned. 'You blokes keep comin' over 'ere,' Jack went on, 'and all the English'll be on the dole.'

'You mean,' said Seamus, 'that they'd have to be workin' if we didn't come. We're the boys that sets to and does all the dirty work for ye, so that ye can sit down on yeer fannies and count all the money ye take from 's.'

'Garn,' said Jack, and they went.

Pat was still stiff, but his eyes were clearer. They were no longer misted with the reflection of his own sufferings. He noticed that Seamus was almost a head taller than he. That would put him well over six foot. He was a very good-looking chap too, Pat decided. You wouldn't notice it at first on account of the size of him. His face was big, but his features fairly regular. He had a nice-shaped head which wasn't spoiled by the big ears that stood out from his head.

'We could talk t' Jack the ganger if you like,' said Seamus. 'We could mebbe persuade him that it might be healthier to give yeh a lighter job.'

'No, thanks, Seamus,' Pat said urgently. 'Don't do that. This is my own battle and I'd prefer it that way. And besides, victory is in sight from my own efforts. Ye'd only spoil it now.'

'All right' said Seamus. Mebbe it's better that way. Jack is a good ganger, y' know, and for a man that's not too big, he has courage. He's not afraid a me or anyone me size on this job. I never noticed him like that before. He doesn't like most 'f us, mark yeh, but he's just enough. Only gives's a few lectures about joinin' the Sacred Heart Sodality and doin' our duties be the Church, and he gets a bit sore whin yeh laugh at 'm.'

'I know all about that,' said Pat. 'Ye laugh at him. But then he considers that yeer practically lost souls, anyhow. But I'm a nearer man to him. I'm at hand, a brand to be saved from the burning.'

'See you afterwards,' said Seamus, flinging off his coat and pulling the shirt over his head.

'All right,' said Pat, doing the same, but much more carefully. Before he went into the ditch he stood on the embankment and looked around him. All away from him, for miles it seemed, were men who got smaller and smaller with the distance, digging and burrowing and climbing. Great cranes were swinging their arms, and engines were chugging and on either side of the embankment, a forest of roofs stretched away to the horizon, their criss-crossed contours broken here and there by the tops of real trees raising themselves above the buildings. Then, also, taller buildings raised themselves above the trees, and the dull sun could be seen glinting on the white face of a gigantic factory raising itself, vulgarly bare-breasted, blowsily blatant over the modest houses. The scene was too immensely sprawling to be comprehended in a glance.

He went into the ditch and reached for the pickaxe.

To his delighted surprise he found it less hard to work it. True, his muscles groaned for the first few picks and his hands reacted violently, wincing away from the glossy wood, but after that his muscles settled down and his hands adopted their best grip and he worked away. Regular. Pick, pick, pick; bend, lift stone, up, out stone; pick, pick, pick. Then up pick, back hand, in shovel, under earth, twitch knee, pull handle and out she goes.

He started to hum later on, thinking, Well, I am coming on.

'How are you getting on?' the voice asked beside him then.

'Fine,' said Pat. 'Fine.' Not looking up, knowing that Jack was up there looking down at him.

'You're a bit slow with it,' said Jack.

'Well, I'll improve,' said Pat. 'Rome wasn't built in a day.'

'No,' said Jack; 'and you wouldn't dig that ditch quick enough in a month a Sundays. Come ou'r that! I have another job for you.'

'But I like this one,' said Pat sweetly, looking up. He still thought that he didn't like Jack's face, whatever Seamus and the others thought about him.

'You'll do what you're told,' said Jack.

'Yes, sir,' said Pat, touching a forelock. He saw Jack's face getting red at this, but he controlled himself.

'Get over there,' he said, 'and feed the concrete mixer.'

Pat liked the thought of that. It was a fairly easy job. Just shovel sand at the open gob of the machine. He got out of the ditch slowly, then looked back at it and said sadly, 'I liked that oul ditch.'

'Go on,' said Jack; 'we haven't all night.'

Pat went. He thought, another win for Moore in the second round. Because he had the ditch beaten, he was shifted. He was sure of that. He thought that he wasn't at the end of his shifting, but what the hell, he thought. If I can lick that bloody ditch, I can lick anything on this job. He walked with his shovel towards the machine, where two chaps were working. Then he heard Jack shouting at them. They passed Pat, winking their eyes, and before they knew where they were, the two of them were digging the ditch and Pat was feeding the mixer on his own. That was the snag – on his own. It was, Hurry up there, Moore, for God's sake! D'yeh want to hold up the whole job for mortar? Various other endearments. Pat was mad. He felt like breaking up the mixer and throwing its parts at the horizon, but he held himself in and fed it sand, while he also noticed that the two men in *his* ditch, although working quite casually, dug more in ten minutes than he had dug in the two and a half days. It began to dawn on him then that a good labourer was as much a professional as a doctor cutting the guts out of a patient on the operating table. It was silly of him to think about working as a labourer as if it was something very déclassé, honouring it in fact by his presence, when it was a very skilled job that would require years of experience. Well, he thought, it's another lesson learned, and he flung the sand viciously into the revolving maw of the machine.

He walked home later with Seamus.

He had gone in the bus before, but now he walked. He felt like walking now that his eyes were open to other things. They didn't talk much, an odd sentence here and there, but Pat felt quite happy that way, and thought how good it was to be walking along an English street like this with Seamus. Then he thought, if they were both at home, he the smart aleck from the town and Seamus the tall country boy driving the ass-load of turf to the town to sell it in the Square, if they had been like that, would he have walked with Seamus and felt as much pleasure in it, or with the silly, petty, frightful snobbery of the small Irish town would he have walked and felt his neck red, and sweated lest any of his pals should have seen him in close converse with a country gob?

It is good, thought Pat wisely then, for man to leave his home town. He patted Seamus on the big back, and when the other turned his head for the reason, Pat winked and laughed, and although Seamus didn't understand what it was about, he laughed too, and both of them felt good, with the warm feeling you get in the pit of your stomach.

He liked the streets where they walked. No speed limit this side of the shops. All sorts of cars whizzing by. Beautiful long cars, purring with haughty-looking lassies at the wheel, cigarettes in their mouths. Or fat men with Anthony Eden hats and white collars, probably provided by the fellows with the vans and the white collars advertised on the sides of them. The Keep Left signs and the barbers' poles with the bulbs on the top of them, where the pedestrians walked. And then the shopping centre, which they felt was their own, since it was put there for them. All sorts of shops with all sorts of things in the windows, and the butchers' shops, the strangest of all. He even stopped to look at one. All the pieces of meat carefully cut into pieces and laid on marble slabs with the price marked on them.

'Not like home that,' he remarked to Seamus.

Seamus grunted. It didn't mean much to him. At home he saw meat on the table about four times a year. That's what he was thinking.

Pat was thinking of the butchers' shops at home. The wide open doors with no windows. The carcasses of cattle and sheep, hanging up whole with all the insides out of them and the heads gone. I want a pound of steak, you'd say, and me man would get his huge knife, sharpen it, and go over and cut into a carcass right there in front of you. A cow's head laid on a side table looking at you. And a heart, maybe, beside in pools of blood. The flies in summer and the butcher slapping at them with a swatter. Hah, ye bastards! Dead flies and fresh beef, and the great chopping-table, once two feet thick of solid wood, now weary and worn away in the middle from the blows of the chopper on the bones. He laughed and they passed on.

'Will yeh come over to an oul dance on Saturday night?' Seamus asked him as they paused where they separated, Seamus to go off right past the shopping centre, Pat to go on past the church and turn left.

'Are they any good?' Pat asked.

'What the hell does that matter?' Seamus asked, wide-eyed.

'That's right,' said Pat, with a laugh. 'I will so.'

'Good man,' said Seamus, and swung away. 'See you tomorrow.'

'If I'm alive,' Pat shouted after him.

He went home then. He felt alive. He felt hungry and he thought of the tea Mary would have for him, and he didn't give a damn about the unctuousness of Jack or the depressions of Jack's home. Not now, he thought, that I have begun to see and to enjoy.

He turned into Acacia Avenue and he was whistling.

4

P at stood and watched for a while at the door, with his
hands in his pockets and a cigarette in his mouth.

He was conscious of his new suit. Blue pin-stripe with the
stripe not too noticeable. Double-breasted looking well on his
slim figure. Very natty, £2 12s. 6d. at the multiple tailors. A nice
cut. It made him feel much better, as if with this new suit bought
in England he was at last becoming part of the place, getting rid
of his former identity. He was new all the way. A cream-
coloured shirt with a soft collar; a blue tie with a stripe, and
under that brand-new underwear; soft leather shoes with the
toes not too pointed; a white handkerchief sticking out of his
breast pocket to show that he had the makings of a gentleman.
Any girl's fancy, he thought, grinning. And God knows there
were plenty of girls. All sorts and sizes here in the brightly
lighted dance-hall. Tall and short, fat and thin, and just right.
Dancing around to the strains of Mac's Melody Makers, blowing
themselves out of wind, lifting the roof with doleful sighs as they
played awhile and sang awhile, all together, 'I can't give you anything but love, Baby; that's the only thing I've plenty of, Baby.
Dream awhile, scheme awhile, and you will find, happiness and
I guess . . .' and a deep blah-blah-blah from the trombone and the
trumpet.

It was a successful dance. You could feel that from the atmosphere. People were really enjoying themselves. It wasn't a terribly big dance-hall. It was a sort of a club place, and it reminded
him of the boat-club dances at home, with the streamers strung
from the rafters and the racing boats they called needlers hanging

over their heads. It was a long and narrow hall with the door here and the band at the far end on a platform. Seats at the side decorated with the seated flowers, looking at their successful dancing sisters pretending they didn't give a damn if nobody ever asked them to dance.

Pat could make out the figure of Seamus. He smiled. Seamus danced these modern dances as well as he could, but he still brought a bit of the Connemara dance into it, a sort of a hop, and holding his partner away from him, looking down to see his big feet shuffling on the floor. Then you would hear a loud 'Hurroo', well over the noise of the band and the singing and the shuffling feet on the powdered floor, and Seamus would rise up in the air and down again, and through the throng Pat could see the small dark girl he was dancing with laughing at him, her eyes crinkled and her teeth white and reflecting the light. Seamus was always good for a laugh, and when he got into that mood he was irresistible.

The Irish were well represented, well leavened with all the other nationalities. He recognized some of the other chaps from the job – Mick from Tralee and Walsh from Roscommon, Jimser from Dublin and Raymond from Antrim. Many more, all dressed in their best. Funny, he reflected, how they always called one another by the counties or towns they had come from. He was Pat from Galway. Why, he wondered? It would be better if they didn't hang on to their counties but tried to become part of the land they were living in. Naming you from your own place sometimes gave rise to nostalgia.

He saw the manager of the place, a middle-sized man in a dinner-jacket. He was squat and broad and bald and wore a countenance of worry. He was always afraid of his life that a row would start up and get his place into bad odour. Everyone knew that the Irish were that way inclined, that they would start fighting on the drop of a hat, particularly if they were drinking and sometimes if they weren't. There had been famous fights here before, but Pat had never seen any signs of trouble on the three Saturdays he had danced here. There was a sort of rivalry all right between the working gangs. If you were working on one job, like themselves on the railway, you took a poor view of the other Irish chaps who were working on that factory job in Willesden. He saw some of them now. Their principal was a very big man from Kerry, called, simply enough, Kerry Mick. A tall man, rangy like the Kerry-men, with sloping shoulders and long arms with great power in them. The back of his head flat, going into a long neck. His face red, ears large and sticking out from his head, and a most amiable grin on a long face, which had big teeth in it. That's why Seamus called him Horsey. They didn't like one another. They left it at that, but every time they happened to be in the hall together, the manager seemed to become restless and went from here to there, smiling and rubbing his hands nervously.

Pat threw his cigarette on the floor, stamped it out with his foot, and started to worm his way to the band platform, where he and Seamus generally sat in the intervals. He pushed and apologized. It was very hot in there now. You could feel the sweaty heat coming from the bodies as they danced. The sweat from big bodies and the whiff of cheap perfume mixed up with bay rum or carnation hair-oil. Most of the girls dressed in light-coloured frocks or blouses and skirts, the blouses pulling up a bit from the stretching of their arms and showing pink slips or pink flesh. They were nice girls in the main, carefully powdered and lip-sticked. You could have been at home. It would have been the same except for the accents of the girls. Some of them Irish all right. Some of them passed for English, which could mean anything here, Scots or Welsh or really London.

He hadn't taken any of them home after the dance. Just that he didn't feel at ease yet. One had to find out what the custom was. It was international, he knew. But he hadn't met anyone to date that he felt energetic enough about. Nice pleasant conversation about the hall and the dance and Hot, ain't it? And, What do you think of the band tonight? And the usual; and the humming of the dance numbers as they were played.

It was when he was sitting on a seat in front of the band that the image of Jojo came into his head. He felt quite excited. It was the association of ideas really, because Jojo and himself had never missed a dance within eight miles of the town after they left school. And then Jojo was supposed to be in England too. At least, he had slipped away from the town one day and when he asked, Where's Jojo? Has anyone seen Jojo? somebody said, Jojo, is it? He's in England, I think. A picture of him came clearly to Pat's imagination now. About the same height as himself, only broader built, and black hair that was parted at the side, and always came down a bit over his forehead. A broad forehead with black eyebrows. A sort of square face with a chin coming out and a split in the middle of it that he would find hard to shave as he got older. Brown eyes that always had a sly smile at the back of them. What could have happened to Jojo, he wondered, or where could he be! He wouldn't half like to see him now to have a chat and start on the Do you remember stuff and say, Does this remind you of . . . They had drifted a bit after the first year or two, when they had got their Leaving Certificates. Jojo was a very bright boy, scholarships and what-not, and Pat was surprised that he hadn't gone on to the university. But Jojo got a job instead, the same as his own somewhat, temporary clerking – but not in the same place. So they hadn't seen one another on that account; and then the next thing he hears Jojo has gone to England. In fact, now that he came to think of it, that might have been at the back of his own head too, might have made him restless to think that Jojo could go off to England, so why the hell couldn't he go too?

A singing voice behind him broke into his consciousness then. It was the voice of a woman. She was singing, 'I can't give you anything but love, Baby,' and he noticed that the voice was husky and came from the chest and sounded like a few of the women crooners he had heard on the films, standing in front of a mike, dipping their heads and spreading their arms and clenching their fists and uplifting their already uplifted breasts to the roof, pulling in their stomachs and smiling, smiling all the time, like an advertisement for toothpaste, even when they might be saying things like, I'd die for you, Baby, or Angel, or Buddy. All the crooners or croonerettes who came to the dance-hall every Saturday night with the different bands were always the same, the sob in the throat, the scoop of the voice, and the smile. He turned now and had a look at this one.

He was surprised. She was a very beautiful girl. He twisted further on his chair to look at her. It was the figure you noticed first. Most of the boys dancing had stopped to raise their heads from the whispering or the humming or the caressing to have a look at her. She wasn't moving her body in the usual way. She remained perfectly still and let her mouth work on the words and let herself do the rest. She wasn't lifting her chest. It was all right in the natural position. A little full, like her hips. The green dress she was wearing was tight-fitting and you could see the shape of her thighs under it. It was a short dress to just below her knees, and her legs were spread a little, most shapely legs ending in a small foot, covered in delicate sort of high-heeled shoes.

Pat didn't know that; but it was only when his eyes had travelled from her chest to her feet that he raised his eyes to her face. It was framed by sort of rusty-coloured hair with a shine, worn loosely and coming down to her neck, where it curled up again. Her skin was white, her eyebrows and eyelashes a black contrast, and her eyes green. It was a rather full face, with almost perfect features. He could see the top of her white breasts, rising from the frock, and arms, a little plump, ending in small hands.

He felt something happening to him inside. A sort of squiggling going on in his stomach, and he thought, My God, this girl is grand, so she is! I wonder how could I meet her. I wonder how could I get her to look at me. It didn't matter that she couldn't sing; she wasn't singing really, just speaking the silly words with the band as a background, but suddenly Pat thought that the silly words weren't silly any longer, that they had taken on a meaning, just as if Byron or Shakespeare had composed them after severe soul-struggling. For God's sake let her look at me, he prayed, and as if St Anthony had been listening to his pleas, she turned her head and her eyes fell on his own. Time stood still for him for a few seconds as she looked at him. He felt her eyes going over him, and coming back to his eyes again, and he was sure, he was certain that it wasn't the casual look that one throws away, to photograph a thing and then never develop it. To his surprise, he felt his hand shaking, and his leg too, resting on his toe, the heel off the ground as he turned his body. She was at the end of her song and then her eyes went away from him – reluctantly, I hope, so I do – and she turned away, nodded at Mac, the leader, and went and sat on a chair near the drummer. The music died with a groan and the clapping broke out all over the hall. She stood up then and bowed and smiled, and he could see that her teeth were small and white behind the full lips.

It was a blow of Seamus's big hand on his back that brought him to himself again.

'There y'are,' said Seamus, 'I've been lookin' all over for yeh.'

Seamus was wearing a plain blue suit. The trousers were wide and baggy at the knees and the big muscles of his arms and shoulders had made big creases in the coat he was wearing.

'I want yeh to meet the girl next door,' he said then, his hand on the shoulder of the dark-haired girl he had been dancing with. Pat looked her over casually. She was a nice little thing, he thought, with a friendly smile. Dark hair, big eyes, a snub nose, nice lips and a smile. She was nicely built and neatly dressed; but she hasn't got green eyes, he thought, his heart thumping as he thought of the girl behind him.

'Hello,' he said, shaking her hand.

'Hello,' she said.

'Isn't she grand?' Seamus asked proudly, as if he was displaying her at a flower show or the Connemara Pony Show, Pat thought with a smile. 'Maureen Potter is her name.'

'A nice name,' said Pat politely.

'You're Pat Moore,' said Maureen. 'Seamus has been telling me about you. Isn't Seamus grand? I call him Seamus Mor. He's teaching me to talk Irish.'

'Is he really?' Pat asked.

'Go on and show 'm, Maureen,' said Seamus. 'Say the one I taught yeh comin' in tonight.'

'The one you wouldn't tell me what it meant, is it?' she asked.

'That's the wan,' said Seamus.

She screwed up her forehead and thought for a little, and then she opened her lips cautiously and said, *Tabhair 'm póg.* She had her eyes half closed as she said it. She looked like a child thinking up its prayers at night, and obeying an impulse and for the joke of it, Pat bent down and lightly laid his lips against hers. Her lips were soft, but they didn't register much with him. Seamus started to laugh, slapping his hand on his leg.

Maureen looked at Pat, her eyes wide. 'What's that for?' she asked.

'That's what you asked me for,' said Pat. '*Tabhair 'm póg* means Give me a kiss.'

'Didn't I catch her on grand?' said Seamus, sitting down. 'Wasn't it lovely the way I caught her on?'

'Very neat, thanks,' said Pat.

They sat on the seat with Maureen in the middle of them. She was looking at Pat closely. She liked the look of him very much – the way his brown hair waved off his forehead and the clear white of his eyes and the thin, sensitive-looking face. She looked at his lips and thought how nice it had been to feel them on her own. Suddenly and for no reason at all, as she told herself, her heart started to beat more loudly than usual.

'You work with Seamus?' she asked.

'Well, I'm on the same job,' said Pat, 'but I don't know that you'd call my part of it working.'

'Don't mind 'm,' said Seamus, leaning across her. 'That fella is comin' on fine, so he is. In a little while now he'll be better than meself, so he will!'

'I don't want to be,' said Pat. 'I'd want to work twenty-four hours a day, so I would, to be equal to you.'

'He's awful big, isn't he?' said Maureen, turning to look at the bulk beside her. Seamus laughed and beat his fists on his chest.

'I'm the best man that ever kem outa Ireland,' he said. 'Isn't that right, Kerry?' plucking at the coat-tails of the big Kerry Mick, who was crossing the hall near them with a girl in tow. The big Kerryman stopped to look down at them.

'What's that?' he asked.

'I was just sayin',' said Seamus, 'that I'm the best man that ever kem outa Ireland.'

'You are in me tail,' said the other, when he had assimilated the question. 'They grow bigger than you on the bushes in Kerry, so they do.' He laughed like the neigh of a horse, Pat thought. He talked in a sing-song way high up in his head, like the other tribes from the south.

'Listen,' said Seamus, rising then to face the other, Pat idly noticed that the Kerryman was taller even than Seamus, but not nearly so broad. 'In Galway when any man is born under six foot we throw 'm outa the county and sind 'm down to Kerry, so that people'll think he's a giant.'

'All right,' said the Kerryman, 'so ye think yeer wonderful. Ye were all born with big mouths on ye, anyhow. And while yeer talkin' about how wonderful ye are, we're doin' all the work for ye.'

'Now, listen——' said Seamus.

'Ara, stop it Seamus,' said Pat. 'You're not a child any longer. What the hell does it matter which of ye is the biggest?'

'Tha's right,' said Mick. 'It doesn't really matter.'

'What are we argin' about so?' Seamus asked unreasonably.

'I do' know,' said the Kerryman. 'Do you?'

'No,' said Seamus, 'I don't.'

'Well, good-bye,' said the Kerryman, 'so.' And he departed after looking into Seamus's eyes in a most unfriendly fashion.

'I'd like to murder that fella,' said Seamus, looking after him.

'Why?' asked Maureen. 'What has he done to you?'

'Nothin',' said Seamus. 'Just he bein' there. I can't stand the sight 'f 'm. Always sneerin', he is.'

'That's just his teeth, Seamus,' said Pat. 'He can't help his face.'

'I'd love to alter it for him,' said Seamus, sitting down growling.

Pat noticed that the little interlude had altered the shape of Seamus's face. His eyebrows were pulled down over his eyes and his lower lip was pulled up from his chin. One of his fists were clenched and was being pounded on his knee.

'Here, Seamus,' he said, 'snap out of it, will you!'

Seamus looked at him blankly and said 'Wha?' and then thought and smiled and relaxed his face, and laughed.

Maureen was bewildered. 'What's it all about?' she asked.

'Nothing,' said Pat. 'The resurgence of the primitive.' Out of the corner of his eye then he saw her getting down from the bandstand, joining a man there, and both of them making for the door through the crowds.

'Here,' said Pat, rising, 'let's go and have a drink.'

'I'd prefer to dance,' said Maureen.

'Ah, come on,' said Seamus, rising and pulling her to her feet. 'I could do with a drink bad, so I could.'

'We'll only have a few,' said Pat, watching her out through the door, noticing that she looked very nice from the back too, and that she didn't waggle as she walked. He turned and looked at Maureen then. She was regarding him shrewdly. He wondered if she knew where he had been looking. 'We'll come back then and dance all night.'

'All right,' said Maureen, moving forward.

They walked through the hall, the crowds closing in behind them as the band started to play. It was a relief to get into the fresh air for a while. There was a nice breeze blowing and it was good to feel it on your forehead and exploring the openings in your clothes. First left and they were in the pub. It was a big place, all one: a semicircular counter, an old-fashioned place with the new look. What had been marble pillars and heavy gilt mirrors trimmed and redecorated. Round, glass-topped tables and soft-bottom chairs that enclosed you so that you might be really comfortable and wait as long as possible.

When they went in through the glass doors, Pat's eyes searched the place and saw that his guess had been right. She was sitting over in the far corner of the crowded bar, and there was a free table beyond them.

'There's a table over there,' he said, pointing and leading the way.

'Here,' protested Seamus to his back. 'What d'y want a table for? Isn't the counter good enough for yeh now, isn't it?'

Pat didn't answer, so he followed them, complaining, 'It was far away from tables in pubs that you were dragged up, me boy.'

Pat sat so that he would be facing her. He held a chair out for Maureen, who sank into it. She saw him looking at the woman then and turned her head and saw that the woman was looking at Pat. Maureen felt herself getting a little red in the face, but saying to herself, Don't be silly, you! she looked at the woman, smiled sweetly, and said, 'Hello, Lelia.' She felt Pat looking at her then. 'Enjoying the dance very much,' she said. 'We did enjoy your singing.' Like hell, she thought, a little viciously, and surprised at herself for being vicious.

'Thank you,' said Lelia.

I'll have to do it, Maureen thought. 'This is Pat Moore and Seamus. Lelia Manning.'

Pat couldn't believe that it was happening just like this. He was going to rise and shake hands with her. He thought better of it. He knew what his hands were like now. The large lumps of healed blisters and corrugated flesh on the palms. It would be like shaking hands with a nutmeg grater. And the cuts on the backs from flesh being rubbed off on occasions when you were careless and stones fell. He contented himself with putting his elbows on the table and more or less hiding his hands. 'Hello,' was all he said, but he had to cough before he said it. She was looking at him. He felt for a few moments that there was nobody in the place but themselves.

Seamus shook her by the hand as if she was his fourth cousin up for the Galway Races. 'Howya?' he asked. 'Yeh have a vice like a blackbird, so yeh have. Yeh took's all for a walk, so you did.'

'Thank you,' said Lelia. She turned to look at her partner. He was smiling. A pleasant-enough looking chap, Pat thought grudgingly. His head was shaped somewhat like a pear, the top of it small, with black hair sleeked back with oil and parted in the centre; his ears small and close to his head. His jaws were bigger than his forehead, a long thin nose and good teeth, two of which were sort of bound with a piece of gold wire. He had a nice pleasant smile. All of him was pleasant. Dressed very well too. Spotless white collar and crisp tie. A suit of grey, sort of spotted with almost invisible white. Pat knew it was a very expensive suit and felt shabby in comparison. 'This is George,' said Lelia, waving her hand.

George rose and shook hands with the lot of them. His hands were long and thin and very red in colour.

'Hello,' he said to Pat and Seamus. Then to Maureen, 'Hello, Maureen, how is your mum and dad?'

'Fine,' said Maureen.

'You all know each other,' said Pat in a surprised tone of voice.

'We ought to, chum,' said George, with a laugh. 'Practically neighbours, we are. Ain't that so? Me in one street, Lelia in the next, and Maureen over the road.'

'George is our butcher,' said Maureen, not maliciously she hoped.

'That's right,' said George breezily. 'Best meat in the place. Never a complaint. Here, why not be matey? Pull in the chairs there and we'll get together. A chat and a chow. Here, come on, move over.'

They moved over, and however it happened Pat was sitting beside Lelia, and trying to ignore the pleasant feelings it gave him to be so close to her.

'What'll it be now?' asked George, taking over, a thing to which he seemed to be accustomed.

So they were soon getting matey. Seamus and Pat quaffing a bottle of stout, Lelia drinking a gin and tonic, George smelling at a glass of whiskey and Maureen toying with a sherry. The talk was loud. Pat hadn't much to say. Just feeling sort of breathless, knowing that she knew that he was feeling breathless, and conscious of him. Seamus and George had got on to Ireland. George had been there on a visit and took a poor view of it all, and Seamus was trying to be an agent for the Irish Tourist Association, telling him how he must have been in all the wrong places, that he should have come back to Connemara. That's the place. Enough to stop the heart in your throat. George obviously remained unimpressed and Seamus became more fervent, so in the end, quite politely, George enquired if it was such a bleeding heaven why the hell had Seamus ever left it. Then Seamus told him why he left it, and became almost blasphemously lyrical about how his country had thrown him out, not given him the ways of making a living. And so it went on. Pat stood the next round and Seamus the one after that, and then they had three more rounds and time seemed to have flitted until the bartender in the white jacket went around switching lights off and switching them on, saying 'Now, now, gents, if you please, if you please.' Pat noticed in his befuddlement that he seemed to ignore the fact that there were ladies drinking too. Apparently that wasn't recognized as being a fact *per se*. He noticed very little apart from that except that sometimes his knee touched Lelia's knee and a sort of burn seemed to move from the touched part all over his body, and once or twice they looked into one another's eyes and drank deeply. Then they turned and listened to Seamus and George talking, and now and again for appearance sake Pat put in a laugh, or a Sure, or a Now, now, Seamus; and Maureen just sat there drinking her sherry and looking at Pat with her mind. A little backchat with Lelia about her mum and dad, and Lelia's mum and dad, and also Pat noticed that Kerry Mick and his pals were in the pub, as well as some of their own crowd from the railway.

It all became a bit muzzy in the end, from the smoke and the fumes and the alcohol rising to the head, and when he got up to go out he seemed to be walking on air, and he remembered escorting Lelia outside, and it gave him a chance to put his hand on the naked part of her am and he would never forget how smooth and cool her skin was under his palm.

Then they were in the dance-hall and he was dancing with her. No asking or permitting, or any stuff like that; just walk into the hall and take her in his arms and they were floating over the floor to the music. Pat was a good dancer. He ought to have been, considering all the dancing himself and Jojo had done at home — good old Jojo, and where are you tonight, I wonder. Lelia was a grand dancer. They seemed to have been turned out of a mould by God so that when they came together they fitted one another like the grooved teeth on that bloody concrete mixer. He could feel the bulk of her breasts against his chest, and the arm of her on his shoulders pulled his body nearer to hers so that his right leg was between her thighs, and the world seemed to stand still. The feel of her hair against his face, and once she raised her head and looked at him and then she put the side of her face against his own and pressed it there for a few seconds, and pulled her body tightly against his; and his heart was a dull thump like the loud beating of a muffled drum. Her skin was as smooth as the water of a deep river and there was perfume on her breath, not the perfume of the gin and tonic, but just perfume. He had never before in his life felt smothered with love of a girl as this. It was like being wound in a cocoon of cotton-wool impregnated with all the perfumes of Arabia and the powders of the poppies of China. She left a void between him and the world when the music stopped and she left him to go and sing again. The front of his body was cold. So he just sat that one out and looked at her while she sang. She sang to him, and time stood still again. Of course logically his mind said to him, You feel this bad because you are after drinking six or seven bottles of stout; but he discarded that thought and knew there was more in it than that, that this feeling was also there under the porter.

After that she danced with George, and he had to restrain himself from going over to George and beating him into insensibility for daring to let his butcher's body come near hers, his hands, that were dyed with the blood of beasts, from touching her pure skin.

He was dancing with Maureen.

'Do you like Lelia?' he heard Maureen asking him.

He just looked down at the shrewd eyes looking up at him. 'Oh, Lelia!' he said. The way he said it, it was the concentrated production of an orator, the impassioned pleading of a forensic giant.

'It's easy for her to look well,' said Maureen. 'She never does a stroke of work. Her father keeps her. Just sings occasionally at a few dances. If we were all like that we could make men go gooey over us. I thought you would have more sense, that you were a level-headed young man.'

'Why should she work?' Pat asked in horror. 'Is it her to stain those little white hands of hers? Wouldn't that be a crime, I'm asking you? She shouldn't sing either. Why should she throw the pearls of herself before those swine?'

'My God, you have it bad,' said Maureen, 'or is that just the Irish in you or the Guinness?'

'Tell me,' he asked, 'is she engaged to that butcher chap, or anything?'

Maureen thought it over and with a sigh decided to be honest.

'No,' she said, 'he's just one of her men.' Maybe, she thought then, it would have been better to have been dishonest.

'What do you mean?' he asked, horrified. 'One of her men!'

'She always has battalions of men around her,' said Maureen. 'Why wouldn't she? Isn't that all she has to do all day – doing herself up so that she can attract them all?'

'You shouldn't be talking like that,' said Pat. 'Isn't it terrible how a beautiful girl can never get any other girls to have a good word for her?'

'What do you mean?' Maureen asked indignantly. 'I'm being very kind about her. If I wanted to be catty I could tell you things about her that you wouldn't believe.'

'I certainly would not!' said Pat.

'That's what I thought,' said Maureen. 'So I'm not going to say anything at all about her.'

It was just then that the row started. It was announced by a girl screaming, and then a space in the centre of the floor was cleared as if a man had swept it with a scythe.

'It's Seamus,' said Maureen.

So it was. He was standing there in the middle, his big body crouched and his arms held out from his sides. It was no surprise to Pat to see that Kerry Mick was facing him, his long body held upright and his long arms swinging. Pat had just time to shout 'Seamus!' when they came together. Their bodies met and they held one another's arms, while fury shot from their eyes and a string of words in Irish from their mouths. From Seamus Pat could just distinguish, *'Sgoiltfidh mé thú, a dhaibhail Mhumhanaigh!'* and Kerry Mick throwing more words back at him in Irish, and then they separated and swung at one another. It was not scientific, just two wild blows that if they had landed properly would have decapitated a bullock. Seamus was the more successful. He took the blow of Mick on his arm, and his own landed on the other's face. Back Mick went, and his feet gave from under him on the slippery floor and he went down on his back like a boy on an ice slide. He was quickly up again as Seamus moved towards him. At that point the little fat manager – quite courageously, Pat thought – tried to get in between them, his arms held out appealingly. Seamus just swept an arm without looking at him and the manager went sailing down the floor with a most ludicrous look on his face. Then the two giants met again. Girls stood on the seats at the side and screamed, and Pat saw the little manager crawling on all fours towards the crowded doors. That means the police, he thought.

Something hit him then on the back of the head and he hit the floor. He was bewildered. He shook his head and looked up and saw Maureen pummelling a large man with her small fists. He recognized one of the Irishmen who was a supporter of Kerry

Mick. He got to his feet, unsteadily, his blood boiling, had time to see that various scraps were going on all over the hall before he pulled Maureen away and went for the man who had hit him. It was a short encounter. He just feinted with his left hand and then buried his fist in the other's stomach, and as the man bent in two, Pat, before he hit him in the face, noticed that he had red hair. So he hit him in the face and felt the shock run up his arm.

Then he heard the police whistles and saw a tall policeman in blue making his way furiously through the panic at the door. Pat was amazed at the clarity in his head then. He grabbed Maureen by one of the hands that was held up to her mouth and pulled her towards the bandstand, where the passage went to the back. He had to push his way through struggling bodies to do so. Arrived there, he paused, his hand on the switches that controlled the light.

'Get out the back!' he said to her urgently then, and pressed all the switches.

Darkness descended on the hall, and the screaming increased in volume. He made his way back to the spot where he thought Seamus might be. He was assisted by the one light coming from another cloakroom at the top of the hall. Then he was standing over the two bodies that were twitching and cursing and welting at one another in the darkness. He reached down and felt hair, so grabbed it and pulled back the head.

'Seamus!' he roared. There was a grunt so he knew he had the right man. 'The police are here. Come on, you eejit!'

It was a little time before Seamus became sensible. Then he raised his hand again and brought it down. It hit the floor with a crack. 'Christ!' ejaculated Seamus, and put his fist in his mouth. Pat pulled him up then and made his way back to the place where he thought he had left Maureen. They reached it, fumbling with their hands. He heard Maureen shouting, 'Pat! Pat!' and then she was under his hands and he headed back to the end of the band-stand, where the door should be.

They found it and fled down a long lighted passage. At the end there was another door with the key in the lock. Pat opened the door, ushered the other two out, and then switched off the passage light. He went through the door himself then and followed the others. A long yard and at the end of it a not very high wall. Seamus had already hoisted Maureen up on top of it. They jumped up then themselves, hopped down the other side, and then lifted Maureen down. Up the long lane outside with the mud on it. A few muttered curses as they splashed into a few puddles, and then they were out into the street, with the lighted shops and the buses passing by, and the people and the trolley cars.

Arrived there, Pat turned to look at Seamus. He was furious.

'You son of a bitch!' he said viciously, and then, because Seamus looked at him so sheepishly, rubbing an eye that was turning blue, and because Maureen was breathless, leaning against a shop window with her hair all tossed, he couldn't help it, he started to laugh, holding his stomach. And the other two laughed for some time, stifling it from the passers-by, and after that they waited at the Request stop and got into a bus that brought them towards home, the tyres whining on the shower-splashed concrete.

5

It was fairly crowded on the top of the bus. The passengers were mostly male, talking in loud voices and permeating the closed atmosphere with the smell of stale beer, porter and brown ale.

The three did not really relax until they had lit cigarettes and paid their fares. Then Pat, who was sitting in a seat in front of the other two, turned and fixed a stern gaze on Seamus.

'What did you do it for, Seamus?' he asked.

Seamus was uncomfortable. He was holding a hand up to his right eye, which was swelling and was now the colour of a decayed orange.

'Ah, that Kerry Mick!' he said.

'Listen,' said Pat, 'something told me from the beginning that you wanted to start a row with him. It wasn't of his making. Don't try and tell me that.'

'Nor me either,' said Maureen. 'What on earth would Mum say if she could have seen me in the middle of a row like that?'

Seamus was indignant. 'Anyone'd think,' he said, 'that it was all my fault!'

'Well, wasn't it?' Maureen asked.

'It was not,' said Seamus. 'There I was on the flure, dancing nice and quiet with a little lady, and up comes me man and stands on me foot, and into the bargain called me a name in Irish that I couldn't repeat in front 'f a lady. So I had t' clatter 'm.'

'You were tempted awful quick,' said Pat.

'Go on,' said Maureen. 'Don't mind him. He loves to be fighting. And the other chap the same. There they were, snarling and spitting at one another, and anybody could see that they loved it. And you had no right to knock down the poor little manager. My God, I can still see him sliding along the floor with a surprised look on his face.' She giggled.

'It's no laughing matter,' said Pat, putting a cautious hand up to his ear, which looked very red and was sore to the touch. 'I did nothing at all to anybody and I get a clout on the lug. What'll people think of us at all? Is it any wonder they talk about the Irish? It makes me ashamed of me life to think about it.'

'Yes,' said Maureen; 'what would Lelia say?' There was a little edge on the words which Pat didn't notice.

'My God,' he said, 'that's right. I forgot all about Lelia. What happened to her? I hope she wasn't hurt.'

'Why don't you go back and find out?' Maureen asked.

She was afraid for a minute that he was going to do so, but he sank back in the seat again. 'George was with her, anyhow,' he said.

'Lookit,' said Seamus. 'It had to happen, I tell ye. That Kerry fella has been tanglin' with me since I kem to England. Mortal man couldn't stand the look 'f his ugly sneerin' kisser'. It had to come to a showdown sooner or later, and it kem tonight, and that's all about it.'

'It's not all about it,' said Pat. 'We'll be all lucky if we don't end up in jail. Wait'll the police get after us.'

'Let them come,' said Seamus. 'I'm an innocent man, so I am. Wouldn't a bishop do the same thing that I did if a fella called 'm the name that your man called me?'

'All right, we'll forget it,' said Pat. 'Do I look all right? I'm in bad enough now with me landlord and ganger. I don't want to be chucked out into the cold, cold snow.'

'You can always come over to our house,' said Maureen.

'Can I really?' Pat asked.

'Well, there's a spare room,' said Maureen, 'and we kept lodgers in it before, so anytime you want you can move in.'

'Are you joking?' Pat asked.

'Why on earth would I?' said Maureen. 'We're poor people with nice manners, and a lodger is a help sometimes.'

'That's something to know. My present digs are a little

oppressive, to say the least of it. Mary is nice, but the man gets me down. I have a feeling that I never leave the work behind me, and there's a terrible struggle goes on for my soul. What's troubling me is that if I change my digs I lose my job.'

'Well,' said Maureen. 'you can always get another job. You don't want to be a labourer all your life, do you?'

Pat looked closely at her, as closely as the remaining fumes of the drink and the fug of cigarette smoke and the pain in his ear would allow.

'Aren't you the little fount of wisdom!' he said. 'No, I don't suppose I do.'

'What's wrong with it, anyhow?' Seamus asked. 'What's wrong with being a labourer? It's honest, isn't it?'

'It is,' said Maureen, 'but maybe some people are more fitted for it than others. I'll bet Pat is more or less a total loss as a labourer.'

'He's not very hot at it, all right,' said Seamus.

'Now look here—' said Pat, indignant, as he looked back at his weeks of suffering.

'Look at your hands,' said Maureen, raising the one near her, which rested on the back of the seat. 'Look at that.' The hand was clean, but the nails were black and broken, black from concrete and clay, impossible to remove. The hand was well scarred at the back too, and the skin broken and healed, broken and healed.

Pat pulled back his hand.

'You mind your own business,' he said then, annoyed, his face getting red.

'I will,' she said, leaning back in her seat, her face also getting red, furious at herself because she had liked the feel of his hand in her own.

'For God's sake,' said Seamus, 'don't let ye two start now. Haven't we had enough rows for one night?'

'I get out here anyhow,' said Pat, looking out at the lighted streets and rising. 'Good night.'

'Will I see you at eleven Mass tomorra?' Seamus asked.

'You might,' said Pat, 'if you're not in jail.' He was on his feet then, going back to the stairs, but he paused and rested his hand on Maureen's shoulder. 'I'm sorry,' he said to her. 'I didn't mean to bite and you're very nice.' She was too, he thought. She reminded him of his sister Cissie, a younger Cissie, more good-looking and all that, but a very kind little person. It was a good job he didn't tell Maureen what he was thinking or it is doubtful if she would have softened and smiled up as she did.

'It's all right,' she said.

He went down and alighted at his stop. He stood there until the tail-light of the bus became like a star in the distance, and then he turned down his own road. He was staggering a little, but it passed off as he shook his head. His thoughts were confused. Too much had happened in one evening to be able to sort it all. His mind refused to settle down for him. One minute a picture of green eyes and copper-coloured hair, the smell of perfume, the feel of her body close to his own. Then a wince as he felt the blow on the side of his head, the sight of the polished floor coming up to meet him. A picture of George with his teeth and his head high, saying, 'Let's all be matey' and the taste of the first glass of stout going down his throat. The feel of his fist sinking into a stomach. The sight of a red head bent. The shock of a blow. Confusion. Then the sight of steady brown eyes over a snub nose looking at him candidly. He grinned as he thought of her. Mustn't see too much of her, he thought. We'd be fighting. He seemed to have that effect on her and she on him. Then he started to hum, 'I can't give you anything but love, Baby,' and he felt the chill coming up from his stomach again as he saw her looking at him and sensed the waves that came to him from her.

There was a light in the living-room, he saw. Not gone to bed yet. He automatically reached up and straightened his tie, and rubbed his hands on his hair. Ridiculous, at his age. Like a school-boy. Where's my wandering boy tonight? Have to leave. There was always the danger that Jack might conquer him in the end. That he would become flaccid, like Mary; take it all in the name of Jesus Christ. Bow the head to a false religion like the one Jack professed. His had very little to do with faith, hope and charity. A sort of an inhuman hodge-podge with a God of stone: stone and bad pictures on a wall. He shivered as he closed the gate behind him. Yes, he would have to leave. No proper atmosphere in this place: no happiness, nobody ever smiled or rumbled the belly with a laugh. Mary, because all her laughter had been oppressed out of her like the juice out of a grape. Jack didn't laugh, because his God didn't believe in it. To his God a laugh was the foot in the doorway of hell and damnation. He believed all this too. Pat thought at first that he didn't, that it was just a sort of surface business that he showed the world. But he did, firmly and judiciously. He thought that he was saving all the rest of the Irish with his prayers – like St Patrick or Croagh Patrick beseeching the angels of God to give him the souls of the Irish race. Jack probably saw himself as another Matt Talbot, chaining himself for the cause. Difference was that Matt Talbot believed and suffered in and on himself, whereas Jack thought you had to suffer yourself and make others suffer with you.

To hell with it all, thought Pat, and he opened the kitchen door. It was dark inside and he didn't put on the light. He would make his way to the bathroom cautiously and from there to his own room, and none of them would be any the wiser. Unfortunately his head was not too clear yet and reaching for the table in the middle of the floor, he knocked over a chair. He held his breath. It made a lot of noise, that chair. Then he said to himself, What the hell am I sneaking around like a rabbit for? and he pushed his way manfully towards the kitchen door.

He reached it and opened it and closed it behind him again, and was stretching his hand for the bathroom door when the door of the living-room behind him opened and the stern figure of justice was standing there, a thick book held idly in his hand.

'Come in here,' said Jack. It was a tight voice he spoke in.

Pat debated with himself. Will I tell him to go to hell? Will I say nothing at all, just go into the bathroom? He said, To hell with him, and walked into the living-room. Mary was sitting on the far side of the table. There was a frightened look on her face as she gazed at Pat. Then her eyes dropped.

'Hello, Mary,' said Pat.

Jack walked past him to the other side of the fire. He turned then and fixed his eyes on him. They were red-looking.

'This is a house of God,' said Jack.

'Who are you telling?' said Pat.

'People in this street respect us,' said Jack. 'We have always been decent. This has been a quiet house. I'm not goin' to have you or anybody else comin' in here at twelve a clock at night, staggerin' down the street – as you must ha' done from the smell a drink that's on yeh now. I won't put up with that, d'yeh hear?'

'Listen,' said Pat. 'I'm grown up, amn't I? And I'm not drunk. I had a few drinks all right and if you ask me, you would be the better too of having an odd jar. You might be the better Christian for a bottle of stout.'

'I'll live me own life the way I want without any advice from a young squirt like you,' said Jack. Pat noticed idly that his face was getting pale and that the skin was tightening on his jaws.

'You wouldn't get me botherin' me tail about you at all if it wasn't that me own brother asked me to look after you. So I did. I took yeh into me house and I got you a job, and the least you could do after that was to have a bitta respect for me house and not to be bringin' disgrace on it.'

'What kind of disgrace?' Pat asked, feeling himself getting angry. 'What harm is there in going to a dance and having a drink? What harm is there in that?'

'I know what harm is in it,' said Jack, coming closer to him. 'I've been watching young fellas like you all me life over here. What harm is in it? What harm is there in coming over and going to dances on a Saturday night when yeh should be on yer knees gettin' ready to go to the altar on a Sunday mornin' if you were a good Catholic? What harm is in it when you start drinkin'? And then you stay in bed on Sunday mornin', scootin' out to catch the tail end of the last Mass?'

'Isn't that my own business?' Pat asked.

'It is not your own business,' shouted the other in reply. 'It's my business to see that you don't lapse from your faith like so many of the others before yeh. Yer late for Mass on Sunday. That's the first. Later on you'll be so late that you won't bother yer fanny goin' out to Mass at all. The next thing that'll happen yeh'll be atin' meat on Friday. And after that the next thing, that'll happen is that yeh'll forget to go to Mass altogether. You'll become a bloody pagan, like the people all around you. You'll whore and you'll drink and you'll become like the pigs.'

76

'Well, that's my own business,' said Pat. He was shouting. 'It's my soul, isn't it? And if I want to send it to hell in me own way, that's what I'll do. I'll send it to hell and I'll send it all the quicker for your standing up there telling me what I should do. Who are you, anyhow? Are you a small ganger on a building job, or are you God? Did God lean out of heaven and make you His deputy, or what? What the hell right have you to be going around telling people what they should and shouldn't do? You can tell whoever you like after this, but you're not going to tell me. I'll do just as I like, me brave Jack, and if you don't like it you can bloody well lump it!'

The other looked at him calmly after that, but it was the calm look of intense hate.

'I won't have you in me house any longer,' he said then. 'Go in now and pack your bag and get out of here.'

He stretched his arm. Pat, if it wasn't so tragic, would have felt like laughing. But he didn't feel like laughing.

'I'll leave all right,' he said then, 'but I'm not going to go now. I'll go in the morning, but not now.'

'Get out,' said Jack.

'In the morning,' said Pat, feeling his body tensed.

'I won't have filth like you in this house for another minute,' said Jack. 'I ought to have known that Jim had married into a bad lot. He married Galway gutter when he married ye. Let him suffer; but by the good Christ I'm not going to suffer for him. I won't have me own house polluted any longer be the likes of you. I'll give yeh two minutes to get your stuff and clear out of me house, now!'

'In the morning,' said Pat. I mean it too, he thought. The look of Jack would have frightened anybody. His face was white and his eyes were red-rimmed and there were sparks coming out of them. Maybe three weeks ago he might have frightened me. When I was soft and different. Well, he has changed me himself, with his pick and shovel. He has made muscles grow where there were none before. He has built up my body to his own destruction, and for every ache, every pain which he forced on me, I'll give it all back to him. I'll crucify him. He felt that all his life he had been waiting for a moment like this just to beat this man who

77

stood opposite him. He had only known him for a short time, but he had never known unhappiness of an evil kind until he had met him. If he has taken God from me now and replaced Him with the devil, it is his own bad luck.

Jack bent down and picked up the poker. It was a big poker and a heavy one.

Pat thought, when he hits me, I'll take the first blow of the poker on my arm. I must tense the muscles and it may not be too bad. On my left arm I'll take it so that I can hit him with my right fist.

'Get out,' said Jack, and he raised the poker.

Mary screamed then. Not a loud scream. Just low and fearful. Funny they had both forgotten that she was there. Pat saw her on her feet, stretching out her hands towards Jack's arm.

'No, Jack,' she said.

'Get out!' said Jack, and raising his free hand he brought it up and back and struck Mary across the mouth. She moaned and fell into the chair behind her.

'You bastard!' said Pat.

'Get out,' said Jack.

The mist ebbed from Pat's eyes then. He saw that Mary was there in her chair, terror in her eyes and the blood from her cut lip flowing on her hand. He had seconds to make up his mind. It was the look of Mary that defeated him. He didn't know quite what all this was about. There was something else besides just hating Jack. But if he persisted now, somebody besides himself and Jack would be hurt. Mary would be, more than she was now. You couldn't hurt Mary. It would be all right prosecuting revenge, or whatever it was, for the sake of his own ego. But that wasn't the most important. There was Mary. She had never done anything to him. Just angered him at times with her complacency under what he thought was an evil dictatorship. But no man could alter that now, unless Jack's God liked to step in and save her. So now he had the choice of satisfying himself and hurting her, probably more than Jack. Or he could acknowledge defeat and leave.

The very fact that he had paused to decide was enough in itself. There was really no other answer, he thought.

'All right, Jack,' he said. 'I'll go.'

Jack lowered the poker a bit.

'I'm sorry I ever met you, Jack,' Pat said in a low, controlled voice, 'and I'm sorry I ever took anything from you. I will always feel unclean for the rest of my days because I ate your salt, even though I paid for it. And I'm sorry I met you too because one time I thought I had my religion all fixed. I thought that God and myself were getting along all right. Now I don't know. You've fecked up that on me too, because if God is the kind of a Man you make Him out to be, I don't want anything more to do with Him.'

Jack raised the poker again.

'Stop it' he shouted. 'You blasphemer! Stop your filthy tongue and get out of here! Do you hear! Don't let me ears hear any more of the pus flowing from your rotting soul or as sure as God is my judge I'll destroy you. Get out, do you hear! Get out!'

He moved towards him. Pat looked at him once, and then went out of the door, closing it after him.

He switched on the light in his room and pulled his suitcase from under the bed. It didn't take him long to pack. All he had to do was to squeeze in all the things he had brought from Ireland. He had nothing extra except the clothes he was wearing now. He felt that he must be in the middle of a nightmare. Who would ever think that things like that could happen in a modern world? It was like the flaming things you read about in the Bible. But in this century did things like that happen? If anybody had told him about it he would have laughed heartily. It just wasn't credible. And yet it was happening to him. It an made him feel sort of soiled. Why in the name of God should he have been put in the position of the devil's advocate? What had it all got to do with him? If Jack was frustrated in some way, why should his frustration have to descend on the head of Pat Moore?

He clicked the case shut and looked around him. The room was cold and uninviting under the light of the naked bulb. It was not troublesome to part with it. He had suffered a far deeper wrench leaving his own smaller room at home. He had given nothing to this room. So he had nothing to take away or nothing to leave behind. It was just four walls with a small window looking on to a garden that you could not see. A garden of God too, he thought, with a sneer; every inch utilized for the good of man: spuds and cabbage and cauliflower and lettuce and small white turnips. And no flowers. It would have been nice to have smelled a flower, to have woken in the morning with the sniff of the perfumed wallflower, to have come home at night to the crispness of the scented stock. No — rotting potato stalks, like his own soul according to Jack, and decayed turnips. Good-bye to it. May it rest in peace.

He opened the door and switched off the light. Then he closed the door behind him and went into the kitchen. The light was on and Mary was at the sink, dabbing at her mouth with a face towel.

She turned when she heard him. He looked at her. Her eyes were frightened. He waited to see if she would speak. She tried to, he thought, but then after her lips, swollen now, had moved a little, he saw the tears coming into her eyes and then she turned her back on him

I'm sorry for her, he thought, as he opened the door and went out, closing it softly behind him; I am very sorry for her, but what can I do? It's her life. Years ago she should have made the fight. Perhaps she did too. But not hard enough. Maybe even the poor bitch loved Jack. He thought of Jack as he had last seen him, and shook his head. No. How could anybody love that? Wouldn't it frighten his own mother even? If he had a mother? Maybe he was born from a 25 per cent wax candle. It was when he had his hand on the gate that the probable solution came to him.

Jack was mad. He turned back as the thought came to him and moved a pace to the lighted kitchen. Then he stopped and shook his head. Not that mad, he thought. He's not normal, that's sure, not with that look in his red-rimmed eyes. What could I do, any-how? Couldn't pull Mary out of the place by force. She wouldn't come. He couldn't support her, anyhow. I wonder, he thought, if I shouldn't have hit him? Maybe it might have brought him to his senses. No, it wouldn't either. Or was I afraid? That would be bad. Was he thinking of Mary really when he retreated, or was he afraid of his own skin? He didn't think he had been afraid. He had been too full of rage to be afraid. That look in Jack's eye though? No, not even that. It was Mary. The sinking you got in your heart when you saw her there again, crouching back in the chair with the blood from her mouth pouring over her hand.

To hell with it, he thought, then, and to hell with him and her and the whole lot of them. It's got nothing to do with me. So he stood outside the gate and looked at the empty street (so still and suburbanly respectable, with the tiddly gardens, pretty flowers, neat housewives asleep in single beds, away from their spouses for the love and honour of hygiene). The neat lights evenly spaced. The trees growing on the footpaths, evenly spaced. How little they knew of what has gone on in Number 48. Or how little they cared.

He stood there. 'Now where the hell do I go from here?' he asked the night.

Seamus, of course, was the only answer. He was the only one he knew. So he sighed, lifted his case, and set off up the road. He had been in Seamus's digs once or twice to call for him. A nice place; English people. They were fond of Seamus too, particularly the kids. Always something in his pockets for them. The lady of the house was proud of him – on account of his appetite. It was like having a tame hippopotamus – the size of him and the gargantuan meals he could consume. The poor woman couldn't have made a lot of profit out of Seamus. But then look at the fun they had in the house with him. The difference, he thought, between that house of pagans – again according to Jack, since anyone who wasn't Catholic with him was a pagan – and Jack's austere abode. No use thinking like that, he thought. It doesn't get you anywhere pleasant.

He came out of his own street and turned up towards the town. They all called it the 'town'. It was the centre of their suburb and had a W postal address, so that they could just call themselves Londoners, whereas the poor people a quarter of a mile away were practically country boys, since their address was Middlesex. It was a neat island suburb. On each side it was hemmed in by two great traffic routes to the west, great concrete roads with traffic islands and cycle-paths and footpaths. They were double-hemmed really, because two underground routes paralleled the roads, even though the railways at this point weren't underground but overground, which sounded very Irish to Pat. The town was within this triangle of the roads, and its western end was sealed again by a road that joined up the other two. So that here you had their town in this triangle, and even now Pat was beginning to have an affection for it. It was nicely self-contained and all the big factories were outside the orbit of it, so that it was a pleasant suburb for the housing and feeding of the people and you didn't, as in other places, have your dirty workshops for making this, that and the other staring you in the kisser every time you got up in the morning.

He passed the Catholic church now, a small building with a tin roof, so different to the giant cathedrals at home. Beyond the church you came to the town proper. A cross it was, with shops of all kinds built along the arms of the cross. Not too many shops, just enough for the needs. A modern cinema, as ugly-looking as cinemas anywhere else, and at the other end a public library, which Pat had already investigated and found wonderful. Turn down right then and into more streets of houses built in and around the local park, a big place where you could play tennis for a tanner, where they didn't care about the colour of your blood or who your father was or how much you had in the bank or whether you wore white trousers and played patty ball. All they were interested in was whether your tanner was good or bad. You could even play golf here too under the same conditions, for ninepence a round with clubs on loan.

He turned right again beyond the park and came into another network of roads, avenues, and drives, and walked up the street Seamus lived. It was called Burton Avenue. They were big semi-detached houses, two in a block. The usual gardens front and back, the lot paled by angled creosoted boards.

The house Seamus lived in was dark. He stood outside the gate and looked at it. He felt very diffident about knocking them up at this hour of the night. He didn't know where he might be able to sleep there either. Four rooms fully occupied by the family and Seamus. In the room Seamus slept in there was a single bed, and by the time the big body of Seamus rested in it there wasn't room left there for a flea even. So sleeping with Seamus was out of the question.

Suddenly he thought of Maureen and their talk coming home in the bus. His jaded body wakened up as he thought about it. Providential in a way, wasn't it? But had she meant it? He thought she had. But where the hell did she live? Wait a minute. What's this Seamus had said when he had introduced her to Pat first? The girl next door, wasn't it? Yes, it was. H'm, but which next door? After all, there were two next doors if you looked at it. But then since the houses were semi-detached there were two houses together in a block, therefore Seamus must have meant the house in his own block. That would be the house beyond it.

He walked to the gate of that house. There was a light in one of the windows downstairs. He didn't stop to think any more. He opened the gate firmly and marched up the concrete path, saying to himself that if he didn't strike oil here he could hop over the gate into the park and sleep on the grass. It was a fine night; it wasn't cold.

He knocked timidly. No answer. He knocked more firmly, and then the light was switched on in the hall, the door opened the length of the safety chain and a voice said 'What do you want?'

'I want a bed,' said Pat. His heart had jumped and a feeling of satisfaction had come over him when he had recognized her voice and her features.

'Pat Moore!' she said, as she loosened the chain. 'Come on in.'

He went past her into the hall.

'Go in there,' she said, pointing to the lighted room.

Pat went in. It was a living-room – very nice: cream paper on the walls, done in big panels with decorations at each corner. A low modern fireplace with a fire dying in it. Standard lamp on the floor, tall with a tasselled shade on it. Two big comfortable easy-chairs and a couch. Delicate china cabinet in the corner. Bits of Maureen scattered over the place and a sewing-box open.

'This is a nice time for a girl to be working,' said Pat.

'What happened?' she asked, coming in.

'I had a row with Jack,' he said. 'He fired me out.'

'My God,' she said, wrinkling her forehead. She was wearing a dressing-gown over pyjamas, an oldish dressing-gown. No make-up on her face. All rubbed off with cold cream. Her hair tied up on top of her head with a ribbon. Made her look more like a child than ever.

'Don't be looking at me,' she said. 'I look awful.'

'You look very nice,' he said.

'Sit down, anyhow,' said Maureen.

He did so. It was comfort to sit. He realized suddenly that he was very tired.

'I was sewing,' she said, indicating the things.

'So I see,' said Pat. 'Listen, were you joking about having a spare room?'

'I was not,' said Maureen. 'Why on earth would I be joking about things like that?'

'I don't know,' he said. 'It sounds too good to be true.'

'I don't know about now,' said Maureen. 'There's a bed there, but the clothes haven't been aired or anything and I'll have to see Mum.'

'She mightn't like me,' said Pat.

'That's true,' said Maureen. 'Anyway, I'll go and ask her. Make yourself comfortable. I won't be long.'

She was gone. He started to sweat a bit then. Terrible, he thought. Imagine. He thought of himself as Maureen's mother, awakened out of a sleep. Got a new lodger below, Mum. Fired out of his digs, drunk and disorderly. Heh, Dad, pop on your pants and get the police. Keep him talking until the cops come. That's it. He worked up a terrible sweat. Then he heard her at the door. He stood up. He realized how he must look. Rumpled clothes. Tousled hair. What felt like a cauliflower ear. Must look most disreputable.

She was the image of Maureen. A small, neat little woman. Looking neat even at this hour, disturbed in her sleep. Introduced. You look tired. Her hand small and a little rough from work. Or maybe that was his own. A smile in her eyes too. The snub nose; he stuttered; he stammered. He shuffled his feet. 'Do sit down, please, Mister Moore.' A smile on her face. She probably thinks I'm harmless – who wouldn't? 'Maureen, go and dress the bed in the spare room. The linen is in the hot press.'

'All right, Mum.' 'And put on the kettle. We'll have a cup of tea You'd like a cup of tea, wouldn't you, Mister Moore?' 'I would, ma'am, thank you very much indeed.' A rush of words because she was so nice. A lift of the heart because she seemed to understand. No questions. Just sit down there at the fire stirring the dying embers into an efficient blaze. Most kind. No talk about the funny hour of the night or what happened or anything. Just, 'You're from Ireland, Maureen tells me. Not long here. You must be lonely.' 'No, ma'am, not now.' A smile again. 'Your mother misses you?' 'I have no mother. She died when I was small. Father dead too in the Great War.' Tut-tut. A click of sympathy in her tongue. 'I have a sister Cissie. She's nice. She'll miss me a little. But I like it.' Little questions about other things. Nothing pertinent. He could have hugged the woman. Fell in love with her straight away – like coming into the sun after walking a long road under storm-clouds.

Later Maureen comes in with a tray. Pot of tea and all the doings. Mrs pours the tea and dishes it out as if she was a queen in her own parlour. Little chit-chat. A wink from Maureen as she nibbled a biscuit. Noticed that Maureen had put on lip-stick in the interval and grinned. The cup of tea and another cup and a smoke. No, Mrs didn't smoke. Old-fashioned maybe. But Maureen smoked. Yes. Her father had spoiled her. 'Now, Mum!' 'Yes he has, dear.' Oh, very, very pleasant. Drowning in a sea of kindness and lack of curiosity. Just a calm acceptance. We like you and that's that.

Maureen showed him his room. It was at the back of the house. A small room, but very pretty. The touch of the woman's hand. Little knick-knacks. Cretonne curtains. Cretonne cover on the bed and on the chair. Bed, dressing-table, and wardrobe in a light wood. Very cheerful. Maureen turned down the bedclothes and paused in the door to say good night.

He found it hard to speak.

'I won't ever forget this, Maureen,' he said. 'It . . . well—'

'Ah, fish!' said Maureen.

He laughed.

'Sleep well now,' she said. 'You'll meet Dad in the morning. He's very fierce. He might fire you out again.'

He knew she was joking. It was plain to see that Mum was the power. What a grand power! Now, if she asked me to say the Rosary eight times a day, I would and no bother. So different.

'Good night, Maureen, and thanks.'

She goes.

He lay back in bed then with his arms under his head. Another move on whatever road I am going, he thought. He thought of Jack then. He will probably get me sacked, but I don't care. I will get another job. I feel now that I could move the world on the palm of my hand. So good-bye, Jack, and may your shadow never grow less. He was less cheerful when he thought of Mary. The contrast between this home and the one he had left. It's no use now worrying anyhow, he thought before he fell asleep. I'm finished with Jack for ever.

But he was mistaken.

6

He was awakened from his wanderings in another world by an urgent hand shaking his shoulder, and the voice calling, 'Here, Pat, Pat!'

He managed to open his eyes, squeezed them against the light of the bulb, and said sleepily, 'What? What is it?' He recognized Mr Potter then, his full body encased in the red woollen dressing-gown, his scanty hair tousled.

'Are you awake?' Dad asked then.

'Yes,' said Pat, really coming awake and sitting up. 'What's wrong?'

'There's a wee woman downstairs wants you,' said Dad then.

'A woman? Me? What time is it?' He couldn't assimilate it.

'After one in the mornin', lad. Better go down. It's urgent.'

'Oh, sure,' said Pat, pulling back the clothes and sitting on the edge of the bed rubbing his head.

'No time for scratchin',' said Dad, pushing at his shoulder. 'Down with you.'

'Who is she?' Pat asked.

'She didn't say. In too much of a hurry. Just asked for you and then said get you quick. So I got you.'

'Thanks,' said Pat, reaching for his overcoat in the wardrobe and putting it on over his pyjamas. He hadn't risen to a dressing-gown yet. That would come in years and years when he was as old as Maureen's dad.

'She's in the living-room' said Dad then, ushering him out the door and standing there on the landing watching him going down the stairs. The carpet felt rough on his bare feet.

It was Mary who was standing in the room waiting for him. She was dressed anyway, her hair loosely gathered.

'Mary!' he said. 'What on earth's the matter?'

She came over to him quickly.

'It's Jack, Pat,' she said. 'For God's sake will you come with me quick? He's gone out.'

'What's up with him?' he asked her.

Her eyes were terrified, her movements vague. She seemed to be shocked.

'He went out,' she said. 'There's something terrible wrong with him. I don't know where he's gone. I didn't know what to do. So all I could think of was to come over for you. Will you come quick, Pat? We'll have to find him.'

'But, Mary, what's wrong with him?' Pat felt that it was a bit too much that he should have to be pulled into Jack's life again like this. It was over a month now since he had broken free from him. It had been a nice month. A month of normal living with a nice ordinary family, where he had fun and comfort and he didn't have to be using his mind. Why should he be brought back now into Jack's affairs? 'Maybe he went for a walk,' he urged on her. 'Maybe he couldn't sleep.'

'No, no, no!' said Mary frantically, holding her hands until the fingers whitened. 'You don't understand. He has been getting queer. I don't know what it is. I woke up and he was getting out of bed. He was muttering all the time to himself. Low things under his breath. Pat, I'm afraid he's losing his mind!'

'That's nonsense, Mary,' he said, taking her arm. 'You're imagining it.'

'No, I tell you,' she said. 'I'm not imagining it!' Her voice was shrill. 'I . . . I . . . ' – how could she try and explain it to him? It had been going on for a few weeks. He didn't talk to her much any more, not even about holy things, as he used. Reading his books and holding up his head to say, 'Listen to this, Mary,' and then he would read to her a bit out of it. Always about a saint. What he had said and what he had done. But he had stopped reading lately. He would just come home from work and sit there in front of the fire, looking into it and mumbling, queer things, prayers and things all mixed up. And she would say, 'What is it

Jack?' and he would just look at her with burning eyes, and seem to come from far away, and lift his hand to his forehead, and say, 'What? What's that?' And she would say, 'Is anything wrong?' and he would say, 'No, no. Why should there be anything wrong?' And then he would read maybe, but his eyes would be blank and she would have the most appalling feeling of terror; and when they went to bed she would lie beside him, her body shivering, but not from the cold, since the weather was warm. He would fall asleep then, but he would be mumbling words in his sleep and flinging out his arms, and she would pull away from his hot body, get as far away from him as she could, and tremble. She would sleep eventually. He would seem all right again in the morning. Just the same as before. He always got up and went to seven o'clock Mass, and he'd be back for his breakfast and she'd have his lunch tied up in the pail for him, and he would go and she would say, Thank God, he's gone and he won't be back for eight hours.

'He was looking into the fire all the evening,' she said to Pat, 'and he was talking away to himself, and when I spoke to him he didn't turn his head to look at me at all. Just went on mumbling. Until later. Then I said, "You better go to, bed, Jack," and he didn't seem to hear me, so in the end I had to go over and put my two hands on his shoulders and lift him and I guided him into bed. He sat there on the edge and he was still talking, and even though he was looking at me, his eyes didn't see me. I had to take off his clothes and put him lying down. I went to bed too, but I knew his eyes were looking all the time. And he was talking, talking. That was horrible, I tell you. Mixed up things, incoherent, no sense to them. I thought I would go mad myself listening to him. I don't know what happened; I must have dozed. I woke up suddenly and I heard the door closing after him. I got out of bed, but before I could get anything on he was gone. I looked up the street, but there was no sign of him. So I put on some clothes and came over to you. Pat, we'll have to find him. There's something wrong with him!'

Pat felt a cold chill running up his spine. She had succeeded in putting her fears across to him all right. He knew that there was something wrong.

'What about his clothes?' Pat asked. 'Had he dressed himself?'

She looked at him, her eyes wide.

'I don't know,' she said. 'I didn't think. I didn't look. All I wanted to do was to get out and come over to you. I wanted to talk to somebody. I was afraid.'

He had a sudden picture of her in the house: silent, waiting, with all the coloured faces looking down from the walls. There was always something not quite right about Jack. He should have recognized it – not to have been doing the smart guy, picking him up.

'I won't be a second, Mary,' he said. 'I'll just chase up and put on a few clothes.'

He went out the door quickly and raced up the stairs. Maureen was on the landing with her father.

'Is anything wrong, Pat?' she asked.

'I think there is,' he said. 'Look, Dad' – he had got into the habit of calling him Dad too, like all the others – 'would you ever go out and get Seamus. Tell him to fire on his pants and meet us at the front. It's Jack, you know, where I was staying before I came to you. I think he's lost his mind. We'll want Seamus if we can find him. I wouldn't be enough on my own.'

'I'll get him,' said Maureen. 'I'll slip out the back way and over the fence.'

'I'll go down with you,' said Dad, and they went quickly and efficiently. Pat went into his own room, deciding to keep his mind blank deliberately. He pulled on trousers over his pyjamas, and a jacket, and slipped into socks and shoes. It didn't take him long. Then he went down again to Mary. She was standing exactly where she was when he left her, her eyes wide and her face bleak.

'Mary,' he said, 'you know Seamus, the big fellow on the job?'

'Yes,' she said.

'Well, he lives next door,' said Pat. 'We better bring him with us. If we . . . never mind.' He didn't want to put a picture into her mind of Seamus and himself struggling with a madman – if he was a madman. 'Are you sure, Mary, that he didn't just go for a walk because he couldn't sleep?'

She didn't even answer him. He knew he was only trying to comfort himself.

'Come on so,' he said then. He took her arm and brought her outside.

He looked up at the house next door. There was a light in Seamus's room. While they waited it flicked out, and shortly the door opened and they saw Seamus coming down the steps, pulling on a short coat over a shirt that was gleaming whitely in the light cast from the street standards. Seamus is good, Pat thought. You can always depend on Seamus. He didn't even ask a question. Just stood there beside them waiting.

'You know Mary, Seamus,' Pat said.

'Howya, ma'am,' said Seamus, in a sort of whisper, and then the three of them turned and made their way down the street.

It was a fine, warm summer night and the streets were deserted.

They didn't talk. There was just the sound of their hurried footsteps on the pavements, the heavy, long strides of Seamus, the trip-trip of Mary's small steps, and Pat's a little longer. Up by the park and turn left and down then into the town. Turn right at the cross and down towards the church.

'We better go to the house first,' Pat said. 'He might have come back.' He glanced idly at the church as they passed. There was the reflection of the light in there, the red sanctuary lamp before the Blessed Sacrament that is never allowed to go out. They turned down Acacia Avenue then, and Pat wondered at the distaste that turning down the street brought to him even after this long time.

They went in carefully. He knew that the three of them were holding their breaths as they followed Mary to the door. She opened it with her key and then Pat put her aside and went in first. Seamus followed him. It was very silent. Into the living-room. He switched on the light and then noticed that there was a light in the passage beyond. It came from Mary's bedroom, he thought.

'There's a light in your room, Mary,' he whispered.

'I left it on,' said Mary. 'I was afraid of the dark.' Poor Mary, he thought.

They went into the bedroom cautiously. It was empty. Pat had a peculiar sensation, like the feeling you get in a room full of people where one of the people is a simpleton. Everyone talks and acts normally, but always at the back of your neck there is the chill knowledge of the half-mind, the lack of reality.

'What'll we do now?' Mary asked in a whisper.

'What clothes has he?' Pat asked.

Mary looked carefully.

'His pyjamas are there,' she said. 'His trousers are missing.'

'Is that all?' Pat asked.

Mary nodded her head, a frightened and bewildered look on her face.

Pat thought of the church then. He didn't know quite why it came into his head. Just that it did. He thought of the reflection of the light from the sanctuary lamp. Wasn't it too bright for a small red light?

'Mary,' he said, his hands on her shoulders, 'will you wait here now? Seamus and myself will go out and look for him.'

He felt her body shivering under his hands. 'No,' she said; 'I'll go too.'

'It might be better,' said Pat seriously, 'if you waited.'

'No,' she said. 'I'll have to go. I'll have to know.'

'All right,' said Pat abruptly. 'Come on.' He led the way out of the room. They switched off all the lights and went out again into the empty road. Pat walked fast. Seamus caught Mary's arm with his big hand and helped her on. She could feel the kindness of him.

They paused outside the gate leading into the church. It was open. They approached the big doors. They weren't very big doors really. Not if you had been used to the towering arched doors of the churches at home, with the big black, medieval-looking hinges on them and the squat-headed bolts. It was a small plain church like a small cinema with the four walls and the roof of corrugated iron. A door at the front – double door with a small porch. The altar was at the far end, and there was another door there going into the tiny sacristy, where the priests robed themselves for the ceremonies. Six big windows in the walls on each side to let in the light. Just plain glass windows. Here no towering stained glass exquisitely executed by the delicate hand of Harry Clarke. It took money to put in stained glass and to build a big church, and it was just now as he looked at it that Pat realized that the priests here must be poor. It just flashed across his mind and then he walked down the side of the church, caught hold of a window sill, and raised himself up so that he could peer in. The lights were on at the far end of the church. He brought his eyes up there, and then caught his breath.

Jack was there all right. He let himself down again.

'He's there, Mary,' he said.

She put her hand to her mouth.

'How did he get in?' he asked. 'The front door is closed.'

'He has keys for the sacristy door,' she said. 'He helps to dress the altar and that.'

Pat remembered. At Mass, at the Gospel the green-covered plate being passed around and the figure of Jack in the aisle, in his Sunday suit, looking at each hand that put money on the plate. A picture of Jack doing this and that in the church. Helping, holding the brass jug for the holy water. Answering responses. Jack sometimes serving Mass when the altar boys were doing something else. What do we do now? Pat wondered. He walked up by the side of the church, his feet loud on the gravel. He heard them following him.

He paused at the sacristy door. Tried it. It swung open on a touch.

He turned then to Mary.

'Go in and get the priest,' he said.

'No,' Mary said, 'I . . . '

'Mary, for God's sake go in and get the priest, will you!' he said it harshly so that it penetrated. She looked at him, a frightened flash from her eyes, then she turned and walked past the church. The priest's house, a small brick house, was built at the far end of the enclosed space. They stood and watched her. Heard her knock on the door. Remained there until a light flashed on high up. Then Pat nodded his head at Seamus and he went into the sacristy.

The light was on. A plain little room with distempered walls and only a cross hanging up above the sort of counter where the robes of the priest rested as he draped himself for the Mass. Brightly polished candlesticks and the smell of incense. There was another door opposite that led out to the altar. It was closed. Pat tiptoed over to it and opened it slowly – just a little so that he could look out. Then he signed to Seamus to come over. He felt the bulk of him behind. Heard him suck in his breath, expel it again slowly. What do we do now? Pat wondered.

It would turn your heart in your chest. Jack, kneeling there in front of the altar, inside the rails, naked except for his trousers, his hands spread wide, the light above shining on the bald part of his head, his eyes wide and staring, horrible in their complete blankness. His lips moved to a jumble of incomprehensible words, foam at the corners of his mouth. While they hesitated he rose to his feet, his toes gripping the smooth mosaic floor. There were four statues, two on either side of the altar: the Sacred Heart, the Blessed Virgin, St Joseph with the Little Child holding his hand, and St Peter. They were small statues with flowers in small bowls at their base. Not gaudy statues. Very simply executed. Peaceful-looking. Serene.

Jack went from one to the other of them, bent and kissed the feet of the statues, then looked up at their faces with his blank eyes and mumbled his words; knelt down before each one and bowed his head, rose then and went to all the others; and when he had completed the rounds of the four statues, he returned to the front of the altar and knelt and held out his arms and looked up and mumbled.

Pat felt the hair rising on the back of his neck. He knew that Jack's mind was no longer there. It had soared its way to another world all of its own. Jack had returned to a sort of peaceful childhood of his own. He was away in a land where no normal mind could penetrate. Pat felt that if only his actions had been violent or his speech loud the whole thing would have for them taken on an air of awful reality. But not this. Not this man with the blank eyes and the eternal mumbling. All you could make out was the tail end of a word or a phrase, nothing coherent.

'This is terrible,' said the voice of Seamus behind him.

Pat's mouth was dry. He had to shuffle his tongue around it to try and talk. 'We better go and get him,' he said, in a hoarse whisper.

'All right,' said Seamus. 'I'll get the far side of him.'

They went in. They were shut off from the main body of the church by the altar rails. Seamus lifted his leg and crossed them and then walked along until he came to the double gates in the centre. He opened those and went in, ending up on the far side of the kneeling man. Pat closed in then from his side. He had a terrible urgency to get Jack out from the altar rails. Standing there he felt that he shouldn't be there himself and that it was wrong to have Jack there. From his youth he had been trained to appreciate what the altar side of the rails meant. That it was not meant for unconsecrated men, that the peace and mystery of the tabernacle was something to be assimilated from afar. Maybe, he thought, if we could only get him out to the body of the church that things wouldn't seem so bad.

They went towards him. Pat hesitated to lay his hands on him. He didn't know what would happen. He expected Jack to come alive, a roaring maniac, struggling in their arms, shouting at them, breaking the peace, anything.

He put his hand out firmly and grasped the stretched arm. It was taut and cold to the touch, terribly cold, even though looking down now he could see sweat on the balding forehead. Seamus had grasped his other arm. Now for it, Pat thought, his stomach tightening, his whole inside waiting for the struggle to come.

There was no struggle. They raised him to his feet. He didn't even notice them. His eyes just strained forward and he kept his mumble going. They walked back through the gates of the rails. He came with them. He didn't resist or assist, and they put him sitting on the first bench. It was then Pat thought that he would have felt better if Jack had exploded in a welter of words and deeds. Anything but this. The arms and body gone flaccid, the head erect, just looking, and the eternal jumble of words. Pat bent down and looked into his eyes.

'Jack,' he said. 'Jack!' and he shook his shoulder a little.

It was entirely useless. Jack didn't see him or hear him.

Pat felt like crying. It would be better, he thought, for a man to die and be buried and to rot than to have him like this.

They heard a shuffle on the floor of the altar then and they turned as the priest came out through the gates. He was a medium-sized man. Pat didn't know him to speak to, just knew the look of him from seeing him saying Mass at eleven o'clock on a Sunday. His hair was black, going white at the temples; his body slight, with long, thin hands. His face was narrow and the eyes were deep-sunken, and Pat knew how they could twinkle when he made a humorous remark during the sermon. It was all the more unexpected to see his face lighting up because his eyebrows were black too and thick and you would think that he was a most glowering man until you heard him speaking in his soft, precise voice with a laugh at the back of it. They fell away from Jack as he knelt in front of him.

'Hello, Jack,' he said then, his hand on his bare shoulder.

Jack just looked and mumbled.

'Ah, the poor man,' said the Father then, just as if he had been called because Jack had a sore foot or hand or limb. That was good. It returned the other two to near normality. Then Pat saw Mary framed in the sacristy doorway.

'No, no, Mary!' he said in an urgent whisper. She didn't heed him. She came in.

'It's all right,' said the Father to Pat. 'It's no harm. The poor man is just sick.'

Mary knelt in front of Jack then and she placed her two hands on his arms and she looked into his eyes and she called his name. It made no difference, so Mary's head fell into her hands and she started to cry, silent tears that flowed out through her fingers – like, Pat thought, the blood that had flown through them not so long ago.

'Now, now,' said the Father, putting his hand along her shoulders. 'Now, now; there, there.' It was very little to say really, but there was a wealth of comfort and understanding in the timbre of his voice.

He raised her to her feet.

'We better go into the house,' he said then. 'Would you lads carry Jack? We'll have to get him in out of the cold and get the doctor for him.'

He led her away to the sacristy. Seamus bent down then and took Jack in his arms, just as if he was carrying a child. It was no effort to him, Pat noticed. Pat let him go ahead and switched off the lights and closed the doors behind them. They put Jack on the black leather couch in the priest's study and covered him with a blanket. Then they sat there on the chairs and waited for the doctor to come in answer to the priest's telephone call. It was terrible, that wait. It was an austere room, something like the sacristy. Distempered walls, with only a cross in the centre of the wall over the couch. A large table in the centre of the floor, of polished mahogany. Four chairs with the curved backs covered in the black leather. A breviary on the table. A bookcase in one corner beside the fireplace and a bookcase in the other one. Large books, leather-covered. The night was quiet. There was nothing to disturb it except the mumbling of Jack.

The priest came back. 'He'll be here shortly,' he said.

He sat close to Mary and asked her questions. It was a relief to her to talk. It was a relief to the others to listen to her and to try and shut out of their ears the talking of her husband.

'I'm sorry, very sorry,' the priest said. 'He was a great assistance to me. Great assistance. A good man. Maybe he took it all a little too seriously. When did you notice that he wasn't quite right?'

She told him. The words poured out of her, and her fear. The priest wasn't surprised, but he didn't say that to Mary. Jack had frequently harangued himself about the whole business. It had become an obsession with him. At first he had been between two minds whether Jack was a saint or not. Then he knew that Jack wasn't quite balanced. He was too vociferous to be as holy as he tried so hard to be. Strange the workings of the mind. He had met cases of religious mania before, of course. More distant though. Never as close as this. Funny thing was that it wasn't a lot to do with religion, really. It was a culmination of small things, other things, weighing on the mind. Going after the religion was an endeavour to escape. Not the true faith one strove so hard for – just an escape. That wasn't so good.

The doctor came then, and they all went into the hall except the priest who stayed in there with him. The floor of the hall was parquet; chairs and a hall stand. Mary sat and the others stood and tried to talk, but what on earth could one talk about? Seamus was very uncomfortable, just shuffling his feet and looking huge and sad.

Later the doctor came out. He was a youngish man, Irish too, and his name was O'Neill. Pat recognized him from having seen him going around in his small car. Short and inclined to be fat; brown hair going grey; a small nose and a big face and cheerful eyes.

'You better go home now,' he said to Mary kindly, 'and leave him to us.'

She stood up.

'What are you going to do with him?' she asked.

He hesitated. 'He'll have to go away,' he said, trying to be kindly diplomatic.

'Where?' she persisted.

'We better go now, Mary,' said Pat, taking her arm.

'Where are you going to put him?' she asked, resisting his arm.

'He'll have to go to Hanwell,' said O'Neill uncomfortably.

Really, he thought, there's no difference between the telling of this and the telling of approaching death. It's a hard life. She looked such a nice woman too. Neat and long-suffering. Maybe, he thought, it will be better for her in the long run to be separated from her husband. She was crying again.

Pat thought of Hanwell, not so faraway. High walls; buildings not seen from the road, the unease that came over you when you passed an asylum.

'Come on, Mary, please,' said Pat.

'Look,' said O'Neill. 'He's not too bad — honestly. He's bad enough, of course. But it won't last. It never does. It's a comparatively mild form of — eh — mania. He can be cured.'

'How long?' she asked.

He was uncomfortable again. 'Not too long. Can't say with any certainty. But it's very mild. Maybe a year, two years. It's happened before. It's more in the nature of a brain storm, you see. Not too bad. A sort of nervous breakdown. That's right. Think of it as that — a nervous breakdown. You better go now. There's nothing you can do. Leave him to us.'

He was afraid for his life that she would wait until the others came, the police surgeon and the police with their car. That was a terrible thing for her to see.

They got her away when the priest had come out and spoken to her and patted her shoulder, feeling a little helpless but infinitely sorrowful.

They walked down the road again and went to the house. They sat in the kitchen and Seamus set about making a pot of tea. It was a relief to him; it gave him something to do.

Mary sat there for a while, dry-eyed now, her head on one side. Pat remembered other people before whom he had seen with their heads on one side from sorrow. It was always that way, as if the neck had lost its power to hold the weight of the head. There was little he could say, because he had not liked Jack and had little to do with either of them, because in his youth and freshness he had thought Mary had allowed herself to be beaten into submission by her husband. Once only it had flashed across his mind that there was something wrong with Jack to account for his behaviour. He hadn't pressed the thought very far. Just adopted the evidence of his own preconceived ideas. He had seen sorrow before when he had lived at home – the death of his mother: a stiff figure laid out in a brown habit on an iron bed in the room, lying on a white quilt. He had seen the woman who had cut her own throat. He had seen the old lady who had drowned herself in the canal. These things had mattered very much at the time, but he was young then and they hadn't taught him to be helpful to Mary.

'I loved Jack, you know,' she said then, almost shocking them with unexpected speech. 'I know you don't think I did, Pat, and that you think that I was a fool to put up with him. It wasn't all that you saw. You saw him at a wrong time. I knew him when he was different. I knew him when he could laugh and the flesh would crinkle around his eyes. He was quite clever too. He used to read different things. We had fun, long ago. He used to tease me. Yes, he used, and tickle me long ago. We would both laugh. Because he wanted a child very bad, and I knew he would laugh then too and he would have spent hours tickling the child. I saw it all.

She paused then. There was little sound except Seamus carefully leaving a cup on the table. They stifled their breathing.

'He didn't have a child,' she said. 'I don't know why. We

prayed enough for one. We went to doctors too, and that wasn't nice. We should have had one, but we never did. I don't know why. He became sad then. He used to stop and play with the kids on the street. He used to come home always with sweets in his pocket for them – in the street where we were before we came here. And then he didn't play with them any more and he didn't bring sweets in his pocket and he stopped laughing. I prayed to God until I was empty and couldn't pray any more, but there seemed to be no end to his praying. It became very intense. Maybe it became too intense. I don't know. I'm not very clever about things. All I know is that I remember him like he was. Maybe all those prayers, the good ones and the bad ones even, couldn't go astray. Maybe he will get better soon, and that he will be like he was before. Maybe he will laugh again. Do you think so, Pat? What do you think, Pat?'

He put his hand on hers leaning across the table.

'That's the way it will be, Mary,' he said. 'It's too late for now to be sorry, but I am. I didn't understand.'

'How could you?' she said. 'You're young. He was like that too, one time. Impatient. It's impatience that makes life worth while sometimes. It makes situations and laughter. If I thought that Jack would laugh again, all this would be worth it.'

'Here,' said Seamus then, clearing his throat, 'have a sup a tay.'

They sat there and drank the tea.

'Mary,' said Pat then, after a time, 'would you like if I came back and lived here again? I mean, you'll find it hard now. If I came back the money would be a help. If you had a lodger again.'

'Me too,' said Seamus; 'couldn't I come too? That'd be two you'd have.'

She smiled wanly.

'I have a sister in the north of England,' she said. 'I'll go to her for awhile. I'll be all right. We didn't spend much money you know. Jack had good wages. He saved. I'll be all right. I want to go away, and then come back again.'

Pat was relieved. A terrible thought, but he was. He still didn't want to come back here. Even with Jack out of it.

They left her as the dawn was breaking palely in the sky. She went into the bedroom, and they waited a little and then they left, closing the doors after them. They started to walk home slowly.

Seamus was the first to break the silence between them. 'Sometimes, Pat,' he said, 'I think it's a rale stinkin' oul world.'

'It is,' said Pat, smiling a little at the idea of two young people like them trying to philosophize.

'She's a grand little woman too,' said Seamus. 'Why does it always have to happen to nice little women like her?'

'I don't know,' said Pat. That was true, what Seamus had said, he thought. He remembered all the other nice little women from his own very poor days. The women with the streaks of grey in their hair and the sad eyes. Mostly women with shawls, who thought it all was the will of God and in the end cracked a little joke about their seemingly perpetual misfortunes. It was false, he thought, to think of those women as being weak. They were not weak. They were able to adapt themselves. He thought of the life Mary must have had for the past few years with a husband slowly going mad. Nobody would ever know the resources in her own soul she had to call on to be able to bear with it. But she had. She bore the signs of it etched for eternity on her face. You could dismiss her as being weak for bearing with her lot, but she had gained something else in her eyes, a look of what was it — courage, fortitude, patience? Or something else that she would never have had if she had broken away.

'I don't know,' said Pat, with a sigh, 'I don't know what the hell the whole thing is about.'

'Jack is better off than us now, anyhow,' said Seamus surprisingly. 'He doesn't have t' bother any more what the hell it's all about.'

'There's that in it,' said Pat.

They parted at their gates. They had two hours left before they would have to get up and go to work again.

Pat got into bed, but he couldn't sleep. He felt very tired and very sleepy, but he couldn't go to sleep. He was afraid that if he dozed, he would see those sightless eyes, hear that awful mumble. His mind was a jumble of flashing pictures. his heart was a jumble of mixed emotions. He didn't know whether to feel horror at the sight of Jack or sorrow for what he had come to. He didn't know whether to cry for the look of Mary or to applaud something in her he couldn't understand. But he did know one thing. He had learned something, whatever it was. He thought that tonight might have taken the immature stars out of his eyes. He didn't feel that he was the same young man who had awakened to the shaking of Dad. He wondered if he would ever forget tonight, hoped that he would, and fell asleep on the hope.

It was a short sleep and a long lesson.

7

'Ah, lookit, hurry up for God's sake, Maureen!' Pat shouted into the open Potter door. 'It'll be time to come home before we start at all, so it will!'

'Yeh might just as well have patience,' said Seamus behind him. 'Roarin' at 'r won't hurry 'r up.'

'My God, women!' said Pat, jiggling at the brakes of the bicycle impatiently.

Mrs Potter came out the door then, with a tissue-paper packed parcel in her hand.

'Here are the egg sandwiches, Pat,' she said. 'Better not go without them.'

He took them from her and opened the black leather cycling bag attached to the saddle of his bicycle. It was a nice bicycle. It shone bravely in the August-bank-holiday sun, a sort of a racing bicycle painted cream and picked out with blue stripes. Thin tyres and lowered handlebars with thick rubber grips. A pound down and three bob a week until it was paid off, but it was worth it all. It was the pride of his heart, the first bicycle he had ever owned. If it wasn't that he was so fed up waiting for Maureen to appear, he would have great joy out of it. He put the sandwiches into the already filled bag and strapped it down.

'What's keeping Maureen, Mrs Potter? he asked. 'What in the name of God is she doing with herself at all?'

'I don't know,' said Mum. 'She's been up in that room of hers for hours it seems to me. I'll go in and try and hurry her.'

'Tell her if she's not here in five minutes we'll go without her,' said Pat determinedly. At that moment she appeared on the doorstep. She was clipping a bandeau to her hair. She looked very nice on the step in the sun, wearing a white blouse and blue shorts. The shorts were as short as their name and it was obvious to the most casual eyes that her legs were very shapely.

Seamus whistled.

Pat shouted.

'For God's sake stop titivating yourself, will you, and come on,' he said to her. 'Are we going to wait here all day for you?'

Maureen looked at him calmly. 'Nobody asked you to wait,' she said. 'You can go to hell if you like.'

'Maureen,' said Mum.

'Well, he'd give anybody a pain,' said Maureen.

'We can't be keeping Lelia waiting,' said Pat.

'And why not, pray?' asked Maureen, coming down the steps. 'Is Lelia more important than me? Is she?'

'Ah, lookit!' said Pat, exasperated.

'For goodness' sake, Maureen, can't you get going?' said Mrs Potter. 'This arguing is no way to start a holiday.'

'Who's arguing?' Maureen asked indignantly.

'All right, all right,' said Pat. 'I'm sorry. And now can we go?'

Maureen came out then, stopped as if to argue further, thought better of it, and put her tidy behind on the saddle of her bicycle, which was propped against the kerb.

'Good-bye, Mum,' she said then, waving a hand. 'We won't be too late.'

''Bye, Mrs Potter,' said Pat. ''Bye, ma'am,' said Seamus, throwing a leg over a rather disreputable bike borrowed from one of the lads on the job, and then they were away. Pat was wearing a new white shirt with an open collar and grey flannel trousers. Seamus was wearing a shirt that wasn't white but striped, no collar, and his navy-blue trousers were held to his big waist by one of his ties. Seamus was always that way. He never seemed to have the proper things at the proper times, and he didn't give a damn.

'Have a good time now, let you,' said Mrs Potter, waving at them as they departed and then, sighing, saying to herself, Well, thanks be to heaven they are out of my hair at last; and then went into the house and determined to go upstairs and root Dad out of his bank-holiday bed so that she could get on with things.

'Are you sure you have everything now before we get too far away?' Pat asked. 'I don't want to be coming back again for something you forgot.'

Maureen looked at him and her glance was furious.

'I think you're a frightful smug, insufferable idiot!' she said.

Pat looked at her in amazement.

'What did I say?' he asked.

'Ah, lookit,' said Seamus, 'can't ye get into the proper spirit of this thing, can't ye? Don't ye realize that we're supposed to be happy an' gay, don't ye? I thought this was supposed to be a holiday and that we were goin' on a holiday. Look, if yeer goin' on like that, wouldn't it be better for's not to go at all?'

'I'm sorry, Maureen,' said Pat. 'I didn't mean it. It's just that I'm excited I suppose.'

He was excited too. This was the first day he had been on a bicycle of his own going into the green English hinterland. He had never been out of the town since he had come, and he felt that it was something to be going out to see green fields and beech trees and sit under them, with Lelia. That was what had him really excited. Lelia. He had seen her only twice since the famous night at the dance-hall. He had been to the pictures with her once. He didn't remember what the picture was about. All he remembered was the warm feel of her beside him. He had taken her hand too, but she had gently disengaged it after a time. You had to go slow with Lelia, he thought. You just didn't get down with Lelia and go to town. It made it all the worse as far as he was concerned, that he couldn't get near her. But he would today. He didn't know how it came about that the four them should be going for the day to Burnham Beeches on bicycles. He thought it had come from Lelia, and he had elaborated, and he didn't know how it had ended up in a foursome, but he didn't mind. Maureen was nice and Seamus was nice, and great fun, and Lelia would put the tin hat on it for him. Yes, this would be a great day and he felt as stirred about it all as he had felt long ago, counting the days until they would all be off on the school excursions.

'I didn't mean to be an eejit,' he said.

'That's all right,' said Maureen, and gave him a smile. Maureen had very nice teeth, he thought, and she looked very nice today the way her hair was pulled back from her small ears, and then he forgot her as they stopped outside Lelia's door.

'Will you get her?' he asked Maureen.

Maureen alighted reluctantly.

'All right,' she said, and opened the gate and went up to Lelia's door. They saw the door opening and a fat lady with a fat smile opened it and they heard her say, 'Just a minute, dear, and I'll get her,' and then she went back, and called, 'Lelia!' and Lelia appeared at the door and came down the path in front of Maureen. Her hair was tied with a ribbon and she wore a scarlet jersey that fitted her very closely and had short sleeves so that her arms were bare and you could hardly miss seeing the outline of her breasts pushing belligerently against the wool. She wore shorts, cream coloured, very nicely cut, and the way her thighs tapered to her knees made Pat hold his breath. When she stood beside him pulling on cream gloves so that one of her breasts rubbed against his arm, his heart started the pound that only Lelia could induce.

'Like me?' she asked, looking up at him.

Pat could only answer her with his eyes. She turned then to Seamus.

'Would you get my bike out of the shed, Seamus?' she asked. Seamus dismounted good-humouredly.

'All right, alannah,' he said, as he propped his bike and went into the gate, going up to the door of the shed built beside the house.

'We'll have good fun,' said Lelia.

'We will indeed,' said Pat. He noticed that she was wearing sandals. Her feet were very small, like her hands.

'You were, late, weren't you?' Lelia asked, turning as Maureen joined them.

'A little,' said Pat.

'That was my fault,' said Maureen. 'I delayed them. Of course I had to help Mum get the grub and then I had to dress, but nobody would think of making allowances for that.'

Pat thought that Maureen looked hot and couldn't help comparing the immaculate coolness of Lelia with her. Maureen looked grand and neat, but it was funny how she almost disappeared when Lelia appeared. Maureen, looking at him, noticed it too, and she felt like crying or stamping on the pavement. But she just glared at Lelia's back, and told herself again that she was a fool to come, and what was it to her if a bit of an Irish labourer couldn't see through this woman and was looking at her with a light in his eyes as if she was the Blessed Virgin of his religion?

They got away eventually and as they reached the main road Seamus and Maureen went on ahead and Lelia and Pat cycled behind them. It was some time before Pat became conscious of his surroundings. He was too conscious of Lelia. She would sometimes stretch a hand and leave it on his bare arm. He was conscious of the slightly gleaming perfection of her skin and her shapely legs as they rose and fell on the pedals of the bicycle. Her teeth shining in the sun through her parted lips as she spoke, and when he got behind her to allow a speeding car to pass them by, he noticed that she was as well shaped at the back as she was in front, and he couldn't help feeling from the looks she gave him that she liked him. Maybe, God, he thought, she would even be feeling the same breathlessness that I feel myself every time I touch her or feel her touch on mine. But he didn't think so. She was very cool. What did they talk about? He didn't know. Lelia was talking most of the time, about her mummie and dear daddie and how good they were. She was an only child, you see. But she was a trifle delicate. Had always been. So they wouldn't dream of letting her work. Gave her a very good education, so that she could have a proper appreciation of poetry. She often pitied poor girls like Maureen who had to start working for their living at an early age, so that they missed learning about the higher things. It must be so hard on poor Maureen to be stuck in an old office all her life pounding away at a typewriter.

Pat said he thought Maureen rather liked it, because she met a lot of interesting people. To that Lelia answered, commercial types. She couldn't stand those. They would drive her mad. And Pat had a little sneaking feeling that he ought to stand up for Maureen more, because God knows Maureen never said anything hurtful much about anybody and she was nice too, but he thought this might offend Lelia, so he agreed that an office wasn't exactly the place to meet anybody cultured and said it was a pity about poor Maureen, and to that Lelia said she wouldn't say 'poor' exactly – that owing to the upbringing she had, she would be well able to look after herself. Pat, remembering frequent arguments with Maureen over things, agreed heartily. And Lelia said what could you expect when her poor father was merely a driver on the L.C.C. Pat said weakly, he's a very nice man. I like him very much. Of course, why not? said Lelia; but it helped a bit to have a father who was something in the City, like her father. A very cultured man. She got her love of poetry from him. She didn't tell Pat that he was a clerk in a shipping office, and that the principal extent of his poetry, when he came home tired from work and his rather careless wife hadn't got a meal ready as yet, was for him to enquire why that lazy bitch of a daughter of hers couldn't stir herself and do something about the house. Whereat Mrs would tell him what she thought about him, and didn't he know that Lelia wasn't strong, to which Mr replied that cows weren't strong either, but they did something useful, like giving milk or chewing the cud, anything but sitting on a couch like lazy bitches all day, munching chocolates and reading filth from the cheapest circulating libraries. He wouldn't get very far, because Mrs when she married him had a bit of money and she still had it, and they couldn't possibly live on his salary if Mrs didn't dip into her stocking on occasion. So he would have to let the matter rest, whilst Lelia ignored him and Mrs went out and bought her lovely daughter another box of chocolates or a new pair of panties or an uplift bra, like the Genie of the Lamp serving faithfully her daughter's lazy and idle dreams.

'You'd love Daddy,' said Lelia.

'I'd like to meet him,' said Pat. 'He must be very good-looking to have turned out something like you.'

Lelia smiled and turned that away. 'You can't meet him now,' she said. 'Mummy and he have gone off to Brighton for the three days. Poor me will be all alone in the house. I hope I won't be frightened.'

'Why didn't you go with them?' Pat asked.

'Oh, well,' said Lelia, with a look to him out of the corner of her eyes, 'I had arranged to go to this place with you, and I didn't want to disappoint you.'

Pat felt very good at that answer and fell silent, and Lelia thought that she liked the look of his face and the profile of him and the nice neck sunburned going into the white shirt. And she liked the way the tendons stuck out on his lithe arms, lightly covered with short golden hairs.

'I like you, Pat,' she said then, and Pat looked at her and their bicycles came close together and she put a hand on his shoulder and could feel the muscles under her fingers. So they sighed and separated again.

It was a long, concrete road stretching a grey finger into green fields.

Maureen, ahead of them, appeared to have recovered her good humour. She was wobbling on the bicycle as she laughed at things Seamus was saying to her, turning her face so that you could see the shape of the small firm chin and her teeth shining. You could hear her laugh too, which was a sort of a gurgle, and Pat felt he might be missing something and felt a little peeved, and then thought, that is nonsense, because I have the better part of it, and he rested a hand on Lelia's back and could feel the cool flesh under his fingers where the neck of her jersey stopped short.

'Seamus has a wonderful back, hasn't he?' she said then.

He had. The shirt he was wearing, which was an outsize, was stretched tightly on his body and you could see the bunched muscles of his shoulders dancing under the tightened material.

'Seamus is a great guy,' said Pat, feeling that deep down in him he loved Seamus.

'Pity he's only a labourer,' said Lelia.

Pat felt something going cold in his chest. He looked at her. Her face hadn't changed. It was just a remark. She probably didn't know how it would hurt. Not that Seamus would mind. Still, if it had been anybody else who had said it . . .

'There's nothing wrong with being a labourer,' said Pat. 'It's an honest living, hard work. You rob nobody. You give value for money. I like it.'

'So unambitious, though, isn't it?' she asked, turning to look at him.

He couldn't deny that. 'I suppose it is,' he said thoughtfully. 'There's no future in it.'

'That's what I meant,' said Lelia, still looking at him.

All of which means, Pat thought grimly, that if I want Lelia I will have to cease to be a labourer. Maybe that was what he wanted. Somebody like Lelia to say, You must cease to be a labourer.

There were all sorts of vehicles on the road. Bicycles even more rattly than the one Seamus mounted, with the loosened mudguards waving wildly and the tinny noises emanating from it. There were tandems, with little carriages at the side for carrying the baby. Long, sleek automobiles passed by with a gentle hiss. It would have been slander to call them motor-cars. There were motor-cars too. Rattlers and bangers and belchers, and steamers, all sorts and sizes. Ones that had been built twenty years ago and still held to the road by the grace of God and far-away honest engine-builders. Flashy little sports models, with young men who leaned out and whistled at Lelia and Maureen, knowing that their speed would save them from the ire of their cycling partners. Everything mechanical and moveable seemed to have been resurrected for this sunny holiday. They swept by, their noises sounding different, their tyres making different music on the concrete. No speed limit here. They just whizzed by, streamers of them.

It was nice too, the land. It had been a long time since Pat had seen green fields with nothing else on them but the grass and cows. They had come to the edge of the building boom, had left behind the black belch of the ulcerating factory chimneys. The great two-way traffic road came to an end and they got into the country proper. Narrow roads winding through leafy lanes. All the hedges high and created from different kinds of thorn bushes, woodbine and tall trees. The kind of English lanes he had read about in books but couldn't credit, being used to his roads bounded by stone walls, loosely put together, gathered from the rocky fields of a hard and barren land. No sea to roar or murmur behind the walls, just undulating land lush and heavy, its period of pregnancy finished, the fruits of its womb given up with a sigh to the maw of the huge harvesters.

A village too. Incredibly neat, with its green. The tree in the middle and the wooden bench surrounding it. The mathematically thatched cottages. The village pub with the seat outside, where old country gentlemen sat and held tankards to whiskered faces. You found it hard to believe that it was real. It was too like the exact replica of what the English novelists had written. The old-fashioned mill there beside the stream, with the great wooden paddle stilled, either by the holiday or growth of the machine, all that. Too like . . . Hogarth, was it? who had painted it . . . and Reynolds. You felt as if somebody were having you on. Placed this here in your path with a sort of a leer of exactitude just to show that the writer didn't lie, that the painter's brush was true.

They paused in the village to drink tankards of ale and watched the procession pass them by. This village, timeless. And then these machines going by in a cloud of dust and pink faces. Others going by. Girls in shorts, pink flesh and brown flesh; and the men with sweat showing under the arms of khaki shirts, with packs on their backs and heavy socks and shoes on their feet. Incongruous, like a witch of four hundred years ago sitting and foretelling the incredible future.

They pushed on again.

They were all quite happy, even though it was more difficult now to cycle in the middle of all the traffic. Honking horns. Ringing bells, grinding gears. A mad medley of mass humanity, escaping for a few hours into a once washed, now begrimed and glorious countryside. To Pat it was all new. He found it hard to believe it all – this apparently mad movement to the country. It made you think of the real size of London; of the millions escaping for a single day; of the rivers of human beings pouring from all the London roads like water hosed from a pipe. All good-humoured, smiling to strangers, waving a hand; sitting at the side of roads with packs open eating sandwiches, drinking beer, making tea.

The closer they got to the Beeches, the slower became the going. At first sight it was magnificent. Miles of trees stretching away to cover the acres. Incredible. All this for the people.

Then Pat saw the rest, and his heart sank. A garish swimming-pool painted yellow. Signs up advertising this and that. Stalls set up, selling ice-cream and sweets and chocolate and oranges. Thousands and thousands of oranges, whose skins would litter the earth. Thousands and thousands of bananas, whose skins would blacken and rot and form a mucous mess under milling shoes.

They parked their bicycles and made their way into the woods. It was incredible. People everywhere. Lying on the ground in the patches of sun. Kids up on the branches of every tree. Mammas laying out the lunch on white tablecloths. Papas lying with newspapers over their faces and their shoes off their feet. Lovers lying under trees, clasped in an impassioned embrace, unmoving and unmoved by the mill of people around them. Every square inch covered by racing or lying or walking or talking bodies. You had to step carefully over bodies. Acres of bodies, left, right and centre, up in the trees and around the trees and about the trees. The sounds: crying children, and screaming children and laughing children, snoring people and loud-voiced people and laughing people; the clink of bottles, cups and plates. The smells: beeches — over all, but not all; the acid smell of oranges, the sickly smell of bananas and cold meat and bread and beer and the littered earth; also children relieving themselves as discreetly as possible against the butts of the trees, in the bushes, in the open. That smell too, rising triumphant over all. The indestructibility of man, the power of man, the conqueror of the earth and the woods. The blinding colour of the scene: the brown and dark red of the beeches, and then the flagrant blaring colour of man, his very flesh a challenge to camouflaged nature; his decorations, the paint of the wooded aborigines; his coloured shirts and his coloured dresses, scarves, headgear, over-gear and under-gear; his tropical orange-peelings jeering obscenely at the once tranquil trees. What did the trees think of it all?

Pat had to grin. The others didn't seem to mind or notice. They had been here before. Seamus had. Lelia or Maureen wouldn't know any difference. They had been born in London. They had had to adapt their pleasures to crowded living. It was all one to them. It didn't mean a thing. This to them was coming to the country. And to the thousands of others too, even to the poor hot-faced mammas who had to arrange it all, and fix the food and unpack it and serve it. More trouble than at home. But it was a day out. They had spent a day in the country, the lovely woods. And for all he knew they would remember it until next year as being peopled solely by themselves and the gently falling leaves and the birds.

Pat laughed joyously, and threw himself to the ground where Seamus had found a clear spot for them.

The other three looked at him.

'What the hell are yeh laughin' at?' Seamus asked him.

'Oh, I was just thinking,' said Pat. He could see only a little of the sky through the closely knit branches above his head. 'I was thinking of all this and the difference at home. You walk for five minutes and you are alone, completely alone. We have cycled miles and miles and miles today and we are less alone that we would be in the middle of London.'

'What's so funny about that?' Maureen asked.

'It's just that I thought of it,' said Pat, leaning on an elbow and then moving his bare elbow from the way of a slippery banana skin. 'I used to do a lot of walking with another chap. When we were at school and we were on the beryl – mitching you call it here, I think. We used to like the solitude of the lake and the lonely beach by the sea. I just thought what he would think now if he was here with us. He was always a sort of a lonely chap. He's in England too. I wonder did you ever come across him, Seamus?'

'What was his name?' asked Seamus.

'Jojo Keaveney,' said Pat, lying back again.

So he missed the start that Seamus gave, the stiffening of his body. Maureen noticed it all right, but didn't pay much attention. Lelia was occupied in arranging things so that she could lie languidly on the grass.

'No,' said Seamus; then, after a pause, 'I never met him.' He went on then to cover up another pause, perhaps because Maureen was looking at him closely. 'You remind me a the story of the country fella asking the Yank if he knew his Tomeen. The Yank says no, and where would Tomeen be? He himself was from New York. And the countryman said, "Well, sure Lord God, if you're from New York you must know him, that's where he is."'

They laughed and Pat said, 'All right; I stand corrected.'

Then they spread a scarf and ate their lunch

It was a nice lunch, like all the food that is eaten outdoors when the day is fine and the heart is light. Conversation was limited. Pat was too conscious of the body of Lelia beside him. She appeared to be unruffled by the heat and the exertion and the crumbs. She ate slowly and daintily and kept the crease in her shorts. He could smell perfume from her too. It was wafted to him every time she moved. Then he remembered the dance and how closely he had held her to him.

'Did you ever come across Kerry Mick since, Seamus?' he asked.

'I did not,' said Seamus, 'not since the court.'

Pat laughed, because justice had caught up with Seamus. He was so big and recognizable. That was his trouble. And everybody knew where he worked. So the police just went to the job and picked out the biggest man on it, had a chat with him and served a summons. It had been very funny. Seamus and Kerry Mick acting the big innocents. Not exactly committing perjury. It was just that right was on their sides as they saw it. Seamus saying that it was Mick's fault on account of the name he had called him in Irish. 'What was the name?' the Justice asked. 'I couldn't repeat it, your honour,' says Seamus; and the Justice looks at him over his glasses, and says, 'H'm, maybe you'd write it out for us.' 'What's the good of that,' Seamus asked, 'when it was in Irish and ye wouldn't understand it?' 'Well,' says the Justice with a grin, 'translate it.' That shook Seamus. 'But it's a very bad word, your honour.' 'The court is used to bad words,' said the other, so Seamus had been handed the bit of paper and had bit on the pencil and written something and handed it up, and everybody in court was dying to know what it was, but the Justice read it and crumpled it in his hand saying, 'H'm, colourful as well as alliterative,' and then he had asked Mick what about it and Mick said it was nothing to what Seamus had called him. This was also written down, read and digested and the whole thing had ended with a fine of fifteen shillings on both parties, and a binding over to keep the peace. It was a nice case. Everybody had enjoyed themselves. No harm done, except to the little fat manager of

the dance-hall, who complained about loss of goodwill or something, but nobody was interested much in him, and he was told
that it was up to him to run his dance-hall properly, see that the
proper persons were admitted and to quell disturbances.

Later they went to the swimming-pool. A mess of bodies like
worms in a jar. Pat was conscious of his stripped body standing
on the edge of the pool waiting to dive, Seamus beside him.
Maureen looked at both of them standing there, and she thought
it was like the sword and the sheath. Pat the sword, built narrow
and flowing, and Seamus with his enormous body, his rounded
chest almost on a level with his square chin, arms like legs and
legs like trees. He was completely unconscious of his body, just
wanted to wet it and flounder about in the water and roar and
laugh and have fun, swimming under and catching Maureen by
the legs and pulling her down.

Lelia didn't wet herself at all. Just put on her two-piece costume on her perfect body and relaxed, said she couldn't possibly
go into that water. She was sure it was dirty. So she would just
sunbathe. Pat thought it would be a pity to wet the costume she
was wearing, it was so pretty. Kind of silk stuff with a little skirt,
a bare midriff and covering for her breasts. The only thing was
that he felt it was a pity she didn't have a proper background for
it. A shore and sand and great rollers coming in from the open
sea. Not this – just enough room to sit down; people pressing
and laughing and running and diving on either side of you,
splashing water; no room to talk, no room to breathe, no room
to feel the waves that came to him from her and made him want
to hold his breath. Maureen was wet beside him: a small figure,
making her look more and more like a little girl. Her hair wet
and going into curls. Small breasts and a flat stomach and narrow
legs. Lelia was a woman in comparison, he thought. She looked
so cool and confident. Built beautifully so that she would almost
make two of Maureen. But in shape she was matured in all the
right places. Not that Maureen wasn't matured, but she was built
on less generous lines.

And later they squeezed their way past all the sprawling bodies and dressed and got out of the place and on to their bicycles
and they made for home.

However it happened, for part of the way he was with Maureen. They had a long chat, a friendly one for a change. He pointed out all the places he had noticed when they were coming and talked about the difference there was between them and the places at home. She was interested too, and he made her laugh talking about this and that. Maureen was grand, he thought. You could really talk to her about things like that. About Jojo and the times they had, forgetting to go to school when they got to the gate, and the long walks on the winter days, ending up somewhere near a desolate sea-shore. Nothing but themselves and the sea and the birds and a man loading seaweed on to a cart. How they had gone to swim with nothing to cover them but a length of seaweed, although nobody could see them but God.

Of course, he reflected, when they were separated again and Lelia was resting her hand on his shoulder, you couldn't expect Lelia to be interested in things like that. Lelia always seemed to live in the present. Maureen was different. Lelia quoted poetry at him. Very pleasant stuff. She had a good voice for it too and she was an apt quoter, even though they were all love poems, which suited him very well now, when Lelia bathed them with significance. She knew one or two of Shakespeare's sonnets which he had never had much time for. She said them well. Gave them significance. Not like when they were at school and daily doses of Shakespeare being shoved down their necks, the only kick they got out of Shakespeare then was to try and get hold of unexpurgated editions and read the *Rape of Lucrece* under the desk, hoping that they wouldn't be caught. All this in the warm flood of adolescence. In some way now, here on this English road, cycling along, and Lelia saying sonnets, he seemed to have a flash of those illicit days of puberty and felt the sweat on his stomach.

The sun went down and the moon came up. They reached the concrete road again and cycled along it, blinded by the approaching headlights. The smell of the dust was in their nostrils and the approaching smell of the city. Rubber and lamps strung on standards . . . Keep Left . . . One Way Only . . . lights and a red glow coming from its heart like blood on the moon. They were feeling tired too. Their limbs were beginning to feel the stiffness.

Aches starting from where you sat on the saddle and going down the backs of your legs.

Seamus and Maureen were waiting for them outside Lelia's house.

'Tell them you'll be after them,' said Lelia.

'I'll be after you,' said Pat dutifully, and saw them remount their bikes tiredly, and go on and turn the corner into Maureen's street.

'Come on in for a while,' said Lelia, lifting her bike on the path and opening the gate. He followed her.

All the talk had been knocked out of Maureen.

Seamus opened the gate for her and let in her bicycle.

'Are you tired?' he asked her.

'I am,' said Maureen.

'It was a good day, all the same,' said Seamus. 'I feel full a fresh air.' This hitting his chest.

'I'm sorry I went,' said Maureen, leaning against the gate. 'Seamus, I don't like her.'

'Lelia?' he asked.

'Yes,' said Maureen.

'She's a bitch.' said Seamus.

'He thinks she's wonderful, doesn't he?' Maureen asked.

'He does,' said Seamus. 'But maybe he'll get over it.'

'I don't think he will,' said Maureen, shaking her head. 'You know it wouldn't surprise me if he wanted to marry her.'

'It's wanting he'll be,' said Seamus, 'take my word for it.'

'What do you mean?' she asked.

'Listen,' said Seamus. 'He's a labourer, isn't he?'

'Yes,' said Maureen.

'There you are,' said Seamus. 'He'd want to be a first cousin to the King of England before she'd look at him. That or a near relation to the Bank of England. Listen, go in and have a good sleep and forget him.'

'I wish I could,' said Maureen.

'Remember Bruce and the spider so,' said Seamus. 'I have the second sight, so I have, even though I'm not the seventh son a the seventh son. Stop worryin', will yeh? A nice girl like you. If

I thought you'd look crossways at me, I'd ha' been after you long ago.'

She got on her toes then and kissed him.

'Good night, Seamus,' she said and went in.

Seamus watched her for a while, shook his head a little, scratched it, looked at his closed fist, shrugged, and went in the gate to his own house.

Pat was sitting on the couch in front of Lelia's electric fire. She had changed out of her shorts and was dressed in a housecoat. He could see her bare neck and her leg where the coat had fallen away. It was smooth. He raised his hand. Idly he noticed above the pounding of his heart that it was trembling. He rested the back of it against the inside of her thigh. She left it there, and then reached out, took it up and fondled it in her own two hands. Small hands, that were soft around it. She examined his hand then, front and back, and pressed it into her breast.

'Your hands are ruined,' she said.

Pat found it hard to speak.

'They are,' he croaked.

'You'll have to stop ruining them, Pat,' she said. He had never heard his name spoken like that before. A short sharp name, on her lips now it sounded like clear water in a stream.

'I will,' said Pat, 'in the morning if you want me to.'

'I wish you would,' she said.

He was looking into her eyes. Every other thing around seemed to be shut out from his vision except her eyes and then he lowered them a little to the hollow of her neck. There was a pulse there and it was beating very fast. As fast as his own heart. A sparkle of joy came to him. She can't hide that, he thought. She's just as stirred as I am myself, even though her mouth doesn't seem to be dry like my own, or her limbs shaking like mine. He looked into her eyes again. A flicker of triumph. Then he brought up his other hand and rested his forefinger on the pulse. He looked at her again. Enquiry in his look. She left his hand where it was, freed her own two from it and put them around his neck. His hand on her breast thought that it was fondling cool silk and then her mouth was on his own.

For him it was the end of time.

Maureen waited in the living-room. She made tea and smoked a cigarette. He won't be long, she thought, putting the hot tea-pot near the dying coals.

But the coals died, and the tea-pot became cold, and the cigarette packet emptied itself into her lungs before she gave it up. She washed her own cup and left the one prepared for him on the cabinet in the kitchen. She put out the lights then and went to bed. She lay in bed with her window open and the door open because it was very close. It doesn't really matter, she said to herself. He's not really worth it. I got on all right before I ever saw him and I'll get on all right again when he's gone. He's only an Irish thick with a smattering of education, and he's not really good-looking if you examine him piece by piece. It's just that when everything is put together he fools you. And even though Mum and Dad like him very much, it's just because they can't see through him like I can. Below in the room the chiming clock beat out its silly strokes. Bells jingling for a hanging every quarter of an hour, and then the deep bing-bong, like a miniature Big Ben, while she tossed in the bed, threw the bedclothes off and pulled them on again.

There was a hint of dawn in the sky when Pat carefully opened the front door. That brought the thought into his mind of another dawn he had seen; but he put it out of his mind with a shiver. This was no dawn for it. His eyes were alight, and he felt replete, like after a good meal when you are starving. He could feel Lelia all around him. He felt that he was not on solid earth at all. He wanted to hold on to the feelings he had because they might never come again. They would never come again like this. I could die now, he thought and everything would be all right, if I wasn't in love and big with the future, a future rose-coloured with Lelia in all sorts of forms. Lelia in a kitchen with a neat apron, Lelia at the door waiting for him to come home from work, Lelia asleep with her wonderful hair glinting on a white pillow.

He tiptoed up the stairs, past Maureen's door. She heard him.

'Is that you, Pat?' she whispered.

He looked in the door. She was in bed, leaning on her elbow, a vague figure. He went in to her and sat on the side of the bed.

'What kept you?' she asked.

'I was talking to Lelia,' he said, rolling it on his tongue.

Maureen could smell the perfume from him, recognized it. Coty, Paris. So much a bottle. It flooded from him. Maureen felt sick at the stomach and turned her head away from him.

'Look, Maureen,' he said, 'you know that chap you work for, the insurance bloke. You were trying to get me to go and see him. Didn't think it nice having a labourer for a lodger' – a joke this, because the Potters liked him and didn't care if he was a public lavatory attendant – 'Well, fix it up for me, will you, when you go to work? Make a date for me. I'm finished with being a hand worker. Now I'm going to work the head and wear a white collar.'

'What changed your mind?' she asked.

He hesitated. Will I tell her, he wondered? All about it? No, not because Maureen wouldn't understand; she would, being a good pal, but I want to hold this for a while and savour it and dream about it, just for myself.

'Nothing,' he said, 'I was just thinking.'

'All right,' said Maureen, 'and now get out of here and let me go to sleep.' She turned away from him with a plop. 'Sorry,' he said and went to the door. 'You bloody bastard!' said Maureen, to her pillow. He turned back then.

'What's that?' he asked.

'Good night,' said Maureen.

He went in his own door. I am in a beautiful nightmare, he thought. Why on earth would I imagine that Maureen called me a bloody bastard? He grinned as he undressed. That's a joke. That's what love does to you.

His dreams were beautiful. Remote but beautiful.

8

He approached Lelia's house whistling.

It was the moment he had been secretly waiting for and working for and building up to, and not even the cold October blast sweeping up the street, driving before it the flotsam of the gutters and madly whirling the ends of his overcoat about his legs, could chill the heat of his coming triumph.

He was twenty-two years old today. His hair was carefully brushed, a lick of oil saving its orderliness from the searching wind, there was a shine on his newly shaved face, a glitter from his polished shoes, the visible ends of his trousers had an edge like a Sheffield knife. And there was a great gleam in his eye. He had to restrain himself from shouting to the sky, from jumping in the air and racing down the street like a spring colt.

It was all fixed. He would collect her as they had planned, and they would go to London as they had planned, to celebrate his birthday, and when the day was over Lelia would be the prospective Mrs Pat Moore. He would save it up as long as he could hold out, which wouldn't be long, he told himself with a grin and the part that would really stun her, was when he told her about the new job. Today, Saturday, the first one in October, had been his last few hours as a labouring man. Monday morning he would don his white collar, mount his bicycle, and become one of the great middle class with a crease in his trousers, clips on his trousers, an insurance book in his hand. No more digging ditches. No more scraping mud from under his nails. No more blinding blasts to jar your eardrums as rocks were pounded into dust by that loathsome gelignite. No more dirty clothes to change at the end of a hard day. No more anything but Hello, Mrs Jones. Nice day, isn't it? How's the kiddies? And your old grannie? Have you got her insured now? When she dies, you know, you will be put to some expense on account of the funeral. Had you thought of that?

Pat grinned and patted the pure white handkerchief peeping out of his breast pocket. Good old Maureen. It was a birthday present from her. The neat box of hankies. She had worked the job too, although luck had played its part.

Pat was a little awed when he thought about it. Into the office. Glass and light wood counters. Maureen winks and goes into the little place at the back with Private written on it. She comes out. You may go in now, Mr Moore. Through that door. Pat goes in, closes the door, and looks at the man sitting at the desk. A pause as they look at one another. Pat's heart thumps. I know him. Where the hell have I seen him before? Small man, pudgy, with a little diamond pin in his tie. Puzzled look on the other's face as well. Screwing of eyebrows like Pat. Both speak. 'Now where . . .?' A laugh. Now I remember. The little man on the boat coming over. No, it couldn't be. He rises, holds out his hand. Now I remember. You were the young Irishman on the boat. I gave you my card. So it was! Sit down. Talk about coincidence. Pat felt a little guilty too. What the hell had he done with that card? Had he kept it or had he thrown it away? He had heard Maureen talking so often about her Mr Johnson. Better try that. Well, this is a strange thing, Mr Johnson. So you know my name? Yes, you gave me your card, remember. Well now imagine that! Who'd ever think?

It was only a matter of time after that until Pat was to become an insurance agent. There were a lot of preliminaries. Sign a bond. No running away with the firm's cash. Put down twenty-five pounds as a sort of deposit of good faith. Another twenty-five to be paid at so much a week out of salary. It would take time. Meanwhile meet the boys. Go around on a book or two with them to find out what it's all about. Then the assistant will take you around for a week or two. After that you are on your own. No limit to the amount of money you can make. All depends on yourself and the gift of the gab. Commissions on

sales and a salary of three pounds a week basic on your collections. You can make ten, fifteen pounds a week if you are good
enough. It all depends on yourself. Pep talk. Smiles. Gratified
feeling in the stomach. He knew the boss. The boss would look
after him. Felt that he had a sort of prior interest in this young
Irishman. Took him into the office and told them all about it.
Holding him by the arm. As if he was exhibiting a prize flower
at the Show. Amazement. Laughing. Maureen's face flushed with
pleasure. Thumbs up.

'I'm putting all my eggs in one basket,' he hummed as he
skipped; 'I'm betting everything I got on you.'

Wait'll Lelia hears it! His appointment only came through
today.

The boss on the job: so you're going, are you. Just when we
had made an honest workman out of you. Just when you were
beginning to earn your keep. You Irish all over. Never satisfied.
Always 'oppin' from one thing to another like fleas in a doss
house. Seamus was quietly glad. You were a poor investment on
a job like this, so you were. You'd hurt any honest man to the
quick watching you. He clapped his shoulder and laughed, and
they both thought how fond they were of one another. You won't
look at the side a the road we're on now. Oh, won't I, Seamus!
We'll be together for always. You'll be my best man when I'm
married. What's this? Are you gettin' married? You never know
– it could happen. And not only the best man but the godfather
of me first child. Roars at this and a little bout of bawdiness.

He's a great lad, Seamus. Everyone is great. I'm the greatest
guy in the world and nowhere is there a lark more happy than I.

He opened the gate to Lelia's house, pausing to look at the
shiny new Austin car standing outside. The smell of new leather
from it. He could see himself reflected in the gleaming black
paintwork of it. His whistle died then, and he went to the door.
A ring on the bell.

Lelia's mother. Fat and steaming as always. Big smile. 'Hello,'
she said.

'Lelia in?' Pat asked. 'I have a date with her.'

'Come on in,' she said. 'The more the merrier.'

What does that mean? Pat wondered, going past her into the

hall and waiting politely until she closed the door and preceded him into the living-room. Oh, living-room of beautiful memories!

He stopped short then when he saw George. He was sitting in the big armchair and Lelia was sitting on the arm of it, very close to him. George was beautifully turned out – glistening oiled hair, hard white collar, and an obviously new suit, good stuff and well cut. He was smiling, as always. George's careless smile. Nothing could ever wound George while he had that look of affluence and that careless smile. His teeth big and shining; good-humoured look.

'Come in and sit down, Pat,' said Lelia. 'Did you see George's new car? Isn't it smashin'?'

'It's a very nice car,' said Pat carefully, sitting on the arm of the other chair. Always it was the same when George appeared. What had seemed to him to be good and gleaming became bad and dull when George appeared. Still, George could have his smile and his car.

'It ought to be,' said George, 'with what it cost me. What say I give you all a little run in it? Nice, hah? Let's go out and take a trip.'

'That'll be grand,' said Lelia, clapping her hands.

'But how about—' Pat began to say.

'We can go miles,' said Lelia, 'and around our town here too. I want the others to see me in it.'

'But—' said Pat.

'Aren't they a scream?' Lelia's mother asked. 'The pair of them. Look grand in a car, our Lelia will. Always said, I did, that she wanted a car as a background. To show her off like.'

'But I thought, Lelia,' said Pat desperately, 'that you were coming up to Town with me.'

'Oh, not now, Pat,' said Lelia.

'You better tell Pat,' said Lelia's mother. 'He'll be the first to know, after myself.'

'Tell me what?' asked Pat.

'Will we tell him, George?' Lelia asked, leaning over him, almost touching his forehead with her lips.

'Why not?' George said laughing. 'You can go up and shout it in Piccadilly for my money.'

Lelia left the chair then. She came over to Pat, holding out her hand.

'Isn't it grand?' she asked. 'Isn't George a genius?'

'Not a genius, ducks,' said George; 'just a bloody good butcher.'

He laughed at that. Lelia laughed and Lelia's mother laughed.

Pat was staring at the engagement ring on Lelia's finger. It was a very good ring. He had been looking at rings himself recently. He felt himself sweating when he thought of the comparison between this and what he had been interested in. His mind was just a dull daze.

'Do you like it, Pat?' Lelia asked, taking her hand back and holding it up and twisting it from side to side.

'You and George——' Pat said, forcing out the two names from the whirligig in his head.

'Been chasin' that girl for ages,' said George. 'Blimey, she didn't half give me the run around. Chasin' her like a knight in armour, I was. Like St George and the dragon. Pinned her down in the end. Didn't I, ducks?' He leaned out then and caught her by the arm and pulled her on his knee. Pat could see his red hand holding her breast under her arm, quite openly. The gesture of the winner; the bond of the owner.

'Oh, George,' said Lelia, bending and rubbing her face on his, and then coming forward again to hold up her hand and admire the ring.

'You could have knocked me down with a feather,' said Lelia's mother, 'when I looked out and seen George coming out of that there car. It's George, Lelia, I says, and he has a car. A new car. Like a ruddy millionaire you was, George, comin' out of that car. Pity he hasn't a cigar too, I says. That'd put the finishin' touch on him.'

'I'll impress her, I will,' said George. 'That's what I said. Wait'll Lil sees me outside her front door in a brand-new car. She won't half come runnin' into me arms. All done by kindness, eh, Lil?'

'You type,' said Lelia. 'You always knew I was soft about you, George. You didn't have to trot out the new car for my benefit. Always knew you'd get me, I did, right from the beginning. Are you surprised, Pat?' She turned to him for this. He couldn't believe it. She really had nothing at all in her face except a reflected light from the ring and probably the car outside the door. She was looking into his eyes. Nothing stirred in them. No appreciation of what they had been to each other, of why he was here, all dressed up and nowhere to go. His stomach turned over.

'Excuse me,' he said, rising and making his way to the door. His fumbling fingers found the knob, twisted, opened it, and then he was out on the path and down the street walking very fast, still feeling the sweat of disbelief under his arms, on his chest, and under the band of his trousers.

He felt that his face was blazing, but Maureen, who was walking towards him, thought that his face looked pale and drawn. Although his eyes were resting on her, he didn't seem to be looking at her. They approached and he would have passed her by if she hadn't stretched an arm and pulled him up.

'Pat!' she said.

She saw the blank look in his eyes then giving place to recognition, and that was worse, she thought, because behind his eyes she could see a deep hurt.

'What is it, Pat?' she asked.

He tried to speak to her, to focus his mind on the fact of Maureen, that she was looking at him with worry on her face and at the back of her kind eyes.

'Nothing, Maureen,' he said in a choked voice, 'it's just nothing.'

He left her then and walked on. She called after him, but he just raised a hand without turning his head and walked on and on up the street until a corner took him from her sight.

He didn't know for some time where his feet were taking him. He was conscious of people brushing by him and a scream of tyres once as he crossed a road, and he heard the driver cursing him in a loud and penetrating manner. But it didn't get through to his consciousness. His main feeling was of feeling unclean. He had dressed himself so carefully. Now he felt as if he was shoddy and down at heel. Coming out, his head had been in the clouds, but now his head was in the dust with his feet. His crumbling dreams seemed tawdry and pitiful. His three pounds a week basic with an insurance company had seemed to mean a lot of wonderful things. He shuddered when he thought of what it meant now.

He deliberately didn't think of Lelia, not for some time. It was so incredible that Lelia the beautiful, Lelia the sympathetic, Lelia who had filled the world for him, could hand out such barbed cruelty with those small, casual hands. Had he, then, meant nothing at all to her but a body and a face and scarred hands? He couldn't believe that! If he was to believe that, what became of his self-respect and his ego? Didn't that mean that he was the blindest man in all the world? That he hadn't recognized Lelia's impassioned love as being merely a hobby? That if it hadn't been him, it would have been somebody else? That he had meant no more to her than an instrument to satisfy, a pawing lust on a living-room couch?

He couldn't believe that. Even if it was true and Lelia had been like that, where did it leave him? It left him feeling so small that he could crawl into a drain and live with the rats and never let anybody look on his foolish face again. He burned now as he thought of it, and raised his hand to wipe the sweat from his eyebrows and he groaned aloud. Christ, he thought, it couldn't be like that!

He thought of the house he had just left, the bright car, the gleaming ring and the mother with the fat, satisfied smirk on her face. The possessive George and the complacent Lelia. For she had been complacent – he would have to recognize that at least. Maybe she had been overwhelmed with the thought of herself married to a man who could afford cars and rings? That the thought of herself riding around in gleaming cars and wearing shining rings for the rest of her days was too much for her? Maybe so; but why in the name of God had she treated him, then, as if he was the butcher's boy who had called to leave the meat, or, he thought with savage hurt, the insurance man who had called to collect his weekly premiums? This date that he had been planning with her for a month, that she had taken such an interest in, that they had been looking forward to? He could have sworn the last time she was with him that there was nothing else desired more than this simple excursion they had planned to celebrate Pat's birthday. But all she had said was, Not now, Pat . . . Not now, Pat . . . Not now, Pat.

Surely nobody in the world could be as casually cruel as that? Surely she must have realized that it all meant far more to him than stolen moments of passion? He could still feel her body under his palms. It wasn't just a body; it was Lelia. It might, indeed, have been St Lelia the way he felt about her. Of course he knew that Maureen didn't like her much, or the other girls who knew her. But you could understand that. She was so beautiful and they would resent that in her. On that account they would think her a bit of a bitch, because she didn't have to work and because she could devote more time to making herself look well. She wasn't a bitch really. She couldn't be. Even though she had been a bitch in that room . . .

You could understand George. He didn't dislike George. George was a downright individual. George knew what he wanted and he set out to get it. Just like selling a lump of meat. Make it attractive to the customer. That's all you had to do. Make it look nice so that you would start saliva and charm the money out of the bag. So with George. He had made himself attractive to Lelia, and she had taken him. It was only a problem of sales resistance to George.

But Lelia had bigger things in her than that – she must have! He thought of their times together. Surely she knew that he wanted her for ever, that he had changed his job so that he too might be more attractive to her. Surely she knew that he loved her as he had never loved anybody else before, and that he wanted to marry her. He hadn't said so, but it had been so implied. He had been such an eejit in love. Sometimes he had felt himself that he was an eejit, he was so soft about it all but he had shrugged and whistled and said, If you're in love you show it, and so what after that? Nothing. He hadn't time for playing games. He was downright too in his own way.

He found himself staring at the Underground station and was amazed to know that he had blindly walked that far. He hesitated for a moment, pulled his mind away from his inferiority complex, and walked into the station. He bought a ticket to London. He was going to celebrate his birthday. Lelia wouldn't be with him, but he could think of nothing else to do.

I am alone, he thought as the sliding doors swished to and the tube train whined its way out of the station. He wasn't alone in the long car, but he had never felt so alone in all his life before. Not since his mother had died. He was small then, but he remembered. A woman in a bed under a white quilt. You could see the steam rising from her forehead. Her eyes were glazed and she was raving. Talking about things that Pat had never heard. An ambulance outside the door and the covered figure of his mother being carried out on a stretcher. The gliding sound of the stretcher being put in. The banging door. The grunt of the engine. And the next time he saw her she was laid out. He felt alone then, all right. But not too long alone. There had been too much kindness and too many people to drop tears with you and for you. The unrestrained sympathy of the poor – they would share their crusts with you or they would share their hearts with you. It was all one to them. They had nothing to lose, everything to gain from kindness and charity.

Who could one go to now? He looked around him. At the people sitting stiffly in their seats. At the people standing holding straps looking at nothing. He had noticed this before. Everybody was on guard. Tensed in case you would talk to them. A horrible silence. A voice raised created raised eyebrows and a look of surprise that any man could have the temerity to raise a voice in the sanctity of the tube train. Like urinating in a cathedral, singing obscenities in a cloister. He could understand it in a way, and failed to see why men should not have thrown up their hands and left it all. The life of a suburbanite who worked in the City. Rush for a bus to catch the tube. Scramble to catch the closing doors. Acrobatics to read the morning paper. Arrive. Rush out like a damned soul. Rush to the escalator. Not fast enough, so you run up. Out of the train. Rush to catch a bus to the office. Stop. Rush out for your lunch. Rush back to work. Stop. Rush for the trains again. Beat your way to the throngs on the platforms. Wait. Train. Opening door. Rush. Squeeze. Acrobatics again to read the evening paper. Home. The whole thing took almost twelve hours. Eight hours of actual work. Four hours of exhausting rushing to and fro. He couldn't understand it.

It was a pastime to keep his mind off himself. He smiled at the advert on one of the panels in the train. The Man Who Coughed in the Tube. It was a good thing about the English that they could at least laugh at themselves and their customs. But what a life! He decided that he'd never work inside in the black maw of the city. He could feel an incipient ulcer now at the thought of it. How was it that afterwards you could never remember a face of a person you had seen in a tube train? Other trains or the boat now. A pretty face, a stern face, a laughing face. Or a nice figure or nice legs or a nice suit. They weren't just casual. Afterwards you would remember. A flash.

They went into the tunnel and crawled down into the ground of London like the electrified moles they were. Lights come on. Something happens to your ears. You squeeze them to get them back to normal. The new rush of the charged air below. The smell of the underground. The difference in the whine of the wheels. Pulling from blackness into the opened stations below, like cuts in the body. The opening doors, the rushing people. Out and up the stairs. The endless escalator. The stepping on. The looking at the advantageously placed advertisements. The step off. The meeting of God's air outside.

Pat went to Euston. He just went there to look at it again, and remembered with not a little sneering the blue-eyed simpleton who had one day (was it twenty years ago?) arrived from Ireland with his cheap suitcase in his hand. A lost soul who had been afraid to chance the tube. He chanced it now and came back to show what he was like. He got out and went to a variety theatre. Lelia had wanted that. He sat alone in the gloom and watched. People acrobating. People singing. The man in the grey suit who told the story about the little dog lost in the black wood, and the tall tree leaning down and saying, Dear little dog, please have this one on me, and the little dog saying, No, thank you, I have just had one on a house. Gales of laughter. Blaring band. Coloured lights, flashing flesh. Into a cold street where night had fallen and become artificial day under the glorious glare of the neon tube.

Almost automatically his feet continued the pilgrimage they had arranged, even though he felt like a death's head, the gaunt skeleton at the feast, pushing food into gaping jaws so that it rattled on empty ribs as it went down.

It was an American restaurant near the theatre. Small, and nice smells. To his amazement he found himself eating. It seemed to him to be slightly obscene to have an appetite at a time like this. American layer cake. Probably that's why Lelia wanted to come here – full of cream and as luscious as herself. You're getting nasty now, he thought. Double-decker sandwiches, with chicken and lettuce and things between slices of toast. Very tasty. A great clattering in the restaurant. Very few Americans. Good honest English burghers lapping it up, like himself. The whiff of the American toasted cigarettes taken from the slot machines. That made him remember back to the American liners coming into the Bay at home. Lighted up at night like floating fairylands. Jojo and himself had always managed to get out to them. A brief glimpse of luxury. The feel of thick carpets. The smell of cigars and all the money that went with them. Lovely ladies, talking through their noses and dressed like princesses. The small bar where you drank lager beer before the customs men came to seal it up.

He went into the night again. Over towards Piccadilly. Around the Circus and then he found himself outside another theatre with pictures of gorgeous-looking lassies with lovely smiles and visible navels, bare breasts, their thighs clothed in a speck of gauze.

He went in. It was there that he really got to thinking about the whole thing, calmly, despite the coloured lights on the stage and the naked women, beautifully formed and standing in their birthday suits, in historical tableaux that had little to do with the more vigorous part of history. Bald men with opera glasses, dissatisfied with the naked eye. Not so good; not so bad. It was the sight of all the bodies that brought Lelia to his mind. All sorts and sizes of bodies. But still bodies, some of them looking a little blue, because it was cold enough weather. It showed that his reflexes were sane enough when he could pity some of the girls because their skins were blue from the cold.

Lelia was a body. Pat sat up straight in the seat as the thought came to him. What had Lelia got for him apart from a body that made your limbs tremble every time you came within a correct distance of the waves emanating from it? She wasn't interested in anything that he had to tell her about himself, about the things he was thinking, about things that had happened to him in the past, about his present life or his hopes of the future. Why, he talked more with Maureen about the things that mattered than he had ever talked to Lelia. All he did with Lelia was to make love to her, and in the interims listen to her quoting poetry at him. Now that he came to think of it, he realized that there had been times when the love of theirs was sated, that he had felt a little bored. He had pushed the thought away in horror. How could any man be bored with Lelia around? But there had been pauses. Blanks in the conversation. What the hell will I talk about now? he had to think furiously, a sweat coming over him. This can't be true – not with Lelia. It didn't make any difference to her. She could have sat there for hours without talking. Would it be, he wondered, because her mind was a bit blank? Good God, surely not Lelia? But it had been hard to think of something to say at times. A glad-to-get-home feeling, since I don't have to be acting any more.

No, he thought. Just because I've got the bum's rush, I'm trying to find a way to save my ego. But it was strange about Lelia, the woman he had been dying to marry, that she knew far, far less about himself and his feelings and his life than Maureen did. He knew all about her. She was at school and she left school and her mother adored her and her father adored her, although Pat had begun to doubt the last bit, having seen her father looking at her once or twice. That was a point, he thought. I was dying to marry. That's the operative word. The thought of being deprived of Lelia's body now made him move uncomfortably. The thought of the butcher's red hands appreciating something he had come to regard as his own was one that forced a low groan from him. But he was feeling a little better. What have I missed, after all, he wondered, except a body? He knew he was only trying to soften the blow that had been dealt him. But all the same it was something to think about. It had miraculously cleared his mind a little. There wasn't the same awful feeling of unreality pressing on his mind. His chest didn't feel so tight.

So he looked at the girl on the stage, set as a bedroom, who came in from a dance singing that her love loved her and she hoped he would be true to her for ever, and she proceeded to undress herself, to clothe herself again in a diaphanous nightie, and to get into bed and put out the light. Very nicely done, like a girl at a convent saying her prayers. Pat laughed and left.

He was surprised at the light feeling that had come over him. The black despond had left him. The wounded ego was slightly healed. It would be scarred a little. But maybe, he thought, that was a good thing for it. Lelia might have been a good surgeon, for all he knew.

He ambled into Piccadilly. He could see it now with clearer eyes, and the huge lighted sign of Johnny Walker seemed to have a meaning for him. A man with a smile who had kept going for a number of years. Pat winked up at him and walked around towards the tube station. The people everywhere. Beautiful dames in evening dresses and wraps being escorted to night clubs and eating-places by beautifully turned-out men in evening suits and top hats and coats shaped to their bodies like gloves. Discreetly peeping white scarves. Younger lassies, incredibly beautiful in white fur wraps. The smell from them as they passed, ignoring the common throng. The old woman who sold newspapers and watched them pass. Her asides to another seller with decrepit trousers and cap and a dirty red scarf wound around his throat, his thin body shivering in the cold wind. Their laugh. And their words that he couldn't get. Their accent was too much for him. Some day he would. Other people just wandering. The rush and hurrying were over for a while. Traffic not so terribly crowded. Sleek cars and red buses with straining drivers. Lights, colour, movement.

Then he saw Jojo. If an angel from heaven had come down and hovered over the place he couldn't have been more surprised. He had heard before that if you wanted to meet anybody from any part of the world all you had to do was stand in Piccadilly for a few hours.

Jojo was hurrying from the Circus into the street where tall graceful buildings wound themselves out of it in a delicate curve. He was hatless, wearing an old raincoat, and his hands were sunk in the pockets of it. He slouched along as only Jojo could slouch.

Pat jumped, literally, and yelled. 'Jojo!' he roared, and then he dived into the middle of the throngs of people and traffic. There was the sound of brakes going and tyres screaming and a blast from a police whistle. For one historic moment in his life Pat upset the calculated movement in the heart of a great city as he bounded across the intervening streets towards Jojo. He was afraid that he would never reach him, that he would be gone, swallowed up by a multitude, blotted from his sight as miraculously as he had appeared. He got into the right street after him and ran like a hare, dodging and side-stepping, ignoring the outraged glares that respectability shot at his unorthodox rushing.

He saw him, shouted 'Jojo' again, and panting, stretched out a hand and caught his shoulder, pulled him to a halt and went around to face him.

'Jojo!' he said then again, his hand stretched out and his eyes shining. The same Jojo, he thought, with the black hair and the thick black eyebrows. A Jojo who was paler than Pat had remembered him and whose face was drawn into lines, but still Jojo.

Jojo spoke. 'You bloody fool!' he said, in a low sort of savage whisper. 'Who the hell do you think you are, shouting my name all over London? Let me go, will you, you eejit, and go about your bloody business.' He threw a look over his shoulder then, pulled his shoulder from Pat's arm, and was away in a quicker slouch before Pat had got over his surprise.

He stood there staring after him, until he had well vanished. No, he said to himself, this isn't true. Things like this couldn't happen to me, not twice in the same day. It was Jojo, wasn't it? My pal Jojo? Of course it was. He couldn't be mistaken about that. But why? Why in the name a Jaysus should he have done a thing like that?

'Lost your friend?' a voice enquired behind him. He turned quickly.

A bulky, unobtrusively dressed man in a soft hat, squarely placed on his head. A square face, squared-off level eyebrows and grey eyes. For some reason which he couldn't explain, Pat's heart started to pound. A slight fear entered his mind. Apprehension? Why should an ordinary question like that make him apprehensive?, Why was Jojo looking over his shoulder?

'He's not my friend,' said Pat. 'I made a mistake. Thought he was somebody I knew, that's all. I was mistaken.'

'You called him Joe, didn't you?' the other asked.

'Did I?' asked Pat.

'Something like that,' said the man. Pat wondered why this kindly-looking person should bring into his mind a picture of the big garda sergeant at home directing traffic on the main street. 'I know him slightly,' the other said with a smile, 'and his name is Michael.'

'See how easy it is to be mistaken?' said Pat.

'You are Irish, aren't you?' the other asked.

'That's right,' said Pat. 'Excuse me now. I have to get home.'

The bulky gentleman stepped back and Pat went towards the tube station with his mind in a whirl. It's too much, he thought. I really can't take any more, so I can't Why me? What have I done to be kicked around like a ball on a field? From Lelia over to Jojo. Back again. Somewhere in the process he had become a burst ball.

Down the stairs. Ticket. Waiting on the platform. Not many people. It was an in-between time. He got in and sat down. He had the carriage to himself almost. Himself and the gentleman in the Burberry coat who got in with him. A hiss, swishing doors, and the train pulled out.

Pat was staring for some time at the deep black headlines on the paper which the man opposite him was holding, reading the inside of it, exposing the headlines to Pat's hurt and puzzled eyes. He was staring for some time at them before the sense of them percolated to his mind. Another Explosion, said the headlines. I.R.A. Outrage. Even at that it was quite a time before things made a connection in Pat's brain. The paper moved and he was conscious of the man opposite looking at him and then flicking his eyes away to an advertisement, like all tube travellers. Pat noticed a signet ring with a tiny blue stone in the centre of it on the man's hand as he lighted a cigarette, and then Jojo, a Jojo who was afraid, with a drawn face, came into his mind and he thought of the headlines that he had seen in the paper. His body stiffened.

Not Jojo!

These bombings had just started. They were amusing for most people, this business of dropping explosive letters into pillar-boxes and post-offices. Like games that boys were playing. Big boys. It hadn't meant much to Pat. It had meant as little to him as it had to the Irish at home and the ones over here. People just laughed, shrugged to suggest escaped lunatics, and forgot it. It came back to Pat now. Jojo? No, surely not Jojo? A picture came to him of Jojo at school, with his intense eyes, that could twinkle and laugh as well. He thought of their talks and their walks and all the rest. But no, he just couldn't fit Jojo into it. Then why, why had he done it to Pat? This awful business. He knew that Jojo had recognized him. It was just that. He recognized him, and had wanted nothing to do with him. Why didn't he stop and say, 'Pat! Well, you old bastard, what are you doing here?'

Christ, Pat thought, he could have said hello. He felt a burning behind his eyes, and he remembered that this was the second time today that he had called on Christ to witness a humiliation of him.

I don't care, he thought, I'll forget him. He can go to hell. He had been feeling a little better too, about Lelia, and then he had to meet Jojo. Well, at least, Pat thought, Jojo cauterized Lelia. They cancelled one another out.

Pat did some heavy thinking after that and a lot of weighing up. It kept him busy when he reached his own station, and it kept him busy as he decided to ignore a bus and walk home. He reviewed his life before and after England, and he thought over the people he had met, what they had done to him and what they had meant to him, and out of all this thinking a solution came to him that straightened his drooping shoulders and brought his head up, and started a slow pulse re-beating in his heart. A solution that had been there inside himself all the time, if he had only stopped to recognize it for what it was. He recognized it all right, but would other people? – because it was something you couldn't argue about. You just said it. You knew that it was true, that you meant it; but a different complexion could he put on it altogether. So he alternately hurried his pace and slowed his pace, until finally he decided, and after that he pursued his course with determination.

He didn't notice that the man with the signet ring walked behind him out of the station and followed him down to the door, and waited on the opposite side of the street until the door closed behind him, walking away then writing something in a little notebook.

Pat flung off his coat in the living-room, switched off the light, and chased up the stairs. He went into the bedroom without knocking.

Maureen was sitting in bed reading a book. She dropped her book, looked at him surprised, examined his face and showed her gladness that the pale strain had gone from it, a strain that had been in front of her eyes since he had left and had taken away her appetite.

He came over and sat on the side of the bed. He looked at her. For the first time he noticed how big her eyes were, how snub her nose, and that one of her teeth was appealingly crooked.

'Maureen,' he said then, 'will you marry me?' Let her understand now, God, he thought, because I can't say it all. It's too mixed up. It would want a genius to figure it and an orator to sell it.

There were a lot of things Maureen could have said then after her eyes had opened in surprise. An awful lot of things! She looked deep at him, and she thought, wrinkling her forehead.

'I will, Pat,' she said.

Pat let his breath go and relaxed there, a hand on each side of the bed. They looked at one another and neither's eyes moved.

'I love you, Maureen,' said Pat, and then he got up and went out, closing the door softly after him. No kisses; nothing; but when Maureen finally slept, she went to sleep smiling.

9

They were married in the sacristy of St Peter's Church on a Saturday morning in November. It was a more or less furtive ceremony. They had found that it wasn't as easy to get married as they had imagined.

The trouble was that Pat was a Catholic and Maureen belonged to the Church of England. Of course, if Maureen had been willing to be converted it might have been easier, although they would have had to wait a few months longer while she was being instructed in the Catholic Faith. Pat had first gone to see the Father to tell him he was going to he married and would he fix it up. He was talking to him in the same room where they had waited the night long ago whilst the doctor was coming to see Jack.

The Father congratulated him and then asked who was the girl. Pat told him. And then the complications started.

He went back to Maureen. She thought it over. She belonged to the Church of England, although they weren't church-goers. Maureen had been in her church the day she was being baptised and also fifteen years later when a friend of hers was getting married. Pat explained the business to her.

'No,' said Maureen then, 'I'm not going to become a Catholic.' Her chin was set. There was a bit of a row. Pat wanted to know why the hell she wouldn't become a Catholic. Sure her own church meant nothing to her anyhow, since she never even looked the side of the road it was.

'That makes no difference,' said Maureen. 'It's the principle of the thing. I was born in the Church of England and I'm going to die in the Church of England.'

Pat wanted to know what was the difference. Why had this sudden love spurted in her for something she had ignored all her life?

'Well,' said Maureen, 'even though I ignored it, I was born in it. What's the use of changing over to something else that I know nothing at all about? Won't I only ignore that too? So thank you very much, but if you want me you'll have to marry me as I am.'

The trouble was that Pat had no arguments. He believed in his own faith and tried to be as good as he could. But he couldn't believe that it made all that difference. He was grounded in the rudiments of his religion, but he wasn't grounded enough to open Maureen's eyes to the way of the light and the truth; and in a way he could believe in her holding on to something even if it was only a principle. So they went along to the Father together.

Maureen was prepared to be stubborn with him. God knows what she imagined – that he would give her the third degree or practise a bit of the Spanish Inquisition on her. She ended up of course by liking him very much. He was reasonable, pointing out to her that some day serious differences might arise between them on the question. That Pat would have to comply with practices with which she wouldn't agree, like not eating meat on a Friday, for example, a small thing; but he pointed out, laughing, how hard it would be for poor Pat to be digging his teeth into a lump of codfish and watching Maureen polishing off fried steak and onions. Maureen was practical on that and said she didn't like meat much, anyhow, and if she couldn't buy it for Pat on a Friday she was damned if she would buy it for herself. The Father laughed and pointed out that he had only brought that up as an example, but when they talked some more, he realized that he was up against the buried English Puritan in Maureen, a throwback to the Reformation. If she had known more than the barely vague belief that she wouldn't change her religion, he might have got somewhere. But that was all she had, and she was sticking to it, and that was that. Fair enough.

Now, he had said, if you won't turn to marry Pat, there is a thing that you will have to do. Papers will have to be signed that the children of the marriage will be brought up Catholics.

Maureen jibbed again.

Not that she cared greatly, but she said she thought that this was an infringement on the rights of personal freedom. Pat's eyes opened when he heard Maureen talking like this. It made him grin and feel good in a way. He was getting to like Maureen more and more. It was a solid thing, he thought, like the layers of concrete being poured into an embankment to hold up a railway.

'If you don't do that,' the priest said, 'then I'm afraid Pat can't be married by us at all.'

'Who'll marry him?' Maureen asked. 'He'll have to be married in a register office,' she was told. 'What's wrong with that?' she asked.

'Nothing,' the Father said; 'it's legally binding in the law, but in the eyes of his Church Pat wouldn't be married to you at all.'

She thought that one over. 'You wouldn't like that, Pat?' she asked, turning to him.

Pat was thinking at the moment that he would be married by a witch-doctor to her if she wanted it. But he couldn't, of course. He would really yield if she pressed him, although according to his beliefs then he would be merely committing adultery with her, or was it living in sin? But he wouldn't like that, he wouldn't like it at all. And he would want his kids to be Catholic. He knew that. He knew that some of the kids around the place could do with some religion, no matter what. He had found out since he started to go from door to door that there was little thought about religion in the area he travelled. He had seen a parochial magazine; the local clergyman's plaints; the articles in the papers. They were all true. Religion as far as he saw at the moment was in a slump. And if he and Maureen had kids, a thing he couldn't visualize now – because how the hell could they afford them? – he would want them at least to know that there was God in heaven and that it wouldn't do any harm to pay Him attention.

'I'm afraid I wouldn't like it, Maureen,' said Pat. 'But it's your choice.'

'Pat, Pat,' said the Father, 'what has become of your faith?'

'It's there, Father,' said Pat. 'But I love Maureen too.'

'I'm afraid, Pat,' said the Father, 'that you'll never become a saint.'

Maureen yielded, and it was arranged – all about how the permission would have to be got from the Bishop and how they would have to be married without a Mass, quietly in the sacristy, since there was no getting over the fact that Maureen was a heretic. Poor Maureen, Pat thought, sitting there neat and determined.

'I love heretics,' said Pat.

'You're not the first,' said the Father, 'and probably you won't be the last.'

Another young priest came in then with papers and things for them to sign. He was a young priest and he had an Irish accent, just like Pat, so Maureen got on well with him, and they chatted and smoked cigarettes.

The Father talked with Pat, and said, 'You have a duty, Pat, you know.' And Pat said, 'What's that?' and the Father said, 'To be a very good Catholic. It will be up to you,' he said 'to show Maureen that the religion her children will be brought up in is a good religion. You can't argue about those things,' he said. 'You will have to demonstrate them.' Pat said, 'I will try to be better than I am, Father,' and he meant it too, so the Father patted him on the back, and said, 'Good man. She's a very nice girl you're getting. Treat her well for the love of God.' 'I will cherish her,' said Pat, and he meant that too.

So they left, after smoking and chatting at the door.

'I like you very much,' said Maureen to the Father, as she shook his hand at the door, 'and your son is very nice too.'

'My what?' the Father asked with a shout.

'Your son; the young priest,' said Maureen.

The Father took it very well. He collapsed into gales of laughter. Pat laughed as well, and the young priest got a bit red, because he was young, but he smiled. You'd have to smile anyhow at Maureen's face.

'What's wrong with that?' she asked.

'I'm sorry, my dear,' said the Father. 'But we're not like your ministers. We are all celibates. We don't marry at all.'

It was only when she had gone, still looking puzzled and embarrassed, that it struck him that his answer had been ambiguous. He wondered if she thought that the young priest might he illegitimate. That sent him into gales of laughter again. He didn't tell the young priest his thought, because he was very young and still very intense, and he mightn't see the humour.

Pat was still laughing as they got out on the road. She was a little annoyed.

'Well, I'm glad,' she said, 'that I can make you laugh, anyhow. I'll be a jester as well as a wife.'

'Ah, you're killing me,' said Pat.

'I don't see the point,' said Maureen primly.

'God, what did you say that for?' he asked. 'Don't you know that Catholic priests are celibate? That they never get married?'

'How was I to know,' Maureen asked, 'without being told? Do you mean to say they never have a bit of fun at all?'

'No,' said Pat, 'they don't.'

'Coo!' said Maureen, and was silenced.

So here they were in the sacristy, Pat and Maureen standing in front of the Father, Maureen's father and mother, Dad all decked out in a new suit and a hard collar in which he was highly uncomfortable. You could hear the breath of protest whistling through his moustache. Mum, very neatly attired and absolutely determined not to cry. It was so ridiculous, these mothers who persisted in crying at their daughters' weddings. Seamus, big and towering, also in a new suit, his face red but pleased, dwarfing Maureen's bridesmaid, a little girl named Margie, who was raising her nose in the air sniffing, tying to pin down the smell of incense, wondering what on earth it was. The little man representing the law who would have to more or less marry them again when the priest was done, so that it would be recorded for all time that Pat Moore, insurance agent, was married to Maureen Potter, spinster, on this Saturday morning in November.

Pat noticed that Maureen's head came to his shoulder, and he liked the feel of her hand on his arm. She was wearing a grey coat simply cut and it made him feel all the more strongly that he was marrying a child. He could feel the tremble of her fingers and he could see from the moving of her pink blouse that her heart was beating very fast. He thought of Lelia, and he winced. He knew what he was doing was right. Knew it from the warm feeling deep down in him as he felt the presence of the confident little girl beside him. A warm feeling. Maybe it wasn't love at all, but it was what he wanted. It bore no resemblance to the feeling he had had for Lelia, but now he thought that having suffered that feeling, he didn't want any more of it.

The ceremony was soon over and they were sitting around the table in the crowded dining-room in Maureen's home.

It was a crush. The table stretching from window to window and chairs and borrowed chairs down each side. Mum and Margie were serving. Not a lot of people. Just themselves and the Father and Maureen's uncle, a man almost the spit of Dad, with the moustache and the same manner except he talked more and drank more. He was an L.C.C. driver and he said that ale was good for his ulcer. Pat could believe that a London bus-driver would have stomach trouble. Maureen's uncle said that all bus-drivers died at an early age from stomach trouble, so why wouldn't he have a bit of fun before he passed out? The people next door were in as well, the lady and her husband and daughter who had the pleasure of having Seamus boarded on them. The husband was a postman, thin and tall, with little flesh left on him from all the walking he had to do. His name was Percy, and he talked all the time about the wicked dogs tearing at the backside of his breeches whenever he opened a gate to deliver a letter. He hated dogs in any shape or form. Pat could sympathize with him, because since he had started the door to door business, he was quickly losing his love of dogs. Percy's wife was there too, a nice warm woman, with little to say. She was fond of Seamus and she loved it when he was insulting her food or her behaviour, pretending that she and himself had great fun and games whilst Percy was out having dogs tearing at his backside in the course of duty.

And Mary was there too. A different Mary, Pat thought, watching her now, laughing at Seamus. She had more flesh on her bones and the pale, drawn look had left her face. She was working in a factory, one of the shadow factories that were springing up like mushrooms in the London suburbs. She was dressed well and she looked ten years younger than the night when Jack had been taken away from her. Yes, Jack was still the main thing in her life. Just now she had told Pat that she had been over to see him yesterday and he had almost recognized her. Yes, he was getting better, they thought. It would take time, of course, but he would be better, they thought. And it wasn't just wishful thinking either on her part. She knew, down deep in her, that everything would be all right. Pat had been over to her house. It was as changed as herself. She had it all repainted from top to bottom, done by her own hands. All the paints were bright paints, that captured the rays of the sun and retained them when the sun had gone. A lot of the pictures had departed. There were too many of them, she had explained – but that was Jack. No matter where he went, he always came back with a picture. Now there were one or two, good engravings, remaining small and discreet on the walls. She was happy. She would never be the same again. Pat didn't think, no matter what happened, that she would ever go back to being the pale shadow of her husband.

The food was simple. Roast chicken and roast beef and some vegetables, and of course tea. And then the bottles of beer and the bottle of sherry. No hard tack. Nobody in the room was fond of the hard stuff. Just the beer or the stout, to distend a belly, caress an ulcer, and just give you enough bounce to feel that you were at a wedding. Jellies and trifles and biscuits. Very homely; nicely cooked. And after all, it was just the same food as if they had gone to an hotel and had it dished up at so much a head. No difference except that in the hotel it would have been disguised in a few ways.

It was uncomfortable, like all wedding parties. That was why at home Pat had always got drunk when he went to a wedding. It's a thing nobody could explain, why a wedding should have a depressing effect But it's true. Personally Pat was wishing that it was all over and that he and Maureen were out of it altogether.

It didn't take so long really. It provided a chance for the older people to become young again for a while.

First Dad, who was as shy and embarrassed about saying the few words as if he had to make a maiden speech in the House of Commons. Short and sweet. He liked Pat, but one could never be sure of the Irish and he hoped that he'd never get fed up with England and take their Maureen away out of it. He knew those Irish. Always coming and going like gipsies. But if Maureen had to go to anyone he was glad it was Pat she had picked. Because Pat was a nice lad. They had known him for some time now and he was sure she would be happy with him. Then he spoke about the time he had got married, and became a bit braver and spoke a little near the knuckle, while Mum remonstrated with him, her lined face actually becoming flushed, and for a moment you looked at them and you didn't see them with the biggest half of their lives behind them, but stripped of their lines and their grey hairs and young again, like Maureen and Pat, and Pat felt if Maureen got old like her mother it would be all right with him. Applause.

Percy spoke at length, because he had a few under the belt now and the whole day off. He brought the dogs into it, of course, hoping that as soon as Pat and Maureen got going that they wouldn't keep a bloody hound that'd tear the backside off the poor postman when he called to deliver registered letters. Then he spoke about me and my old woman. How she had been in the house when he was only an apprentice postman and used to hand him out a cup a char on a cold December morning when nobody was looking, and he took them through his long courtship and eventual triumph, skipped lightly over the marriage bed, spoke of his fears and ambitions, the tragedy of wet clothes and damp feet, about the postmen's union and what was wrong with it. The men at the top and what they were doing to withhold the rights of the common man. He attacked the Government fiercely then, and said they'd better be kind to the postmen because if they weren't what did they think would happen when the war came if the postmen went on strike. What'd happen to the red tape then, he wondered. He went on like that for a long time while they ceased to listen to him, and his wife eventually pulled him down into his chair.

Then it was Maureen's uncle. He was a bachelor. He told them why. He was a better talker than Dad. And more long-winded. Pat just listened to him with his mind somewhere else. His right hand holding Maureen's under the table, everyone knowing he was holding her hand and not giving a damn even so. Maureen's uncle told them why he was a bachelor. It was like a serial to be continued next week, about all the beautiful blonde

146

females that almost had him in their clutches over a lifetime. His shifts to get away – tight corners, triumphs.

Mum here interjected to say that it was the grace of God really that nobody had ever married Harry. Think of what the poor woman would have to suffer with him! Laugh.

It merely drove Harry to greater lengths, explaining about the evils of marriage, the undermining of the nation; too many people in the world anyhow, and he hoped Pat and Maureen weren't going to add to their numbers. Consternation and a little ribaldry. It got the party going, anyhow, and the tables were cleared and the bottles on the sideboard were broached and they sat around the fire getting ready to have a good time as soon as the newly-weds took their embarrassing presence away. It took time.

Maureen upstairs in her mother's room comforting her for the tears that had broken at last. Pat impatient and going up to add to the comfort. What's the use? It always happens. Even the lassies that get married in long white gowns and carpets up the church steps and the minister bowing his head, Rolls-Royces waiting to swish them away, even their mothers acted just the same when their daughters got married. It was something going out of their lives that they had created, reared, and nurtured over the years. Nobody could be like a mother to them any more. Blowing of noses. Wiping of red eyes. Downstairs again to shake hands and kiss where applicable. A strong handshake from Seamus, and a good look into his eyes.

Then they went on their honeymoon. They hadn't far to go.

Out into the street, turn left, down by the park; turn left again at the trees surrounding Maureen's church, up the hill. An avenue of newly-built houses. Up to the door. Insert the key. They were on their honeymoon in the new flat. At least they were on their own.

It was a very nice flat. Modern. A hall-way with a built-in cupboard and off that a living-room which would have to be a dining-room as well on state occasions and bonfire nights. Past the living-room a cream-painted bedroom with a wide window and built-in wardrobes and electric fire. Opposite that a small bathroom, and past that the kitchen with more built-in cupboards all convenient to the hands of the housewife, the kitchen window looking at the kitchen window of the flat a few feet away. That was the only drawback. And off the kitchen a small spare room, also looking out on the garden. Twenty-five shillings a week. It was a lot of money out of three pounds basic.

They closed the door behind them and solemnly surveyed it.

They had managed to furnish quite a lot of it. The living-room had a carpet and two easy chairs as well as the dining table and four chairs to match. A second-hand writing-desk for Pat. A small bookcase on the other side of the fireplace. A nice lamp-shade. That was that. They summed it up. They went and looked at the bedroom. Nothing but the bed. Double. Pat insisted on that. No hygiene for Pat, thanks very much. Two chairs. That was the lot. It would have been hard to fix anything else into it, anyhow. The kitchen was furnished of its own accord with the folding table and the built-in presses. Just two kitchen chairs to buy as well as a pot and a pan and a kettle and a brush. The whole lot cost over thirty pounds, after they had pooled their resources. As they stood they had their furniture, a flat, the clothes they stood up in. Some more in the wardrobes, twenty-two pounds eighteen shillings and elevenpence in the Post Office savings account, delf, cutlery, and a few other useful doo-dahs from wedding presents, and of course they had each other.

They found it hard to talk when they had finished surveying their domain. A sort of tension seemed to have sprung up between them. They avoided one another's eyes.

'I better light a fire,' said Pat. 'It's cold.'

'Do,' said Maureen. 'It's cold.'

He opened the kitchen door and went out to survey his coal bin. Coal on one side. Coke on the other. He just raised the lid and stood there looking at it. Maureen pushed her head out of the door.

'You don't want coal,' she said. 'Don't you remember we set the fire last night?'

'That's right,' said Pat, and came in again.

'There's a nice bit of garden out the back there,' said Pat, 'I must start digging it in the spring.' He felt like a farmer.

'That'll be nice,' said Maureen.

He followed her into the living-room. She sat on the chair, her coat held tightly about her, while he set a match to the piled paper and sticks, and nursed it into a blaze. He was good at lighting fires. Often had to do it at home, getting up first in the morning. In the Boy Scouts too. One of the tests – light a fire in the open without the assistance of paper and with only one match.

The fire blazed successfully.

'Amn't I a good fire-lighter?' he asked.

'Massive,' said Maureen. 'A genius.'

He sat in the other chair. The evening was drawing in. The flames flickered at the walls and lighted up her face as she stared into its heart. What will I say? Pat wondered, searched and found nothing.

What will I say? Maureen wondered, and remained silent too.

Pat managed it at last.

'I'm sorry, Maureen,' he said, 'that we couldn't have had a honeymoon. Like other people. Some day we will. Some day I'll give you a great honeymoon.'

'I'm sure you will,' said Maureen.

There was no chance of a honeymoon. He had only been about four weeks in the job anyhow, and it would have been a bit too much to have expected a honeymoon. Not with the money they had. They had to hold on to the little bit of money, in case.

'Some day, maybe,' he said, 'we'd go to Ireland. So that you could see it. In the summer maybe when I get the fortnight's holidays.'

'That would be nice,' she said, trying to infuse interest into her voice. She was afraid. She felt lost and lonely as if somebody had placed her in this firelit room with a complete stranger. What do I know about him? she asked. Nothing really, except that I took to him the first time I saw him. I felt something inside my chest clicking. But apart from that? Apart from the fact that I like the look of him and the way his hair grows and the way his eyes crinkle at the corners and his long hands and the ease of him, even sitting down, what do I know about him? That he is Irish, from the West of Ireland, whatever that is like. She had a sketchy knowledge of Ireland, like most other ordinary English people. It was just a piece on a map that sheltered England from the worst Atlantic gales. Her idea of Ireland was poor people with straw houses, brogues, and bad tempers, shooting people or beating people and upsetting English history. It had seemed to her at school that just when everything was going nicely for everybody, a King or Queen, who after a lot of wars and things and intrigue and what not, had fixed it all up, and when they were on the point of sitting down and taking off their shoes and putting on slippers to relax with a sigh, a dusty rider arrives at the palace, disturbing the regal rest, and says, 'The Irish are at it again.' So everybody said, 'Those Irish!' buckling on their swords again with a sigh of resignation.

She knew Pat came from a big town where there were schools, universities and cinemas and theatres, but she found it difficult to believe. So, reduced to its essentials, she had nothing to go by but Pat himself and what she thought he was like. Suppose she was wrong?

She looked at him now. He was staring at her intently with a worried look on his face. Poor Pat.

'Come on,' she said, 'and we'll go and get something to eat. Our first meal in our own house.'

His face lighted with relief and he jumped up.

'That'll be grand,' he said.

They went out to the kitchen. Pat scratched at the flint with the gas-lighter and the gas burst to flame and was soon caressing the virgin bottom of the new kettle. Maureen got the pan, put grease in it and put it on another flame. She reached again and hauled down the food. She paused then.

'You know, Pat,' she said thoughtfully, 'I'm afraid I'm not a very good cook. I have never done much of it. But I've watched Mother at it.'

'Listen,' said Pat. 'Even a burnt offering from your pan will taste sweeter to me than manna fried in elixir by the hands of an angel.'

She laughed. 'Wait'll you taste it first,' she said.

The tension eased a little and she did what Pat had been hoping all the time she would do. She took off her coat and wrapped a new apron around her waist. It was a small waist and the apron looked nice on it. Pat relaxed. It was good to see her coat off. For a few minutes in there he had been afraid of his life that she was going to get up and walk out on him. She must be going to stay awhile, he thought, now that she's taken off the coat. It felt good watching her dressed in an apron, with a fork in one hand and the handle of a pan in the other.

'Will you lay the table inside?' she asked.

'I will,' said Pat. So he got the virgin cups and washed a little of the shop dust out of them and brought them inside and laid their virgin saucers on the top of the virgin table. Cutlery from the canteen that they had got as a present. There was a smell of rashers coming from the kitchen. All my own, he thought. Imagine! He went back and got the bread then and sliced it with their new bread knife. They were quite thin slices for his first effort. At least, they were thin at one end.

They ate their first meal before the blazing fire and the drawn curtains. They laughed quite a bit. Because the rashers had somehow got a bit burnt, and the bottom of the eggs was more than brown and the top of them more than hard, and the sausages had a wilted look of outrage, as if they had been assaulted by a piledriver, but Pat really thought that he had never tasted anything like it, and told her so.

'There's no need to tell me that,' said Maureen; 'you couldn't possibly have ever tasted anything like that.'

They washed the dishes at the sink, Pat drying up, his eyes straying to Maureen's neck at the back where her hair curled away from it, and the slim rounded arms in the soapsuds and a very warm feeling came into him all over inside. But he still didn't feel at ease. He knew there was something that he should say that would establish them where they wanted to be, but it eluded him. They were laughing all right, but their eyes were still guarded. It wasn't a matter of leaning over and putting his arms around her waist and kissing her. Not until he had cleared up something else that seemed to be between them. They had kissed before. Not like the kisses he had got from Lelia and the ones he had dished out. With Maureen it was kind of advancing by slow and growingly interested degrees, like a man beginning to explore a foreign land, and find it nicer and more pleasant as he went along, knowing that one day he would get to the heart of it and never want to leave it again. But how to get that across to her? That was the rub.

They went back to the fire again and sat in front of it. Not near to one another. Automatically they went to separate chairs and sat in them, almost as much apart as before the meal, except that there was a burnt offering shared by them and Maureen didn't have her coat on.

'Maureen,' said Pat after a pause, finding it difficult, 'are you afraid of me?'

She looked at him, startled.

'No, Pat,' she said, 'Why should I? I'm not a little filly.'

'I don't mean that,' said Pat, 'but there's something in your eyes, not fear maybe, but uncertainty. Are you sorry I rushed you off your feet?'

'You didn't rush me off my feet,' she said.

'We haven't talked about it at all,' he went on then. 'You have been very patient. You haven't asked one question or anything. The night I came home from London and asked you to marry me. You remember that night?'

'I do,' said Maureen. As if she would forget that!

'Well, I had gone over to Lelia's house that night with matrimonial intentions. Did you know that?'

'I more or less guessed it,' said Maureen.

'George was there before me,' said Pat.

'I guessed that too,' said Maureen.

'I will always love George more than I would love my own brother if I had one,' said Pat leaning forward in his chair to her. 'I thought then that Lelia was God's gift to a disillusioned world. If it hadn't been for George, I might have been left with Lelia. That thought, Maureen, freezes my stomach with terror now when I think of it.'

'Does it?' Maureen asked, brightening a little.

'It does,' said Pat intently. 'I left that house of theirs sweating with embarrassment, hurt, and what I thought was suffering. I look back on that night like Columbus must have done when he thought about America.'

'Do you really love me, Pat?' Maureen asked him, facing him squarely.

He thought a moment before he answered her. He wanted to get it right, just right, so that never again would a threat of it come between them.

152

'Maureen,' he said, rising to stand in front of the fire, looking down at her, 'if I loved Lelia, then I don't love you. I wouldn't want to, not if it was like what I felt for Lelia. I thought a lot coming home in the train that night. It seemed to me that I was like a man who had been drinking in a pond with green slime on it, and then you came to me, so clear, like a stream on the side of a hill, like you had flowed right into me and taken away the stagnant pond water. It's silly. This trying to get you to understand, but, Maureen' — and he got on his knees in front of her, his hands resting on her leg so that her eyes were almost on a level with his own — 'what I feel for you is as deep and as permanent as the waters of the Atlantic Ocean. When I look at you I feel inside me like I used to feel standing on a cliff at home looking at the white gulls hovering, or white sails on a boat in the bay, or white clouds in the blue sky. What I feel for you is everything in nature that is clean and fresh, like the rain washing a granite rock, a river going over a waterfall, a . . . Christ, I'm trying too hard, amn't I?' he asked her, his head falling a little.

'I don't think so,' said Maureen softly; 'I think you're doing fine.'

She raised her hand and put it on his hair. He looked at her. Her eyes were soft, so he took her hand and put it on his cheek.

'I have been looking for something like this, Maureen,' he said, 'and I think that it is more wonderful than I had any expectations of it being. We're two ordinary people, with just ordinary educations and ordinary jobs, but I feel things for you that are so vast and deep and satisfying that I'd want to be a poet to get them into words. And I'm no poet. It seems just like the climax to living to be here, the two of us, alone, in a flat costing twenty-five bob a week that we'll find it very hard to pay for out of a small screw, but I wouldn't be anywhere else in the world and I wouldn't be anywhere else with anybody else in the world. And I'm telling you now, knowing, as firmly as if I was an old gentleman of ninety-eight, that you will always be the one for me and that I'll never want anybody else but you.'

'Oh, Pat,' said Maureen, her head falling on his shoulder, her face soft against his own.

Later he looked at the dark night through the window. Maureen's head was on his shoulder, his arm around her, and she was sleeping gently. He felt her breath on his neck and her body lying against the length of his side. This is it, he thought, this is it all right, just as I knew it would be, and nobody will ever take it away from me. We'll be two ordinary people, ordinary suburbanites in a great city, like millions of others, and we'll have great happiness, and nothing will ever touch us but simple things. We'll go along masking our joy like everybody else does, like a miser keeping a jewel in a cupboard, and nothing and nobody will ever come between us. It will be a square sail on a calm sea, a dull suburban sea, undisturbed, equable, unsullied.

It was a nice dream.

10

'**G**ood morning, Mrs Smith,' said Pat. 'A lovely morning, isn't it?' It wasn't a lovely morning really. It was a raw January morning, and Pat shivered as the fingers of the wind explored the crevices of his clothes, but one had to have those little niceties. They became a reflex. Everything is all right with the world and the weather. Keep the customer smiling.

Mrs Smith looked at him. Jaysus, Pat thought. No money this week either.

'I'm sorry, Mr Moore,' said Mrs Smith. 'It will have to wait until next week. My husband is on short-time again and my little girl isn't well. We had to have the doctor to her, poor thing.'

What could you do? Pat wondered. The Mrs Smiths he had on his books were the people who made him dislike his job very much. He felt that he was exploiting them. Mrs Smith endeavoured to pay three shillings and sixpence insurance every week, mainly because she had been talked into the policies by good insurance agents. She couldn't afford it. She would pay for a few years and then the bad time would come and Mrs Smith would have her policies lapsed. In order then to save his commission on the lapsed policies the new agent would have to rewrite new policies for Mrs Smith dating from the present. Mrs Smith would comply and would pay for a few more years until the next time, when they would be lapsed again. Pat wondered why in the name of Christ it never struck Mrs Smith to put her money in the Post Office, so that it would be there when she needed it, instead of sending it into the maw of a great insurance company that could well afford to do without it. He reckoned that Mrs Smith had been paying money to an insurance company for ten years need-lessly. It would have been as well for her to go and flush the money down the lavatory.

The trouble was that it wasn't up to him to tell Mrs Smith to put her money in the Post Office and to have nothing whatso-ever to do with insurance companies. He had to live too, like the other agents. He would have to lapse her policies, and the com-mission paid to the agent who had persuaded her to take them would be taken out of his wages if he didn't persuade her to take them on again, fresh. It was a nasty business.

'You owe eleven weeks now, Mrs Smith,' said Pat, 'and if you don't pay next week, your policies will have to go.'

'I'll manage next week,' she said. 'Things will be better next week.'

But they wouldn't, he knew. Next week he would see the same look on her face.

'Is there no way at all,' he asked, 'that you could try to pay up the back money you owe? If those policies lapse now you'll only get a paid-up policy, a fraction of the value you have paid in, and you will be at a loss on everything.'

'I'm afraid not,' she said. 'But it doesn't matter. I'll pay them again. They were lapsed before.'

'But don't you realize,' Pat asked, 'that when you take them again you take them fresh and that you lose practically all you have paid?'

'I always took them before,' she said, 'when they had to be lapsed.'

It was no use. You couldn't explain it to her. She would prob-ably go on doing this for the rest of her days – every year that passed she would have to pay more for less, and it would never strike her to think about it, to realize what a hare she was being made. You couldn't talk sense into the pale blue eyes, so he sighed and left her, mounted his bicycle, closing his coat collar to the piercing wind, and cycled on to his next client.

He was glad there weren't a lot of Mrs Smiths. It made him uncomfortable about the work he was doing. Most people who paid insurance weekly didn't stop to realize that they were pay-ing dearly for their cover. In fifteen years they would get back scarcely as much as they paid in. If they paid their money yearly or half-yearly or quarterly they would get a good return. It was the same way with the world. It was the man who could afford to pay who got the best return. Pat wondered how many insurance agents there were in the country and how many Mrs Smiths were on their books. At least two to every agent, he imagined – which meant that there were thousands of people making presents of money they couldn't afford to big insurance combines. Which made Pat feel in some cases that he was a bit of a confidence trickster.

His next call was different, and it cheered him up. Mrs Manleigh was a big woman, whose house shone like a polished diamond. He always reached her at eleven in the morning of his Saturday morning round. All insurance was collected between Friday and Tuesday. Good business, because any other times all the wages might be spent, so you went as near to the general payday of the people as you could. Otherwise the money for the insurance agent might be gone on this or that and it would take a few extra weeks for them to pay off what had been spent. All reflecting on your collections and your salary. Apart from Mrs Smith, Pat rather enjoyed being an insurance agent.

It had been difficult at first. He hadn't realized that he had such an Irish accent that people just couldn't understand him, nor he them. It was funny really. He would be talking away there to a blank look of politeness, and the sweat would break out on him. They were very polite and listened to him kindly, which made it worse. Fortunately he had been with Maureen's people for some time and had heard the others speaking, so that he more or less knew, but there were always some words he said that meant nothing to the clients, and words that they said that left him blank, but they gradually got on a footing of understanding; he making an obvious effort to lessen the way he flattened his words, and they slowing their speech a little to the frowning concentration of his furrowed forehead.

Mrs Manleigh had been his first real hand of friendship. He had stood on her doorstep the first week he had been going around alone and tried to tell her that she should insure her old grannie for an extra threepence a week which the law allowed her. He talked feelingly about the expense of funerals going up, and would she be sure she had enough to bury the old lady, when she passed out? All for the sake of four shillings and sixpence commission on the threepence a week. Mrs Manleigh just stood and looked at him and smiled and said. 'You don't say!' at intervals, and then broke him up by saying, 'Come on in and have a cupper tea. You must be dry, dear, with all that talking.'

He followed her into a spotless kitchen and was soon sitting at the table drinking a cup of tea and eating chocolate biscuits. He discovered that it had always been the habit for the agent to come in and have a cup of tea and a chat, if she liked him, that was. She liked Pat, said it was the first time they had ever sent her an Irish one. She liked the way he talked, even though she couldn't understand half of what he was saying, but she was a very friendly woman and she talked to him about her neighbours and the dogs next door and about her children and what they were going to be, and about her husband and what he was.

It became a ritual for him to call on Mrs Manleigh and drink her tea and talk.

There were others like her, friendly people.

As time went by he discovered that an insurance agent to some of the people was a sort of safety valve. They got rid of a lot on him. And when people died or you had to pay out on policies, you discovered a lot about their way of living – about the old lady of sixty whose husband when he died wasn't her husband at all, but they had been living in calm and peaceful and loyal sin for thirty-two years. He discovered simple men at simple jobs who when they came home tried to express themselves by painting pictures or drawing pictures of their children. Also there were unhappy houses where wives were dirty and discontented, husbands hard and bellicose. There was no house without humanity, whether good or evil, and he realized what a mistake it was to accept the calm, serene, picture-postcard fronts of suburbia as being the outward expression of what they contained inside. No house without love or hate or greed or lust or honour or beauty or nobility or degradation behind the clean curtains and the mowed lawns. And an insurance agent got a glimpse behind the curtains, because the people appeared to treat him as a sort of an emotional eunuch. They told him things that they wouldn't tell their clergymen — about their lives and families and private ailments, because he also paid National Health money on the side and had to have certificates from their doctors to prove that they weren't trying to get their fifteen bob a week sick money by underhand methods. Oh, a very interesting way of living, if you didn't have to be trying to persuade people to take out policies, a lot of which you didn't believe in. You had to have faith in your goods, like a shopkeeper, and Pat felt that some of the goods he had to sell were of faulty manufacture.

He chatted to Mrs Manleigh and drank his tea and told her about Maureen, and how she sent her thanks for the recipe of the cake Mrs Manleigh had sent her through Pat. Oh, very pleasant. And then he faced into the cold wind again and headed down to the house near the bridge.

It was a flat really, and his last call before going under the bridge to the other calls on the far side. More ritual. He would call, collect his money, pass on, turn at the far side of the bridge and wave to Seamus, who would be up there on the job, his old job. Seamus knew what time he passed on Saturday and was always on hand for the wave, standing big on the embankment in his shirt-sleeves, even though the weather would freeze a bishop in fur underwear.

Pat didn't like the house by the bridge. There was an Alsatian there and he didn't like callers. Pat could flash his mind now over the houses on his rounds with dogs who didn't like callers. There were dogs everywhere, but some of them were spoiled. He had come to the conclusion that the people appeared to have lost the religion they had and had replaced their religion by the worship of dogs, just as the ancient Egyptians had worshipped cats. There were all sorts of dogs from Poms and Pekinese to St Bernards and Great Danes. They all appeared to be fed like princes and slept in special places with blankets and what-nots. He felt that he had been bitten and frightened by every known make of dog, until by this time he had arrived at a detestation of all dogs and bemoaned the fact that Noah had ever taken a bitch into the Ark. Since you had to be polite you couldn't reach out and give the snarling dogs a kick in the belly as you would at home. You just remained on the defensive and smiled in a frozen manner as you listened to a tale of the dog's astuteness, perspicacity, humanity, the beast curling a lip at you and you wanting to strangle him. You couldn't do that. Not if you wanted to keep your business. So you hid your fear and hoped it wasn't true that dogs could smell the sweat of fear and go for you before you had time to close the gate after you, you having walked so nonchalantly to the gate hoping it wasn't obvious that every second you expected sharp teeth to be fastened agonizingly in the cheeks of your behind.

He knocked at the door of the flat at the bridge. The door opened of its own accord. There were steps inside, and he saw the Alsatian coming bounding down those steps at him, with his teeth bared.

Pat was completely taken by surprise. He was automatically used to knocking at the door and feeling the muscles of his stomach tightening at the loud bark of the dog. Then the door would open and Mrs Gosper would appear holding the books in one hand with the money inside them and the collar of the straining dog with the other. That dog didn't like Pat. He always looked at him as if he was three-quarters of a pound of raw beef which he would love to gulp.

Pat fell back a little. His main emotion was to give way to ignominious flight as he saw the dog coming, his hind feet already tensing to launch his big body at the figure in the doorway. There was a low wall at the side of the steps, and as Pat's hand went back he felt something smooth and as the dog sprang for his throat he grasped it, raised it high and brought it down hard on the side of the dog's skull.

Action after that was fast. The dog whined loudly, and slithered at his feet; whined again, turned and went bounding up the steps with a definite wilt to his tail. Pat was surprised, pleased, and triumphant as he looked at the empty milk bottle in his hand. He reflected that the Express Dairy had never done a better job of work than this morning. His triumph waned swiftly as the doorway was filled with the figure of Mrs Gosper.

She was a small, stumpy woman almost as broad as she was tall. Her arms were big and bare, her neck was big with fat and the main features of her face consisted of a mouthful of splayed

teeth. The teeth seemed to come out of her mouth in all direc-
tions, acting as a sort of separate sounding-board for the words
which were being flung from her mouth now, like bullets from a
machine-gun. He listened in a sort of daze.

From it all, he realized that if Mrs Gosper's dog didn't like
him, he was only reflecting Mrs Gosper's own emotions. A nice
state the country was comin' to indeed, when they were lettin'
all sorts of trick-o-the-loops into it. Savages, that's what they
were. Never did she think she'd see the day when men in England would be permitted to go about the country hittin' poor
defenceless dogs with milk bottles. She would complain to his
manager. She would complain to the Government. She would
complain to the Express Dairy. That's what kyme of not keepin'
England for the English. Openin' the country wide to filthy Irish
that kyme over in a savage style, ignorant louts like the man on
her doorstep now, so that they could go around the country'
assaultin' innocent dogs. Wasn't it enough that they were
blowin' up the poor English? Couldn't get a letter now. Have to
send letters by pony express. Imagine in this day an age. All be
put in jyle they should, bag and baggage.

'I'm really sorry—' Pat tried to interject.

She just raised her voice louder.

Never liked them, she didn't. Too sly. Just like them Welsh
comin' down from the coalmines. Why couldn't they all sty at
home? That's what she wanted to know. Tried to blow up the
reservoir last night with bombs. Wasn't that gratitude? She
wouldn't be surprised if he was up to something last night.
Wouldn't surprise her at all if he was the one that put the bombs
on the bridge. Any man who could go around hittin' dogs on the
heads with milk bottles wouldn't surprise her what he'd do.
She'd see her M.P. She'd see the Chairman of the Council. She'd
put a halt to his gallop. She'd write a letter to Mr Churchill, the
only man in the whole country that seemed to hate the Irish as
much as she did herself. No wonder they wouldn't bring him
into the Government. Let them bring him into the Government
and he'd soon put an end to the I.R.A.

Pat felt he ought to try and defend himself – to use a bit of
logic, point out that the dog was vicious and that it was her own

fault that he was; that you couldn't keep a big dog like that confined to a small flat in the suburbs. It wouldn't be any use. He let her go on. Her voice must have been audible up in Buckingham Palace. The tirade flew around him until he felt his ears burning with the whip of the words. He just contented himself by saying, You old buck bitch, under his breath; made no further effort to defend himself.

Wait'll my old man comes home from work and I tell him about this. Wouldn't surprise me if he took a dog-whip to you, it wouldn't. And now take yourself away from my doorstep and never stand on it again to the longest day you live, or I'll have the police up here, I will, you bleedin' monster. She heard what they did to the donkeys in Ireland, the beatin' with sticks, the sores as big as saucers. Well, he wasn't in Ireland now, and the sooner he went back to it, the sooner this country could come back to peace and prosperity.

Then she banged the door in his face, opening it again to shout something about the Manager, the Government, and the Express Dairy, and banged it to again, and left him standing there, in the terrible vacuum of silence that is created after a noisy berating.

He was petrified and cautiously looked around to see if anybody besides himself had been listening to her. There was a postman on the opposite side of the street, a milk roundsman this side at his barrow, and a woman two doors up cleaning her windows. Pat's face was red. He couldn't tell from the attitude of the listeners whether they had heard or not. They must have. They showed no sign of having done so. He came down the steps and went out the gate, mounted his bicycle, and paused again to look around him. Nobody paid him the least attention except the milk roundsman, who, pausing on his way with a packet of butter, closed one eye in a significant and sympathetic wink.

Pat laughed and cycled away. There's a lot to be said, he thought then, for the air of isolation which the English people carry around with them. It was annoying to others sometimes, the aloofness from their neighbours' business. If they had been at home a sizeable audience would have gathered, more appreciative of the oratory than anything else. They might even have assisted in the flow or for the sake of an argument they might have taken the opposite side and started up an argument of rhetoric – bawdy and beautiful, vernacularly invaluable – which would have excited them for an hour or two. It was tough to be on the receiving end all the same.

He crossed under the bridge and remembered when he got to the far side to turn and look for Seamus. He was there, all right, up on the embankment. Pat waved to him, feeling warm that there was somebody around who liked him. Seamus waved back at him, and then he turned and continued his round, most of the unpleasantness, he hoped, being past.

Seamus stood and watched him until his cycling figure was swallowed by the canyons of terraces on top of the hill.

Good old Pat, Seamus thought, as he bent to his work again. Pat so serious for his youth, never intense, just interested. Seamus thought that Pat must be a sort of copybook edition of the common or garden man, getting enjoyment out of small things and making adventures out of simple things. He wondered how Pat would feel if he was presented with adventures on a large scale that were so much bigger and truer than the ones he was accomplishing. He imagined how he would react. He would think them over and probably reject them. Not that he hadn't the stomach for them. Just because he couldn't throw himself into them from a surge of the spirit. He would have to be directed by a power he himself believed in implicitly, and he would have to be sheltered by the law, because it was the common man who created the law, for his own protection, and it was the only thing he would ever fight to protect, the intangible laws that had been created by himself for himself.

Seamus wondered what Pat would say if he could hear him thinking like this. Pat looked on him, he knew, as a very nice lad from Connemara, a little inferior in intellect and education. No, not that. He knew that Pat liked him and certainly he liked Pat, probably because there was no bad in him worth talking about, and you had to be a little bad as well as a little mad to be able to undertake the things Seamus and the others were doing. Seamus wondered why he was doing them. It was love in a way of a bigger kind than you could have for a mere man. It was an intangible affection that made all risks seem worthwhile. Risks – there was that in it too. The thrill of taking a risk. The knowledge that you were something like a badger or an otter, that you were on your own, that you had to kick out a burrow of wilderness in a world of civilization.

It was a little later that he saw the two men and the manager going into the wooden shed that housed the explosives. He straightened himself and automatically felt for his coat.

His pulse was pounding, but his head was cool. It's come at last, he thought. What am I going to do now? He had very little time in which to decide. The explosion at the reservoir last night had been a little close. It was obvious that they would nose out the men on this job sooner or later. It was too apt. So many Irishmen; so much explosive. It had to be. He thought of his chances. After all, there must be over a hundred Irish as well as himself on the job. It would take time for them to get around the lot of them. Yes, but that would mean that they would reach him in the end. They would have to. There were many little things that it was impossible to hide from the trained eyes, and they with all the sources of enquiry they had at their command.

He decided almost immediately. He would go. Now was the time. If he left it any later, he would be too late, like hesitating to take a leap into the sea when someone was drowning.

There was a bunch of chaps near him at the concrete mixer. They hadn't noticed anything. It meant nothing in their lives that two big men in hard hats and city-type coats should be visiting the powder-house of the job on a cold January morning. He pulled on his coat and moved away from them.

'Hy,' one of them shouted after him, 'where are you off to?'

Seamus made a gesture indicating a call of nature. They laughed and he went down the embankment casually, his mind racing. He had very little time. He hadn't time to go home and collect his things. That would be very foolish. He would have to get into London, to a place he knew which hadn't been raided yet. By bus? No; it was slack times and the bus driver would remember. They would cover the buses and the trains. Trains were dangerous things because they passed through stations and stopped there. All that was needed was a phone call. Besides, they couldn't miss him. All they had to say was he was a very big size and the way he was dressed and he would be dragged from the train like a rat from a trap.

He passed the rough latrine, got behind it, and climbed the fence separating the job from the road. It was a galvanized fence with the wooden supports on this side. He was sheltered by the latrine. Over he got, smoothly and quickly, and then his feet were on the road. It was a side road and nobody saw him. Pity, he thought, that I couldn't have taken one of the bicycles. But they were on the far side. He would have been noticed. Bicycle? He thought of Pat then immediately. Somewhere up there on the right-hand side of the main road in the maze of terraces, he would find Pat and his bicycle. He could of course whip the nearest bicycle, but that would tell them the direction he had taken.

He quickened his pace. He didn't go by the main road. He would have been seen by the others on the embankment. He took the side lanes going up by the left of it, reached the terraces further on where new houses were being built, and then when he knew he was out of sight of the embankment he turned on to the main road and plunged across. Pat would be somewhere along here. It should be easy to find him. The houses were built in long rows regularly. A street stretching to the horizon crisscrossed by another shorter street and then another long street stretching to the horizon. He went down one and searched its length with his eyes. Blank. He walked down it and turned into the criss-cross street and searched the next. Blank. Into the third.

He saw the blue and cream bicycle half-way down that street, leaning casually against the kerb. He walked down to it.

He stopped short of the bicycle and looked at the house. Pat was there chatting to a young woman who still held the book in her hand. She was laughing. There was a pleased look on her face. Good old Pat, Seamus thought; the old personality – the quiet kind; we all fall for it. Where he was standing, a lane went up by the side of the house to the long lane at the back servicing the houses, with coal and things and dustmen and what-not. He drew back there a little and waited for Pat to finish his business. Voices. Banter. The sound of Pat's feet hitting the concrete path. The closing gate. Seamus stepped out a little. Call.

'Hey, Pat!'

He had to laugh at the startled look on Pat's face before he found where the voice was coming from. He turned. Widened eyes.

'Seamus!' he ejaculated then, coming towards him. 'What the hell are you doing here?'

'Look, Pat,' said Seamus, 'I'll have to talk fast. I have to get to London in a hurry. I can't go the proper ways. So would you give me the old bike?'

A look of puzzled anxiety on Pat's face, but no hesitation. Just like him.

'Of course, Seamus,' said Pat, bending down to slip the bicycle clips off his trouser ends. 'Here, you'll want those.'

'Thanks,' said Seamus, bending and clipping them on. He straightened then to find Pat looking at him.

'What is it, Seamus?' he asked.

'Look, Pat,' said Seamus, 'it'd be better for you not t' know anythin' at all. What you won't know you won't be troubled by. And if you are asked any questions, you can't give answers to somethin' you know nothing about.'

Pat searched his mind furiously. Seamus and trouble – they were two things you could take together. But Seamus running away from trouble meant something else altogether. Something serious – like bombings say? Startled, he looked at Seamus again, at the broad face looking kindly at him split by a large grin.

'You'd never believe it, would you, Pat?' Seamus asked.

'Why didn't you tell me?' Pat asked. 'It's terrible you going away like this. With no chance to say good-bye.'

'I couldn't tell you anything, Pat,' said Seamus, 'because I know you too well. You show too much on that oul dial of yours. You weren't ever meant to be mixed up in things outa the real ordinary. Yer a good honest man, Pat. It was nice knowing you, and bein' with you was just like being at home with the lads. Small things were drama for you. Like about what happens to people and not what they do. You wouldn't feel right, Pat, knowing about the other things, because you couldn't see only the ordinary man's side of it. You couldn't see why, only what. And I didn't want to have a row with you. You'd probably be tryin' to convert me. I couldn't take that, so I couldn't. Not from you. Because I know you'd want to, however much you tried not to. And then maybe we couldn't have been as friendly as we were. Do you see?'

'Where are you going?' Pat asked him. 'How will you get out?'

'I'll sweep in by the Wembley road,' said Seamus waving an arm, 'and I'll hope for the best. I have a good chance of gettin' through this way. If I can get into London, I might be all right. There'd be ways a gettin' out from there I hope. If you don't read me name in the papers inside a month you'll know that I got away. And if I get away I'll write to you maybe. I'm not a good hand at it. But just to let you know.'

They walked out to the bicycle together, Seamus already cautious, looking up and down the street first. It made Pat's heart contract to imagine what this cautiousness meant. He couldn't find anything to say. The whole business had been sprung on him too quickly. Seamus mounted the bicycle. He held out his hand.

Pat shook it, marvelling again at the size and firmness of it. Imagine not having Seamus around any more!

'Good-bye, Pat,' said Seamus. 'I'm glad to have met you. And we'll meet again some day too, so we will.'

'I hope so,' said Pat.

'If I get away,' said Seamus, 'your bicycle will come back to you. If I don't get away you better say that it was stolen. Give me a day or two and if nothing happens don't say anything about it, because that'll mean that you'll get it back. But if anything does happen and I'm caught, go to the police and complain about the bike. That's the best way.'

'All right,' said Pat hoarsely.

'Give my love to Maureen,' said Seamus. 'She'll be shocked and she won't like it. Also to Mrs Percy. I couldn't get back to the digs. The police are probably there now. Tell her if you can that you are sure I'm sorry for getting her house into trouble. She was a nice woman. It was a nice digs, but there you are. So, good-bye now, oul son.'

They looked into one another's eyes for a few moments. Seamus was thinking, poor oul Pat, it's a shock to him, to know that

167

somebody could be different to what he had them all fixed out to be. Pat was thinking that, but he had started to learn earlier never to judge from your young impressions. There was Jack. There was Mrs Gosper and the dog. He was thinking not so much about Seamus being different to what he had imagined, as that Seamus was nice. He had got used to him. It was a comfort to see the bulk of him and the cheerful face, and the easy pleasantness that had covered this other business. He should have known from his eyes, because looking at them now he saw there was far more behind them than the eyes of the young man who could drink a pint of porter and laugh, or do two men's work on the job and laugh, or paste a chap in the kisser in a friendly fight and laugh. There was going to be something missing with Seamus absent.

'Take care of yourself, Seamus,' he said.

'Don't worry,' said Seamus, with a laugh, 'I will.'

He cycled away then, without looking back, and Pat stood there and watched him. bulking over the slender build of the bicycle, until he turned at the end of the street and vanished from his sight. For a few seconds then he stood there on the street and he felt lost – like, he thought, the way I felt when I came first and stood on Euston station with that cardboard case in my hand. Seamus had been a tenuous link that had bound him with home. To look at him was to see men trundling turf bar-rows on a bog with a great mountain rising behind them. Or men in a currach struggling with their cork on a scornful sea. Or the smell of hay newly cut by a swishing scythe, and bulging brown muscles raising forkfuls of it to the top of a cock of hay. Or the smell of porter in a pub in the evening. Or the clatter of milk churns on a common cart. All so far away, and so different to this carefully worked out civilization of which he was now a part, with his flat in suburbia and his tiddly job, and the warmest part of it his Maureen of the English limpid eyes. For her it was worth all of it, but he felt that Seamus going had taken away a part of something. It didn't matter about why Seamus went. He put that out of his mind, the wrongs and the rights of it. It was Seamus as a person and what he had meant. But Seamus will be all right, he thought. Seamus will get away. He knew that no matter what Seamus did, he would pray for him to get away.

He turned then and walked to the rest of his calls. First all the houses on this side of the main road and then all the houses on the other side of it. His feet told him after half an hour how big was the space he covered effortlessly every week on his bicycle. He found it hard to put on the good old smile, to show the teeth, to pat the heads of the curly-headed babies, even though he liked most of the people and liked smiling with them and liked babies and liked to be patting their curly heads. It was an effort. And Seamus was brought back to him at every door, because it was the prevailing custom for the agent and the client to spend a few minutes discussing the news in the morning paper. They talked about high finance and politics and murders and human interest, and he came to realize how much the lives of the people swung around the news in the morning papers. The papers this morning were full of the unsuccessful reservoir bombing. So they talked about that and questioned him. After all, since he was Irish he might be expected to know what the whole thing was about. It was getting more serious now. One or two people had been killed and the bombs had moved from the humorous letter-box stage. So he agreed and tsk-tsk-tsked with them, and tried not to remember Seamus riding off on a bicycle with a very efficient police force hot on his tail. He knew the way these people would all regard Seamus if his picture appeared in the paper. It would be an impossible task to try and draw a picture for them of the Seamus he knew and what he was really like.

So he walked his book on the right of the road and then he crossed over and walked his book on the left. Rows and rows of houses with their gardens. New houses in blocks and semi-detached and detached, with their shopping centres and small cinemas and the smell of fresh cement and lime in the newer areas. And he met the same people. The other insurance agents and the milk roundsmen, and the postmen and the bakers' delivery men with their hand barrows, electric barrows, bicycles, cars and vans.

And then he met Lelia.

A screech of brakes beside him, a frightened jump, a cross look at the motorist, and there was Lelia, leaning out the door of the car to him with a sparkle in her eyes.

'Why, Pat,' she said.

'Hello, Lelia,' said Pat, as if he was talking to one of his clients. Idly he wondered how long ago it was since he had seen her and how little she meant to his life. He could even smile when he remembered the flux into which she had once thrown him.

They shook hands. Her hand was as soft as ever, but he thought from the feel of it that it was better covered with flesh. Her rings sparkled.

'What are you doing up here?' he asked.

'Why,' ejaculated Lelia, 'we're going to live up here. We are buying a new house up there on the hill.'

She pointed back where a forest of scaffolding raised its head with tall trees of the nearly digested countryside forming a background.

'And what are you doing?' she asked.

'Working,' said Pat, 'on my rounds, you know. Collecting the jolly old insurance, what.'

'Walking?' she asked, her eyes wide.

'I punctured my bicycle,' said Pat. 'Had to leave it in to be fixed.' Lie One, he thought, already.

'Well, come on,' said Lelia, 'and I'll drive you around. I've time to spare.'

'Oh no,' said Pat.

'Oh yes,' said Lelia; 'hop in,' opening the door on the other side.

She drove him around the rest of his calls. She was well-dressed and he smelled the same perfume from her, and once when her arm brushed his hand he felt the smoothness of her skin. Her hair was burnished and beautiful and she was probably the worst driver that ever crucified the workings of a motor-car. She chattered. About George. About Daddy. About the new house. About the fortune George was making from meat. And Pat, his business sense working, realized that he was an insurance agent and that cars had to be insured and he could insure them, and shops had to be insured and he could insure them, and lives had to be insured and he could insure them.

He became a little pleasanter to Lelia, joked about George and insurance and what would happen to Lelia if George passed out. She thought it over.

'Why,' she said, with a look at him out of the corner of her eye, 'I don't think George is insured much. We'll have to see him about it, won't we?'

'It would be an idea,' said Pat. 'No wife should have an uninsured husband.' George should be big stuff, he thought. Maybe a thousand. That would be ten-quid commission. Then the car. He started to count it up and decided it behooved him to be nicer to Lelia. So they laughed and he finished his calls, ignoring the pointed looks of the ladies at the beautiful chauffeuse he had suddenly acquired, and then she drove him home.

Stopped outside the gate.

'Well,' said Pat, 'you were a great help to me. Thanks very much.'

'I must go in and see Maureen.' said Lelia, switching off the engine.

'Oh no,' said Pat, 'I don't think you ought to really. She'll be a bit upset – getting the dinner and that.'

'It's ages since I've seen her,' said Lelia, getting out of the car. 'Besides, we'll have to fix a date for you to meet George.'

'All right,' said Pat, walking up the path to his flat with her, wondering how Maureen would accept the *fait accompli* and wondering if insurance could be garnered at too high a price.

11

Maureen wasn't very pleased to see Lelia. Apart from the fact that she already had a visitor, who was holding her back from getting their midday meal ready, causing her to run from the living-room to the kitchen to see if everything was all right there, and running back again, she wasn't feeling so good these days. She felt harassed and her stomach was upset, and she felt that she was untidy, and she felt that Pat was taking her troubles and annoyances with too light a heart – that he could have been a little more sympathetic. So when Pat opened the front door with his key and then walked into the living-room with Lelia, she got up from the couch where she was sitting, took one glance at Lelia, ignored her, and attacked him.

'Where have you been all this time?' she wanted to know. 'What kept you? You are hours late.'

Then she became conscious of the sobbing Mrs Percy in the chair in front of the fire.

'Poor Mrs Percy has been waiting hours for you. The police were at her house. They were looking for Seamus. Where is he? What happened to him?'

'Isn't it awful, Pat,' Mrs Percy asked, looking up at him with red-rimmed eyes. 'Hello, Lelia, you look very well I must say.'

'Hello,' said Lelia, sitting on the couch, carefully pulling her coat about her plump knees. My God, Maureen wondered in exasperation, will I ever see Lelia unconscious of her body?

Pat closed on Mrs Percy, standing in front of the fire looking down at her.

'What happened, Mrs Percy?' he asked.

'It was awful,' said Mrs Percy, waving her dampened handkerchief. 'Never happened to us before, it didn't, having the police right in our own house. Knocked at the door, they did. I go out. Two of them. Big fellows. Shove cards under me nose and say they want to look at Seamus's things. You could have knocked me down with a feather. "Here," I said, "what's all this here? You wait until my old man comes home before you go pryin' about. Where's Seamus then?" I say. "What's happened to him? What do you want to look at his things for? What authority, I say, have you to look at his things?"'

She paused dramatically.

'And then they told me,' she said.

'What did they tell you?' Lelia asked avidly.

'That they wanted him for the bombing at the reservoir last night,' said Mrs Percy. 'Can you imagine that? Seamus! The nicest boy you'd meet in a day's walk to be doin' things like that. I got pale, dear, and I had to sit down. "Here, ma," said one of them, "take it easy." "I'm not your ma," I says back at him, "God forbid; and I don't believe that Seamus would do anything like that." "Where is he, then," they asked, "if he isn't here? Why did he run away from the job? Oh, he did it all right," they said. "We know that now. Has he come back for his stuff?" "No," I says. "Then maybe he'll be back for it," they say. "We'll wait for a while." And then up they go into his room and pull it about and they come down with his suitcase. Sit there, they did, for over an hour, lookin' at their watches and lookin' out the window. My Perce didn't half give it to them when he come home! "What you mean knockin' my old lady about?' he says, puttin' his arm around me. "It's a free country," he says. "You can't go about makin' women cry in England," he says. "What about the Magna Carta?" Oh, Perce give it to them all right, he did. Not that they weren't nice. They were. Oh, very polite, callin' me "madam" and Percy "sir", just as if he wasn't a mere postman. But Percy was shocked when he heard it, he was. "Here," he says, "what's this? Me that was fightin' for King and Country for four years until I gets this," and he pulls up his trousers then to show them where the bullet went into his leg, time before we was married and he was in the war. "Me," he says, "to be harbourin' an enemy of the people. I didn't know," he says, "or he wouldn't have been here. Not that he wasn't a nice lad, for an Irishman," he says. "He was, but I wouldn't harbour me own father," he says, "if he was doin' things like that!" A regular scene it was. I tell you. But I couldn't stop cryin'. I like Seamus. The laughs he used to give me. I couldn't believe it, I tell you. It would be like if me own son turned out bad.' She finished her speech in a burst and blew her nose resoundingly.

'Well, it doesn't surprise me,' said Lelia smugly. 'I always thought there was something wrong with him.'

'How very perspicacious of you,' said Maureen.

'Of course,' said Lelia, 'he knew I didn't like him.'

'It was mutual,' said Maureen.

'What annoys me about the business,' said Lelia, ignoring her, 'is that they all seem to be labourers or carpenters or such. It wouldn't be so bad if they were gentlemen.'

'I hope,' said Maureen, 'when you get a bomb in the belly some day that it will be planted by a blue-blooded hand.'

'What's wrong with you, Maureen?' Lelia asked with raised eyebrows. 'You are not yourself today.'

'Oh,' said Maureen. 'I have to go and look at the dinner,' and she went out. Pat was looking after her with worried eyes.

'I better go home myself,' said Mrs Percy, rising. 'I've been in a dither ever since it happened. Can't lay me mind down to anything. I had to come over and see you, knowing how friendly you were. Maureen and Pat will be shocked, I says, when they hear it.'

'Did you not know, Pat, that he was mixed up in the business?' Lelia asked. He felt the two of them looking at him closely.

'No,' he said, 'I didn't. He's the last man I thought of.'

'It just shows you,' said Mrs Percy, 'that you never know, do you?'

She went to the door.

'Do you think they will catch him?' she asked from there.

'I don't know,' said Pat.

'I hope they don't,' said Mrs Percy. 'It's wrong of me, I know, and he was a very bad boy to be going around with bombs. But he was so nice. He'd get up early in the mornings sometimes and before I'd be awake he'd have a cup of tea up on a tray to Percy and myself. When he knew I was very tired. Little things like that. He couldn't be all bad, he couldn't. He didn't mean to hurt anybody, I'll bet. I do hope they don't catch him, or if they do I hope they'll be nice to him.'

Her grey hair was straggling around her head and her eyes were red and her long nose was red, and you could see the apron under her coat. She made a lost sort of pathetic figure standing there working it out. Pat felt sorry. He went over to her.

'Here, Mrs Percy,' he said, 'I'll see you out.'

'I hope they catch him,' said Lelia loudly. 'A nice way for him to repay hospitality and a good job. Biting the hand that feeds him, I call it.'

He said good-bye to Mrs Percy at the door, assuring her again that friendly as he was with Seamus, he knew nothing about his activities. He could see that she wanted an assurance of this, because she was so friendly with Maureen and her people, and she had visions of him being escorted to a cell with Maureen wailing behind him.

'He was great for making you laugh,' she said on her way to the gate.

'You have quite a nice little place here,' said Lelia to him when he went back. She was summing it up. He bet that she had the price of everything in it to a T, hence the derogatory faint praise.

'Would you like to see the rest of it?' he asked, wishing that she hadn't come, that she was anywhere else but here. He wanted to talk to Maureen about Seamus. It was unfortunate that he couldn't get to talk to her on his own, before all the others had broken it to her. Lelia looked casually at the bedroom and the bathroom. Pat, looking at their meagre furnishings, thought they were very nice indeed, and thought how clean and shining Maureen had everything. But to the eyes of Lelia he supposed it was very poor-looking. To hell with her, anyhow, he thought; she'll never have as much happiness in a two-thousand-pound house as we have here. The kitchen then. Maureen bent over a pot on the stove. Her face averted. He knew from the way her chin was that she was displeased. But what could he do? Short of physical violence, Lelia could not have been kept out.

176

'A nice little kitchen.' said Lelia. 'Tiny, isn't it?'

'It suits us,' said Pat.

'Well, I'd better go,' said Lelia. 'George will be home for his dinner. I hope Mother has it ready for him.'

'Excuse me,' said Maureen then, holding her hand to her mouth and hurriedly leaving them. Pat saw that her face was pale as she passed him. They heard her going into the bathroom.

'What's wrong with her?' Lelia asked.

'Her tummy is upset,' said Pat.

'Is that so?' Lelia asked with interest.

They went back to the living-room. Pat found it hard to say anything to Lelia. When you examined your mind there was really nothing you could talk to Lelia about. Lelia didn't mind. To her there were no blanks in any conversation. Maureen joined them shortly.

'I'm sorry,' she said. 'I don't feel so well.'

Lelia looked at her closely, at the slight fattening of the face, the small breasts just a little bigger than she remembered them.

'Why, Maureen,' she said, 'you're pregnant!'

If she had thrown a bomb at the pair of them, she couldn't have got a better effect. Maureen looked at her with a pale petrified face and Pat looked at Maureen with startled attention and growing comprehension. Both of them thought of Maureen's stomach being a little upset, of the powders and bottles they had bought to soothe it. The joys of married life – finding out that your sweetheart had such a vulgar thing as a stomach and other functions apart from the romance. It would have been funny in a way if the discovery had come any other way. After the shock they might have laughed at the powders and things, about how two people could be such fools closing their minds to something they didn't want to happen. But how could you laugh about it when it had come like this, and Lelia of all people!

'Didn't you know?' Lelia asked. 'You are a babe, aren't you?'

She sat on the couch then, a light of enjoyment in her eye.

'Lucky I came at the right time, wasn't it?' she asked. 'It's quite simple dear, really. All you have to do is to get a very hot bath. Hop into it, and while you are in it, drink a half-pint of gin. You won't even notice it after that.'

Jaysus, Pat thought, what brutality!

Maureen didn't speak. She rose from the chair again, looked at Lelia with widened eyes, out of which the tears suddenly started to pour, and then she was gone. He heard the bedroom door closing after her and the slight creak of the spring as she threw herself on the bed.

'My God, you are a bitch, aren't you, Lelia!' said Pat.

'Why, what have I done?' Lelia asked practically enough. 'I only wanted to help her.'

'But holy God,' said Pat, and was stuck there. 'You better go now,' he said then, 'and leave me to handle her. Honest to God, I don't know why you are still alive. It's a wonder some girl hasn't gutted you long ago.'

He took her by the arm and ushered her to the door.

'Girls don't like me much,' said Lelia. 'They're jealous. I always have their boys after me.'

'Well, for the love of God,' said Pat at the door, 'remember you're a married woman now.'

'Oh, George understands me,' said Lelia.

'That's what I'm afraid of,' said Pat grimly.

He smiled good-bye at her. She was a hopeless case really. There was nothing you could do, short of drowning her, but to smile at her. Lelia had only one commandment in her conscience; what Lelia wanted to do was right, what other people didn't want her to do was also right. No half-way house. In that she was like an evil, selfish child, capable of doing deadly damage and being surprised that she didn't receive bouquets for it. He closed the door and came in as she went from the kerb with tearing gears. He stood in the hall and thought. Then he went into the living-room and lighted a cigarette and thought some more, before he moved to the room where he knew Maureen would be lying across the bed, her tears fat on her cheeks. Poor Maureen!

What a way, he thought, for both of them to make such a discovery! Maybe it wasn't true? Alas, he was sure it was. They had both been so ignorant, so stupid in an age when people weren't supposed to be, about things like that. How had it happened? He didn't know. By all his reckoning it shouldn't have happened.

They didn't want it particularly. When you thought of his salary, barely enough with the hard-won commission to keep them going, how in the name of God would they manage all the rest? The Irish always said, God will provide, when the wife said she was expecting her tenth. Maybe there was something in it. He hoped to God there was. They should have been more cautious, of course. It was his fault in a way.

Trouble was, he was a Catholic. Church said, No contraception except in compliance with the natural law. He still remembered the shock of embarrassment he got when he saw his first English rubber-goods shop. Open. Like that. Everywhere. When you went to the barber for a hair-cut, there were the little packages on the glass shelves in front of your nose. Remember the first time? Looking at them for about twenty minutes. Trying to figure them out. What could be in the little rectangular boxes? Green and gold, with a flourish. Had, to his shame, nearly asked. Then he got a better look at the words on the box. He could still feel the flush that rose all over him. Why? Because he had been brought up differently. Came to look on those things as a mortal sin. Still could not think about them without a stirring of embarrassment. Imagine going to Confession. How would you say it? You'd have to tell the priest that you did. 'Father, I used a contraceptive.' God above! He stirred restlessly now, threw his cigarette away, lighted another one.

Ireland too. It was different there. Completely anti-contra. All the jokes were about commercial travellers caught with suitcases of french-letters for the use of the amorous burghers. Smuggled goods. The savour of forbidden fruits. Their sale banned in Ireland. Now and again discreet paragraphs tucked away in the back pages of the newspapers. So-and-so at such-and-such a court today. Fined twenty pounds and costs for the illegal importation into the State of contraceptives. He could see the little paragraphs now, set in minion type. Fearful lest the people might get to know that it was possible to get what-you-know at a price. Why? Because we were all good Catholics? Or because they were afraid of not having enough babies to grow up for export? Now, now, Pat, don't be that way. It's just the innate decency of the Irish people. Oh yeah! Anyhow, thought Pat, that way is out for me. I have been taught too long that it is wrong. To hell with the whole thing. I have to think of us now.

How did he feel? About becoming a father?

Fine, he thought suddenly. I don't mind at all. Imagine that! It was just making the discovery that way. Shades of delicate whispers in the night. Blushing bride. Sinking flaming face on hubby's broad shoulder. There, there, dear. Or the modern miss. Hey, cock, you're going to be a daddy — you must have slipped up somewhere. Pat grinned. He felt good. It didn't matter really. Just that it would have been far nicer if it hadn't been for that bitch Lelia. And then there was Seamus. My God, why did everything have to happen to him and all at the same time?

He straightened his shoulders, threw his cigarette at the fire, tasted his dry mouth. Why, he wondered, did your mouth go dry in a crisis? Why did your chest crave for nicotine? Why did a cigarette, even though you wanted it, taste so insipid?

He went into the room. He sat beside her on the bed. She turned her face into the pillow. Pettishly, like a child. He put his hand on her hair and ruffled it. It was soft and silky, as it had always been.

'Poor Maureen,' said Pat out loud.

That brought her up. She turned and sat on the edge of the bed, produced her handkerchief and blew her nose loudly.

'There's no need to be sorry for me,' she said, her head averted.

'I'm not,' said Pat. 'I think you're wonderful. I think you're the bee's knees. I think you're the best thing that happened since Brian Boru.'

She looked at him, her eyes wide.

'It's all your fault,' she said.

'That's right,' said Pat.

'You and your laws of life,' said Maureen.

'A slight misinterpretation of the rules,' said Pat airily.

She giggled. That's good, he thought, she giggled.

'You can only be wrong once,' said Pat; 'but I'm glad.'

'Are you really?' she asked.

'Yes,' said Pat.

'I hope it keeps fine for you,' said Maureen. 'It's all right for you. What about me?'

'I'll look after you,' said Pat. 'You're my dish.'

'My God!' ejaculated Maureen, starting up. 'The dinner!'

They ran into the kitchen. Every pot on the stove was steaming. The kitchen was fugged. They threw open the windows and Pat flipped at the steam with a dish-cloth. They laughed as they burned their fingers taking the pots away and pouring the meal on to the plates. They sat down then and ate. Pat felt good. He felt light inside and knew that he had a sort of brightness in his eyes. Yes it was all right for him, but what about Maureen? Maureen would be all right too. After all, she was sensible. Everything she did, no matter what, she did well. This would be the same.

'Maureen,' said Pat after a while, 'you didn't take her tip about the gin seriously, did you?'

'Why,' Maureen asked, 'do you want me to?'

'Holy God, I do not,' said Pat.

'It's probably efficacious,' said Maureen, 'coming from Lelia. She ought to know.'

'That's a nasty one,' said Pat.

'She makes me feel nasty,' said Maureen. 'I would have liked to tear her eyes out. What brought her here? Why did you let her come in?'

'She more or less insisted,' said Pat. 'Old pals together. But there's another thing.'

'What?' Maureen asked, a little coldly he thought.

'George is a biggish man now,' said Pat. 'It's about time he took out a nice fat insurance policy. Also he has mechanically propelled vehicles – his car and a van for the shop. And then the shop itself. I think it would be a nice gesture on George's part to switch his insurance over to me. I could do with it. We could do with it now specially. You can't have babies on hay in this day and age. They're a luxury.'

She digested that. 'That's true, I suppose,' she said then reluctantly. 'But I wish you didn't have to.'

'Listen,' said Pat, 'it's George I'll be courting, not Lelia.'

She laughed. 'I hope so,' she said.

They chewed cheese for a time.

'What worries me, Pat,' said Maureen then, 'is the way all this makes me feel changed.'

'How do you mean?' Pat asked.

'I don't feel as stable as I used to,' said Maureen. 'I want to cry for nothing at all. I don't feel like getting down to work in the flat. And a flood of hate comes over me for things. Even for you.'

'Good God,' said Pat.

'I suppose it's natural,' said Maureen. 'But it takes time to get used to the feeling. Sort of as if something was loose inside of you and that you had lost control over something. I can feel myself flying into rages about simple things that don't matter really, even when I'm alone. I wasn't that way before, was I? Even when we had rows?'

'No,' said Pat. 'I always admired you in a row. You had a terrible cool way of saying hard things that made me feel like climbing up the walls.'

'That's what I mean,' said Maureen.

'Forget it,' said Pat; 'you were bound to feel that way.'

'How do you know?' Maureen asked.

'I don't,' said Pat, 'but I suppose everyone does.'

'I wonder,' said Maureen.

They washed the dishes after that and then went into the living-room and sat in front of the fire. Little talk. It was taking time for them to assimilate what was happening to them and the changes it would make in their lives – radical changes. Things would never be the same for them again. They both knew that they were in the middle of something which was the last whistle of good-bye to their personal freedom from one another. The new element would mean something to be shared. Something that in a way you thought would never happen to you. Exciting one minute, filling you full of fear and doubts the next minute. About things you had given little thought to before – mortality and birth.

'If you came home in her car, Pat,' said Maureen suddenly. 'what happened to your bicycle?'

He hesitated a few seconds before replying. He would tell her anyhow. He never kept anything back from Maureen. Besides, he thought, she liked Seamus.

'Well,' he said, 'I was—' The doorbell pealed.

They gave one another a who-could-it-be look.

Probably a client, Pat hoped – a motorist seeing his sign on the window about Third Party Insurance Cover Here.

'I'll get it,' he said, and went into the hall.

He opened the door. His heart started a dull pounding, a sort of a jerk and a pound and then back to normal. Because neither of the two men on the step could be looking for Third Party Insurance. He didn't think so. They were tall burly men, heavy belted coats, one brown, the other a sort of inconspicuous grey. Soft hats placed evenly on their heads. Hard white collars, scarves, faces very well shaved and a little red now from the cold wind. His eyes travelled from the one to the other before they spoke. The man on the step he didn't recognize at all. But a fleeting impression of having seen the other chap came to him. Where? The man in the brown coat spoke first.

'Mr Patrick Moore?' he asked.

'That's right,' said Pat. He was a nice-looking man, fairly young, with grey eyes. His voice was soft and pleasant. There was a distinct smell of tobacco from his clothes. He put a hand in his inside pocket and took out a leather-covered card and flicked it at Pat.

'Smith,' he said. Pat didn't get the rest. He didn't need to. The rabbit pound in his chest had told him they were police when he opened the door. The sort of stray feeling that came back to him – the whiff of a memory of when he was young. Armed police; sandbagged barracks; men with rifles in tearing lorries. Fear. Racing up back streets after singing 'Kevin Barry' to annoy the approaching patrol. Kids. With hearts pounding in the middle of youthful bravado. Just like now. The man in grey was called Wren. Pat looked at him. Where have I seen you before? A picture came to him then. Piccadilly, wasn't it? Calling Jojo and the voice of the kindly stranger in his car, 'You called him Joe . . . His name is Michael . . . You're Irish, aren't you?' Like a voice in a dream. Funny they should both have grey eyes with the same sort of squared-off eyebrows. Not that they were really alike. Just that.

He stepped back. 'Won't you come in?' Might as well get it over with. They stepped past him, removing their hats. Waiting politely for him to close the door. 'In here,' he said, showing them the living-room door. Followed them in.

Maureen stood up, apprehension in her eyes.

'This is Mr Smith and Mr Wren, Maureen.'

Maureen, in a tight voice: 'Hello? Sit down, won't you?'

They, very polite: 'Thank you, Mrs Moore.'

How did they know she was Mrs Moore? She could have been his doxy for all they knew. But they knew. Both of them, sitting colossally on the couch, their big bodies and coats practically hiding it from view.

Maureen sat back on the chair slowly. He sat on the arm of it beside her – to feel the warmth coming from her.

Small talk. 'Very cold weather, isn't it?' 'Ah well, never tell now until the Spring comes.' Glue like that. But kind. Giving time for their racing minds to settle.

'You knew Seamus well, didn't you, Mr Moore?' Smith asking.

'I did,' said Pat. 'He was a grand guy. He was kind to me when I came to work here first. He was staying next door to Maureen before we were married. He was my best man.'

'You know about him now, of course?'

'Yes, Mrs Percy was here a little while ago. She told us. She was crying.'

'Yes, I'm afraid we upset her. She was very fond of him apparently.' A shrug with that. How could anybody be fond of a man like that, a man doing his best to blow up her country-people? To be expected. Couldn't expect them to see that Seamus was Seamus. Not what he did, but how you felt about him. Looking at them he thought of big Seamus and saw his smile, and saw his smile from behind a window with bars on it. Not that! Not for big Seamus, who was part of the air and the sky.

Smith spoke again, casually: 'Did you know that he was engaged in those – eh – activities?'

'No,' said Pat, 'I didn't.' No elaboration. Not that they wouldn't know anyhow, he thought shrewdly. They probably knew by this what he had for his breakfast every morning.

'If you had known, would you have approved?'

That wasn't a fair question. 'I don't know,' said Pat. 'You see, you didn't know Seamus. He was a very nice chap to know and to be friendly with. He came from near my own place at home, not very near. You couldn't help liking him. If I had known I might have tried to use influence on him, if any, to make him stop; but if you mean by your questions that I would have told you what he was at, then I don't think I would. If Seamus had murdered my mother, I wouldn't have been able to do that. He was very nice. You didn't know him.'

Smith laughed. His eyes disappeared in the crinkles around his eyes.

'No,' he said, 'it wasn't a fair question.'

Then right on top of that admission, he shot out another question, 'Do you know Michael Brodel?'

Pat's blank face was sufficient answer. He really didn't know a Michael Brodel. 'No, I don't.' It was only when he had said it that he remembered the other man and his remark, 'I know him as Michael.' He tried not to look at Wren, who was watching him closely.

'You ran after a man in London some months ago,' said Smith then. 'You called him Joe. Who did you think he was?'

'As I told your friend here at the time . . . ' Pat began. They looked at one another; Smith smiled.

'You have a good memory,' he said.

'I never forget a handsome countenance,' said Pat. They laughed. The air became a little warmer.

'I thought he was a friend I knew at home. Not from the same town. We played football against them. From Ballinasloe he was. Name of Joseph Bentley.' That's a big lie anyhow, he thought, but what the hell did they expect me to do? Trot out Jojo's name and occupation and home address when I don't know what the whole thing is about? Let them find out all about Joseph Bentley. There was one, but as far as he knew, Bentley was still there ploughing his father's farm. It was true about the football. Memories of oval balls kicked through the air. Tackling bodies. Running, stocking-covered legs. Shouts. Dinner in the hotel and drinking shandy out of the big silver cup.

He could almost see them memorizing the name and address.

'It must have come as a shock to you to hear about Seamus,' Smith went on.

'It did,' said Pat, and they believed him.

'If he comes back again you'll let us know, won't you?' Smith asked.

'Did you not find him so?' Pat asked.

Smith looked at him quizzically.

'No,' said Smith. 'For an obvious man like him, he disappeared very quick.' Pat felt a load lifting off his mind. It was just for Seamus, himself. He didn't know how he ought to feel.

'Well,' said Pat, 'if he does come back here, I'm sure that you'll know about it yourselves quicker than I will.'

Smith laughed again, and stood up.

'You know, under the Emergency Regulations to cover the present events,' said Smith, rolling his hat in his hand and looking down at it, 'that it is possible to deport people, Irish people, who might make themselves undesirable by assisting others who break the law. You know that, don't you?'

'No,' said Pat. 'I didn't know; but I know it now, and I'm grateful for your telling me.'

He could feel Maureen tensing behind him.

'Just a precaution,' said Smith smiling. 'But then maybe you'd like to be sent back to Ireland, fare paid.'

'I wouldn't,' said Maureen. They looked at her in surprise. She was standing up. Her face was pale. Pat felt disturbed, looking at her.

'Sorry,' said Smith. 'I didn't mean that of course. Mr Moore is a hard-working citizen who behaves himself impeccably. I was just being facetious, to match Mr Moore's humour.'

Pat liked Smith. It could be all a front, his niceness, but he didn't think so. He was a kind man, Pat thought.

They left then, shaking hands. Was that a good sign? Murmured farewells. Talk about the weather on the doorstep. Pat closed the door and waited there until he heard the outside gate closing after them.

He came back into the room again.

He stopped still on the threshold.

Maureen was standing in front of the fire. Her eyes were blazing, her hands were clenched.

'You knew,' she said. 'You gave him your bicycle?'

'I did,' said Pat.

'Why?' she asked. 'Why? What's it got to do with us? Why should they drag us into their lives? What have we done that they should leave us open to police calling in on us? You shouldn't have helped him, do you hear?'

'What should I have done?' Pat asked tightly, trying to keep the coldness out of his voice.

'You should have minded your own bloody business!' she shouted. 'I liked him too. But I wouldn't like him if I knew what he was at. Do you expect me to? I think it's despicable of him to do what he did. Taking us all in. Smiling at us and all the time he was at the other thing. Suppose they arrested you? What would I do? If he was half as fond of you as he said, he wouldn't have let you in for it. What is going to happen if they find out you gave him your bicycle? Why didn't you stop and try to think of me?'

'Look, Maureen,' said Pat desperately, 'you don't understand—'

'I understand enough,' she said. 'You are as bad as he is. It was nothing to do with you, and I hope they find out, do you hear? I hope they do and take you away to hell out of my sight!'

She brushed past him going out. He didn't try to stop her. She reached the room before the tears fell. He heard the key in the lock. Stood looking after her.

What has happened to the even tenor of our ways? he wondered.

What has happened to my bicycle?

12

His bicycle came back. It was a night some six weeks later. Not night really, but evening. Pat had come to realize that there was a difference. At home when you said to a chap or a girl, I'll see you tonight, it was understood that you meant any time at all after tea, which would be at six o'clock. The word "afternoon" was merely an affectation used by polite people with British educations. He had to unlearn quickly enough. When he had talked a wife into letting him see her husband about taking a policy and said, 'I'll be around tonight so'. At her amazed look he had to correct himself and say, 'This evening, I mean.' It was all very confusing for a while, the fact that night really meant night and not tea time. He had to learn to roll his tongue around the word afternoon, which meant just what it said, but he had used it so little up to this that he found it hard on his Irish tongue, but he was intrigued with it. Wasn't it little things like that, he thought that went to make up the difference between foreign peoples who used the same language?

It was destined to be a fairly busy evening, this Tuesday evening in late February.

It was the evening when he had to make up his week's accounts. Tot up what he should have received against what he had in his pocket, hoping to God that he hadn't given wrong change. He had done that several times when he had started. Given a person the change for a pound when it should have only been ten shillings, and discovered it when it was too late and had to suffer the loss. He put his takings on a sheet, subtracted his salary, counted out what went to the company after paying his commission, and the rest was his own. Simple, but it was a headache, and he was inclined to get a bit hot under the collar about it, and a few sharp exchanges generally occurred between Maureen and himself, so it had become Maureen's habit to go and visit her mother every Tuesday evening and leave him to it. I refuse, she had said, to be the nearest implement at hand on which you can vent your arithmetical rage. So she went, and returned again when the storm had passed. He grinned now as he thought about it. It was a practical solution to a problem, and typically Maureen.

He was finished with his own accounts now, but he had other accounts to do. Strange ones.

The Father had called. He was welcome too. He was the only one of Pat's visitors that Maureen really welcomed. The other visitors meant Lelia and George, who had got into the habit of calling occasionally. He was working hard on George for insurance, but it was a hard fight. George, as he kept reiterating, was a 'business man'. Presumably a business man was a man who was under the constant impression that somebody was always trying to do him, so to convince him he had to make out more figures and estimates than an income-tax man for the province of Connacht. Their visits always put Maureen in a bad temper. He couldn't blame her in a way, because while he was sweating over George, Lelia would be giving advice to Maureen. About how to cook, although Lelia never cooked; about sewing and darning, although Lelia neither sewed nor span; about cleaning and china and beds and flies and fleas and cats and dogs and every conceivable domestic problem under the sun. Pat had to admit that it was a bit trying. Lelia as a preacher would convulse a bishop, and when he thought it might be becoming a bit hot, Pat would generally go to the rescue, which eased things for a while until Lelia would put her hand on his hand or lean against him and rather tactlessly bring up little personal things that had happened when Pat had thought she was the answer to the riddle of the universe. No matter how coldly he reacted now or how cautiously, he couldn't persuade the mind of Lelia that he had really changed his thoughts about her, that he now regarded her as being the answer to the Theory of Relativity.

190

But Maureen liked the Father. He didn't try to convert her. He just came and sat deep in the chair and smoked his pipe, and had a cup of tea and talked about a lot of interesting things, so that time flew when he was with them and he made you feel invigorated and alive when he had gone. Maureen was still 'my little heretic' to him, and he was fond of her. Anybody could see that. His coming this evening had been funny. The usual rat-tat-tat. You know, the one that goes to the rhythm of: 'How's your oul one?' Pause. 'Très bon.' Or 'Game-ball,' depending on the way you were brought up.

'Come on out,' he had shouted when they opened the door, 'and see what I have!'

They went out, expecting to see God knows what, and were duly surprised to see an old bicycle leaning against their wall. It was very high — must have been built in the penny-farthing period, but it was gleaming with new paint and new pedals and new tyres. A most dignified-looking crock.

'Isn't it lovely?' the Father asked, waving at it. 'It's a present. I got a present of it. Thank God there are still some good Christians left in the world. I've been complaining for months about my corns. How hard it is on me to be chasing erring Catholics of the parish with them. A subterfuge really,' he said then, coming in to the fire, 'because I was hoping that somebody would take the hint. And they did. What a nice thought! It makes life worth living, so it does, to get something like that.'

'They could have made it a new bicycle,' said Maureen.

'Now, now,' said he, standing tall, his back to the fire and his hands holding up his coat-tails to get the heat better, a habit he always had. Pat bet he'd even do it in summer when there was no fire at all. 'Let us not look a gift horse in the mouth. It's a very dignified-looking bicycle and I'm sure it will add considerably to my stature to be seen riding around on it. Oh, I'll have all the Irish buckos on the hop now that I'm mechanized, so to speak. I couldn't get near half of them up to this on account of my poor feet. I'll round them up now, all right, the rascals, and get them to go to Holy Mass on Sundays. I'll become the terror of the parish, so I will. A tall, gaunt black figure on a bicycle.' He laughed heartily at this picture of himself. He was genuinely pleased, Pat thought, to have been made a present of an old bicycle that another man would be ashamed to be seen up on.

Pat looked at him more closely then, and for the first time he noticed that the Father's clothes were far from being new, that there were places in his clothes that had been carefully darned. It was hard to notice them in the black cloth. And when he raised his arm you could also see that the ends of his shirt-cuffs were slightly frayed. It struck him that it was not all tea and roses to be a priest in England, where congregations were small and mainly poor – not as poor as that, but with just enough money to keep themselves going. And out of their pittances the Father had to build his church and keep it going. You forgot you were not in Ireland, where everyone was a Catholic and where there were huge churches on every side and enough money to keep all of them going. He couldn't think of any priest at home who would have been so overjoyed because he was presented with an old bicycle.

It was another thing that made you realize the difference between yourself and those people whose language you spoke.

So the Father sat and had his cup of tea, and then he had pulled out the tattered looking copy-book. 'I want you, Pat, like a good man,' he said, 'to go over these figures and tot them up for us. To tell you the truth, we're not much good at the sums down there, any of us. You might be called an actuary owing to your profession. These are the parish accounts for the year. We've added them all up ourselves and we think they are right. But as you know, the Church is only infallible about matters of faith and morals. There's nothing laid down in the rubrics about mathematics.'

This gave him another good laugh. He always brought his hands together when he laughed, the tips of his fingers touching, and he would lay them on his chin and throw back his head – infectious.

'All right, Father,' said Pat. 'I'll do it, if only to see that you are not swindling the income-tax people.'

This gave him another laugh.

'Ah, the poor creatures,' he said. 'I feel sorry for them. But what can we do? Nobody would be happier than myself if the day

192

ever dawned that we would be owing them something. But alas! Ah well!'

So they had tea and talked and then Maureen put on her coat to go around to her mother, and the Father rose too and said he would be a bit of the way with her, that it would add pride to her walk to be seen in the company of his aristocratic bicycle.

He turned at the door. 'By the way, Pat,' he said, 'Jack is back.'

'He's what!' said Pat, standing up.

'Yes,' said the Father, 'he's back. Looking very well too. Cured, they say. Mary is very proud of him.'

'That's great,' said Pat.

'Um,' said the Father, choosing his words because Pat had talked to him about his stay in Jack's. 'You might call in on them. Nice gesture, you know. It would please them very much, you know. He's changed a lot. For the better. He was sick, you know, Pat, as I told you. It wasn't really his fault. It was in the mind, poor chap.'

Pat thought about it. 'Of course,' he said then, 'I'll go and see them.' He thought it was worth it to see the way the Father's face lighted up. Another small bit off the multifarious load of lives he carried about with him.

'Good man, good man!' he said. 'Well, good-bye, good-bye, and don't get these accounts into a bigger mess than they're in now.' This got him out on another laugh, so Pat set to and tackled his own accounts and then tackled the Father's.

It was a sobering experience. When it was all totted up and added up and subtracted, what it meant in effect was that the Father and the two curates were endeavouring, when all their bills were paid – the upkeep of the house and the small church – to live on a sum of money that varied each week between four pounds and five pounds. No wonder, Pat thought, that his clothes are darned. No wonder he takes such pleasure from the gift of a second-hand bicycle. It made him think that life in England wasn't an beer and skittles for the priest any more than for the labourer. Was that good for the priest? Certainly, Pat thought, he had never met a man from whom goodness so emanated as from the Father. Because it was such a struggle, was it? Because they were near to the Man who had instructed them about giving up everything material, living on the charity of the people? Pat didn't know. He was sorry in a way to have seen it. It sort of bared the Father's poverty. Not that he would mind. It was comforting in one way to know that a priest was finding it as hard, if not harder, to live as Maureen and himself on their small wages. Ups and downs. It was nearer the kernel, here – the survival of the fittest, despite its state of high civilization.

Further cogitation was interrupted by the ringing of the doorbell. Pat muttered a curse and then went out to open it.

'Hello, Pat,' said Jojo.

Yes, it was!

Pat's first impulse was to let a great shout out of him, calling his name to the high heavens, and then he remembered the last time he had done it and its consequences. So he restrained himself apart from the shout in his eyes.

'Oh, hello, Jojo,' he said quite coolly, as if he had been playing snooker with him yesterday evening, instead of the lads from the office.

It shook Jojo a little, but not much.

'I brought back your bicycle,' he said.

Which shook Pat. 'Oh,' he said.

'You might ask me in for a minute,' said Jojo a little impatiently.

'The last time I saw you,' said Pat, 'taught me not to be impulsive any more.'

'Oh, that,' said Jojo. 'I'm sorry about that. It was one of the reasons that I brought the bicycle myself.'

'Come on in,' said Pat, holding the door wide. Jojo was wearing a cap and a soiled raincoat, belted. Pat idly noticed how Jojo's quick glance took in the hall and the rooms beyond a little nervously before he followed Pat into the living-room. To gain a little time Pat went to the fire and stirred it with the poker. Then he turned and faced him. Jojo was looking around the room, more from caution, Pat thought, than assessment. His cap was in his hand. His black hair was as thick as ever and inclined to turn over on his forehead, but his square face was a lot thinner. The bones were pressing against the skin and there were dark circles under his eyes. Pat felt sorry then. He spoke more warmly.

'Here, Jojo,' he said, 'come on and take off your coat and sit down at the fire.'

'Thanks,' said Jojo, opening his coat, but not removing it, and sitting on the chair which Pat placed for him. Sitting on the edge of it cautiously looking at the fire, his eyes distant. That was what made Pat feel uncomfortable. The distance between them. It was as if Jojo had on an invisible cloak of impenetrable material that he was pulling around him.

'You shouldn't have shouted my name like that,' said Jojo. It was the sort of apology that you would make to a child with whom you have been too severe when the child has done wrong. 'They were watching me then. They are always watching me. They don't know my name. You shout my name. They find out who you are and where you came from and the name of your friends, and it's easy to find out who I am.'

'I see,' said Pat. There was silence between them then for a time. The embarrassed silence of I wish he hadn't come, I wish that I hadn't come.

'I didn't know,' Pat burst out. 'Here I am in London. I had heard you were in England somewhere. And then right out of the blue I see you. I felt like jumping over the moon. I wanted to meet a friend just then. You seemed to be the answer to a prayer. It was no wonder I shouted after you. How was I to know that it would injure you?'

Jojo looked up at the sound of his aggrieved voice, his eyes cleared and he smiled. For a moment he was the Jojo of long ago, with the quirk and the mallet-like humour, devastating.

'Ah, I'm sorry, Pat,' he said. 'It was just that you startled me out of my wits. I would have bitten the nose off me own mother then. It was only afterwards that I thought about it being you, and how nice it would have been to have roared at you too and slapped your back, and we could have gone to a pub and had a pint, and talked about normal things, and started the Do-You-Remember. It would have been nice. Nice and normal.' His voice was wistful. Eyes on the fire for a moment, head on one side. He leaned back in the chair then, fumbling in his pocket for cigarettes. He captured them – a small Gold Flake, crumpled packet, flattened cigarettes. Offered them. Pat took one, shoved

195

it in his mouth and held a match to Jojo's. Noticed how deeply stained were his fingers, how thin his hands had become, but still so muscular. Nobody at school could break Jojo's grip. He was the champion handshaker. His nails were cut short, almost to the quick.

'Tell me all about yourself,' he went on, when he had sucked smoke into his lungs. 'Seamus tells me you are married. Is she in? Where is she?'

'She's not in,' said Pat. 'She's out with her mother. Tell me, Jojo, how is Seamus? Where is Seamus?'

'Seamus?' asked Jojo. 'Seamus is away. Seamus is at home now, at this moment probably drinking a porter in a Connemara pub or out poaching' salmon on a Connemara lake. Seamus is at home with his mountains.'

'That's great,' said Pat heartfully.

'You liked Seamus?' Jojo asked quizzically.

'Yes,' said Pat. Enough said.

'He was a good man,' said Jojo. 'Useful too. Adroit for a man of his size. That was his trouble — his size. He was too notice-able. Well, he's all right now, Seamus is. If the others over there leave him alone. They'll have their eye on him, of course. He sent his regards to you. Said that some day he hoped you would meet when he was going into the market to sell a load of turf.'

What pictures that conjured up!

'I better go now,' said Jojo, standing up.

'Oh no,' said Pat. 'Don't go yet. Will you have a cup of tea? You can't leave my house, dammit, without having a cup of tea.' He felt that he had to hold on to Jojo, to try and get back a bit. If Jojo went now without their getting some basis, he felt that something would have gone from his values. He noticed that Jojo had become thin. They were almost of a height. But Jojo was no longer young, he thought. Jojo was a man. His face, almost hag-gard, settling into lines. 'Come on out and I'll show you the place.'

Jojo considered it.

Before answering he walked to the window and flicked back the curtain with a practised movement. Looked. Turned.

'All right,' he said. 'Let's see the mansion.'

Pat showed him the bedroom, told him how much everything cost, and then went into the kitchen and put on a kettle. While waiting for it to boil he talked about Maureen. How he had met her and the job he was doing. He talked too much. He knew it, and Jojo knew it, but there was nothing else for it. He couldn't burst back into the do-you-remember straight away, not with Jojo taut the way he was, every nerve of him seeming to be on the alert. Got a cake from the cupboard and brought in the cups and things on a tray and put it on the table. Drank tea and ate cake. Still talking. All small stuff. Jojo trying to show interest. Eventually the well had to dry. They were smoking cigarettes after their tea. It was Jojo who spoke.

'You don't really understand, do you, Pat?' he asked.

Pat thought it over, sighed, leaned back, and in a voice far different from his former prattle, he said, 'No, Jojo, I can't understand.' He tried to think, to bring out his words, words perhaps, that had been gathering questioningly in him since he had found Jojo. 'I never thought when we were at school. Even when I had left school. I knew you liked history, that you were very good at history. I can still see the 99 per cent marked on your Leaving Certificate. Mine was so low. We laughed about that. I could never remember dates and I always got my battles mixed. You never did. I remember you didn't like the Government much. But that wasn't strange at the time. None of us did. We were all agin it. But I didn't think that you were serious.'

'Look, Pat,' said Jojo, 'it's not a matter of being serious. It's a matter of fact.' He spoke carefully, almost relaxed, again as if he was lecturing a child. 'The roads of Ireland are littered with stone monuments to the dead. Many centuries of them. They were erected because some day men thought the voices of the dead would be lifted in a song of freedom.'

'So they were,' said Pat, wondering at how calmly and low they were speaking, almost in a whisper. 'They won a Government.'

'They won a Government,' said Jojo; 'they didn't win a nation. And that's why I'm here, why I may possibly be left here too, but without the monument. That Government that was the heir of the revolution betrayed the revolution. They didn't get

Ireland. They got a castrated corpse. I am here so that we may restore the corpse to full virility.'

'But why here, Jojo?' Pat asked desperately. 'What have the ordinary tom-tits got to do with an eagle?'

'Look,' said Jojo earnestly. 'There is only one way to make an eagle give up its spoils, and that's to drop powder, scalding powder, on its tail. That or get into the nest of the eagle and frighten its young, so that the mother will drop the spoils from its talons to protect its eaglets. They have to squawk beforehand, though.'

'Look, Jojo,' said Pat. 'I meet about three or four hundred people here every week. They are a mixture. They are English and Scots and Welsh, Cockneys and suburbanites and emigrants and immigrants and exiles. Listen, Jojo, they know no more about Ireland, the ordinary people of them, than a Fiji islander. They think that Belfast is the capital city, when they think of it at all. Dublin is a vague spot on a map which they had to learn at school. They are surprised to hear that we have universities and what they regard as the amenities of modern living. One in a thousand of them might have heard of the Black and Tans or 1916. Names that are household words to us leave them blank. They have never been to blame for anything that happened in Ireland. It's the people that ruled them.'

'A people,' said Jojo, 'are responsible for their rulers. You say they don't know anything about Ireland. Well, they know now, don't they? They have come awake to the fact of Ireland and what has been done to it. Isn't that what we wanted to do, isn't it, all our lives, to make them aware, so that they would say to their rulers that we must have justice?'

'But some of them have died,' said Pat uncomfortably.

'Innocent people have died with the wicked in all wars,' said Jojo.

'I'm afraid, Jojo,' said Pat, 'that I could never see it. All I want is a chance to live my own life. There is a Government at home. Even if I don't agree with it, I would obey it. If they called me out to join an army and go and get back the part of the country that was lost, I would go reluctantly, because I don't really care, Jojo. What I care about is the number of poor people there are in the country, with empty bellies. You ought to remember those

too. We lived with them. It seems to me that it is more important to give them food and good houses and a way of life than it
is to go after the other thing.'

Jojo stood, up.

'Poor Pat,' he said. 'The poor old puzzled man. You can't see,
Pat, and I'm afraid I can't show you. It's only much later on that
you'll understand. All the men who went out in Easter Week
weren't understood either, and the original battles were all won
by a handful of men, without the support of the people. The
people were like you then too, Pat. They said the Government
we have is good enough for us; let us be satisfied with it, in the
name of God, and have no trouble. Mostly, Pat, freedom is not
won by the masses, but despite the masses. So you can remember that in the days to come. I know you, Pat. You're not made
of the stuff to be able to do the things I feel are right. I don't
blame you for it, either, because there are so many like you, all
blinded by the carrot tied to a stick in front of the donkey's nose.
Look – have a good look at me, Pat, and tell me what you see.'

Pat looked at him.

'I don't see the Jojo,' he said then slowly, 'that I knew one
time. You've gone away, Jojo. And to tell the truth to God, I
don't know whether to envy you for an intensity and determination about something that I could never feel, or to be sorry for
you because I feel that you are wasting it all on a shadow. I don't
know. I don't know at all. I wish to Christ that we were all young
again and that we never had to grow up.'

There was so little resemblance now to the Jojo diving off the
rock into the sea in the summer and stretching his compact body
on the hot sands, little resemblance between that Jojo and this
gaunt young-old man with the fire in his eyes and the determined
intensity in every fold of him from the toe to the crown. He was
as if he had been tempered in a forge fire, and now he was as he
was and nothing would change him. He made Pat feel bloated
and spineless and in the wrong.

'You see, Pat,' said Jojo, 'how the years have changed us.'

'The short years,' said Pat.

'That's right,' repeated Jojo, 'the short years.' He thought
over that for a few moments. Then he said, 'Well, I'd better go.'

'I'll see you as far as the bus,' said Pat. 'Or is it the train that you're taking?'

'There are more people in trains,' said Jojo, which brought Pat up short as he struggled into his coat. All this seemed like a dream. It couldn't he happening, not to them, not to Jojo. By the police and the outraged citizens he would be regarded as a brutal, callous criminal. No allowance to be made for the fire in his eyes and the belief that burned in him. His belief that what he was doing was right and just. Again, like Seamus, it wasn't these things that mattered, but the persons of Seamus and Jojo themselves, what they were like inside. Jojo, if he was put to it, would never hit a poor dog on the sconce with a milk bottle as he, Pat, had done. He had a way with animals when he was at home. The special way that some people have. A snarling dog would drop his head and his tail and come under Jojo's bent hand to be patted. He was the same with horses. He had the touch, they said about him. And yet here he was and here was Pat, going out of the house casually, unconsciously taking the back way, speeding their feet across the busy main road, getting again into the shelter of another tree-lined avenue, discreetly lighted, with a breath of relief. Pat was more conscious of fear than Jojo. Jojo never relaxed. Time had made him that way. He seemed to be watching with his whole body, where Pat just watched with his nerves and danced at shadows. The long avenue under the embankment, which Pat's mind shied from, and then across, and further along, and a turn to the right and on to the main road, Pat feeling that Jojo was naked under the green daylight-lighting tubes.

And then the station. They hadn't talked. There was just nothing to talk about. Jojo had put his youth behind him. All that mattered to him now was today and tomorrow. Pat couldn't seem to get away from yesterday and today, comparing them. Is that because I'm pretty useless and lazy, he wondered, because I don't want to face tomorrow? But all the same he knew that Jojo was conscious of the fact that they were walking together and it warmed him a little. Pat thought so. He felt the same and told himself defensively that if they had had more time together he might have got Jojo back. Jojo would have laughed if he heard that, because yesterday had really ceased to exist for him, and it was the fact that it hadn't for Pat that made Jojo like him, however exasperated he might feel at his lack of consciousness about the problems of his castrated country.

They stopped on the sheltered side of the station.

'So long, Pat,' said Jojo, taking his hand, 'and thanks for the tea.'

His hands were cold, his fingers as strong as ever. Sure of themselves, like Jojo.

'So long, Jojo,' said Pat. 'I'm glad you had the tea. It was nice seeing you again, only I wish it had been different. If you ever want me you know where to find me.'

'I don't think I will want you, Pat,' said Jojo. 'We're like the saint and the sinner, and the man who couldn't tell one from the other or which was which. I am alone, Pat. And that's the best way to be. For me. A man is his own best company. At least you can't betray yourself.' His voice was bitter. But he had already left Pat and was thinking in terms of something completely outside them, something about which Pat felt he didn't want to know. He didn't want to think away from the fact that he had loved Jojo and that this was a bit of Jojo, and he kept his mind firmly on that track.

They parted. Pat walked home slowly. Why do things like this have to happen to me, he wondered, to make everything complicated? Why can't things flow along in a nice easy manner, nice and dull and ordinary, so that I don't have to feel twisted up inside going from one emotion to the next? He felt very sad about Jojo, like you would feel sad about losing something valuable. They had got on always, disagreed about things but never to the detriment of a link that bound them. The link was gone now.

There is an antidote to every ill; a pain in one place is lessened by a pain in another place, like a red-hot poker placed on a wound.

Maureen met him at the door. 'There are some people to see you,' she said, her voice tight.

He groaned. Lelia and George he supposed. God, not now. I don't want this and the row with Maureen that is bound to happen when they've gone. He had the row with Maureen all right, but it wasn't about George and Lelia.

Mary and Jack were sitting in the room. Jaysus, Pat thought, Maureen could have told me! It wasn't fair not to. Probably, he thought, she wanted me to get the shock that she got herself. Mary first, colour in her face and was it an appeal in her eyes?

'We came over to see you, Pat,' she said. 'Look, he's back! Doesn't he look wonderful?'

Pat shook hands with Jack, but he didn't look wonderful.

'This is great, Jack,' he said. Jack's grip was flaccid, but then it had always been so.

'I feel grand now,' said Jack.

He was dressed in his navy-blue suit that he had always worn on Sundays. It was hanging very loosely on his body. The shoulders of it drooped over his shoulder-blades. It hung in folds behind him, because he wasn't able to fill it. Sweet God, Pat thought, he must be nothing but a skeleton. It was his face that was hardest to look at. His bald spot had become much wider and the hair cropped closely around it had become almost white. The bone structure of his face was very prominent and the skin had a sort of yellow pallor. Frightening, sort of. Until you looked at his eyes. They pulled you up and took your mind off his pallor. The eyes weren't the Jack's eyes he had known. They were quiet eyes, tired eyes inclined to fix themselves on you. It was just as if someone had taken them out of his head and held them over a fire until the fever and restlessness had been burned out of them.

'I think he looks marvellous,' said Mary. 'Don't you?'

Pat laughed. 'Well,' he said. 'He could do with a bit of fattening. A proper skinny-ma-link you are, Jack.'

Jack laughed, a real laugh. He seemed grateful to Pat for the remark.

'That's what I tell Mary,' he said. 'You can see right through me. I'm like a walking X-ray picture, so I am, but she tries to tell me that I'm not.'

'Well, he won't be long putting it on,' said Mary defensively. She was glad at the way he was talking, glad that he was refusing to be treated as a child. That's what her first inclination had been.

'I'm thinking of going home to Ireland for a while, Pat,' said Jack. 'To go home for a while — it would be nice maybe. Build me up again. Do you think that's a good idea?'

'It's an excellent idea,' said Pat.

'That's what I thought,' said Jack, 'and then when I come back perhaps people will have forgotten that I was in a lunatic asylum.'

He said it quite calmly. Pat heard Mary pulling in her breath.

'I enjoyed it, in a way,' said Jack. 'Afterwards, when I knew where I was. You don't mind when you wake up. You have become used to the people around you. It makes you think too. And, of course, it's nice to come home. Oh, so nice to come home.'

Maureen in the background felt like crying, but as she told herself, that was nothing, since she could cry now at the drop of a hat.

'When you know you are better, it makes you feel almost sorry for all the others, mostly very nice people, who will never get better. There's a consolation in that, a sad sort of consolation. They would have let me come home sooner, but they were trying to fatten me up. I couldn't be fattened, not until I came home. It's changed too. Did you see what Mary has done to the house?'

'I did,' said Pat. 'She's a great woman. It seems to be filled with sunshine.'

'That's it, bright, nice and bright,' said Jack. 'Ye must come over and see us before we go away. You and Maureen. She's a nice wife you got. How did you manage to capture one like that?'

'The old personality,' said Pat, laughing.

'The old bully,' said Maureen.

'We better go,' said Jack, rising slowly. 'I'm supposed to go to bed early for a while. I like going to sleep. You know all the time that when you wake up in the morning you'll be at home. Isn't that great, now?'

'Terrific,' said Pat.

'What I want to do now,' said Jack, 'is to hurry up and get fat and get back on the job. They held the job for me. Wasn't that nice of them?'

'Why wouldn't they?' asked Pat. 'Aren't you the best ganger

they ever had? But you'll have to get the muscles on again. You can't tackle the lads unless you have the old muscle.'

Jack laughed. Mary was delighted. He could see it in her eyes. No doubt there. She knew Jack was all right. She had always known that he would be all right.

'Thanks,' she whispered to Pat, before going out to the gate with Maureen. Pat walked behind with Jack.

'I notice,' said Jack, in a sort of whisper, 'that you are to be a father. I hope it's a boy, I do.'

'Lucky dip,' said Pat. 'Anything that comes, I'm ready for it.'

'Jim will be glad,' said Jack, 'to know that you've settled down. I'll tell him all about it. I'll be glad to see Jim again.'

'He'll be glad to see you,' said Pat, and then an idea suddenly came into his head. He didn't give himself any time to think about it. It just seemed a sort of an answer to all that had gone on between Jack and himself. 'If you're back from Ireland in time,' he said, 'how would you like to be a godfather?'

It stopped Jack. He looked closely at Pat in the light of the street lamps. Went to say something. Stopped. Was it to say Do you mean it? He didn't. He walked on.

'I'd like that, very much,' he said, and Pat knew he meant it and knew that he had been right to say it.

Pat told Maureen about it back in the house again. She didn't mind. She was sorry for Jack. She said that he went through her, that she couldn't see in this old man the sort of monster that Pat had made him out to be.

It was a little later that she thought about the other thing.

'The bicycle came back,' she said, looking at him with fear in her eyes, and anger behind the fear.

So he told her. She told him. The safety-valve went into operation. It ended the usual way. She slept alone behind a locked door, and Pat had the couch.

13

It was late October of that year when Pat's life started to whirl its way to a climax.

It was a period of time when the whole world seemed to be holding its breath and the word *crisis* was the most overworked word in the language of all nations. Even the drums in Africa must have been beating it out. There was nothing else of importance in the newspapers. All subsidiary news was read casually and with wonder that other things could be happening anywhere. Pat started his rounds in the morning with it and carried it through the days with him. His memory of it afterwards was to be the blank, breathless faces of the housewives handing him out his few shillings. A slight layer of careless dust seemed to have fallen over the world. The most hardworking of housewives forgot to do their million chores in order to stand and talk with folded arms and furrowed frowns to their neighbours, or to the milkman or to the postman, or to the club man calling for the pennies to bury them when they died.

It was epitomized for Pat in the dirt that was allowed to be beaten into the red tiles or the green tiles on the doorsteps of the houses. Every other time those tiles would be gleaming and shining, wet or fine, and frequently the women would have to rise from their knees when he called to put aside the tin of Cardinal polish, wipe their hands on their aprons, say, 'You are a nuisance, you are,' in order to go and collect their books and money. It would be as much as your life was worth to step on the gleaming red of them. Even the dogs avoided them with their paws, from ingrained habit. Husbands who had been trained early went in the back way in order not to soil the beauty of them. The tiles were the signs of the times. Like the little toy donkey with the string for a tail. When his tail was damp it was going to rain. When it was dry it would be fine. When Pat started to notice the neglected tiles he knew that the bottom was to fall out of the world.

The crisis had done another thing too, he thought. It had rubbed out Jojo and the others as if they had never been. It was the defeat of their cause. People had been afraid. Afraid of what? Of bombs. What kind of bombs? Almost kindly bombs. They would just be like the swish of damp matches fizzling in a tunnel in comparison to what could happen. Nobody believed it could happen to them. As it happened, it didn't then. They got a small breathing spell, to collect their thoughts and to polish their tiles. The tiles would be neglected again, but never for so long, never in such a colossal hush as had descended now on the universe.

A static period? Oh yeh, Pat thought. If it was a static period, it was filled with the quickened beat of anticipating pulses. Not regular. Speedy and remaining speedy, even, he imagined, in sleep. The world woke in the mornings and thought, and their hearts jumped and pumped at the pulses. The newspapers kept them pulsing throughout the morning. And the radios and the conversations kept them at it until bedtime. Faces everywhere were long and blank and worried. People walked faster and then slowly. Schedules were adhered to in fits and starts. The protective cloak of silence was discarded. You would have chatted with the Devil himself if he had a bit of fresh news or a new light to throw. Pat imagined that it was acting like a gigantic purgative on the whole nation. They would even, in a way, be sorry and feel a little let down when it was over, before they went back to polishing their tiles.

And this was the time he had to choose to lose his job. It came from trying to assert himself. It was paying-in day in the office.

Mostly young men, all the agents, and they wore the worried look of the housewives – the what-was-going-to-happen look. They even paid a little respect to the older men who had suddenly brought out of the dusty cupboard their memories of 'the last one'. And where they were, what they did. It didn't impress the young men. Not now. They wanted no part of it. The blokes that mattered had better settle it, or else. Not for me, chum. I've got my own life to lead. Why, I remember my old man goin' off. Not so long ago. Here, who do they think we are? Worry. Fear. But principally they were taken on the hop. It was too quick. They should have been warned about it. A few men, it is true, tried to warn them. But they might as well have been St Johns in a desert. People didn't want to listen, anyhow. The newspapers sold cotton-wool with all issues so that ordinary decent people wouldn't have to listen to the croakers. All was confusion. Neglect. No talk now about how I talked Mrs Brown into a new bob a week. Or how I insured old Jones' car, even though he had it already with that other bastard from the other insurance company. No talk now about what a smart guy what-you-may-call-him was. Know what he did? Spotted that this lidy – he called on her for the National Health, see – just that. Her old man had this other insurance company. Know what then? Saw she was up the spout, that she was goin' to have a biby. So keeps his eye on her. Nips into the hospital after she had it, the very next day. Flowers and a little note. Know what then? Covers the kid for a penny a week and then captures the old man afterwards for ten bob a month. Smart that? Coo, was the other guy from the other company mad? Told her off proper, he did. Smart though. No looking for the inspector now to come and talk a prospect into taking out a hundred-pound policy or a five-hundred-pound policy, or to come and talk a prospect into a house purchase. Houses? A lot of good it would be now to own your own house. So what? You buy it. Then a bomb, swosh, and you ain't got a house any more. I should think. No bleeding fear, old man. They won't do. Nobody will do. Not until something happens and we can all draw our breath again.

Accounts were checked with a lack-lustre eye by the assistants. No arguments now about drawing too much commission or about the indignant letter Mrs Smith wrote to the office because you had hit her Alsatian on the skull with a milk bottle. Such things. Such behaviour. 'I won't have that savage come near my home any more.' He didn't. It was switched to another agent who had a way with dogs. He ran away every time he saw one come within ten miles of him. So if the old lady had her dog loose, her premiums, uncollected, accumulated. I should get the behind torn out of my britches just to please that old bee.

The manager wanted to see Pat in his office. Mr Johnson was very breezy. He seemed to thrive on crises. The more people fear death, said Mr Johnson, the better for our business. Maybe it will make them think. You can't sing a song of regret to a daisy that's growing over your putrefying corpse. Not that Mr Johnson worried. He was a very good manager and kind to his staff. Treated them like children. Set their feet on the right road. Not much pep talk about him. Not like the official pepper-uppers who addressed them *en masse* occasionally. 'You gotta believe in your wares. You gotta love Mrs Jones like she was your own mother. It is your problem if Mr Jones dies and Mrs Jones is left destitute. It is up to you to take care of her before that happens. Make him see the light. For the love of your district. The Managing Director has his eye on you. There are no limits to what you can do. Look at me! [They all thought of this one.] I started out a 'umble agent in such a place. My first year I increased my book by so-and-so. My second year I was at the 'ead of the Company list. Brought up to Chief Office [the voice here always fell to a soft, awe-inspired caress: Chief Office? Heaven. Shangri-la. Persian Market. Buckingham Palace.] "My boy," the M.D. says, "you are a credit to the Company. The Company [Company? God. The King. The Pope. The Sultan of Baghdad. The Emperor of Japan] is proud of you. You will go far." 'Blow the nose on the handkerchief. Dramatic pause. Tears of emotion presumed. Not knowing, the poor bastard, that all the agents down in the hall, while looking very affected as to face, were blowing raspberries with their pursed lips; that sizzling asides were coming from the corners of mouths. They had heard it all before. The rise of the 'umble. Local boy makes good. From newsboy to big maggot. Garret to castle. Woodbines to Havanas. Wheelbarrows to Rolls-Royces. They were sick and tired of Alone I did it. As if they wouldn't too if they got the chance, or were ruthless enough, or got a leg-up, or gave a damn. Finish of meeting. I will be here until Monday. I want all of you to turn in good sound prospects. I will go with you and clinch them. Furious thinking

– of the hard nuts that couldn't even be cracked with a sledge-hammer. Of a scurrying to find a prospect. To show what a model agent you were. Anything to keep the old boy quiet. To show what a good lad you were. That it was about time you got a bit of promotion. So that you could go to Chief Office, Heaven, Shangri-la, the Persian Market, Buckingham Palace too, and be patted on the head by the M.D. God bless him, and let God put it into his fat head to give poor, hard-working agents a salary they might be able to live on.

Mr Johnson wasn't like that. He had a bit of the jargon. God's disciple! But you couldn't blame him for that. Pat knew he had got a bit of it himself – the Simon Pure stuff. That you were a benefit to humanity. Nothing sordid like money and commission entered into it at all. The Priest of the Premium. The Helper of the Poor and Afflicted. Tears in your eyes when you had to lapse a policy. For the sufferer's own benefit. It didn't matter that if you let it go on too long you yourself would have to pay what was owing after twelve weeks. Surcharge. Your own fault. Can't be soft with these darling children who pay on policies and then can't afford to keep them going. The Benevolent Teacher of the Uneducated.

'What's wrong, Pat?' Johnson asked kindly.

'How do you mean?' Pat asked.

'You're slipping,' said Johnson.

'Am I?' Pat asked, his eyes wide. 'In what way, Mr Johnson?'

'Your kitty is blank,' said Johnson.

Your kitty is blank – your cupboard is bare. It was the same thing. When you put on a bob a week policy, that was a bob in the kitty and you could charge nine shillings commission on every sixpence per week added. If your kitty was blank it meant you couldn't charge commission, which meant that you had only your basic salary minus unemployment insurance, minus national health insurance, minus the half-dollar a week you paid towards your guarantee, minus the three bob a week on your new bicycle, minus the twenty-five bob a week rent, and after that where were you? You were out in the cold. You were running to the little bit in the Post Office and closing your mind to how often you had run to it lately and how little there was left. And you with a baby coming. And this wasn't the Garden of Eden, where new babies could run around naked and pluck their food free from the trees. Not that they would have allowed new babies into the Garden of Eden. They let one in once and look what happened! We had a crisis in the year of Our Lord 1938.

'I'm afraid the kitty is blank all right, Mr Johnson,' said Pat. And so am I, he thought.

'That's what I said,' said Mr Johnson. 'I don't know why. You were very good when you started. You put on new business very quickly. Sound business too. But not lately. You have written up very little new business lately. Is it because you're not trying?'

Trying, Pat thought. Why? Because I just don't like the whole business. Might as well confess that to myself now. But confessing it to Johnson was another matter. Shilly-shally, shilly-shally said Pat to himself furiously. It seemed to him that for the last year he had done nothing but shilly-shally, that he had allowed his life to be moved around for him by other people. Everything that had happened to him had happened outside of himself, because he had allowed himself to be drawn along, in the wake of other people's tide. Time I stopped drifting, he thought, time I tightened up my own lip and followed my own life to a conclusion.

'I suppose I'm just a bad agent, that's all,' he said.

'Now, I wouldn't say that,' said Johnson. 'Your collections are good. But I notice going back over it that you had to pay a lot of surcharge. Not lapsing policies in time. Why was that?'

'Carelessness,' said Pat, knowing it wasn't, that he did it because he hadn't the heart to be lapsing people, always giving them another chance, another chance, saying maybe next week they'll give me something. He should have known. When a thing goes that far it's too late to save it. But he always tried, no matter how many lessons he learned. There you are again. He lacked ruthlessness — or was it just plain indecision?

'I wouldn't think so,' said Johnson.

'Look, Mr Johnson,' said Pat, leaning his arms on the table. 'I want to quit. I give you a month's notice now.'

Nobody was more surprised than himself when he said it. Did I say that? You did. Then to hell with it, that's what I really wanted to do. It filled him inside with a warm feeling of excitement and relief. That was it, relief. It started in his stomach, fluttering, and made its way up until it came through his eyes in a shine.

Johnson was shocked. He thought it might be his fault. But he hadn't meant to be severe.

'Now, now, Pat,' he said, 'don't take it that way. I didn't mean to ride you about this. You mustn't think that. It's for your own good. You won't be able to live if you don't pull your socks up.'

'I know that,' said Pat. 'It's nothing to do with you. You have been very kind to me, and probably long-suffering. It's just that I'm going, Mr Johnson. I'm going now before I get worse. I'd never be able to make you understand, because you believe in all this. Deeply. If you hadn't you wouldn't be as good as you are. But I don't. I can't believe in it. I can't see any sense in all this business of collecting coppers every week. There is nothing to it for anybody. There's too much that's wrong about it.'

'My God,' said Johnson horrified, 'what are you saying? Something wrong about insurance! Where would the country be without it? Where would the individual be without it?'

Pat might as well have thrown doubts on the legitimacy of Mr Johnson's mother.

'I'm sorry, Mr Johnson,' said Pat. 'You see, I'd never be able to make you understand. We're many miles apart. If I had power in the morning, I would declare all weekly insurance illegal and contrary to the law. I would abolish it. I can't expect you to see that. It's just me, because I'm queer. Because I just can't see any bloody sense in it. Because I think too many people lose too many of their miserable shillings on it. That's all. Because I'm a bad agent, in other words. Or if you like, because I'm just not fitted for it. Isn't it better for me to go now, when my slate is clean, than to hang on in something I dislike intensely, and become worse and worse at it?'

Johnson was wordless. Anything else but not this. He was used to the agents who came and went. The ones that went weren't good. They couldn't live on their salaries and took a few bob here and there out of their collections to help them out. They would pay it back, but they could never get around to it. The wolf prowled too permanently for that. So they had to go. But Pat was sound. His books were sound. He could have been good.

'But,' said he, 'you've done well. You have been successful in the big policies you landed and in the motor insurance.'

'Ah, but that's different,' said Pat. 'That's legitimate. That's value for money.'

'Now look here,' said Johnson. He was inclined to get angry, because he was at grips with something outside his experience.

'Please, Mr Johnson,' said Pat rising. 'Don't talk about it. You have been good to me – kind, in fact. Nobody could have had a better and more understanding boss than you. So let's forget it. Will you just take my resignation, and we'll part? Will you do that?'

Johnson looked at him for a while, puzzled. Then he relaxed with a sigh. 'All right, Pat,' he said. 'I'll accept your resignation.'

They shook hands. Inevitably, Pat thought, he'll just come around to blaming it on the fact that I'm Irish, and hence unreliable. It's not that. I'm doing what I feel I ought to do, now, at the right time, in my own time. That's the business – in my own time. And I'll do everything else the same way from now on. I'll do what I feel it is right I should do at the right time.

'What about Maureen?' Johnson asked. 'What will you do about a now job. How will you manage to live? Don't do anything in a hurry.'

'I'll live, Mr Johnson,' said Pat. 'I'll get a job. That's at least one very good thing about here, in this country. If you want to work you can. Nobody gives a damn who you are or what you are or who your mother was or your father. All they are interested in is what you can do and how you do it. If you do it well you'll get on and if you don't you won't. You won't have to follow your father's footsteps. Your father was a scavenger, therefore you must be a scavenger. That business! I'll get a job all right. But don't say anything to Maureen for a while, will you? You know the way she is now. She wouldn't like it. Probably start to worry. Say that I was heaping more troubles on to her. So will you let this be between you and me until I'm on the point of going?'

'All right, Pat,' said Johnson. 'If that's the way you want it. But I'm sorry. I think you are making a mistake.'

'No,' said Pat decisively, 'I'm not. Because I'm doing it off my own bat. Nobody pushed me into it.'

They parted. Pat felt warmly towards Johnson, even though he knew that Johnson wouldn't think the better of him from now on. It would seem crazy to him. Unconsciously he would think that maybe Pat was fiddling with the clients' cash and he would ask the assistant to go around with him and check the customers' books with the office books. Just to be certain. When he found that all was above board, he would be relieved, but more puzzled than ever. He just couldn't get at the other business.

Pat felt like he had felt long ago at school when they had got an unexpected holiday.

He went with the other agents to the coffee-shop across the street, as was their custom. He was very bright. Very cheerful. They drank the coffee and ate the cakes and played the usual game of darts. Laughing. Talking. Nice bawdy talk, as was the custom when men gathered together and there were no women to put brakes on them. Spice. Laced with language. A little hysterical on account of the Crisis. Chaps thought about their wives and kids if they were married. Thought about themselves and the army if they weren't married. But to hell with it, the darts said, as they flew for doubles or twenties. Well-used darts, their tail feathers well plucked, replaced by cut cardboard, soiled. Good fun.

After that over to the billiard hall, as was their custom.

A little guilty. Thinking about the wives at home and the dinners on the stoves. Keeping hot. Always these snooker games started out by saying: Only one game now, lads. My missis, was she annoyed last week? Cold tongue I got. Only one game. Set up the reds and the coloured balls. Pick your partners. Whoever loses pays for the games and the cups of tea and cheese-sandwiches we will inevitably have. Hall rather dirty. Two tables. Good ones. Layer of soot on nearly everything except the carefully kept tables. Utilitarian, that was. A counter in the corner with the tea-urns and the sandwiches. The smell that only a billiard hall can have. Sort of damp smell. And the chalk. And stale cigarette smoke. And men. Only men. No perfume ever, no smell of gentle flesh. The boss behind the counter, a big man, fat, with huge jowls. Looking villainous. Mostly kindly and witty in fact. Just like the Jack of Jack's Pull In, where he and Seamus used to dine so long ago. Two hundred years or so, now.

Off with the game. Snooker behind the triangled bunch of red balls. Laughs. Curses. Potting going on. Becoming exciting. Against your will, becoming exciting. Potting reds. Potting colours. The feel of the smooth wood in your palm. The scrape of the little rectangle of pale green chalk. A lovely colour, like the colour of the sea at home on a fine day when you got into it, into the deep in a hooker, a black hooker looking like a black swan when the sail was distended by a gentle breeze. Oh, God! Game over. Pat and his partner won, more by good luck than accuracy. Reluctant laying down of cues. Must go home now. Dinner will be ready. Think of the wife waiting for the money. Well, just one more game then. Give you a chance to even up. He was reluctant to go home anyhow. Maureen was becoming so much more difficult. As if everything had been specially arranged for her discomfort, even the Crisis. She was taking it all very badly. Sometimes he felt like exploding. But remained as meek as he could. Well, forget it all now for the moment.

Another game. They lost. Have to retrieve their fortunes, so another game. And on it went until the excitement started to wane and the unsatisfactory tea and sandwiches became an uncomfortable lump in the stomach. Settling up. Who paid for who and what. Good-bye to the boss. See you again. When time goes by. If there isn't a war. If we're not all in the effing army. Into the day. Expressions of horror at the time. Blinking your eyes to accustom them to the light outside after the overhead glare of the lights over the tables, the murky light of the hall, with its stained skylight window. Good-bye, chaps. See you next week. No word to them about his leaving. A secret. Hugged it to himself. Actually felt sorry for them. And became fonder of them. Shook hands leaving, to their surprise. Just an excess of affection. Another bird going from the roost. Passing by. The path trodden by so many before.

So he turned his bicycle towards his book and headed for home.

He cycled slowly. Taking it easy. Filling his lungs with fresh air. Watching the avenues of houses with their trees and gardens go by. All the people in them, he was sure, thinking, talking and eating the Crisis. He wondered what Maureen would say when she heard about the job. She wouldn't mind really. It wasn't about things like that they disagreed. Not about tangible things. She would be worried all right until he came up with something else, as he would. All the same, he wouldn't tell her anything about it, not until her own affair was all over. How he wished it was over now so that this wall of whatever was between them might be burst and they could get back again to where they had been.

The Park. He got off the bicycle to look.

They were digging trenches in the Park. They were cutting lines in the carefully kept greensward, and then they were raping the earth under it. A lot of men. They were doing it as if they didn't believe it – a sense of unreality about the whole thing. The entrance was cut up from the wheels of the lorries that were going in and out with timber props and all the paraphernalia of the destructive attack. There was quite a crowd of people there outside the gate watching them at it. They were all very quiet and silent. No chat, no wisecracks to lift their hearts. Just standing there looking. Glum. Unbelieving. Frightened. Glued there to watch when they didn't really want to. Finding it hard to pull themselves away from the sight. Later they would go home and they would say, They are digging trenches in the Park. Horrible. Rooting up the Park. Rooting up our way of living. It made it all seem so real then. You hadn't really believed that there was anything in this Crisis business. A bunch of bastards bluffing. That was all. But when they started to dig up the Park! That was different. It was as sinister as the women neglecting to polish the red tiles.

Pat sighed and went home slowly. He opened the door tentatively. He knew he was late. Knew he was in the wrong. Could imagine it all, and his attempt at a cheerful whistle was the give-away. The act was going forward.

Maureen, in the kitchen, heard his key in the door and the sound of his whistle made her lips tighten and her chin come out. Her eyes were red again, but she didn't give a damn. If she could look and see her eyes not red, that would have been something. It took him a long time to reach the kitchen. When he came in his voice was cheerful, his eyebrows raised. Just as if nothing had happened, as if he wasn't two hours late for his dinner.

'Sorry I'm late, Maureen,' he said loudly, too loudly he told himself, 'but I got caught up in a game of snooker with the lads.'

He took a quick look at her face, decided it would be as well not to endeavour to kiss her.

He wouldn't even give me a kiss, Maureen thought, silently reaching into the oven and pulling out the plate, leaving it on the table where he was sitting. She felt grimly satisfied at the look of it. The potatoes were dry and shrivelled, the peas as hard and as inedible as marbles, and the meat was turned up at the edges. A most revolting sight. Pat tackled it cheerfully, as if he was dining in heaven on ambrosia. That was a mistake too. He should have looked at it, exclaimed, and said, God, I've ruined the dinner on you – I am sorry. Instead he just sat down and proceeded to eat it.

How is it possible, Maureen thought, to hate your own husband with such loathing? She hated the look of him sitting there, hated his assumed cheerfulness, his caution with her, like a cat treading on hot bricks. She had been steadily hating him for some time. She knew it was something to do with her condition, but now it didn't seem to her that he ever did anything at all to please her or make her love him. Nothing except this skating around, trying to avoid annoying her. It was terrible. At night, she would sleep until two o'clock, and then she would wake up to lie there in the bed, tossing and turning wide-eyed until it was time to get up in the morning. He would be there beside her sleeping soundly, heavily, and if at any time her moving woke him, her getting up to go to the bathroom or to get an orange to eat so that she would drive her dry mouth away, he would just open one eye, say, Poor Maureen, can't you sleep? and be asleep himself again before the last word of the sentence was uttered. Or sometimes he would, out of misplaced sympathy, remain awake, and his sleepy mutterings of condolence would be worse, so that she would say, For God's sake go asleep to hell, will you! But that would only serve to make him waken altogether, and the two of them would be awake then, wide-eyed and miserable, he smoking cigarettes until she would say, Please stop smoking, it makes me feel sick. And he would nip the butt with his fingers, so that the room would glow for a second from the sparked reflection, and he would say, Sorry, in a hurt sort of way, so that she would feel that she was a pig and dislike him all the more for making her feel a pig.

Pat thought there was nothing at all he could do that was right, but he put it down to her condition and wished to Christ it was all over.

Sometimes they went out. To the pictures in the afternoon, getting into the cinemas for sixpence before six o'clock. She liked that. It took her mind off to be watching other people's troubles, and she would even laugh and he would hold her hand in the dark, and she would feel that everything was grand again. Inside, that was. But outside was different – coming and going. It seemed to her that she was suddenly surrounded by millions of eyes. All sorts of eyes, but all of them looking at her alone. She would remark viciously about it. Pat would get annoyed. For the love of God, he would say, they aren't bothering their tails about you. They see thousands of women just like you every day in the week. They're staring at me, the filthy beasts, Maureen would say. Look at them! And Pat would say, Ah, quiet for God's sake. There's nobody looking at you.

So you see!

The doctor below too. He was Irish. He had a brogue just like Pat, caressing the same words. He was cheerful as well. She had gone to him because Pat had met him when that Jack had gone off his nut. She threw that at Pat as well. Why should I have a doctor just because he was a nice hand with loonies? That maddened Pat. Always, without fail, so she used it frequently. It was because the doctor was so cheerful. Nothing to it, Mrs Moore, he would say with a laugh; it's just like having a cup of tea! A cup of tea – she could have strangled him, even though he was nice, and made her feel safe and sometimes even got her laughing. But a cup of tea! She'd just like to see himself or Pat having it. Maybe they wouldn't think it was like having a cup of tea then. A cup of tea indeed!

'That was grand,' said Pat, pushing away his almost empty plate. He had left some of the peas and a lump of potato. He had thought privately that he could have eaten them too if he had a pneumatic drill or a sledgehammer.

'I'm glad you liked it,' said Maureen, viciously swishing it away.

Don't overdo it now, Pat's mind said to him, as he tried to think of something to say. Lay off the food anyhow.

'They're digging trenches in the Park,' he said then.

'Um,' said Maureen, making the tea. She didn't mind. They could dig trenches in the middle of Piccadilly and she wouldn't give a damn. She wasn't going to be frightened about all this. Hadn't she enough to be frightened about?

'It's looking blue,' said Pat.

She refused to he drawn. She had her attitude now, cold, indifferent silence, and she was sticking to it. Pat knew it too. He would have to break her out of that, get her talking, even though the talk would fall on his own neck. But you couldn't go on this way.

'I'm really sorry about being late,' said Pat, as she gave him the cup of tea. 'Honest to God I am, Maureen.' His head on one side, his eyes giving her the melting look that wouldn't have failed a good while ago.

'A lot of good being sorry,' she said. 'Leaving me here for hours. The dinner going spoiled in the oven. For what? For playing silly snooker with a lot of idiots who should have more sense. What about their poor wives? Couldn't you come home and have your dinner and then go out if you wanted to? What about me? Wouldn't you think that you would spare a thought for me here at home? It's not nice. I'm miserable enough without all this being loaded on top of me.' And then of course to her horror and dismayed acceptance, the tears started to flow again. God, she thought, I'm like a bloody river!

Well, I broke up the silence anyhow, Pat thought, rising to put his arm about her. He felt sorry for her and full of love and conscious that he was totally unable to help her. Even though she insisted, he didn't think she had changed. Her hair didn't have the lustre it used to have and her face had fattened quite a bit, but Maureen was there all the time, if only she could be more cheerful about it all.

He put his arm around her bowed shoulders.

'Ah, look, Maureen,' he said, 'don't cry. I'm sorry and it

won't happen again.' It's all so daft, he was thinking, all this over nothing at all.

She shook off his arm.

'Ah, leave me alone!' she said, and went over to the sink. 'Go on away, can't you? Can't you get out of my sight?'

He flushed and couldn't stop himself getting mad. Not this time. With all that was happening, their problems should have been so small.

'All right,' he said, biting it out, 'I will. It'll be a pleasure. Anything at all to get away from the inferiority complex you give me. Nothing I do pleases you. Nothing I say pleases you. You make me feel the most spineless son of a bitch that ever lived. If I stay here much longer with you, I won't be able to live with myself.'

With that he went out of the kitchen, banging the door, gathered his coat from the hallway, struggled into it and opened the front door angrily. He was about to bang it after him when she came out of the kitchen.

'Where are you going?' she asked in a mixture of anger and worry.

'I'm going – I'm going over to Lelia's,' he said then in a moment of inspiration. 'Maybe I'd get a bit of peace over there.'

That'll learn her, he thought, as he banged the door behind him.

'Pat,' said Maureen, running up the hall after him. She was too late. By the time she had the door open he was out in the street mounted on the bicycle, cycling away, his face still red. She was going to call after him again, thought of the neighbours and didn't, banged the door again, went into the living-room, sat on the couch, brought out her handkerchief, said 'Pat' into it, cried into it, and felt very miserable indeed.

It's a hard world.

14

It only took a few minutes for Pat's anger to wane, and then his feet went around more slowly on the pedals. Will I go back, he wondered? His heart smote him as he thought of her at home, probably crying again, God blast it. Here I am again, he thought then, indecisive. Will I, won't I? Well, I will. George will be at home anyhow. It's his half-day. He doesn't have to be standing outside his shop in his white coat and apron auctioning off Argentine beef with the chill barely off it. So he settled his chin and headed for Lelia's. Besides, he thought, there's still a bit of insurance to pick up, and I'd better pick it up before I depart. He had managed to get George down for a five-hundred-pound policy. That was five pounds commission. That was nice. There was still the car and the van and the shop. The insurance on them would be expiring shortly with the other company. So there was a reason for going around to Lelia. What the hell do I want a reason for anyhow? he asked himself. I'm going over to Lelia's. I said I would and that's enough about it.

It was a detached house, square-rigged, with a garage against the side of it, a garden front and back, pretty spacious, the whole looking very new all the time. The paint had yet to lose its glitter; the garden, newly laid out, looking stiff and artificial, with the crazy-paving up to the door. The car was outside, so George was probably at home. He parked his bicycle and went up to the door, taking the cycle-clips off his trousers. A ring. The funny doorbell inside, American, went ding-dong-ding like a muted chapel bell. The door opened and the maid appeared. Lelia had two maids – no work for Lelia except in a supervisory capacity.

She was a good-looking little maid too, trim and neat. Lelia despised opposition, Pat thought with a grin, as he asked if George was in.

'No, he's not, Mr Moore,' said she, 'but missus is.'

You can go home now, Pat, if you like, his mind hinted.

'Thanks,' said Pat, stepping in.

The house was very nice. It was painted in bright colours. The hall was wide and panelled, polished parquet flooring with rugs. It still hadn't lost the new smell. Into the door on the right. Very bright. Deep pink carpet. Light-coloured furniture. Modern. A big window leading to the garden with glass doors. Prints on the walls in narrow frames of light wood, modern prints of Old Masters. Women in their baths, at their love, convenient folds of discarded garments discreetly covering little bits of them. Big women, big Italian figures. Heavy breasts, heavy arms, thick thighs, full figures. Pat grinned. Like Lelia would be when she was a little older. Was that why they were there? To show that it was figures like that that painters really went for? Even the cherubs had fine fat bottoms.

'Pat!' said the voice of Lelia behind him.

He turned. She was well turned out. The lady of the manor in an off moment of careful aberration. House coat. Hair piled on top of her head and held by a ribbon. Like a Greek Matron. Mules on her feet. All puffy with some kind of white rabbit fur. Aristocratic rabbit.

'Hello,' Pat said. 'I dropped in to see if I could capture George.'

'I thought you might have come to see me,' said Lelia candidly.

'Well, you're worth looking at too,' said Pat.

'Do you like me?' she asked, carefully draping herself on a wide settee.

'Well, you look new, anyhow,' said Pat, sitting on the edge of a chair. 'The things become you.'

'They're nice, aren't they?' Lelia asked. 'All new. What did you want George for?'

'The usual,' said Pat. 'Still after him for insurance.'

'You are very callous,' said Lelia. 'I don't know how you can keep after your friends like that. Anyone might think you had no other interest in us except stinking insurance.'

'Oh, indeed I have.' said Pat. 'It's a pleasure to be with you both. Where is George?'

'Oh, some meeting or other,' said Lelia. 'I was just going out, as a matter of fact. Would you like to come?'

'Where to?' Pat asked.

'Oh, just anywhere in the car,' said Lelia. 'I'm fed up. You can get George then. He should be home. All this Crisis business.'

'Does it upset you?' asked Pat.

'It's a bloody nuisance,' said Lelia. She rose then. 'I'll go and get dressed. Won't keep you long.' She approached him, preceded by the waves of her perfume. Placed her hand on his hair for a second. 'Amuse yourself until I come back.'

'I'll look at your photographs,' said Pat, indicating the prints with his thumb.

'Are they like me?' she asked.

'Well . . . ' said Pat.

'You ought to know,' said Lelia, going through the door. Pat felt himself getting hot under the collar. That was a dirty crack, he thought. But she didn't mean it. Lelia never meant anything like that. Lelia in her way reminded him of Jojo, living for today and tomorrow. Jojo would be completely horrified if he knew Lelia and heard that. But it was true in a way. Lelia could dish out the most severe punishment to a person and be quite incapable of realizing the hurt she was giving. It just didn't mean anything to her. He still smarted now and again as he thought of the casual way she had given him his congé – a hurt that would have been unbearable if the face of Maureen with the chin and the candid eyes didn't come to him to make him realize what he had missed. I should go home now, Pat thought, rising, to look out of the window. The evening was drawing in. There were dark clouds closing up from the horizon. I've made the gesture, after all. Now I better go back. But he became indecisive again when Lelia returned. A dark blue costume, moulded to her figure; very high-heeled shoes. There's no doubt, he thought, Lelia can dress. She looked very well. Very swish. Like an advert in a posh magazine done in colour. He thought wryly of what would have happened if she had been married to an insurance agent with three pounds a week basic. She should thank him for that anyhow. The fact that he had given George the necessary spurt into matrimony.

'All right,' said Lelia, 'let's go,' pulling on white gloves. Pat went.

'Where to?' Pat asked as she ground the gears. She'd never learn that, anyhow.

'Oh, just anywhere,' said Lelia.

What do I talk about? Pat wondered. Nothing with Lelia, unless delicate talk of love and kisses and clothes. You couldn't start about the Crisis. Lelia wouldn't really give a damn. You couldn't talk about the things you had seen and the people and the effect that it all left on you. You couldn't talk about Maureen. Lelia wasn't really interested in Maureen. Only, he supposed, if you said disparaging things about her. About Maureen! No fear. He became despondent. Where am I going at all? he wondered. It's all right to give up your job and say I'll get another as easy as winking. And Maureen. And how helpless he felt with her. How helpless he felt with everything, for that matter. He had come with the feeling that he was going to set the Thames on fire and all he seemed able to do up to the present was to make people unhappy. Something unhappy always happened to his friends. He hadn't brought much happiness to Mary. There was Jack. He didn't know if he had brought any benefits to George by giving him Lelia. And Maureen, what had he done to her? Wouldn't she have been far happier if she had never met him at all? What about Seamus and Jojo? Wasn't he like an evil finger of fate to everybody he came into contact with? Except Lelia. He couldn't do any bad to Lelia. Lelia could sup with the Devil and get away with it.

'Good old Lelia,' he said out loud, reaching his hand to the leg beside him and pressing it. It was still the same shape, he noticed. Nice. He could feel the silk of her stocking shifting under the cloth of her skirt where his hand rested.

'Nice Pat,' said Lelia, letting her hand rest on his and pressing it into her leg.

'Look out,' said Pat, and she put her eyes back to the road just in time to save them from immortality.

'A woman driver,' said Lelia disgustedly, craning her head after the other car.

'Phew,' said Pat. 'Look, Lelia, pull in somewhere and we'll have a drink.'

After about five miles they pulled into a Red Lion set at a cross-roads. A rearing building, looking Dutch although it was newly built. Leaded pane windows, red and yellow. The only touch of Olde England the sign outside the door with the Red Lion painted on it. All the rest very modern indeed. All panels and noiseless doors and a lounge with deep carpets, and small round tables and deep chairs well upholstered so that you sank into them. Drink in peace, they said. Drink in comfort. Once you got into them you didn't feel like getting out again. Young men with sleeked hair walking around soundlessly with trays. White coats and black trousers and bow ties.

They drank whiskey. Pat felt very sad. They drank some more whiskey and he felt even sadder.

Then the blinds on the window were pulled down and the lights in the lounge were switched off and the television set at the bottom was lighted up. A most peculiar sensation to be sitting in the soft chairs looking at a small screen, miles away it seemed, where two men were belabouring one another and an announcer was getting very excited about it all. And beside him, Lelia. He shifted his foot and he felt her knee against his own. Reached his hand and felt her hand. Tightening. An empty feeling in the pit of his stomach. A flutter of his heart. Not as strong as long ago, which seemed only yesterday. We will leave this, he thought, and it will be the same as it was then. Lelia will be in her own house and I will wait for her in the living-room and she will come out and sit beside me on the couch.

She raised his hand and squeezed it to her breast.

No, thought Pat, it's no good. It's very, very nice, but it's no good. This, he thought, is true appeasement. Walking out on yourself. This, he thought, is the epitome of indecision. But it was nice. He leaned over. She was there. Her head thrown back a little. He felt for her mouth, found it. Her free hand held the side of his face. Her lips were soft, her breath was sweet, but he wasn't lost, as he would have been before. He thought, if they switch on the lights it will be embarrassing. That sunk him. Time was when he wouldn't have thought about the lights going on.

The lights did go up eventually. They were decorous, even if Pat felt the trembling in his legs and noticed that Lelia's hand was shaking and he could see the pulse again beating fast in the hollow of her neck. His head was muzzy. He felt as if he had succeeded in levitating himself, that he wasn't on the ground at all. That was the whiskey of course.

'We'll go,' said Lelia, rising.

They walked out into the air then, her hand through his arm, bringing his body close to her side. It was getting dark outside. He could see that the bank of cloud had come closer. Above it the sky was clear and was the colour of water in a swimming-pool. A far away drone in the sky.

Lelia bent to open the door of the car, fumbling with the small key. She gave it up.

'You open it for me, Pat,' she said.

He took the key from her, feeling the soft flesh of her hand, and he bent to the door. Succeeded, and twisting the handle, stood back. Lelia, behind him, did not give way, so that he felt the bulk of her against his back. Turned then to face her. She was still very near him. He could feel her breasts against his chest. She put her hands on his waist. They were hot. He could feel the heat of them right in through his clothes. He put his arms around her shoulders and squeezed her to him, bending his head to kiss her again. She was pressed as closely to him as her clothes would allow. His blood raced and receded. A funny thought came into his head then. Polished shining lino – just that, the gleaming polished lino in his hall and Maureen on her knees, looking up as he came in, smiling, raising her hand to throw back the recalcitrant lock of hair falling over her forehead.

His ardour waned. The drone in the sky became louder. First a swift whine and then a low, menacing drone. He broke his lips from hers and looked up.

There were small planes passing across his vision, swiftly, and then after them came lumbering shadows, like black flying boxes.

Lelia looked too. He felt her shiver. She pulled herself away from him. 'Come on,' she said; 'let's go home.' She got into the car without another look at the sky. Pat hoped that she would

226

always have some place to retreat to when aeroplanes flew. But it wasn't the aeroplanes. It was just Lelia. If anything arose in her life to threaten to make her think, she always sought shelter, as now.

He got in beside her, and she swung the car out into the road recklessly, and the tyres were soon humming on the tarmac, the headlights pale and anaemic in the twilight. Like myself, thought Pat. Incapable of definiteness until it becomes dark.

Lelia soon forgot the planes. He felt her hand on his knee. He caught it in his own and fiddled with her fingers. Her ring hand. With the beautiful diamond one and the platinum wedding ring. He caught the rings in his own fingers and twisted them hard, so that she would feel. It couldn't be plainer than that. These are yours, Lelia, and you have an obligation with them. Not that it was up to Lelia. It wasn't. It was up to himself. It was his own wedding rings he should have been twisting. But then he didn't have rings, except the ones that were imbedded in his mind. He put her hand back on the steering-wheel. That was enough of a hint. She was a bad enough driver with two hands.

When we stop at the house, he thought, I will get out and I will get my bicycle, the mark of my position, the hallmark of my slavery, and I will say, Good night now, Lelia, and thanks for the trip, and despite blandishments (of which there may, after all, be none) I will go home and I will really be sorry for Maureen and I will work very hard indeed to make her forget today. He determined on that. You will have to pluck up whatever little backbone you have in order to do it, he thought, because the temptation was very strong and he was discovering that he himself was very weak.

The car drew up at Lelia's door.

'Come on in,' said Lelia, looking at him out of the side of her eyes. He knew that look well. He had seen it before.

He didn't answer. He got out of the car and banged the door. Came to the other side, looking for words. That's bad, he thought; I should have the words ready so that they wouldn't look like an excuse. He had his mouth open to speak when the front door of the house opened, the light was switched on, and George was silhouetted there. Pat let the unspoken words escape in air. He had never been so glad to see George even in silhouette.

'Hello, ducks,' George shouted, coming down the steps to the gate. 'Where you been?'

'Hello, George,' said Lelia. 'Pat was looking for you, so I brought him over to the Red Lion for a drink.'

'You could have waited,' said George. 'Hello, Pat.' Pat thought his voice wasn't as friendly as usual, but then that could have been a sort of guilty conscience. 'I could do with a drink meself,' George went on. 'The whole bleedin' world upside down. Makes you think, it does.'

'Come on in and have some tea, Pat,' said Lelia.

He was in a quandary then. He didn't want to go in, but if he didn't George might feel that he was refusing because he didn't want to face the eyes of George. Which left Pat feeling out on a limb, another limb of indecision, he thought, with a tightened mouth.

'All right,' he said, 'I will, thanks.'

George was worried about the Crisis. No doubt about that. He made up for Lelia's studied indifference. He discussed it from all angles and he quoted from all the papers, word for word. He insisted on it. Took up the papers and read it out for them. Lelia wasn't pleased. Pat knew that from the vague way her eyes roamed around. She broke eventually.

'Please, George,' she said. 'We've had enough of it, I tell you. Isn't it enough that everybody else is at it without you joining in? Forget it, can't you? It'll pass, like everything else. Why can't you talk about something else? Talk to Pat there about insurance.'

Part payment, thought Pat, for services rendered. The further Lelia and he advanced, the nearer he would come to the signature on the dotted line.

'Insurance!' ejaculated George. 'At a time like this. Blimey!'

'My sentiments exactly,' Pat joined in.

'What brought you home so soon?' Lelia asked, pouring tea. 'You don't generally get home until midnight from one of those junkets.'

Ho-ho! thought Pat.

'Well, honey,' said George, 'it's the bleeding Crisis. Can't keep your mind on business. Nobody can.'

The poor bastard, thought Pat, practically apologizing for

coming home too early to his wife. What a reversal of the common habits! He felt restless suddenly. He wanted to go home, to get away from here, to get back to living. Lelia was in a bad temper. You could tell that from the way her eyebrows were pulled down. A seething restlessness inside her – it came out in waves. So. Pat thought that Lelia was a peculiar mixture. Funny the way she could send them out, the waves. He wondered if she had a sort of master switch inside of her. Press a button: love. Press another button: anger. Like that. You could tell that George felt it too. He should have got up and kicked her teeth in, but he didn't. He went over to the other side. Little things to please her, very obvious things. Pushing the sugar to her that was already beside her. Lifting the plate of bread with his red hand to offer it to her, when she didn't even have to stretch to get it. It wasn't nice. Would she have made me like that too, Pat wondered, my soul trembling on her whims?

He rose suddenly. 'I'll have to go, I'm afraid,' he said. 'Maureen will be wondering where I am. God, she might even be taken off to hospital while I'm sitting here.'

It was a thought that just came to him then. Suppose he did go home and find her gone? Suppose he got home to an empty flat and Maureen wasn't there, that she had been taken away and died? What then? He felt sweat under his armpits. Not just now, God, he asked, don't let it happen like this, with me going out mad.

'We'll go over with you,' said Lelia. 'Sit down for a minute. We'll drive you over.'

'Ah no,' said Pat.

'George is dying to see Maureen again. He hasn't seen her for ages now. Isn't that right, George?'

'How is old Maureen?' George forced himself. 'I haven't laid eyes on her for ages. Taking it all right I bet, isn't she?'

'Great,' said Pat. 'But I won't pull ye out.'

'It's no bother,' said Lelia.

And that was that. Pat writhed but didn't protest further. What was the use? With Lelia this way, what could he do, unless he burst out into a flame of anger and told them he didn't want them to come over to see Maureen, that he wanted to see her on his own, to make up for the day? That if Lelia came he would have to work eighty times harder when she had gone to make up for her coming and the worms she always left with Maureen after her? He couldn't do that. After all, he had been kissing Lelia passionately half an hour ago. Was it any wonder that she felt she had a claim on him, that he had come within the aura? No, he thought, I will have to take it this time, but as sure as Christ makes rain, there will be no other time.

When they closed the door to go to the car, the rain started to come down. Big splashy drops that suddenly developed into a steady downpour, falling straight from the sky without the assistance of the wind to slant it. It looked like a grey wall under the street lights.

George drove and Lelia sat in the back with Pat.

She arranged it that way, and that's the way it happened.

She caught Pat's hand and fondled it in her lap. It was a listless hand she hid to play with, but she didn't seem to mind. Probably, Pat thought, she thinks that it's because her husband is there in front driving that my hand is listless. Doesn't she feel that it is cold for her for ever?

She didn't mind. Getting out of the car at Pat's flat, she rubbed the side of her face against his. 'Nice Pat,' she said in a loud voice, so that George must have heard it. He didn't seem to have. His face gave nothing away.

They ran for the door and huddled as Pat fumbled with the key. The door swung open and they went into the small hall, shaking the drops from their clothes. They fell on the highly polished lino. Pat opened the living-room door. She must be there. He had seen the light from the street.

She was. Sitting over the fire reading a book. She looked up. Her eyes were not red. She had not been crying. But there was a great indifference in her eyes. They were as listless as his hand in Lelia's lap.

'Lelia and George came over to see you, Maureen,' he said.

She dropped her book.

'Come in,' she said. She didn't rise, just let her wrist take the weight of the book and watched them.

They came in. They sat down.

'I hope you don't mind,' said Lelia, 'but we persuaded Pat to stay for tea.'

'Was it hard?' Maureen asked.

Lelia laughed. 'Not very,' said she. 'But then he and I had been over to the Red Lion for a drink while we were waiting for George, so his powers of resistance were less than usual.' Her eyes sidling to Pat.

If he had been near enough to her he might have strangled her. He looked at Maureen quickly. It didn't seem to affect her. The same look of listless disinterest in her eyes. The trouble was that Lelia was telling the truth. You couldn't deny the truth. But, God, the way it was put! She wasn't finished yet. She seemed to be in a sort of fever. She couldn't sit. She got on her feet and wandered, her small fat hands feeling this and that. And talking. Stopped in front of the fire to look at Maureen.

'Isn't it terrible,' she said, 'how pregnancy makes you so fat? Your legs are huge, Maureen. They say that the proper shape never comes back again. But you needn't worry when you have Pat. Faithful Pat.'

Over to him then, putting her hand on his arm. He shook it off and sat on the arm of Maureen's chair. He felt Maureen shrinking away from his nearness. Oh God, he thought, why can't they go? George looked uncomfortable. His eyes were wincing. For the first time Pat noticed that it was the way George's face was made that gave him the constant look of bon-homie. His two front teeth were a little prominent and his top lip was tight, so he seemed always to have a good-humoured grin. It was deceptive, Pat saw now. A man can smile and smile and suffer, if he has a face like George.

Lelia went back again and sat by George. He was resting his elbows on his knees and massaging his red hands. Lelia thought for a moment how she hated the red hands of George. Pat's weren't like that. Then she forgot and continued. She didn't even stop to wonder why she should have such a fierce feeling inside her when she looked at Maureen. Demure, always curt, so that you knew she was thinking about you and the things she was thinking weren't nice. She hates me, of course, Lelia thought. She married Pat just because I was fond of him. And there she sits with a book in her hand. Just because she knows well that I never read books like that. Just to show how superior she is.

'I'd hate to have a baby just now,' said Lelia. 'Imagine having a baby in a Crisis.'

'I thought you didn't like talking about the Crisis,' said Pat shortly.

'It just came to me now,' said Lelia. 'Of course I'm lucky; George doesn't like children. He insisted that I shouldn't have one. George would be furious if I lost my figure. Wouldn't you, George?'

'Oh, sure, ducks,' said George, 'sure. Can't have those curves knocked about, can we?' Pat wondered if George had any option on the question of the children.

'How you can sit there so patiently waiting, Maureen,' went on Lelia, 'is beyond me.'

'One can get used to anything,' said Maureen in a tight voice.

'Pat is out such a lot, isn't he?' said Lelia. 'I'd hate to be left on my own as much as that. George wouldn't leave me alone so often. He'd be afraid some other nice young man would come along and snatch me away from him. Wouldn't you, George?' playfully tugging George's close-set ear.

'That's right, Lil,' said George, submitting.

'I think you have the most wonderful patience, with the baby on the way and everything. You know, I would go mad, clear stark mad. I know I would. If George was an insurance agent. All those nice young married women Pat has on his books. Talking nice to them too, I'll bet, having tea with them. A change from a pregnant wife, aren't they, Pat?'

Pat got pale. He thought for two seconds before he came to his feet. About what he was going to say. This, Lelia! You are a vile woman, evil beyond imagination. And I'm more evil than you, to have put up with it all, for the sake of what? Of a couple of pounds commission on an insurance policy? Of the weakness in me that can't avoid giving way to the temptation which your luscious curves incite in me? Get out of here now, for the love of God, and take your spineless, poor browbeaten maneen with you.

He got to his feet and opened his mouth. Lelia was looking at him. Her eyebrows were drawn down and her eyes were waiting for what he had to say.

'Lelia,' he said, the muscles bunched at the side of his jaws, and then there was a loud banging on the knocker of the door. Very loud and very urgent. Pat opened his mouth again to continue, but the knocker banged again, so he shut his mouth and looked at Maureen. She was waiting for him. Wasn't she always waiting for him? What was he going to say? Who was knocking at the door?

Pat went into the hall quickly. I should have said it despite, he thought. It was a pity I didn't say it. Now the moment was gone. For the sake of what was going to happen afterwards, it was a pity he didn't.

He opened the door. There was a colossal figure standing there, swathed from head to foot in gleaming black oilskins. Like the picture of the advertisement for Skipper sardines. All that could be seen of the face was the red cheeks and the big white moustache. Small eyes, with a twinkle in them. The black coat went to his shins, and the cascading rainwater from it continued on to his rubber boots. There were three black yokes swinging from his right hand.

'Yes?' Pat enquired.

'Come to fit the gas-masks, cock,' said the man. 'What a night they pick for it, eh? Herbert Jenkins the name. Can I come in? Can't do it out here, you know. Look at the bleedin' rain – like the Flood it is. How many you got in the house?' He stepped past Pat into the hall. Pat couldn't find anything to say. He wanted to say, Listen: go away – not tonight. He didn't like to think of Maureen and this black, ugly-looking figure with the gas-masks. 'It's good to get in out of that. Highly uncomfortable, to say the least of it. Well, where do we go? In here? Got to hurry, you know, have hundreds and hundreds to do yet.' He walked into the lighted room.

Pat behind him heard a gasp from Maureen. He didn't blame her – so unexpected this figure. He stepped in quickly.

'This is Mr Jenkins,' he said. 'Come to fit gas-masks. It's raincoats he should be fitting on a night like this.'

Endeavour to be jocular. A failure, like a squib in the rain. It didn't come off. Lelia was looking at Mr Jenkins with great distaste. Maureen was looking at him with her eyes wide, her face was pale.

'Won't take long,' said Mr Jenkins cheerfully. 'Won't keep you half a mo, I won't. Got into the knack of it now.'

Lelia speaking. On her feet. 'We'd better be going, George. Well, good night, Maureen; it was nice to see you looking so well. Let us know when it happens.'

Maureen paid no attention to her. Lelia moved to the door, Pat ahead of her to see them out. George stopped by Maureen. Took her hand into his own. Spoke kindly, did George.

'Good luck, Maureen,' he said, 'in case I don't see you again.'

Maureen moved her eyes to his. 'Thanks, George,' she said. For some reason George sighed, and then followed Lelia. Pat was holding the door. Mr Jenkins shifted Lelia, anyhow, Pat was thinking. But it should have been me who shifted her.

'Good night, Pat,' said Lelia.

'Good night, Pat,' said George.

I can make one gesture anyhow, Pat thought. 'Listen, George,' he said. 'About that insurance, forget it!'

'Why?' This from Lelia, surprised.

'Because I won't be an insurance agent for much longer,' said Pat.

He looked directly at her. She got it. He kept his face hard. It was quite easy to do.

'But—' said George, looking from one to the other.

'Oh, come on George, for God's sake,' said Lelia. 'We'll be drenched standing here in the rain.' She pulled up her collar, put her hand over her hair and ran for the car. George followed her. Pat closed the door and came in. Mr Jenkins was talking. Mr Jenkins was enjoying himself. Whatever else the Crisis was doing for some people, it was broadening others. Mr Jenkins was blossoming. A chance to step out of the herd again. To be a little boss where you had been a small nothing before. To have the lives of people depending on you. To see the look of fear dawning in their eyes. So it's serious, after all. They really mean business. That was what it meant to be fitting people with gas-masks. There would be many Mr Jenkins now to step out of the herd and be able to order their fellow men. According to regulations. The little badge of authority. To other eyes you would be up a bit. You would be in the know. So you could be a little mysterious, as if you knew more than you did, as if the whole country was depending on you.

So Mr Jenkins was cheerful. He tried to kid himself he was cheerful because people took this gas-mask business so seriously. But it wasn't that. Mr Jenkins was on pension. Mr Jenkins hadn't much to do – he was a man who had been used to having four clerks under him, and he keeping an authoritative eye on the petty cash. Mr Jenkins was in circulation again and so was his blood, and that's why Mr Jenkins was cheerful, why the blood was in his face and the beam in his eye.

'Ooh, a bad business,' said Mr Jenkins. 'I was in the last lot. I know. Got a whiff of mustard too. Bad. Kept me coughing for twenty years it did. Sort of bronchial like.' He coughed hollowly to show what he meant.

'Better get it over with,' said Pat.

'That's right,' said Mr Jenkins. 'Got so many to do before the night is out. Well, here we are. Come in three sizes they do – small, medium and large. You now. You would be large, I'd say. Medium for the ladies and the small one for the kids. Got none yet for the babies, they haven't. Stuff them into a sort of paper bag with a tube, I hear. Now you put in your mouth here first like that, holding the straps in your hands in this manner. Then when you have your mouth in' – Mr Jenkins' voice was muffled at this point – 'you bring up the straps over the head like this and you have it.' He swiped off the gas-mask again. A practised movement. 'Here, sir, you try it now.'

Pat put in his mouth and pulled the straps over his head. He felt smothered and went to take it off again, alarmed at the noises his breath made as it escaped at the sides. Like a man blowing two raspberries at the same time.

'No, hold it there,' said Mr Jenkins. 'Got to adjust the straps now, tighten it up. All right now. Wait until I mark it with a pencil.' He got a small stub of a pencil, licked it and marked the straps at the buckles. 'There you are now. A perfect fit. Got to be perfect, you know. If they ain't perfect it's too bad. You won't know what happened.'

'I see,' said Pat. His hair was ruffled. His mind was wild.

'And now the missus,' said Mr Jenkins.

'No,' said Pat, not even bothering to look at the face of his wife. 'No, I know all about it now, surely. I'll fix her up.'

Mr Jenkins was doubtful. It was part of his job after all. He looked at her. She did look a bit pale. That way too. Maybe not. Can't take it too far.

'Right you are,' he said, looking at her head closely. 'Medium, I'd say. You just be careful about the adjusting of it.' Handing over one of the remaining ones. 'No use blaming me after, is there, if anything is wrong. That's the way. Hard on me poor feet, this job is. Don't know what time I'll get to bed tonight, and me an old man too. That's the way. What a night as well! Won't half get it from the missus when I go home. Don't make any allowances, they don't, for a man out doin' his duty. What keeps you out until this hour of the night, Herbert? she'll say. Blimey! Women, you know the way they are. And the rain as well. Shouldn't be surprised if I get another dose of bronchial out of this lot.'

He didn't look too unhappy about it all. He didn't seem to be in much of a hurry to get going with his other fittings. In fact, it looked as if Mr Jenkins was quite willing to stay there all night and tell them all about it.

'Well,' said Pat, at last making a move to the door.

'That's right,' said Mr Jenkins. 'Got to be moving. Haven't done half-way through yet.' And he left. Pat thought he'd never get him out of the house and yet when he closed the door after him he was sorry he was gone. There was a terrible silence in the house. It was only broken by the sound of the rain outside and the tyres cutting through the rainwater on the road.

He came back in. Maureen was still sitting. Her eyes were fixed on the two gas-masks on the mantelpiece where Pat had left them – most horrible-looking things, like black collapsed skulls.

Pat took one into his hand and played with it.

'It doesn't mean anything,' he said, looking at her anxiously. 'They're still all bluffing, but they have to take precautions.'

'Yes,' said Maureen, taking her eyes from them and leaning back in the chair, her hand up to the side of her mouth. Her eyes were bleak.

Pat sat on the other chair.

'Look, Maureen,' said Pat. 'I'm terribly sorry about today. About the whole of it. I can't feel smaller ever again than I do at this moment. I didn't mean to be so long away when I went out that time. I meant to be home long before tea. I should have been home long before tea.'

'It doesn't matter,' said Maureen. He should have been glad with that, but he wasn't. She just meant that it didn't matter, that nothing mattered. That was bad. There was no breaching that. Not now. Maureen had passed from the stage where things were real and made you suffer to the stage where things were emotions, unreal ones that left a lightness in the head. Not pleasant. So that things that should have been able to elevate you or hurt you were just colours. She was beginning now to see things in colours and to feel away. In fact, she wouldn't have been surprised to have looked out of the window and to have seen herself looking over at herself from the other side of the street. Even that wouldn't have shocked her. She seemed to have passed into a lonely dream, peopled only by herself and little figures that pointed at her and jeered, or laughed or fought. Pat seemed to have decreased in size too. She could look at him and he seemed to her to be a tiny Pat, as if she was looking at him through the wrong end of a telescope. Even the worried wrinkles on his forehead were very clear, and made her sad, so that she would have liked to smooth them out for him.

But she couldn't. He was too far away now. She would have had to have a long arm stretching away miles to be able to place her finger on his forehead.

'Do you feel well, Maureen?' she heard his voice, piping from a distance, like a horn in a distant wood.

'No,' said Maureen, and she wondered that her voice didn't seem to be part of herself either. 'I'm going.'

'Where?' Pat asked.

'To bed,' said Maureen. 'I want to get away from the black.' Ever since that man in the black coat had come the colour she was seeing was black. Like those two things up there on the mantelpiece. She rose out of the chair. She felt his hand upon her arm, helping her.

'Will I get the doctor?' she heard him ask.

'No, no,' she said. 'I'll be all right. It's just that I feel queer.'

She was soon in bed, listlessly sitting on the side of it as he helped her to undress. It was good to lie back and close her eyes. It shut out such a lot of things. But not to sleep. She hadn't slept now for such a long time. So many people had gone away from her, and she felt so lonely. And if she slept it was worse, because then it was just herself, an awkward, ugly figure, calling, calling, wearing her smock, and nobody at all around.

She felt Pat beside her then, along the length of her. Felt his hand on her arm. But he wasn't able to get near her. Not even Pat now could stretch a hand into the world where she was segregated.

She slept later, an uneasy sleep. Pat, lying beside her, wide awake, knew that it was uneasy, and wondered if he should after all go for the doctor. He thought that never before in his life had he felt so miserable or so helpless, and he wondered if God would ever bring this time to an end.

It was nearing twelve when the knocker on the front door banged again.

15

For some reason, the knock frightened Pat.
It wasn't like the knock of Mr Jenkins. That was loud and
blatant and peremptory. The man on the job – open up.
This one was a sort of entreaty, a hurried call of urgency. Nonsense, said Pat to himself, swinging his legs out of the bed and
feeling for his slippers. It's just this queer feeling of unreality
that's hanging over the lot of us. The awful pent-up feeling of
what's going to happen next. He switched on the light. A brief
look at Maureen. She was lying on her side sleeping, her arms
outside the bedclothes, one hand open and her fingers closing
convulsively. She didn't waken. He wondered whether to go out
just as he was. Another knock decided him. To hell with them,
he thought, they can put up with me as I am – who do they think
I am, the gatekeeper in *Macbeth*?

He went into the hall and felt his way up to the switch, which
was near the door; pressed it and the light came on. His hand on
the lock of the door, he hesitated again. Maybe I shouldn't have
opened it at all, he thought. Maybe I should have pretended to
be asleep and let them go about their business whoever they are.

He opened it. Jojo came in quickly.

'Close the door, quick, for God's sake!' he said. Pat closed it.

They stood there looking at one another. Jojo was wearing no
cap and his hair was plastered to his skull with the wet. His
clothes were drenched and dripping there in the hall. He needed
a shave. His eyes were wide and his chest rose and fell hurriedly.
He had been running. And now Pat felt really frightened. He felt
as he had often felt before when they were young and in school,

239

waiting in the morning for the advent of a particularly brutal teacher, who used his cane and his fist on them for little reason. You'd sit there in the desk with the flutter of fear in your stomach, keeping your legs together in case you'd wet your pants with fear. Just naked fear. Like now. He was afraid and the terror showed in his eyes. Not a specific fear. Just a throwback. Jojo didn't have this look in his eyes. But his eyes didn't look as old now as the last time Pat had been looking into them. They were young again, and for a few moments Pat had the terrible feeling that they were both wearing short pants and that they were back again.

'I was wrong, Pat, wasn't I?' asked Jojo. 'I said I would always be alone, didn't I? And that I would manage on my own. Well, here I am, Pat.'

'Jojo!' said Pat, swallowing.

'They're after me,' said Jojo. 'They've been after me for the last three weeks. But they got closer. Rounding on me like ferrets. I'll just stay a little while, Pat, to rest, and then I'll leave. I didn't mean to come, but I seemed to have been channelled out here to you.'

'Oh God, Jojo,' said Pat, 'I'm sorry. I'll—'

Almost before the knocker fell, he sensed that it was coming. Every muscle in his body was waiting for it. Jojo was leaning against the wall, the palms of his hands caressing it. You couldn't mistake the knock. That was a knock that seldom came to a door. It was the Open-up knock. If you don't it will be the worse for you. What now? Pat wondered. He was petrified. He was afraid that he would never be able to move again. But he did. He came close to Jojo.

'The bedroom, Jojo,' he said. 'the window.'

He felt Jojo, wet under his hands and his body seeming to be alive, and then he was gone.

Pat dropped his head in his hands and sighed, 'Oh, Jojo, Jojo!' He pulled himself together then and slowly counted up to ten, ignoring the impatient knocking on the door. Ignoring everything, just concentrating his mind on that count of his. One. And I never said good-bye to him. Two. This couldn't be us. Three. It's not Jojo and me, two boys from a little country town. Four.

Please, God, if ever you did it let him get back. Five. Back to Seamus and the sea beating on a rough shore. Six. He didn't mean anything wrong. Seven. It's just because Jojo is intense and decisive. Eight. Jojo would never kill anybody. Nine. For Christ's sake stop that knocking. Ten. He must be gone by now.

He moved to the door, opened it. It was no surprise to him somehow to see the two brushing past him, looking very huge in their belted raincoats, on which the rain had hardly fallen.

Mechanized ferrets. What could be more innocuous, Pat wondered, than to be chased by two men named Smith and Wren?

Smith halted. Wren went to the living-room and then ran quickly down to the kitchen and the spare room below it. Smith switched on the light in the bathroom and looked into the cupboard.

'Where is he?' he asked.

No urgency there. There was no need to be urgent, Pat thought. They have him on the run and they'll get him. In fact the question was put in quite a kindly way.

'You'd better not stand there in your pyjamas in front of the open door,' said Smith. 'You might get a cold.'

Pat wanted to laugh. Imagine that! You might get a cold. At a time like this, when an awful lot of things were crashing.

'He's not there,' said Wren, coming back. 'There's only the bedroom.'

'Did he go that way?' Smith asked again.

Wren didn't wait for a reply. He went into the bedroom and went swiftly to the open window. He called a name through it. There was no answer. He turned back from the window, halted in surprise to see Maureen, now sitting up in bed with terrified eyes looking at him. Pat could see it all through the opening in the door. It was like something you would see on a film. Not real, your mind said to you all the time, just a story that affects you while you are looking at it. He saw a look on Wren's face, the half-way his hand raised itself to his hat, and then he came out.

'All right,' said Smith, 'Go out and see what happened to him. Tell the other chap to turn the car. He can only go north.

Probably towards the stations. They all do. Get him to send a message. Close in all the other cars. Close off the roads.'

Wren went fast, without appearing to be fast.

Pat saw Smith looking at him. Kindly again. Why kindness from Smith? Pat didn't want him to be kind to him. He wanted him to be kind to Jojo, if one could expect kindness from a greyhound straddling a hare.

'His name was Jojo, wasn't it?' Smith asked. 'You were great friends?'

Pat didn't answer.

'We didn't find out from you,' said Smith. 'There are other ways.'

'What will happen?' Pat asked.

'If he doesn't resist,' said Smith, 'we'll catch him and he'll get twenty years.'

Pat sucked in his breath. Twenty years. Add twenty to twenty. Add half a lifetime to another half lifetime ago you get a young man in the flush of youth and an old man with impaired faculties. He tried to see Jojo with grey hair and his body bent from the waist, and the same pallor in his face that Jack had. What was the difference where they shut you up?

'You mightn't catch him,' said Pat with his mouth, and saying with his eyes, I hope to the Lord God you don't catch him.

'I know,' said Smith. 'But we will. He can't get away. He left it too late. If he had wanted to, he should have gone weeks ago. Now it's too late. We'll get him. All you can hope for is that he won't resist. If he does, it'll be too bad. I hope he doesn't.'

Wren called from outside. Smith heard him, and went out, closing the door softly after him. Pat waited there until he heard the car going; it was hard to hear it. One of those low, black ones with little noise from the engine.

And then Pat flushed himself into activity. He would have to see. He went back into the bedroom, reached for his trousers and started to pull them on.

'Pat, Pat! What is it? What is it?' He only remembered Maureen then, but he paid little attention to her. His mind was too full of what had just happened. It never struck him what a frightening thing it was for Maureen and the way she was and felt, to be awakened out of troubled sleep first to see the crouching figure of a man going out through her window, to hear the grunt and moan outside, to hear voices and footsteps in the hall, and to have another man coming into the room and calling out through the window. Wondering if all this was part of the nightmares through which she had slept, and feeling it wasn't, knowing from the stricken look on the face of Pat that it wasn't.

'Oh, you're awake, Maureen,' was what Pat said, pulling the braces over his shoulders and reaching for his short coat.

'Pat,' said Maureen, 'where are you going?

He didn't notice that her voice was strained, that it was a voice coming from her head, driven there by fear and horror and many other emotions he didn't even pause to define.

'I'm going after them,' he said, pulling on his coat feverishly, removing his slippers and shoving his feet into his shoes. 'It's Jojo, Maureen. He came. They're after him. He got away through the window.'

'Pat,' said Maureen, 'please don't leave me.'

'Maureen!' said Pat.

'Please, please,' she went on urgently, raising herself in the bed. 'Don't leave me, Pat. I'm afraid. Don't go out, Pat.'

'But Jaysus, it's Jojo!' said Pat.

'It doesn't matter,' she went on. 'What can you do? Please, Pat, don't go. I don't feel well. Please, Pat, I don't know what's happening to me. In my head, Pat. I feel light. Things are small and they're all coloured. Pat don't go now!'

'I have to go, Maureen,' said Pat, barely listening to her, 'I have to go.' And he went. She heard his feet on the hallway and she heard the banging of the front door.

'Pat!' She called again. Her voice was nearly a scream. She pulled back the bedclothes and got out with an effort. She had to put out a hand to steady herself. She went over to the bedroom door and called him again. Then she went out into the hall and stood there in her nightdress. The hall seemed to stretch to infinity, the door at the end of it was like the door of a rabbit-hutch, small.

'Pat!' she called again. It seemed to her that she was calling his name in a great cathedral. The echoes of her voice came back to her mockingly. She stood and sweated. She knew her eyes were distended. Her heart was beating very fast. She had never felt more alone in all her life. She saw the picture again that she had seen many times before. Herself in the centre of a great plain, dressed in her smock, calling, calling, her hand stretched out. Not even a tiny telescopic Pat to hear her now, to call back from a great distance.

All the lights were on. She moved to the living-room, feeling alone and still crowded all around with nameless things reaching for her. 'Oh, Pat, Pat!' she said again, sobbing at the door of the living-room. No tears to help her. They had dried up. She had shed enough tears to fill the bed of a river. She raised her head and looked and saw the two gas-masks looking at her from the mantelpiece. Grinning, sardonic and black. An effluvium of blackness seemed to be rising from them, engulfing them and stretching out towards her. All black, like clouds of ink stretching across a mottled sky. She pulled herself back into the hall and called again. It was useless. Again the resounding echoes of a cathedral came back to her, jeering. She pulled away and went into the nearest open door. No blackness here. Light things that she was seeing through a sort of a mist. Her hands on the wash-basin, supporting her because her trembling legs were not supporting her. The white cabinet with the mirror on the front of it.

She opened it. It was white. A lot of white things there. White is antidote for black. All white things. She reached in her arm and took down the bottle.

Jojo was running, Jojo was running as he had never run before. Going out through the window, he had been calm. It was not unusual for him to be going out through windows. It seemed to him that he had been going through windows all his life. And then the hands reached for him, the hands of a very big man. He had a mental picture of himself being hauled like a pig to a fair, with flailing limbs. No, this couldn't happen. He reached into his pocket and pulled out the gun. The big man he couldn't see in the darkness had hold of him by the neck and the back of his coat. He raised the barrel of the gun and dug it into his stomach. He felt it going in. He heard the gasp and the man falling away from him, collapsing with a groan. He was free.

He headed towards what must he the bottom of the garden and was brought up against the wooden fence. He jumped it, his free hand as a lever. He landed on rough soil and stumbled, embraced the wet clammy earth. He rose again from that and went forward stumbling, visualizing in his mind the situation of Pat's place. Trying to remember how they had left the last time to get to the trains. There would be no trains going now, but a railway is a good place to hide. It has length. You are confined, but there are always places to hide. Neglected bushes, over-looked by the excavators of civilization. And no people worth talking about. Because you can't rely on people, not here. All you do is open your mouth and they hear the brogue and shout 'Irish!' and you are on the run again.

He raced up by the backs of houses, his flying feet finding the grass and allowing for the bumps and crevices in it. He came to the end of the houses and saw the line of streets below him. He kept them on his right and raced towards where the shaded tree-lined road had been that he remembered.

I am in the air, anyhow, he thought, wiping the rain from his eyes. It blinded him, the rain. It added God knows how many pounds to his sodden clothes. Even as it was he welcomed it because it was air. His last few months had been horrible. He thought about it. The dank little rooms in the East End, near the ships and sometimes back in the rabbit-warren of streets around Soho. The smell of the room. With the grease-encrusted gas-stoves as old as gas itself, where you boiled water and made tea. The stale bread. The suspicious people. And then they were after you again. They had found out. They went from dump to dump, from arrest to arrest, with more knowledge than they should have had. So you went to another small room with the brass beds and the filthy bed-clothes, where you slept with your clothes on and had no argument with the slatternly sluts who took you in. The being confined. You walked and walked the small smelly room. Sick of the peeling wall-paper, sick of the taste of tobacco in your mouth. Your eyes dying for the dark of night so that you could go out like an animal from a lair. To breathe not air but something that tasted like air.

He threw himself flat on the ground at the next fence that stopped him.

He wasn't panting very much. His stomach was too flat for that. He had no excess flesh to carry, anyhow. Not with the food he had been eating.

He looked behind him. Already, he thought. The flash of a torch. He scrambled over the fence and found himself among trees bordering some kind of a walk. He pulled his head close to the ground and saw the bulk of a building on his left. What was it? A church? The sanctuary of the Church. What a hope! He couldn't stay here either. It was nice being among the trees and the low bushes, but they were so obvious. And they dripped so much. He rose and ran across the lawn, felt his feet first on gravel, then on soft grass, and then on gravel again. More trees and another row of bushes. He pushed his way through and found himself up against a fence again. He scrambled over it and found himself in a small lane. Facing him were the sides of more houses.

Houses? Houses must have backs and that's where dustmen go to collect the rubbish, so that there must be a way. He looked right. Away down there he could see the entrance of the lane he was standing in, well lighted by the street lamps.

He cut across quickly and found himself in a lane at the back of the houses. Knew what it was from the smell of decay and the cabbage stalks. Let the road be somewhere at the end of this now, he thought, and I might beat them yet. He raced down. It was easy. Safe underfoot so that you could really run. He thought of Pat standing there in the hall in his pyjamas, and the look of hurt on his face. For Jojo, for him that look was. Why did the bastards catch up with him so quickly? It would have been nice to have sat for a few hours with Pat in front of a fire, and to really explain to him what it all meant, what Jojo and the others were fighting for, what some of them had already died for. It would have been nice all right, because Pat could have been made to see why, even if he could never have been able to take part himself. Poor Pat. Just wanting people to be nice to him so that he could be nice to people. He was always soft, long ago too. It would have been so nice to have stopped with Pat and to have talked. To have forgotten all about the whole business. Because the last day he could see that Pat had been bursting to start on it. He had given him no chance, had he? Was that the reason that you didn't get a chance tonight, was it? There is a tide in the affairs of men. Well, no matter what they were, they had turned that chap out, anyhow. Easy now The line debouched on to the lighted road.

He threw himself on the ground again and hugged the near fence. Great activity. Two police cars passed whilst he watched, the searchlights on the side of them combing the shaded parts of the road. They passed one another very fast and then came back again and passed one another again. Then they passed again and came to a stand in the middle of the road, the occupants making enquiries of one another. Then they started off again, back to back, and Jojo took his chance. He gathered himself together and ran across the road. It was a broad road. A path a track for bicycles, a lane for traffic, a grass-covered island, another lane for traffic, another bicycle path, a footpath and then the gardens of the houses facing him.

He didn't stop. He took a flying leap at the iron fence chain of the nearest house and fell flat on the far side of the low wall. He had succeeded.

His heart was pounding now all right, but he had jumped through the blind eye of the two cars, because they were turning again to come back. He breathed hard and then, looking across the street, he found himself looking up the lane through which he had come to reach the road. There was that bloody torch again at the end of it. He would have to get out of here. He edged himself through the hedge separating the two houses. It was a light hedge. The houses must be new. He crawled across the garden, over the concrete walk, over the flower-beds, over the flowers. What would the owners say in the morning when they saw the destruction? He kept going. Another garden. And another. He felt himself getting desperate. How many houses? Had a sudden picture of himself at the dawn still working his way through thousands of front gardens.

His odyssey came to an end. His last fence had led him into another lane that backed on more houses, probably the houses of the tree-lined road he had remembered.

He paused a while to rest in the shelter of the fence and then he ran on again. Run, Jojo! Run, Jojo! Where had he heard that before? As he ran it came back to him. He wouldn't be feeling like this. He would be running with the wind in his face backed by a hot sun in a blue, cloud-littered sky. He would be wearing short white pants and his chest would be covered only with a light singlet. There would be white lines on either side of him and on his right would be the stand in the sports-ground where the school had their annual. Stands bursting with boys. Boys of all sizes and shapes, with their white trousers and shirts and white sand-shoes and their school ties. Flags waving and men speaking over a loudspeaker. And on each side of him too the kids would be jumping with excitement. Run, Jojo! Run, Jojo! He's after you! Go on, Jojo, run and you'll bate him! Feeling the stimulation in his feet from the roars of the boys. Jojo was a good runner. Everybody knew that. The four-forty and the half-mile, these were Jojo's. You could always depend on Jojo to win points for the school with those. Christ!

He came to the end of the lane with the cheers in his ears and found the fence, a simple wire fence leading to the towering railway embankment. This was the one they had walked under last time. He pulled himself up it and lay along its length at the top and wriggled his body across so as not to show a silhouette. The feel of the steel tracks hard on his chest. He rolled down the other side. What did it matter about getting wetter any more? He rolled to its end, the long grasses and weeds embracing him, and he rested this side of the wire fence before going out on to the road. He could see more houses across the narrow road. Another back lane. He was making his way through the lower wire when the headlights of the car almost found him. He sank his head on his outstretched arms. The car paused, turned, and came back again, and Jojo shot across like a hare. No use waiting to find out. You had to be bold if you wanted freedom.

He got to the back lane in front of him with the hair rising on his neck. Waiting for the scream of tyres, the shouts, the challenging shouts.

They didn't come. He knew what they were doing now. It was very clever. It was a very good trap. They had cars ranging each road to right and left of him, covering every by-way, every side-road, while the hounds behind came on with their torches.

Give me a real railway, Jojo thought, and I'll beat them yet. He knew the one he wanted. It was the one he had travelled back to town on, the day he had come to see Pat. He remembered his eyes ranging it, storing it up for future use, in case it would have to come in useful some day. You never knew. You never knew. All the same, he was feeling afraid. It had been a great game. With all the forces ranged against you. Everything. And you only a mere man. It hadn't been as hard in the city — so many houses, so many lanes, so many places. But he had been flushed out of them all the same, like a grouse being flushed out of a moor.

It's terrible, Jojo thought then, to be alone. You want the courage of three to be alone. Even though you may be safer. You have no one to talk to, nobody to plan with. He was alone now in the wet night, with forty million enemies against him. Terri-bly, implacably efficient. What hope had he against so many men, so many machines? He stopped himself thinking that way. There was the counsel of despair, and as long as a man had limbs and a heart, he was immune. But he was frightened at the thought that he was getting frightened. It was a chink in the armour of his belief in himself and in his cause.

He barely noticed coming to the end of the lane he was run-ning down now. He was tired. He felt as he had often felt at home when he was swimming far out from the land, against all sane advice. The shore looked so far away, the people like tiny dots. The great ocean all round you and your arms beginning to tire at the muscles. You would say then, I will never reach it, and for a few awful moments you would contemplate letting your-self drift down, feeling the soft water pouring into your lungs. But you never did. You always kicked again with your jaded legs.

Like now. He was confronted by a tall paling of concrete posts and netted wire, the whole backed by a miniature wood of small trees. He rested his hands on the fence, breathing hard, and then he worked his weary muscles again and hoisted himself over, the toes of his shoes biting into the wire. He threw himself over, leaving pieces of his wet coat behind him. He should have removed them, but he didn't care now. He went through the trees by touch more than anything else, on a short incline, stumbled free of them, and then felt his body falling as his stumbling feet found nothing but air.

Down and down. Only one coherent thought. Hold on to your gun.

He fell on his hands and knees, the small stones biting into the clenched knuckles around the gun, numbing them. His knees felt as if they had been dropped on spikes. His whole body jarred. He collapsed where he was, the side of his face hugging the ground. The opening of one eye told him where he was, and he felt like crying. He was at his railway indeed. Up from his eye he could see the double row of tracks gleaming wetly, with the raised electrified rail in the middle of them.

It's no use, Jojo thought, I can't go on. Why should I go on? Who is there in. God's holy earth who cares whether I go on or not? In England he was a brutal gunman. In Ireland he was a traitor to his legitimate Government, who pursued him and his kind with even more venom than their English enemies. No paper in any land to say, These men are fighting for a creed they believe in – give them that. No; emergency powers in Ireland; emergency powers in England. From the altars of their own land they were reviled as men who were forbidden to go to the altar of God because they were members of an oath-bound society. Even all that wouldn't have been so bad if you had thought and believed that the people were behind you. The people weren't. The people, as always, were waiting for the cat to jump. You had to be a success to get the people behind you. Nobody, Jojo thought, looking at me now, lying like a dead dog in its own vomit, could call me a success.

That brought him to his knees, and then to his feet. I reached the railway, he thought, and if I reached the railway despite the odds, I can go on from there. He straightened himself and stumbled towards the rails, put his foot over the first one and then saw the one in the middle, the raised one. It would be so easy to die now, he thought wistfully. Just to lift this other leg and lay it on the rail and my saga will be over for ever.

He didn't do it. He crossed that one and he crossed the next one, and then he was brought up short by the rearing concrete culvert facing him. It stretched a long way, buttressing the earth behind it. He had obviously fallen from the top of the one on the other side. He could feel a trickle that wasn't rain flowing down his legs inside his trousers. Blood from his lacerated knees. And the handle of the gun was sticky to the touch. He stood with his back to the wall, resting. I will turn left now, he thought, in a minute and I will go in towards the city.

And then the lights found him. First from a height on his left, where a bridge and a road went over the railway. A short, powerful searchlight. It sought him and found him and fixed him there, like a moth in a light. He turned to flee from that when one on his right came on, from high up too, but farther away. Another bridge, another car. So they had got there first. And then, to complete it, the torches shone from directly opposite him from the place where he had fallen. He straightened himself and took a firm grip on the gun. Jojo's hour had come.

Pat ran out of the house and up the road in the direction the car had gone. He didn't realize he was so poorly dressed until the relentless downpour soaked him through almost at once, disdainfully. He could feel the water slopping in his shoes, the coat of his pyjamas soon wet through and sticking to his chest. He didn't know why he had come out or what good it would do. Just the thought of Jojo away in the night with those after him, and all alone. Even he wouldn't know that Pat was out, and if he did know what good would it do him? He ran on.

It was easy to follow. He saw the car too, turning off the road and going down to search and coming up again and going on at speed, and turning up again to search. It was a terrible thing to see. It was all so casual. It was hard to believe that it was a man they were after, and harder still to believe that it was Jojo they were after. Why the hell didn't he stay at home? Pat thought. Why did he have to come over here at all? Jojo! It couldn't be Jojo really that this was happening to. But it *was* Jojo.

He was some distance away when he saw the car on the bridge with its light settled, and the figures climbing out of the car and standing with their heads shown up by the light. Peaked caps and the glint from the barrel of a gun. His lungs were bursting with his running. He found it hard to breathe. He had to stop for a minute and rest his knuckles on the path with his body doubled up in order to get back a semblance of his breathing. Then he went on again. He kept watching, but the car remained stationary. The men stayed. Their faces looked hard in the light. The gleam was still on the barrel of the gun.

Then the loudspeaker on the top of the car blared. He couldn't hear what it said. His breathing was too loud in his own ears for that. But it wasn't a courtesy car any longer, he was sure, to advise gentle old ladies about crossing the street.

The speaker said, 'Drop that gun, Brodel! Drop that gun, Brodel!'

Twice the speaker spoke, not even the smothering rain being able to envelop and absorb the boom of it.

Jojo below heard it well. He also heard the bodies of the two men who dropped themselves from the top of the culvert opposite him. He couldn't see them, but he heard them and he knew they were there. He didn't blink his eyes against the light of the blinding torches facing him.

'Don't come!' he said, raising the gun, pointing at where they should be.

'Drop that gun, Brodel,' said the speaker. 'Drop that gun.'

Well, this is it now, Jojo, this is the end of it. He had only two choices. He could press the trigger of the gun and bring his own end or he could drop the gun. That's all there was to it. Whatever he did was the end of freedom. To die would be freedom. It would be put to the test then whether God would keep him out of heaven because on earth he had been a member of an oath-bound society. He'd find out then quick enough whether he had been right or wrong. But whatever way, it was the end of the world for him, anyhow. It was the end of lying on green grass on the top of a cliff looking at the sky with its clouds, and the gulls soaring in it. The end of listening to the moan of the sea at night and the booming of the buoy in the west wind. The end of dreams. There was no going back now to the place where the seaweed rotted under the stars and the silver sands moved under your feet, and the black sails of the puckauns creaked as they were raised to slide to the sea under the light of the moon. So many things, God, that I haven't seen enough of at all. I want to row on the lake again and feel a fat trout at the end of my rod. And I want to see the cormorants on the rocks and hear the lonely cry of the curlew flying over the purple heather. I want to see white houses with the yellow thatch in them, and the men with the bainins, slow and casual, like Seamus, and smell the smell of turf from their clothes. Because I hadn't time to see enough of those things. Because I was too young when these other thoughts came into my head and I thought that men should be free and that this was the way to make them free.

He raised an arm and fiercely wiped the rain from his eyes. Pat reached the bridge and leaned over, looking at the scene. One he would never forget! Even when he was dead, it would be implanted on the retina of his eye. There was a great tenseness. Pat was holding his struggling breath. It seemed to him that all the others around were doing the same thing. There was no move to be heard in the night, not a rustle except the falling rain, and that same was soft because the earth had become accustomed to the feel of it. Even the night seemed to be holding its breath for what was to follow. Pat didn't know what it would be, because Jojo had passed beyond him. He couldn't know now what Jojo would do. Christ above, he thought fervently, don't let him die!

Have I failed? Jojo asked himself. If I die what good will it do? He examined his death coldly. Will I be just an unmarked grave in the yard of an English prison, like so many more? Will a nation catch fire because I have died like that, and say this man died for what he believed in and therefore his cause is just and right, and we must make it our cause too? Jojo didn't think they would. But some day, some day. There was always some day. And when the some day came wasn't it better to be live lips, however livid, that could speak, than to be just a skull with fixed teeth that could never talk, never again in this world? So will I live, Jojo wondered, to fight another day, to try and imbue into other men the welter and fever of my belief? Older, sadder, with an irrecoverable youth behind me, burned out of me. Isn't it better to die than to face that, to be watching a small patch of sky no bigger than a postage stamp for the best part of my life? With something gnawing into you with the years. Telling you maybe that you were a fool. That it was all in vain; that nobody gives a damn anyhow. Wouldn't it be terrible to live if solitude and incarceration were to make me believe that I was wrong – that what I have done was wrong and that I was a fool to have believed in it? Wouldn't it be better to die so? Wouldn't it be easier to die now, here in the rain, when I am so tired, and everything is so black except the searchlights of the servants of an injured people? So easy to die, so easy to die. It became a rhyme in his head. So easy. Easy. That was the word that Jojo didn't like – easy. Because nothing had ever been easy for Jojo. His birth had been hard. His life had been hard. Always everything he had got was the hard way. School was hard and his education had been won at night burning candles, filling himself with knowledge until his eyes ached from it. That was hard. Every bit that had ever gone into his mouth had gone the hard way. And now, he thought, it would be harder to live than it would be to die. I could have died long ago by putting my foot on a live rail. That would have been easy, easy, easy, easy.

He threw down the gun. Pat let his breath go slowly, and rested his head on his arms.

He heard the men around him sighing too, as they expelled their held breaths. He raised his eyes once more. His last look was of Jojo there with the gun at his feet, standing straight up and his hands by his sides, his raised face to the weeping, cloud-covered stars. On the verge of the light he saw the two men moving towards him.

'Good-bye, Jojo,' he said out loud, softly, and then he turned away. He didn't want to see any more.

He put his hands in his pockets, not noticing how wet they were and how wet his pockets were. He dropped his head on his chest and allowed his feet to take him along the wet path. I could weep now, he thought, but that would do him little good. I could weep for myself, because I am so small and my troubles are so small, since they are ordinary things that happen to everyday people. My sins in the eyes of man are so small and Jojo's are so big. That's not right. That's not right at all, because how could it be a sin to do what you believed was right? There were far bigger sinners than Jojo in the world who never had to suffer for them. Far bigger. Because he knew that Jojo was good clean through to his soul. Jojo would have worked just as hard or done as much to help a lame dog over a stile as he had done for this. He thought of Jojo being held by strong hands and being put into a car and being carried away. To where? And for how long? And what would he be like after it? What would it do to him? What would twenty years do to any man?

He stopped thinking that way and he heard his own feet slobbering wetly on the pavement. A slow slobbing, with a mournful Irish rhythm. The words of his walk even came to him, in his head with the tune, like this:

Siúbhal, siúbhal, siúbhal, a ghrádh,
Ni'l leigheas le fághail ach leigheas an bháis,
O d' fág tú mise is bocht mo chás.
's go dtéigh' tú a mhúirnín slán.

The rain softened and fell more lightly on the surfeited earth.

16

The front door closed behind him, and he leaned against it, the water dripping from his clothes.

His eyes began to see after a while and he noticed that all the lights were lit in the flat, right down from where he was standing he could see into the spare room. Every light in the place. That wasn't usual. And then he remembered. He remembered Maureen and her voice just before he had gone out of the door. For a moment it seemed to him that he hadn't gone out at all. That he had just come out of the room and he heard her voice calling after him. 'Pat, Pat, don't leave me!' Yes, that's what she was saying and about feeling queer and things coloured in front of her eyes and small. And she had looked funny before that too. So she had called to him and he hadn't heard her. He had gone out. How long had he been gone? An hour, like a lifetime. Where was she so? Why were all the lights still blazing?

His head began to thump dully with fear. It was then that his lowered eyes saw the small bottle on the floor outside the bathroom door, lying flat with the small lid off it and a few of the white tablets spilled from it.

He went over to it slowly and picked it up in his hand, down on one knee. He took just one look before he began to shake. It was an empty bottle of aspirin tablets. He looked at the closed door of the bedroom. Why didn't she call out when he had come in? Right in front of his eyes then he saw the lurid headlines of the Sunday newspapers. Overdose of Aspirin. Flat Suicide. It was so usual. So much had happened to him now in a short time that it seemed almost fitting to him that the worst thing of all should have happened. His eyes were wide with fear as he looked at the closed door. Every nerve of him was waiting and listening to hear a sound, any kind of a sound. Because, he realized clearly, I have been so cruel. We have all been so cruel. All this day she was alone. The dinner spoiled, now, didn't seem funny. It seemed very tragic. His interlude with Lelia wasn't a very pleasant memory now. And after that, Lelia with her gentle cruelty and the man with the masks, and then the frantic coming of Jojo and his flight and the others. Strange voices in the night-time. And Pat's complete desertion of her. God, he thought, don't I deserve anything that's coming now? Haven't I earned it all with my thoughtlessness and indecision? If I had to go out I should have brought her with me, yes, even into the rain-drenched night. Or, better, I should never have gone at all. I should have stayed. What good did I do by going? I helped nobody at all. I just hurt her.

His hand strayed to the knob of the door. It took great effort on his part to nerve his hand to the opening of it. It was one of the hardest things he had ever done, the opening of that door.

Then he flung it wide. It seemed to him that he had ceased to breathe and that his nerves were screaming, every single separate one of them.

His eyes found her lying back on the pillow. Her face was waxen in colour. He could distinguish no movement from her breast, no twitch on her face. Peaceful and pale her face, and dead. 'O God, no,' said Pat.

'Hello, Pat,' she said then, opening her eyes to look at him.

Pat helped himself to the side of the bed with his hand and fell on his knees beside it, stretched a hand to gather hers in it and then let his head fall on his arm.

'Pat,' she said, half rising in the bed, 'what is it? What's wrong with you?'

Pat breathed hard into the blanket and then after a time he raised his head.

'I thought you were dead, Maureen,' he said, 'honest to God, I thought you were dead!'

Maureen had been all set for Pat's coming. An attitude. But it all went away when she saw the look in his eyes. I need never

258

doubt Pat, she said to herself. Pat is really all for me. She raised her other hand and rested it on his wet hair, on his face.

'What on earth made you think a thing like that?' she asked.

'I don't know,' said Pat. 'Everything. Out there in the hall, it just struck me. How cruel I have been to you all this time. Only a day, but it seems so long. And I went away from you when I shouldn't. I saw the bottle out there in the passage, This. I, I thought that you—'

'That I . . . ? Oh, Pat!' said Maureen, 'how could you think that? Not me. I'm too fond of living. No, things were very queer. with me, Pat, for hours. I don't know. I seemed to be living away from myself altogether. It was my head, I think, and other things too. And then I took a few aspirins, and it went. I saw white again.' She remembered that. The drink of water and the white tablets going down her throat and back to bed with that pain beginning to niggle at her. And then she opened her eyes and then everything became sane again. She saw things as she had always seen them, normally, and she was a little bit mad, but that was all, and it was a good sign too. She had even felt sorry for Pat. And what happened to him? Why did he go out in the rain without his coat? She hadn't heard him stopping in the hall.

'What happened, Pat?' she asked.

Pat raised himself a little. 'Oh, they got him,' he said. 'They got him.' His eyes were bleak.

'You're very wet,' she said practically. 'Go on and take off all your clothes and dry yourself out. Don't put on clean pyjamas. Get into your street clothes. And then this time put on a coat and hat and go out and phone for the ambulance and the doctor.'

He got to his feet, staring at her.

'Maureen!' he said.

'Please hurry up, Pat,' she said. 'I don't know much about it, but we'd better get moving.'

The antidote again for Pat. Wasn't it always the way? That you got a kick in the kisser first and before you could become too taken up with the pain of that, you got a kick somewhere else to take your mind off it, so that you didn't know which pain to feel sorry for. He bent quickly and put his wet face against her, and then turned and kissed her.

'I don't really deserve you,' he said.

'I'll think that myself,' she said, 'if you don't hurry up.'

But she was glad. It saved her from feeling afraid, anyhow, to know that Pat mustn't know that she was afraid. And anyhow, she thought, surely nothing could possibly happen to me on account of Pat. What would happen to him if anything happened to me?

Pat was swallowing his adam's apple, trying to sort it all out.

'Please, Pat, hurry!' she said, in order to jostle him into action.

He went.

A fever of movement. Into the bathroom, dropping clothes from him as he went, like leaves falling from the trees. He took a short time out to rub himself down with a towel. Then out to the hot-press for clean clothes, pushing his head into the bedroom door to shout, 'Are you all right, Maureen?' Seeing her only once with her face screwed up. But she stopped and smiled, and that made him feel a little better. He was flooded with so much thought that his head was light and reeling. She'll be all right. Of course she will. But suppose she isn't? A wave of fear, starting in his feet, as he gave a few seconds' thought to his world without Maureen in it. Then a rush at his clothes again to make him stop thinking that way. His clothes wouldn't go on for him, of course. They never do. His underclothes were back to front. The buttons of his shirt were done up when he tried to get it over his head, so that he pulled and burst them off. His head emerging red and cursing. He managed to dress himself, more or less, and went in to her to hold her hand for a second. You'll be all right until I come back, won't you? Nothing can happen to you until I come back?

The rush to the door. The shout from the bedroom: 'Have you your coat?'

A curse from him as he fumbled in the cupboard for his mackintosh. Struggling into it. Back again to the room again. 'You're sure you'll be all right until I get back?' 'Please, go, Pat, will you!' 'I'm going now, so I am.' And out of the door. Into the night, forgetting to close the door and rushing back again to close it. Going for his bicycle and remembering that he had not brought it from Lelia's house. A pause to curse Lelia and then to curse the bicycle. And he was away running to the phonebox, fumbling fingers at the dial. A pause again. Jaysus, what's this the number is? As if you shouldn't know. As if you hadn't got it off by heart for just such an emergency as this. He couldn't think of it. He hit his head with his hand, but it still wouldn't come. Have to look up the book. What? In his condition? Wouldn't he be a fortnight at that bloody book with his trembling hands? He calmed down, opened the door of the phone-box and sat down on the side of the path. In the rain. His feet in the channel where the water gurgled towards its drain. I will be calm and collected, he thought, and the number will come to me. The rain is not as heavy as it was, he thought. And then it came to him, the number. He got up slowly. No more rushing. I'll forget it again.

Deliberate raising of the receiver. Deliberate moving of the dial. That's all there was in it. Please send an ambulance at once to my flat. The address. A soulless voice at the other end. Thank you. My God, how could they be so calm? Didn't they know what was happening? It wasn't just any woman; it was Maureen. And they as if they didn't really give a damn.

Out then, and off up the street, running like a hare, to the dim distance where the red light burned outside the house of the doctor. He was a good chap, anyhow. He wouldn't be so impersonal. Maureen liked him; they got on very well together, even though he had annoyed her about the cup of tea business. Fumbling fingers at the latch of the gate. His breath coming in pants. My God, I seem to be doing nothing but running and running. In to the door. The bell, a big one so that you couldn't miss it. A peal; no stir. There could hardly be a stir in two seconds, but Pat thought it was at least half an hour. Blast it, he thought, I should have phoned him from down below. Instead of this he pealed the bell again. After another two second half an hour he caught the big iron knocker and banged with it. It reverberated. He thought he heard a muffled voice. A pause. The bell again and then the knocker. It's a good job, something told him, that it's a strong door, or it would be flying out the back yard now. The switching-on of the light inside, the pulling open of the door and the figure inside in the dressing-gown and the ruffled hair.

'Jaysus,' said the doctor, 'why don't you pull the bloody house up be the roots altogether? Why don't you take the door home with you?'

It's easy known, Pat thought primly, that he's an Irish doctor, cursing like that in the middle of the morning.

'It's Maureen,' he said. 'I've sent for the ambulance.'

'All right, all right,' said the doctor, 'so what? Do you have to come along here and destroy me abode on account a that?'

'But it's urgent,' said Pat.

'You don't say!' said the doctor, highly sarcastic. 'I thought maybe you wanted to come in for a pee!'

Pat was shocked. And then he felt all the urgency leaving him. It seemed to him that he would look funny to anyone else. So he laughed.

'Ah, God, I'm sorry,' he said. 'I got excited.'

'That's better,' said the doctor, whose tactics had been successful. 'Go on, back now to her and wait for the ambulance. I'll go across to the hospital in the car. No bother.'

'Thanks,' said Pat, and flew away again.

The doctor paused awhile at the door, shaking his head, wondering what on earth ever persuaded him to take up the medical profession, and then he closed the door and went up the stairs, taking off his dressing-gown.

Pat ran all the way back again. All sorts of contingencies were in his head. None of them pleasant. But everything was as he had left it. Maureen had managed to get up and was dressed ready to go out. It shook Pat. She was so calm. So they just sat there and waited. Pat made tea and they drank it. Nothing to say. There was too much to say. So he just held her hand while his stomach shivered. The ring at the door nearly startled them out of their wits. They hadn't heard the ambulance come despite all their waiting and listening.

And then the door was closed and they were speeding away. Sitting down inside, closed in and frightened. The stretchers with the blankets. The terrible cleanliness of it all. The smell of disinfectants and suffering. They were awed. Pat swallowed frequently.

The doctor was waiting for them on the steps of the hospital, a small one, backed by trees.

He helped Maureen out and greeted her gruffly enough. 'The first day I saw you,' he said to her, 'I knew it. Here, I said to meself, is a dame that's going to haul me out at two o'clock in the morning. Without fail.'

Maureen laughed. Pat laughed. Too loudly, he thought. He could hear his laugh running away in the night.

The doctor took Maureen up the steps, Pat following with her case. The doctor asking her questions.

He turned at the top step. 'I'll take that now,' he said, holding his hand out for the bag. 'You clear off to hell out of here.'

'What!' said Pat.

'Go on, beat it,' said the doctor. 'Take a walk by yourself for a few hours. Go and commune with nature or go home to bed or do what you like. I've seen enough of your face for one night.'

Pat was very nonplussed.

'Go on, Pat,' said Maureen, 'do what he tells you. I'll be all right'.

'But . . . ' said Pat.

'Please, Pat,' said Maureen, 'do what he tells you.'

'What does he know about it, anyhow,' said Pat. 'He's only a bloody bachelor.'

The doctor snorted, laughing. 'It's no wonder,' he said, 'after all the eejits like you I have to placate all my life.'

Pat shook Maureen's hand. As if they were friends parting at a railway station. You couldn't break down on the steps and tell her all you wanted to say, how much you loved her and how little time you had had to tell her about it. And how you were going to be from now on, that you were going to treasure her like an oyster with its pearl. Oh, scats of things he had to say that you couldn't say. So he just shook her hand and looked at her and said, 'I'll be seeing you, Maureen.'

'You bet you will,' said the doctor. 'Amn't I with her? Success is my middle name!'

'It better be,' said Pat.

One more look from her eyes, that were clouding with pain, and then he was facing the closed door. Love locked out. He turned away and gave in to his fears then. Walked down the steps. Surprised to see that the rain had stopped. Paused to look at the sky, where the big clouds were broken and banked with a moon riding high.

It was a sheltered old street he walked. Tall trees on either side, planted probably fifty years ago from the size of them. The houses were old. You knew that from the tall, dignified height of them and the cut of the windows, with the pillars on the door-ways. His feet were the only thing to disturb the settled seren-ity, his footsteps and the drip of the rainwater from the branches of the trees. Occasionally a lighted window caused him to won-der why it should be lighted – whether somebody was sick or dying or praying or being killed or being born, or what.

He walked on, street after street, and eventually he came out on to the main road, one of London's arteries. He walked along it towards the city, passed the silent shops with their blinds down and the monstrous sleeping cinemas. All dead. Except for a strolling constable with his torch, resting his hand now and again on the locks of the doors. He looked at Pat as he passed. Stood to look. Probably decided he was harmless, since he let him go with a 'Good night.' Negative, not friendly, not inimical, just a man passing.

He paused after some time when he came to the park. It wasn't really a park, but a sort of large island where the main road separated itself and broke into two streams, just like a river. And in the centre was the island park. Old. Just surrounded by a foot-high iron rail, which he stepped over to feel his feet cush-ioned by the wet green grass. There was a seat at the top of it on which he sat. He looked back. On either side of him the tall trees reared to the sky, their wet tops brilliant in the moonlight. Right down on either side of him they went, to the end where their branches met and closed on one another. It reminded him of the big church at home. The tree-trunks could so easily have been the pillars, a glinting star low in the sky could have been the per-petual light to God in the dark place before the shadowed altar.

It was very peaceful.

It's funny, Pat thought, that I should have looked at the sky. He hadn't been very conscious of the sky up to now. Probably because in a great city you could not see the sky. The sky there would be the vague roof, a rectangular roof, suspended over long streets. Not like at home, where you lived with the sky. Where you saw it from horizon to horizon and looked at it first thing in the morning to see what it was doing. Your life was really guided by the sky and the things that happened in it. And that made him think something else. That he hadn't been thinking of his home so much now. At first it had been all that. What this was like here as compared to that at home. People too. Lately he was drifting away from that. He was beginning to look at things as they were. No comparisons. Just acceptance. That was right too. You couldn't go on the other way all the time. People would get sick of it and sick of you.

Oh God, he said to the star, please don't let anything happen to Maureen.

Panic. And then he swept it away again, forcing himself to think. Of a lot of things. Of a young man standing on a station with a cardboard suitcase. What has happened to that young man? he wondered. He's as dead as the dodo. Pat felt that he had aged at least twenty years in experience, and for no other reason than that he was ordinary. A lot of things had happened to him. He had known disappointment and love and sorrow. But they were ordinary things. That happened to ordinary people. Only Jojo was outside that. It was only Jojo had shaken him from the groove of ordinariness. Because Jojo had made him feel useless. For the first time, he had really met somebody with a purpose. Pat had no purpose out of the ordinary. And he thought now, I don't want any purpose. All I want is to live an ordinary life. With Maureen. To be left alone with her. To go through all the gamut of ordinary emotions.

If only I wasn't so alone now, he thought. For a few moments he felt a terrible hunger in him to be at home again. People around him he knew. To whom you could talk. To roll and laugh with his little nephews and nieces. To hear the broad brogue of the people, drawled in a western accent, the vowels dragged musically to death. Not the clipped preciseness of the English. All that went with the other. The green sea. And the smell of the sea and the touch of it. And the fish-scales glinting on nets swung from yard-arms, and the tumbling estuary littered with the glittering whiteness of sleeping swans. And the ancient hulks rotting in the off-side harbour, where Spanish grandees had once walked. All that. But it was nostalgia. It wasn't living. His fight was here. Something that was worth fighting for too. A chance for your own happiness and a something carved from adversity.

Lord, he said, give Maureen back to me. A slight breeze lifted the heavy arms of the trees, making them sough like the lower register of a great organ.

He got up from the seat then and walked away. He went back the way he had come, his feet alternately slowing and then running, and slowing again, in action with the beat of his heart. It seemed to him that he would never reach the place, and then that he would reach it all too soon. Wavering thoughts came into his head, and snatches of conversation. The conductor on the bus making fun for the other passengers over his funny Irish money. And the lady with the Alsatian and the flow from her, and the winking milkman. All that. And Seamus standing on the embankment, his huge torso bared and brown, and the teeth white in his face. Lelia and the smell of her, from which his mind shrank, and the worst one of all, the light on the barrel of a gun and Jojo with his face to the weeping sky. Thinking what? Seeing what? Seeing the company he had joined that was denied him even by his own? The company of the priest on a horse leading lean men to death with a song on their lips and pikes in their hands. Or seeing a torn tricolour flag fluttering in the breeze over the heads of doomed heroes. All that. Poor, poor Jojo, whose cup was now as full as the cup of any man had ever been. And yet even Pat's thoughts were denied to him now, because Pat was just ordinary. His mind and his heart were filled with the face of a girl. A quiet one or a sarky one, with shrewd, kind eyes and a mind that seemed to run in tune with his own. A great polisher of lino and a mutilator of meat. One whom it was great to hear laughing because she gurgled enough to send up your temperature and make you laugh with her. This is what I want, Pat thought fiercely. This and nothing else. I just want her for ever, and wherever she is with me that's where I want to be. I can always see the sea in her eyes and beautiful things that are beautiful because they are the small things that make living what it is.

He ran up the steps of the hospital, but slowed at the door.

I have often been afraid he thought, but I have never in all my life been as afraid as I am now.

A tired-looking nurse admitted him and showed him into a large parlour place with mahogany furniture, and a big marble fireplace decorated with fat cherubs and a lolling lady just over the fire. A good job she's over the fire, Pat thought idly, or she'd be frozen, since she was clothed in nothing else but her marble birthday suit. It didn't lift the weight from him, because although the nurse had skilfully if a little bluntly evaded all questions, Pat had thought that her face was grave.

So for the length of time he was there he concentrated on the picture over the mantel. A most peculiar picture for a nursing home, a maternity home at that. It was the picture of a woman holding her hands. It was an old picture and a big one and the colours were darkly lush. The peculiar thing about her appearance was that she was the most obvious and downright and unregenerate virgin Pat had ever seen. She was holding fat arms, looking down at him with some loathing and much abhorrence, over a large uncompromising bosom, widely covered in dark red velvet that was closed at the neck with a large cameo brooch. He couldn't take his eyes off her. If he tried to look at something else, she eventually brought him back again to meet the cold, remorseless challenge of her disgust. You Man, she was saying, and what you have done! It's all your fault. Why was Man ever born? How much better the world would have been had it been run by virgins like myself! Probably, he thought, she had founded the home on that thought, to care for the pitiful results of man's passing passions.

It seemed to him that he was a long time under the scalding glare of her green eyes. She had almost thought him into a vow of celibacy. And then he was called.

Later the doctor wanted to drive him home.

Pat thought of the empty flat, every bit of it peopled with thoughts of Maureen, her clothes and her touches, so he refused. The doctor was tired, but persistent.

'It will do you no good,' he said, 'solitude. It never did anybody any good. You'll have to get over it. Go over to her mother and father. You'll have to see them sometime anyhow, and tell

267

them. You can cheer them up. Remember they are old and you are young, with a whole life in front of you.'

'I'll walk,' said Pat.

The doctor looked at him and shrugged his shoulders.

'All right,' he said.

Pat went down the road blindly. He did not allow himself to think until the doctor had passed with a wave of his hand.

The pavement echoed under his tread. The dawn was licking at the edges of the day. I am a father, he thought.

And then, there on that dignified tree-clad street, he did a very strange thing. He leaped into the air with his arms spread out and he roared into the sky.

'Yahoo!' roared Pat, and then he stopped abashed to look around him. The blinded windows chided him, the trees swished him into silence. 'Sorry,' he said then with a wave of his hand, and he walked on, quick and light, like a feather falling from the wing of an angel. He felt that he was airborne. So it's as they said, he thought. But you have to experience it before you believe it. It was the funny part only you remembered from books and looking at funny films. The husband gnawing his nails and doing absent-minded things. And then handing around cigars to impossible people. After the mother-in-law joke and the dentist, it was the number three national joke of every nation.

Maureen waiting for him, her eyes lighted up. So tired. Stretching a hand, squeezing his. Her messages were few. Go and tell Mum and Dad, and five minutes afterwards turning on her side and saying, 'Go away now, will you? I'm going to have the longest sleep since Rip Van Winkle.' And she proceeded to do so, just after fixing a baleful eye on the doctor and sneering, 'You and your cup of tea!' At which he laughed and Pat laughed and they all laughed and it was a great pity he didn't have cigars, because that was true. You felt like giving things away. If anybody would have taken the shirt off his back he would have given it to them.

And the other little business, in the cot beside the bed. It was hard to think of that. You felt so good about it that it was embarrassing even to yourself. All my own work. Imagine! All he remembered having done was drawing his finger down the middle of the little thing's face, right down, as if he was split. As if he were splitting him in two. Half English and half Irish, he said, laughing, although it wasn't funny.

He suddenly took a spurt and ran as fast as he could down the street, his coat-tails flying out behind him, and at the end of his run he did a jump in the air.

Christ, he thought, it's wonderful. I have a son. And then he thought, isn't it wonderful that it's the time it is, when nobody can see me, and I can express myself whatever way I like?

Isn't it funny that life has taken on a different meaning now altogether, that I don't give a damn about anything outside the two of us, no, outside the three of us? I like everything now, he thought, I like everybody. He ran again as his heart commanded him and he kept running, feeling the breeze he was creating on his hot face until he came on to the main road. Paused there. It's a grand street, he thought, even though at this moment it's as bare as a knuckle. He turned down its length and went on more soberly.

You know, it's all becoming part of me now. It doesn't feel so strange any more. Beginning to feel that it belongs to me too, that I'm not just a stranger with nothing to do with it. He liked the overhead cables of the trolley buses, so alien to him formerly, and thought how he liked the silent shine of them and all the people in them, with the strange accents. How nice it was to be watching them, listening to them. The jaded laughs at the end of the day as they went home from work. The smell of their work. The oil from the chaps who worked over engines, and the strange technical conversations. And the red-faced housewives with their baskets and their banter with the conductor.

The strange was becoming familiar. The pubs on Sundays, with everybody dressed in their best, kids and all, outside the fronts, drinking brown ale. Not the kids, but the parents. Enough to bring Father Matthew out of his grave for a second crusade. But so part of the living. And harmless. It was when a man didn't take his wife and kid to a pub that it was getting serious. Pause and try and think of some of the hard chaws at home trotting to the local with the wife and kids.

That made him laugh, and he decided he must write to Cissie and her husband Jim. He had neglected them. But, boy, had he something to write about now! Would they be surprised!

He passed a lighted garage. A huge place where men were tumbling about, getting ready to take the buses out for the early morning loads.

Then he found himself at the turn up to his own town.

He paused for a few seconds to consider it.

It was the same turn-off where he had alighted when he came first, to go up to Jack's place. Well, he thought, when I go up now, I won't be the same man at all. It seemed to him that a lifetime had passed over him since he had first gone up there.

Awed, with everything so strange. Feeling lost and alone. How the long, long streets had impressed him. Now they seemed not so long and very negotiable.

So he moved forward on different feet, seeing in his mind each turn and corner until he would stand outside the door of Maureen's house. He would wake the street with his knocking, and when they opened the door to him he would do a step of a dance on the path, and shout out the news so that even the dead might hear him. Would they be surprised? He grinned and set off up the road at a fast pace.

Just then there was a heavy drone in the sky over from the west and the earth seemed to tremble as the formation of black aeroplanes came from the shelter of the low-lying bank of clouds. The bombers had come out to play. They passed over his head.

He strained to look up at them, to pick them out in the early gloom. Then he pulled down his head and went on his way. I don't care, he thought. Not now.

That's something for another day. No matter what happens now, I will never be afraid again. I will face everything with the determination that flowed through me when I came in the first place. I will never be afraid again. I have no cause to be, because, after all, look what has happened to me. I have company. I am not alone. Not any longer. Never again.

And he walked up the long road, a diminishing figure, silhouetted against the scarlet tendrils of the rising sun, forerunners creeping across the sky from a determined and hopeful dawn.